GRANDMOTHER

and the Priests

BOOKS BY TAYLOR CALDWELL

1938 Dynasty of Death
1940 The Eagles Gather
1941 The Earth Is the Lord's
1941 Time No Longer
         (Under the name of "Max Reiner")
1942 The Strong City
1943 The Arm and the Darkness
1943 The Turnbulls
1944 The Final Hour
1945 The Wide House
1946 This Side of Innocence
1947 There Was a Time
1948 Melissa
1949 Let Love Come Last
1951 The Balance Wheel
1952 The Devil's Advocate
1954 Never Victorious, Never Defeated
1956 Tender Victory
1957 The Sound of Thunder
1958 Dear and Glorious Physician
1960 The Listener
1961 A Prologue to Love
1963 Grandmother and the Priests

GRANDMOTHER
and the Priests

TAYLOR CALDWELL

Doubleday & Company, Inc.

Garden City, New York, 1963

All of the characters in this book are fictitious,
and any resemblance to actual persons,
living or dead, is purely coincidental.

Foreword

THIS BOOK IS DEDICATED to the heroic memory of God's Servants, encountered in Grandmother's drawing-room so long ago, in the early years of this century, and to the equally heroic memory of all other of God's Servants, whose devotion we do not deserve, whose prayers we do not merit, of whose love we are not worthy, and whose endless labors are known only to God.

For those who are not fully familiar with the terms used in this book, all Bishops of all Faiths are called "my lord" in the British Isles, and are referred to as "his lordship." "The edge of purple" was commonly used half a century or more ago in referring to the Monsignori, no matter their Orders or whether or not "the edge of purple" was actually used on their clothing.

I have used Scottish, Welsh and Irish dialect only enough to give an authentic flavor to these various sagas, so they will readily be understood by anyone who is not of these racial backgrounds.

To the Welsh and the Scots, an Englishman was a "Sassenach," and to the Irish he was a "Sassenagh," both terms deplorably not complimentary.

Some say that the late years of the nineteenth century and the early years of the twentieth were "hard years." But all years are "hard," in different measure. I am sure our modern missionaries and clergymen find these days very hard indeed, too, and their heroism as little appreciated as they labor in their particular and stony vineyards. No, indeed, we are not worthy of our clergy, anywhere in the world.

This is a story of heroes, then, whose lives were indeed hard and perilous, and who often, like their Lord, had no place to lay their heads, and only random shelter. They lived in an atmosphere of faith and fantasy and wonder and joy in life, and told marvelous stories about themselves and others. Moreover, though often oppressed, they were truly free men, often lacking in deadly "caution," and never afraid. They, more than anyone else, understood Emerson when he wrote, "For what avail, the plow and sail, the land or life, if freedom fail?"

Taylor Caldwell

GRANDMOTHER

and the Priests

ROSE MCCONNELL SAID TO HER HUSBAND, WILLIAM, turning a ring around on her finger, "I never look at this emerald without thinking how its color resembles Grandmother's eyes. Look. There is a hint of blue in it, too. And it sparkles, just as Grandmother's eyes sparkled when she was up to mischief or some kind of deviltry. But, I never meet anyone like Grandmother any more. She was a product of the nineteenth century, though she lived far into the twentieth. In fact, Grandmother was ageless. Look how the emerald shines, William! It seems to wink at me, as Grandmother used to wink. I used to admire it on her own finger. I'm glad she left it to me. Emerald as her eyes; emerald as her Irish homeland."

William McConnell, who had met Grandmother only a few times, said, "Yes, she was ageless. She seems as much alive today as when I first saw her. Her name was yours, too, wasn't it? Rose Mary. A beautiful name."

Grandmother Rose Mary O'Driscoll was Irish, and the last child of a family of seventeen children, all of whom lived into their nineties and some into their hundreds. But she had been born in Scotland, not Ireland, for her family had moved to Scotland before she was born. They were shipbuilders on the Clyde, and Grandmother's brothers, some of them, later engaged in whiskey or in railroads. But that was later. In the meantime, Rose Mary O'Driscoll was brought up in luxury in Scotland. She was her parents' favorite child, the child of their old age. She was denied nothing whatsoever, and when she was a married woman (having married a Bruce Cullen, a Scots Irishman), she still denied nothing to herself. Discipline was a word Grandmother had never heard. All her brothers and sisters had had strenuous blue eyes, white skins, and the black thick hair of the true Irish, who have Spanish blood. They were also tall and morose. They were silent, but sometimes silently violent. Grandmother was unlike her older brothers and sisters. She was short, lively and gay. Her eyes were blue-green and glittering. Her hair was red, her nose large and Roman, her skin eternally freckled.

She also had tremendous style and flair and liveliness and wit, from the very earliest childhood. No one ever called her beautiful, not even her numerous lovers, which she took after her four sons were born. But she made up for her lack of beauty in liveliness, loud raucous laughter, jokes and utter devilment. She had a voice like a foghorn, hoarse and loud, which must have made her brothers and sisters wince, with their soft Irish voices. They adored her. They called her "our Rose." They forgave her everything and they had a lot to forgive.

Rose Mary would tell her granddaughter, Rose Cullen, that when she was a child she had her home "under me thumb" from her cradle. This continued throughout her life, until her last few years at the mercy of her grim sons, with their Covenanter consciences and their morality and their stiff repugnance at the slightest sign of frivolity and joy. Because they could never understand her, and because of their father, Bruce Cullen, whom they respected and feared, they came to consider their mother as evil. But Rose Mary was merely her usual shouting, laughing, hilarious and devilish self, as she had been all her life, and which, paradoxically, had first drawn her husband to her—he so dour and restrained and joyless, himself. (Her witchery over him was short-lived, unfortunately.) She was never a hypocrite. "Be yeself," she would tell her granddaughter, Rose, her only granddaughter. "And the divil take the sober." Sadly, her husband and her sons were all "sober," something which she never forgave them.

All Rose Mary's handsome sisters, with their deep blue eyes, snow-colored skins and black hair, were well married before their seven-

teenth birthdays. The brothers married well-dowered girls. But Rose
Mary, having a hell of a good time among her legion of beaus in
Barhead, declined marriage. She was seventeen, and unmarried; she
was eighteen and her mother went to Mass every morning and made
Novenas and wept. Then she was nineteen and her father went to
see the Bishop, himself. What was wrong with his darlin' colleen?
The lads were mad for her, but Rose Mary was not mad for any particular lad; she simply loved them all. Besides, she was enjoying
herself mightily. Dances. Walks. Teas. Receptions. The Bishop graciously accepted an invitation to dinner, remembering Mr. O'Driscoll's fine dinners with pleasure, he who rarely had more than a few
days' supplies in his own larder. He talked with Rose Mary, in his
grave and musical voice, and Rose Mary friskily said her heart was
on no particular man as yet. Yes, my lord, she had passed her nineteenth birthday. But, she was patient. The Bishop looked into the
dancing green eyes and thought of elves, and then reminded himself hastily that there were no elves.

Rose Mary loved music of any kind, though she did not care for
female singers, not even Jenny Lind. "A screecher," she once told her
granddaughter. "It's the ears she would tear from your head." Rose
Mary, herself, sang like a parrot, a bird to which she was devoted all
her life, huge birds like vultures, colored wildly and always giving
the impression, to little Rose, of awaiting the exact moment when
they could snatch out a small girl's eyes. But Rose Mary loved the
singer, and not the song, which soon became distressingly evident
shortly after the Bishop's visit.

Rose Mary was delighted by pantomimes, public dances, theatres,
concerts, and other crowded gatherings, no matter who made up the
crowds. There she would glitter in her Paris gowns, her sequinned
gloves, her plumes (fastened to her bright red hair with brilliantes),
her velvet or furred cloaks, her jewels. There she would soon begin
to be her natural self, and eyes would be directed to the box which
she occupied with her parents, and ears would be listening to her
ribald remarks, her hoarse and hooting laughter, the rattle of her
bracelets. She seemed always to be in movement, restless, exciting,
shining. Her audacious grin would glow upon the young men in the

stalls below, and they would be dazzled by the tiny and vivacious girl above them and her winks and her wicked fannings. Her long and fiery curls lay on her small and freckled bare shoulders. If she had a very childish bosom still, it was lighted up with the gems inherited from female ancestors. She had a seventeen-inch waist, garlanded with a belt of turquoises and topazes, set in flexible gold. Her bustles were gathered up with diamond pins. She may have had no beauty, but she had style and fascination in spite of a small and freckled face, a large grinning mouth full of flashing white teeth, a pointed chin with a deep cleft, and a very big nose with coarse nostrils. She had no need of beauty; she scintillated.

She met her fate, as it was called then, while she attended a certain concert with her parents when she was within hailing distance of twenty. The featured singer was a lad all of eighteen, tall, handsome, brooding, with pale and chiseled features, quiet blue eyes, an incipient mustache the color of pure gold, broad and impressive shoulders, and a stern mouth full of Scots melancholy. His voice was beautiful and strong. He sang the ballads of both Scotland and Ireland, and the audience wept, including Rose Mary, the cynic. She had never cared a fig for such ballads before, but she was now suddenly lost in the eyes of a Scots lad and heard nothing but his voice. Rose Mary was deeply and instantly in love for the first, if not the last, time in her life.

She was never quite explicit to anyone as to how she contrived to meet the lad, who was Bruce Raymond Cullen. But contrive she did, under the very noses of her parents. She also met him on other occasions. "He was mad for me from the beginning," she would tell her granddaughter, "and he a Scots Presbyterian and I a Catholic. We ran off to Gretna Green, and were married within a month." But not in the presence of a priest. The lad may have been mad for Rose Mary, but he "wouldna hae a priest," he made it clear. So Rose Mary had him without the priest, a fact which when revealed to her parents caused them impotent agony. Nor would there be a second marriage. Rose Mary was infatuated, and she was to remain infatuated for all of five years, during which time her four sons were born. Then the infatuation ended as abruptly as it had begun, and Bruce was rarely seen at home any longer. He continued his concert work and died when his oldest son was ten years old, and if Rose Mary mourned him it was not evident.

No one had ever accused Rose Mary O'Driscoll Cullen of being a patient lass, and so she took upon herself the proper bringing up of her sons—whom she had found dull and uninspiring almost from their birth—impatiently. They all reminded her of her husband, of whom she had become unbearably weary long before he died. Now that there was no scandalous husband on the premises, involved in a marriage they considered invalid, the parents of Rose Mary came to her assistance, bewailing her dire circumstances. They were hardly poverty-stricken even from the point of view of modern days, for Rose Mary had inherited two thousand pounds a year at her twenty-first birthday from her maternal grandfather, and Bruce Cullen had made quite a bit of money, himself, on his concert tours of the British Isles, and had made even more money among the sentimental Scots and Irish immigrants in America. It is true that Rose Mary had spent most of the fine money on her own small person, and was adding to her store of jewelry, and that her house—now in Glasgow—was modest and not in a fashionable neighborhood. But she and her children were scarcely starving, though the besotted O'Driscolls felt they were. So they established a fund for Rose Mary, and the equally besotted brothers and sisters added to it. (It is of no consequence, of course, that Rose Mary did not tell her parents that her husband had left her considerable money.)

Rose Mary was humbly grateful and affectionate to her kin for all they had done for her; they missed that green and mocking sparkle in her eye. As she wanted, more than anything else, to get her lads from under her feet, she immediately sent them to public (private) schools far from Glasgow. She then took a grand tour of the Continent to renew old and fascinated acquaintances, and there was an interlude with an Italian gentleman of family of which no one in the Isles had ever heard, nor did they ever know. Satisfied, surfeited, and full of the lust for life, she returned to the Isles, lived in London for a while, then became interested in increasing her fortune through investments. As she was restless, she moved from city to city as time went on, establishing fine homes, then selling them at a sound profit.

Her sons married fairly well, but Rose Mary was not interested either in them or their wives or their subsequent children. She did declare, however, that she had always wanted a daughter, and when one of the sons, the third, did produce a daughter Rose Mary was in temporary raptures, invested the child in her own christening robe, and named her after herself. The child, Rose Mary Cullen, had Grandmother's own hair, greenish-hazel eyes and general features, but unfortunately she had also inherited her Grandfather Cullen's sober and dogged personality. So Grandmother lost interest, if she still retained a random affection for her namesake. She remembered the child on her birthday and at Christmas, but saw her infrequently until the little one was about four years old. Grandmother was then living in Leeds in a very fine house indeed, in the very center of a block of houses she was renovating and restoring for later profitable sale.

So it was that little Rose Cullen found herself every winter for considerable periods in Grandmother's house, whenever her parents had their prolonged and bitter rows. She never quite discovered what the rows were about, and never really cared, for she was a child of silences and solitudes. She accepted life with deep and passionate interest, but it was not a personal interest. She almost welcomed the rows so that she could go to Grandmother's at Leeds, where the house was filled with beguiling treasures, a parrot or two to be teased and observed from a safe distance, an air of luxury, and, always, Grandma's vivid if not affectionate presence and Grandma's strange and exotic guests. Besides, Grandma had a cook of an expansive nature whom little Rose found very comforting, and who could be relied upon for dainties from Grandma's table and bonbons and glazed chestnuts and candied ginger and exquisite tartlets. And Grandma's gardens, even in winter, were mysterious with mist and silence and wild birds and rooks, and, above all, there were no wrangling parents.

Rose often said to her husband, William McConnell, "I remember a time at Grandma's in 1904. (She always insisted I call her Grandmother, however; it seemed to her less aged than 'Grandma,' and much less dull and suety.) I remember . . ."

Her first memory of Leeds, England, and Grandmother Rose Mary O'Driscoll Cullen's house, was when she was just under four years of age and a row had blown up at home. Her parents packed a bag for her, put her on a train by herself, and returned home to do unrestrained battle. Grandmother's carriage and coachman met her, silently, at the station in Leeds, and in silence they drove to Grandmother's house. Rose recalled that first lonely occasion very sharply. The dun-colored streets were awash with cold and sooty rain; water splashed on the roof of the carriage. Lights drifted by as they passed lonely houses, and the air was full of the stench of coal gas, wet leather and wool, and smoke. The horse clopped along on the cobblestones. The darkness came down heavily and the carriage lurched from side to side. Rose's hands were numbed with cold, even in their gloves. She listened to the boom of the wind against the carriage, the far wailing of it as it rushed westwards. She was not frightened, nor even lonely, for she was accustomed to loneliness. Carriages passed, their lanterns lit. Once one of those new and rowdy motorcars charged around the carriage, startling the horse, and causing the coachman to curse and threaten with his whip. The gutters chattered; the stones of the street glistened in lamplight. But Rose was excited; she was on her first visit to Grandmother's and to the mysterious world in which that legendary figure lived.

The house was very large and lighted at almost every window, and there was a reflection of red and flickering firelight on draperies not yet drawn. The building had a little portico with about four white, round wooden pillars and a broad fan of brick steps leading to the door from the street. The coachman, with a sour look, opened the carriage door for Rose. Then he was moved to some kindness for the forlorn little girl. He swung her up in his arms with a hearty word, and his rough chin and cheek scraped her face. He carried her up the steps and said cheerily, "There you be, little miss," put her down, banged the knocker, and returned to the carriage for her luggage. In the meantime a smart, uniformed maid stood on the threshold, staring without favor. "A kid in the house," she mumbled, and pulled Rose inside smartly. "Behave yourself, and no trouble," she warned. Grandmother was entertaining at dinner, and there was no time for any greeting. The unfriendly maid pushed Rose irritably up an immense stairway of white wood and velvet carpeting, and then into a long hall filled with closed doors. A lamp burned at its farther end, the light enclosed in a crimson globe. The maid opened the door of a small and arctic bedroom, and lit a candle. Rose saw the big bed with its canopy, its horsehair chairs, its little green slipper love seat, its empty fireplace, its Brussels rug, its blue velvet draperies looped back over fine lace curtains.

"Have you had your tea?" asked the maid, threateningly.

Rose shook her head. The maid sighed. "And now I've got to get a kid's tea," she grumbled. "Very well, you. Sit there and be quiet," and she lifted the child and set her down with a thump on a giant rocking chair whose horsehair chafed her thighs immediately. "Not a word out of you," the maid warned, and slammed the door after her. Rose was suddenly very tired, yawned and drowsed, the chair swaying under her. She came awake to see the maid angrily lighting a small fire. There was a tray on the table of sandwiches, tea, cream, sugar, pound cake, a hot scone or two, and jam. Rose was hungry at once, climbed down from the chair, stood at the table and began to devour the food. The fire caught; the wind thundered in the chimney; the windows rattled. It was a cold night.

The maid scrubbed her with coolish water in a large bowl afterwards, sneered at her flannel nightgown which boasted no lace or embroidered buttons, and thumped her into the icy bed. "Where's Grandmother?" Rose asked.

"Better things to do than to bother with the likes of you," said the maid. "Go to sleep. The chamber's under the bed, and mind you use it properly."

Rose did not sleep for a long time. She watched the small fire on the hearth, and listened to its brisk crackling. She listened to the wind pounding at the windows, shouting in the chimney, growling in the eaves. The rain sounded like a cataract. She was at Grandmother's, in Leeds, the first of many visits, which were not welcomed. But she had already learned that there is little welcome for anyone in the world, and so was not disturbed. She said her prayers tranquilly enough, praying dutifully for dear Papa and Mama and all the Poor. God, she was certain, was standing right there beside the bed. She had known much about Him since she had been hardly two years old, long before anyone had ever spoken His Name to her. Rose turned her head on the sweetly scented bolster, and there, over the fireplace, stood a crucifix, the first she had ever seen. It was very large, and the Body of the Christ appeared made of dark gold. Rose had never as yet heard of Him, fully, but all at once she was filled with understanding. She fell asleep as if under the blessing of a sleepless Guardian.

That was all Rose ever remembered of the first of the many visits to Grandmother's house in Leeds. It seemed to her that those visits never ended all the rest of her life, and she returned to the memory of them as one returns to an old cathedral of one's deepest memories —though Grandmother's house was hardly a cathedral.

Rose was going on five on her next visit, and it was this visit that impressed itself forever on her memory, as the beginning of her friendship with Grandmother's holy men. They were the only holy creatures ever to enter Grandmother's houses, until the end of her life.

Chapter Two

ROSE WAS FOUR IN THE LAST SEPTEMBER and British children begin their education at that age. The little girl was sent to a very small private school run by a dejected but punishing Miss Brothers in the latter's shabby but genteel house. Rose did not like the schoolmistress and was bored by the other children, who ranged from four to fourteen. Children, at four, learned their letters at once, and began to read, or God help them.

After the Christmas holidays she was sent to Grandmother's again. She was delighted to be free of Miss Brothers and her schoolmates and chattered freely while her mother packed her luggage, a uniqueness that caused her mother to eye her with reflection. The train excited her as before. She read a storybook in that compartment filled with adults. They did not smile at her; children in England are not regarded as objects of interest but only as nuisances. The rain began, the dull gray rain of midwinter, and the shouting winds. Hamlets moved sluggishly beyond the windows; narrow little streets were revealed, filled with lorries or hurrying working people. Twilight was coming down.

The train rumbled; gentlemen rustled their newspapers. Ladies knitted or drowsed or conversed together in low voices, pausing only to look outside haughtily when the train paused at some sooty station. There would be the "lower-class" people who were scurrying towards the second- or third-class coaches—mostly the third—their heads and shoulders hunched together against the rain and wind. Rose felt sorry for them. They were the Poor she was always being admonished to pray for every night. There seemed such a lot of them, and they appeared so cold and shabby, so red in the chapped face.

It was dark, and the rain and the wind were truly formidable. "Leeds!" called the guard, and Rose picked up her heavy bag and struggled with it to the door of the corridor. No adult, of course, offered to help her. She was a child and therefore well able to take care of herself. But the guard at the door of the compartment smiled at her kindly, and said, "Here, that's a big lumbering thing for a little lass. I'll give you a hand." She was much surprised. He even lifted her down the high steps of the carriage. He embarrassed her. He made her feel small and incompetent. A new coachman and Grandmother's carriage were waiting, and the train guard tossed her luggage into the carriage while the coachman watched impassively. The train guard touched his cap as if she were a grown-up lady, and as she did not know what else to do to repay him for his kindness she gave him a curtsey. The coachman sneered and spat. "Lookin' for sixpence," he muttered, driving off. "Give him that, did you?"

"No," she said, "I have only three shillings, for emergencies."

She spoke in the chilly accents taught her at Miss Brothers' school, and the coachman became silent. When they reached Grandmother's house he even alighted and lifted her and her luggage from the carriage. "Don't get above yourself," he warned her, however. "It's the Madam as has the money, not your Pa."

Grandmother, of course, was at dinner, with guests, all gentlemen from the sound of them. But what voices! They were the voices of giants, laughing, interrupting, bursting into laughter, arguing. They were also musical, with the brownish burr of the Scots and the Irish. There were snatches of rollicking song. Manly voices, strong and powerful. "The priests, again," said the coachman disdainfully to the maid. "At it again, are they?"

"Ever so," said the maid, in a tone to match his own. "Wot she sees in them——"

"Once a Roman, always a Roman," said the coachman, departing.

"What's a Roman like?" Rose asked Elsie, with interest.

"Never you mind," she snapped. "Just keep out of their sight. Upstairs with you, and mind your tongue." But Rose was older now, almost five. "Watch your own tongue, Elsie," she said with hauteur. "You are not the one to correct me." She had learned a thing or two at Miss Brothers', and a lady was not to endure impudence in servants.

"I'll give it to you!" cried Elsie, viciously. But she did not haul Rose upstairs this time. She followed her with the luggage, three steps behind, muttering to herself. She lit the fire; the room was as bitterly cold as Rose had remembered. Then she went down for Rose's tea. She came back, empty-handed. "The Madam wants you in the dining-room," she said, incredulously. "You! A kid! Wot's the world comin' to, tell me? But then," she added, as if it explained everything, as it probably did, "the priests want to take a look at you."

The "Romans." Rose was filled with curiosity. Also, she was hungry. "I want my tea," she reminded Elsie.

"Ha!" Elsie said, and threw up her hands. "There's a place ordered for you at the table. At the table! Go along with you now, fast as you can. But wash your hands first."

She scrubbed Rose's hands and more roughly scrubbed her face. Then she combed out her hair. "Red!" she said, with contempt. "And not a curl in it. Straight as a stick. Your ribbon is undone." The comb, and her fingernails, dug into Rose's scalp. Elsie even rubbed the dust from Rose's boots and straightened her stockings and brushed down her woolen Tartan frock. "No beauty, you," she said, with pleasure. "All knees and elbows and you not five yet. You'll be as tall as a man, from the looks of you, and the Madam so dainty!" She made it sound as if to be five were rather criminal, but Rose was accustomed to this attitude on the part of adults. One outgrew five, eventually. Six followed, and then seven, and time took care of the guilt of being less than five. She had also learned that time took care of other unpleasant things, too, such as sitting in a form at Miss Brothers'. The summer would eventually come. Christmas had come, hadn't it, just when she had given up hope? (Papa had finally surrendered to the "Popery" of Christmas, at Mama's relentless insist-

ence, for as a true Scot he despised and ignored Christmas and celebrated only the New Year. But Mama had not, as yet, introduced
the enormity of a Christmas tree.)

Rose went downstairs sedately. What would the "Romans" be like,
those strange creatures of whom Papa talked with mingled fear and
disgust, and in a dark tone? She had learned, however, to discount
much of what her parents said, and besides, Mama would often
laugh at Papa's lurid tales of priests and nuns. Rose made her way
through the baize door to the threshold of the dining-room, which
appeared vast, too brilliant, too intimidating, to her. It was all one
dazzle, from the chandelier blazing from the ceiling, to the white
lace tablecloth set with glittering silver and crystal. Worse, it was
full of monumental men with huge red faces. The only lady present
was Grandmother. She was flushed with wine and laughter and joy,
and was dressed in her favorite color, green, satin this time, restless
with gems. There was a great fire on the hearth, and the room was
very hot. Grandmother's hair was piled high on her head, and it was
the color of flame.

"It's Queen Victoria, herself, come to life again!" shouted Grandmother, catching sight of Rose, and gesticulating towards the door.
"The ugly frock and all, and the sober face of her!" She yelled with
mirth and lifted a freckled thin bare arm in a mock gesture of salutation. Her shoulders were astonishingly bare, and small.

The men, all dressed in black, and with odd collars, turned as a
man to look at Rose. For the first time in Rose's life every adult face
smiled in her direction, and every eye was kind and tender. There
seemed dozens of these friendly if gigantic creatures. There were
probably no more than eleven. The nearest held out his hand to her,
beckoning. He said, in a soft and growling burr, "Come to me, little
colleen. I'm wanting to see ye close."

Amazed that an adult could want to see her "close," and fascinated
as well, Rose went to him slowly. Grandmother grinned. "She'll not
be setting the world afire, with that solemn face," she said, hoarsely.
"There's no style in the girl. I was a belle at her age."

The priest stroked Rose's hair and cheek, and there was love in his
touch. "It's the brave face she has on her," he said, and he sighed.

And that is how Rose came to know Grandmother's priests, and all about them, and all the stories they could tell. She came to love and trust them, as she had never loved and trusted anyone else. They had many different faces, and they were strange and sometimes not to be understood by a child, but not one had a harsh voice or a cruel expression, and in spite of their big bodies and the sense of mysterious authority about them, they were gentle.

Well-brought-up British children did not eat their meals with their elders except on special occasions such as Christmas Day, New Year's Day, Easter Sunday, and birthdays, and suchlike.

Therefore, when Grandmother, with another flourish of her diamond-laden arm, indicated that Rose was to sit halfway down at the table between two priests she was dumfounded. She had never, at any time, sat in the presence of adults, at a dinner table, except on the most extraordinary of occasions. She crept onto the damask chair, half fearing that she would be yanked from it immediately for the grossest impertinence, and sent to bed without even a light tea. She was not disturbed by anyone, however. Conversation continued all about her as if she were not present. She saw Grandmother's beautiful Sèvres dinner plate before her, delicate creamy-white with its deep border of dark blue and gold, and her heavy silver-and-crystal goblets filled with a variety of wines. Rose furtively studied the design of the lace cloth, as delicate as a web. A servant placed a bowl of hot broth before her, and she dubiously regarded the tiny brown items in it; she did not as yet know they were mushrooms. Hushing every sound she might possibly make, she sipped at the broth, full of wonderment. Then came a delicious trout in its own sauce and the smallest of creamed onions. This was followed by a thick slice of roast beef, Yorkshire pudding, and the usual British vegetables. By watching out of the corner of her eye at a big hand near her, Rose gathered what fork to use. Then came the savories, and a new wine.

During all this time Grandmother's voice boomed, shouted, and raucously laughed so that the yellow damask walls appeared to vibrate. She was in a very high, good humor. She had wanted daughters of her own, and then granddaughters. But she detested women.

It was rare that she could endure the presence even of the wittiest
and smartest at her own dinner parties, and she never accepted invitations to all-female teas or dinners. She preferred her brothers to
her sisters, her father to her mother, her male cousins to her female.
The only men she had truly disliked were her husband and her sons.
She disliked them because they did not automatically proffer her
what she considered her due: admiration, affection, and appreciation
of her formidable charm and magnetism. She resented a man whose
eye roved from her to another woman, and this did not happen often,
because she was fascinating, effervescent and always beautifully
gowned. Grandmother loved living, and in her presence even the
saddest could find some gaiety in life, something endurable, a fresh
allurement or colorful witchery.

None of these were based on the slightest virtue at all. Grandmother was not immoral; she simply was not moral, in any meaning
of the word. She was given to bursts of extravagance in favor of the
Lad of the Hour, but she totally lacked any real charity. "Help your
neighbor if you will," she once told Rose, "but run fast, lassie, for
your life's sake!" Grandmother never jeopardized her life, and as she
rarely assisted anyone she did not make enemies.

As a lapsed Catholic, or at least as a baptized Catholic born to a
Catholic family, Grandmother was the object of the constant and
earnest prayers of her brothers and sisters, all devout. According to
family legend, her relatives were always at Novenas, at Mass, on their
knees many times a day with rosaries in their hands, praying for
Grandmother's carefree, buoyant and hilarious soul, and for her return to the Sacraments. As they were all well off, they endlessly
visited famous shrines in her behalf. Visiting her, they secreted holy
medals in obscure places, which caused Grandmother high amusement when a servant unearthed them. "They'll be having my soul,
will they?" she would ask, shrieking with laughter. Her father gave
her the big crucifix which Rose had seen in the bedroom upstairs,
and which had been blessed by the Holy Father, himself, at the
humble importunity of her great-grandmother.

As her family had been so devoted to priests and the Religious
when she had been a girl at home, Rose Mary had come to look upon

them all with affection. The priests in her day were not Elegant English Gentlemen, but were men of vigor and strength and imagination. They had to be, to survive in those days in Scotland and England. The weak among them had no chance at all. But even those who survived were chronically poor and hungry, as were most of their parishioners, chronically shabby and threadbare, with neat patches visible at knee and elbow and boot. What woolen scarves they had were made by female relatives, or old ladies in their poverty-stricken parishes. Moreover, most of the priests had large numbers of indigent brothers and sisters, nieces and nephews, not to mention old parents, and to these went most of their tiny stipends, if any, and all of the meagre gifts.

They were not persecuted, of course, in either Scotland or England, but they were ignored by all but Catholics. They appeared to live in a world that found them invisible. They had no friends except those of their own Faith, and if some of the more daring reached out a kind and tentative hand towards a possibly different friend, they were immediately accused of attempting to make converts. Rare was the Protestant minister, however full of good will, who would challenge his own congregation by inviting some starveling young priest to dinner. A minister who paused on the street to speak to a "Roman" colleague was inviting the darkest of suspicions and even darker glances. Sisters meekly collecting for charities in shops were usually roughly ordered out at once, unless the shopkeeper were Catholic, himself.

So priests in England, Scotland and Wales in those days led very rigorous lives, and they needed all the humor, affection, sympathy and kindness they could get from their own people. It was no life for the faint-hearted, the timid or the too gentle, or the openly sensitive. Sons of a brawling people, they did not hesitate openly to protect a victim of a gang on some sordid street. They did not rush for a policeman. They rescued the victims themselves, and punched and kicked with fervor. Their garb did not protect them at a time when they were objects of derision. Many a priest suffered a broken head or a limb on his missions of violent mercy, but one can be sure that they gave as good as they got. Each of them would have eagerly offered his life in martyrdom for his Faith and his God, and considered such martyrdom the most blessed of Graces. But a helpless woman who was being beaten by her drunken husband, or a child who was being tormented by cruel adults, often had reason to rejoice encountering a passing priest drawn by her screams and groans. The deep humility of their souls, which would have prevented them from defending their own persons except when in danger of death, did not permit priests to stand by while the weak were being attacked or tortured. Many priests died of injuries in the slums of London and Liverpool and Manchester, when their attempts to save a helpless man, woman or child failed, or even when they succeeded. They had to be brawny and vigorous men, of courage, steadfastness and strength. They met the devil face to face many times in their lives, and often gave their lives and blood in the struggle against him. But still they preserved their good humor under the direst of challenges, and as they were mighty men they were singularly gentle and uncomplex, the first to help, the first to comfort, the first to offer kindness.

They were, of course, not Gentlemen. Few there were of noble blood, those Scots and Irish priests. Most of them had been born in the working class, in poverty, in the midst of other teeming children, in hunger, in cold. They knew hard labor as soon as they began to toddle. They never wondered if they had a vocation for the priesthood, nor did they dally at ease with the thought. A lad knew, absolutely, if he had a vocation, and he pursued it under the most dreadful of circumstances, often without a penny in his pocket or more than the clothes that he stood in. He knew what the life entailed, and so from the very beginning he could have no doubts. A boy or youth with doubts, or hesitations, never became a priest in those days.

It is no wonder, then, that their people reverenced and loved them, for they knew what these men were sacrificing for them because of their love of God and man. Few Catholics in those days, in England, Scotland or Ireland, were rich. If they were, their homes became oases of refreshment, temporary rest, and food, and what charity could be wrung from rich pockets. It was never a great deal, that charity, for men of substance who have never known pain, sorrow, hunger or homelessness are frequently hard of heart. What little money found its way into the offering plates came from hands scoured, callused and twisted by the most arduous work. Still, the homes of the rich Catholics were open to the priests, most of the time, provided the priests did not press too ardently for cash for a school or new bells or an orphanage or a convent, and used tact during the hour of possible extraction. It was a case of "I won't look if you take anything from my purse, provided you don't call my attention to it."

Grandmother had known priests all her life. As they possessed her own sense of humor, vitality, shrewdness and love for living, she remained fond of them. They also reminded her of her petted childhood, when there were always at least two priests at every dinner. She had respect for them, she who respected no other men. They knew how to survive.

They were all aware of the dire state of her soul, the various members of the family usually keeping all priests up to date on the sins of "our Rose Mary." Her house was open to them, and they came. There is not the slightest doubt that every priest, even while eating the best of dinners and drinking the best of whiskeys and wines in Grandmother's house, was praying for her soul and her return to sanctity.

So the priests came to Grandmother's home, when they passed through Leeds, for though a lapsed Catholic and obviously living in sin in more ways than one, she was still the daughter of a Catholic family and had been baptized in the Faith. There was always the possibility that influence, patience and prayer would bring Grandmother back to the fold. They were also great gossips, bringing messages to Grandmother from Scotland and Ireland from her old friends and her relatives. They were also full of tales, for sagas were still being spoken and written in those days.

They drew the line, these priests, at staying overnight in Grandmother's house, though with mirth leaping in her eyes she invariably invited them and described the comforts of fires, hot water, indoor plumbing and thick feather beds and fine linen. They would look wistful, while shaking their heads. Then, hours after dinner, and after many stories, they would depart for less sinful lodgings, huddled

in their thin coats. "Ye'll be knowin' where to reach me," they'd say
to her hopefully, before leaving, envisioning sudden alarums in the
night when the only help possible would be that given by a priest.
But Grandmother was superbly healthy. "It's not dying I will be
this night," she'd answer, with a toss of red curls, her own and
supplementary others. "Never fear, Father." They wanted to "fear,"
but Grandmother never called for a priest. She outlived all those
she ever knew. But still they hoped.

Rose learned all these things over many years. But even as a
young child, on her second visit to Grandmother's house, and finally
gathering that these "Romans" were "wee ministers," themselves, she
wondered what in hell they were doing at Grandmother's table. It
was so obvious to Rose that Grandmother was a very naughty lady,
indeed.

Rose had never sat at a table with Grandmother, for even when
she had visited her sons in London she had not wanted a child near
her, "the blasted nuisances." So Rose could hardly believe it, that
night in Leeds, that Grandmother had suffered her to be seated at
her scintillating table, in the presence of the eleven priests. The
priests had invited Rose; therefore, Grandmother could not protest
at a "brat sitting in me presence." But she ignored Rose's existence
as she would have ignored a pestilential fly. She continued to amuse
her friends with the most outrageous stories.

But the priests did not forget Rose. An enormous hand gently
took her knife to cut up her meat, and she basked in this smiling
attention. She looked at her assistant timidly; his big red face beamed
at her as if she were not a child at all, but a person whose company
was agreeable. The priest on her left hand was being addressed as
Monsignor, and though, when she looked at him, he gave her a
brief smile, he had a more remote air than did Father McGlynn,
and a certain chill austerity. He was Monsignor Harrington-Smith,
one of the few Englishmen among all those Scots and Irish. But as
he was a priest he was tolerated by his colleagues. He was also distantly related to one of Grandmother's cousins who had married a
Sassenagh. Rose soon saw that he gave a kind of "tone" to the

party, not only because he was the only Monsignor present then, but because of his superb manners and quietness.

A savory was placed before Rose. By this time she was exhausted by all the noise and shine and brilliance, and the heat in the dining-room, and she was a little fuzzy from the sips of wine she had drunk. "I think," said Monsignor Harrington-Smith, "that I should not eat that, if I were you, Rose." An adult's word was law. She put down her fork.

Grandmother, always willing to please a priest, rang for a servant and asked if there was any milky blancmange on the premises, a lowly dish usually eaten only by domestics. There was. A shivering morsel was brought in, on a golden saucer, for Rose, and Monsignor nodded approvingly. Rose ate it obediently; it tasted like paste.

There was champagne, which Monsignor deftly prevented Rose from sampling. She decided that though he was kind enough to endure the presence of a child he was too much like Miss Brothers, who served dry sardines on drier toast as a savory. Monsignor Harrington-Smith, apparently, was no stranger to champagne, for he tasted it critically and daintily, before accepting it. But his colleagues rejoiced in it, the poor men not having much of a palate, of necessity. "It'll be pleasing you, Monsignor?" asked Grandmother, with a wink.

"A good year," he said, a trifle pompously. He examined the bottle which the manservant extended to him. "A good year," he repeated, "though not the best. I understand there was not enough sun during the final weeks."

"It's delighted I am that you'll be drinking it at all," said Grandmother, demurely. "But then, one knows that your lordship was bathed in champagne, at your christening."

"You know very well, Rose Mary, that I am a second son," he said.

She grinned and dipped her head with mock humility. Then she rustled to her tiny feet—which were covered with satin and jeweled slippers—and the priests rose with her. Rose stood up, also. Monsignor Harrington-Smith folded his hands and prayed. Rose was fascinated by all those suddenly solemn faces around her—even

Grandmother's—and was thinking about it during the movement following the prayer when she felt a hard pinch on her shoulder, and smelled Grandmother's hot and musky scent. "Upstairs with you," Grandmother said.

Rose started to obey at once, then a hand fell on her shoulder. Her new dear friend was holding her back. "And why should not the little one join us?"

"An auld head on her shoulders," said Grandmother, somberly, shaking her own, and speaking in her curious mixture of Scots and Irish burr. "It's nae good thing for a lass to have. It's a touch of the divil, himself."

She gave Rose a jumping and warning look, and Rose murmured it was past her bedtime. But she was led into the drawing-room, which she had rarely been permitted to enter before. It seemed to her at least half as large as the street on which she lived in London and was crowded with little gilt chairs covered by vari-colored damasks and tapestries, with rose damask glistening on the walls, and sofas everywhere and tall crystal lamps and portraits and mirrors and tables teeming with exquisite little ornaments and buhl cabinets in each corner filled with objets d'art and Spanish fans. A big fire danced in a fireplace in which a medium-sized ox could have stood, and over the mantelpiece hung a very fine portrait of Queen Victoria, whom Grandmother did not resemble in the slightest. If the dining-room had awed Rose, the drawing-room petrified her with its size and shine and magnificence. The windows, covered with rose shirred silk, over which were looped blue damask draperies, appeared to her to extend upward to infinity.

Father McGlynn led Rose to a little polished steel stool, a sort of hob, which stood beside the fire, and he put a cushion on it, and then lifted her onto the cushion. "There, and that's a comfort," he said, and patted her cheek.

Dazzled, trembling with anticipation of what she did not know, she crouched on the stool. The priests sat around the fire, with Grandmother in the semicircle, and all had big brandy glasses in their hands. There was just a little golden liquid at the bottom of the glasses; they swished the liquid around, inhaled the fumes, said

"Ah!" in deep voices, and occasionally sipped. Rose was fascinated.

Grandmother pulled up her skirts to warm her thin little shanks —she was always cold in spite of the incredible amount of alcohol she consumed daily—and said to Monsignor Harrington-Smith: "It'll be your time to tell your tale, Monsignor."

"You know I am not superstitious, Rose Mary," he said to Grandmother. The priests looked depressed. "Superstition" was, of course, forbidden sternly by the Church, but they believed, with Shakespeare, that there are more things in heaven and earth than Englishmen would ever acknowledge or see or hear. Or perhaps they believed that no Sassenagh would be able to tell a tale that would keep a watchdog awake or curl a single hair of a more susceptible child.

A priest said hastily, "Sure, and I am thinking it is my turn."

"Nay," said Grandmother, with a wicked twinkle. "I remember me that it was to be Monsignor Harrington-Smith's."

"I am not superstitious," said the Monsignor, as if this little interlude had not taken place. "Nevertheless——"

The priests sat up, with more hopeful expressions. Monsignor was shaking his head, and frowning.

"Ah," said Father McGlynn, in a deep, expectant voice. Anything that could baffle Sassenaghs must be really extraordinary. Why, if St. Michael appeared before them they'd be wanting to examine his armor for authenticity, suspecting it had been stolen from Windsor Castle, and they'd doubtless sneer, "Sheffield steel," when running skeptical fingers along his sword.

"So——" said Monsignor, and launched into his story with increasing reluctance, as if, someway, such things did not happen in the orderly course of events, to Englishmen of proper breeding. "It was in Ireland. Of course," he began.

"Ah!!!" said the priests in a body, nodding, and pulling their chairs closer. If it had happened in England—nothing would have happened. But Ireland!

MONSIGNOR HARRINGTON-SMITH AND
THE DREAD ENCOUNTER

Edward Albert Harrington-Smith was the second son of a British peer. He, very early in life, knew that he had a vocation for the priesthood. He was the handsomer lad of the two, and his father had had hopes that his breeding, face and carriage, and undeniable intellect would attract a girl of some family and money, or, perhaps, a rich American. The father had even saved enough to send the youth to America in pursuit of the necessities. But Edward wanted to be a priest. "If only we were High Church," said the father, with a little wistfulness. "We Catholics, even those of us with illustrious names and fortunes and castles, are not truly acceptable in this society. Now, if we were High Church we could be assured that Edward would be a Bishop within a short time."

Edward went to a Seminary, and his priestly superiors were not particularly impressed that he was "a second son." They demanded faith, character, a true vocation, and dedication and sincerity. He had all of them. Eventually he was ordained a priest. However, he had characteristics that did not quite meet the approval of his superiors. He was inclined to be proud, remote and a little disdainful of his "inferiors." His superiors believed that a parish in one of the more destitute sections of Ireland would have a salutary effect on him. ("Ireland!" cried his father, with horror, never forgetting for a moment that he was an Englishman. "I will write a letter at once to his Eminence! Ireland!")

His Eminence was kind, but realistic. "A priest must learn to go anywhere," he wrote to his friend. "It will do Edward good."

Edward was not certain of this. But he kept his doubts between himself and his confessor, who did not have too high a regard for the Irish, either. So Edward soon found himself in a very wild parish, indeed, where his parishioners implicitly believed in the "little people," and fairies and banshees, and were quite "superstitious." Moreover, they were both awed and resentful at having a Sassenagh as their pastor, a man from Oxford at that. Edward tried desperately to be humble, as his Lord had been humble, but he could not help his proud carriage, his high head, his cold and handsome young face, his lack of warm and simple sympathy. He prayed that his nature might be changed, that he could be one with his parish. He would accept the usual reverence paid to a priest, such as a pulled forelock or cap, or a curtsey, but nothing else. His rectory was a small and tumble-down place, and he had no servant. The poor village women, but only the old ones, would take turns cleaning up the tiny rooms. The thatched roof leaked. It was very cold. His stipend was practically nothing. He returned the small cheques his parents sent him. So, he was always hungry. He never demanded anything for himself from his parishioners, and they believed that he "rolled in it." No one offered to clean his outdoor privy, so he did the odorous work himself. "It'll take the pride from him, sure and it will," the men of the parish would chuckle, only too glad to be relieved of a task rightfully theirs.

His church was hardly more splendid than his rectory. He had trouble obtaining altar boys. The old women washed and ironed the simple altar linens; an old man was surly at being appointed sexton, though he had served in this capacity most of his life. The Sisters, who had a wretched convent and little school, were all Irish, and did not like the English pastor, who was given to be rigorous at times and liked absolute discipline. In short, Father Harrington-Smith's life was made a minor hell by his parish, especially by the Mother Superior of the convent, an old lady with a mind like iron and a will like a Toledo blade. She called him "that boyo." When the Sisters giggled at this, she frowned at them in only a perfunctory way. Edward met the hostility head on, and Edward lost.

Edward had only two joys: the celebration of the Mass, and walking the wild and incredibly beautiful countryside. The land was meadow, and somewhat flat, but the cloudscapes! Slowly he began to understand that these cloudscapes were the origins of the

strange Irish legends. One sunset he paused, struck, to observe a
spectacle he was never to see anywhere else.

The green earth was wrapt in a faint mist, and so was anonymous
and without feature. It rolled languidly to the horizon. Now cloudscapes anywhere else in the world have a way of standing in the sky.
But in Ireland they appear to touch the earth, to rise from it, to be
born of it, to be one with it, to merge with it. Edward saw a new
earth, a new land, in the enormous clouds. First of all, looming
against a red sky, stood a perfect castle, with towers and battlements
and walls and a moat and slitted windows. Below it fell away a
complete village, with tiny neat houses, roofed with crimson, and
little winding streets and a green stream moving down to a greener
meadow. Edward could actually discern the forms of sheep in the
meadows, and the tiny figures of shepherds. He saw glows in the
little windows of the houses, a lantern flash at the end of the street.
But it was all so silent!

"Impossible," murmured Edward, with awe. "Fata Morgana."

As he watched the tower drifted into nothingness; the walls
dropped away; the village was wrapt in a pink mist and hidden from
his sight; the green meadows became dim and vanished. The clouds
turned sullen and dark, pierced by one ember-like eye of the setting
sun. A cold wind arose, and Edward heard cowbells and the complaints of cattle as they moved towards their paddocks. Somewhere
a dog barked irascibly. An old man, in a two-wheeled cart, trundled
by, pulling his cap at the sight of the young priest, then shrugging.
The long purple twilight came down, and Edward stood and
thought.

He knew he did not have much imagination. He was too pragmatic for that, and too much of an Englishman. But now he was
full of a strange excitement. Could it be possible that past scenes
and past eras were indelibly impressed on the retina of Time, so
that Time could reproduce them at capricious will? Edward took to
roaming the countryside in his infrequent leisure, and watching and
listening. Of course, the "superstition" of "the natives" was not to
be countenanced by a pious and intellectual priest, even if he did
live in an ancient thatched house full of creaks and moans in the

moonlight, and even if he did hear weird and uncanny sounds in the dark of the moon, like the howling of ghostly wolves and the crying of witches. "There are more things in heaven and earth——" Nonsense, he would say to himself, unlocking the church door at dawn, and looking anxiously down the village street for dilatory altar boys and the sacristan. The sexton was rarely there, and Edward would frequently have to pull the bell-ropes himself, a fact the villagers appeared to enjoy slyly. "He has the muscles on him," the old women would say, pulling the shawls over their heads and fumbling for the rosaries in the pockets of their skirts. "It's no harm it will do him."

The Mass is the central and holy celebration of the Church. Edward had always perceived this intellectually. Now, as he became bemused over the cloudscapes, and all the strangeness of them, he perceived the Mass as a tremendous Mystery. He had always been reverent. Now he was quietly ecstatic. He complained less to his people, so he began to find a simple dinner—apparently placed there by the "little people"—on the self-scrubbed table in his dark and miniature kitchen. A piece of cold goose or chicken, a fish on Fridays and holy days, a covered dish of hot potatoes, a slice of simple cake, fresh fruit in season, a slab of cheese, a pitcher of goat's milk, a pot of tea on the brick stove. Never questioning, he ate voraciously, for he was young. He was simply thankful—and silent—when his roof was mysteriously repaired during an absence. How had his people come to know that he was slowly becoming one with them at last? It was a mystery, but it was also a fact. Even the Mother Superior's old seamed face cracked in a smile for him. But this was much, much later, after the Cunningham tragedy.

He tried, but he knew he would never be truly humble. That was his cross, and he bore it. But he found himself unbending. He stopped to speak to little boys playing marbles in muddy gutters. He inspected little babies he had baptized. He listened, with deliberate patience, to the complaints of housewives; he admonished men who liked their beer too much, but in an understanding tone. (That is why he frequently found a pitcher of beer on his table at night, and occasionally a small crock of raw Irish whiskey.) He was less stern in the Confessional, and more gentle. He sighed, rather than found cold and bitter words, when some shawled girl whimpered to him that she had "not been very good, Father," in the wild fields of moonlit spring with their tiny daisies and buttercups. His inflicted penances were given with a measure of mercy. Sometimes, at dawn, before Mass, he would enter the decrepit little church and stand, in meditation, before the crucifix, and think strange thoughts for an Englishman. He found poverty no longer disgraceful, and the leisurely way of his people no longer "feckless." There was more to life than a fine house and busyness.

When he was called to a cottage by a distracted father who feared his girl-wife was dying during her delivery, and he looked upon the girl as she struggled to give birth, he would invoke Mary's help with all his heart, and without any irreverence at all: *"Salve, sancta Parens, enixa puerpera regem qui caelum terramque regit in saecula saeculorum. Eructavit cor meum verbum bonum . . ."* For, who knew what the coming child would be? Perhaps a great and humble man, perhaps an inspiration and a joy to his people, perhaps a deliverer from war, perhaps a priest who might one day sit in Peter's Chair. Or, perhaps above all, a gentle girl who would give a saint to the Church. All women were one with Mary, in their hour of giving birth. She was not remote in heaven; she was here, with her suffering daughter. He had not thought that before. But this change of understanding did not come to the priest until much later, after the Cunningham affair.

There was only one family in the vicinity which could be called "gentry." The master was Michael, Lord Cunningham, his young wife, Dolores, and his brother, the Honorable Henry Laurance.

"Fine names," said Monsignor Harrington-Smith to his listening audience of Grandmother and her priests, "and a fine Irish family, very old. They went back to the Celtic kings of Ireland, back to legend and history and the Crusades. They were also very poor, as poor I was, myself."

Michael, Lord Cunningham lived with his wife, Dolores, in what once had been a noble castle, centuries before. Now less than a quarter of it was habitable. The rest was crumbling away, the walls littered deep in rubble, the moat dried to a trench which stank in the spring and was filled with a jungle of wild flowers in the summer. It stood upon a low hill overlooking the village. Two of its three towers were only stumps now; the one that remained had been built three centuries later than the others. Nevertheless, it had slowly detached itself from the castle; there was a chink some four feet wide between itself and the castle proper. Roofs on various rooms of the castle had fallen in chaos, so that only jagged fragments stood where once great halls had been alive with festivity. There had been a private chapel; it was now a ruin, smashed by the centuries. The beautiful gardens had decayed into a wilderness of snarled and dying trees. The castle stood against the skies in utter silence, except for the fierce cries of rooks or the sharp utterances of foxes. Gray, desolate, the remaining walls overgrown with ivy, it was hard to believe that anyone lived there at all, and especially not two young people filled with joy and the celebration of life.

The younger brother lived in a hut a quarter of a mile from the castle, and he lived as rudely as his shepherds. What little income the family had came from rents in the village, the sale of wool and mutton to hard-eyed English traders. Even that small income was depleted by taxes demanded by London Town. There was only an old female servant in the castle. Lady Dolores, nineteen years old, was dressed as poorly as any village girl. If Lord Cunningham, twenty-eight, hunted, it was for food and not for sport. He was too poor to be welcome even among his impoverished colleagues in other counties, and as he was quiet and shy he was let quite alone.

Lady Dolores had been the only child of a family as impoverished as Lord Cunningham's, noble and old, if without a title. She had been born in County Mayo, and from birth had been extraordinarily beautiful, with wide, dark blue eyes, skin like the petals of a white daisy, and hair that resembled black silk. Her family had sent her to a convent-school in Dublin, and had had their dreams that one day their Dolores would marry into wealth and a title. They garnered their last pounds before them and gave a reception for their daughter when she was eighteen years old, and invited the gentry and nobility for miles around. Lord Cunningham and his

brother, Henry Laurance, had been invited, and sensing an opportunity for some pleasure, and some free meals and a little dancing
and gaiety, had accepted. There had been considerable scurrying
for the proper clothing, some sale of sheep, some accepted debt. But
when they appeared at the dilapidated home of Mr. and Mrs.
Patrick MacMuir they had created a sensation, for they were fine
figures of young men. Henry was even more handsome than his
brother. Michael was three inches shorter, though still tall; his
smooth brown hair was gold on his brother; his pale blue eyes were
a brighter blue in Henry's face; his overly large nose was patrician
on Henry. He had a gentler chin and a more retiring air than his
brother, and did not stand out in the assemblage.

Still, he would have been considered very handsome—had it
not been for the glowing presence of Henry, Henry who appeared
like a young Irish Tara, with a touch of Apollo in his profile.

Both young men had the Irish indifference to immediate wealth,
and the Irish love for serenity and life. Michael, to the horror of his
people, had enlisted in Her Majesty's Navy, had acquired a bullet
in "some heathen place," and had subsequently received a pension,
which was more than could be said for Henry. Neither of the young
men had been educated to make his living. After all, lords do not
go into the market place, particularly Irish lords. And Henry liked
the bucolic life.

"No one ever suspected, except myself, and one other, that poor
Henry was really stupid," said Monsignor Harrington-Smith. "Beautiful as a Greek god, but absolutely stupid." Monsignor hesitated,
then went on resolutely: "One sees that, in decayed families. Michael
was the one with the brains, though he put them to little use. He
preferred living in their molding castle than to take lodgings in London and learn a profession. He loved his country." Monsignor reflected. "There is a lot to be said for that, even in these bustling,
modern days. Love of country appears to be degenerating everywhere, and when that happens—the barbarian comes in."

Dolores MacMuir was indeed a great beauty. But she had no
money, and her countrymen, even the eligibles, had no money either.
Her parents could count on leaving her only two hundred pounds a

year. Noble sons were all about them, drinking the free beer and whiskey, and hardly a penny among them. Of course, there were rich families in Dublin, but sons of rich families wanted to marry riches, too, and even great beauty and family did not impress the Dubliners, who had learned much from the Sassenagh, the trades-man. Dolores could dance like a fairy; she could chatter in French; she could do fine needle-work; she was very pious; she knew how to manage a household. She appeared to float, rather than walk. She had a saintly character, and a high sense of mischief. She was eight-een, and adorable. But she had no money.

It was soon evident, at the ball, that Dolores was attracted to the Honorable Henry Laurance. As for poor Henry, he was mad for the girl. He walked about in a daze; he visibly trembled when he danced with her. He tripped on her heels when she moved ahead of him. And she smiled on him with radiance. The parents were alarmed, as the days of the festivity passed. (Irish festivities do not end in a day, and sometimes not even in a week.) Henry was only an Honorable, though distinctly a distinguished Honorable. His brother, Michael, was a peer. He would marry eventually, and pro-duce an heir to the title, which was one of the grandest in Ireland. He would always have, and his heirs, what little poor estate there was. Henry would never have anything. He could smile the heart out of you, but that was all. Even an Irish smile could not put a gown on a girl's back, nor conjure a dinner on the table or a sovereign in a pocket.

Michael was also in love—with Dolores. Shyer than his effulgent brother, he could only stare at Dolores from a distance. She would sometimes drift to him and chaff him; his only reply was a stutter or a blush. She teased him; he looked miserable. She floated off, and his heart was in his eyes. And Henry was always at her side, laugh-ing richly, dancing magnificently, smiling like the sun itself. The parents came to the conclusion that Dolores had fallen in love, with Henry.

Their alarm increasing, they called their priest and despairingly laid the matter before him. He had a quiet talk with Dolores. The young men returned to their ruined castle. But very soon Henry

was writing daily to Dolores, and Michael once a month. "And what
are you doing, Father, to help us?" cried the anguished parents.
"Patience," said the priest. As Dolores had spoken to him in confidence he could reveal nothing at all. He only smiled. The parents,
giving up the priest as a bad job, rushed to the rescue of their bemused daughter. If she married either of these poverty-stricken lads
at all, she must marry Michael, Lord Cunningham. They laid down
the law. Dolores listened, her eyes downcast. Then she agreed with
her parents. It must be Michael or no one. She was a dutiful
daughter. They did not see the mischief in her eyes.

("Ah, and she crushed the pour heart in her," said Grandmother
in a sentimental tone, she who was as sentimental as a crocodile.)

The Monsignor appeared not to hear this. He said meditatively,
"There are those who know nothing about the Irish and who
therefore maintain that the Irish are a jolly and effervescent race,
and display all their emotions copiously at any provocation. They
forget that there is much of the stern Spaniard in the Irish, and his
moroseness and his dignity, which prevents him from being vulgar
and spilling out his feelings and the secrets of his soul. These he will
express only in song and poetry."

The two brothers, Michael and Henry, loved each other deeply
but by nature could not express this love except in the companionship of the hunt or the worry over the bills and taxes. "Even Our
Lord," Michael would say, "found the tax-gatherer, the publican,
the man in most need of the mercy of God, for is he not evil by
nature and doomed to hell, lest he repent?" (This was too deep for
Henry, though he hated the publican also; he could only shake his
head and think simply of the mace, a fine iron ball with spikes
sprouting from it. The publican, to Henry, meant the Englishman.)
The brothers had been closer than most brothers from their childhood, for their lives had been isolated and surrounded by the awesome beauty of nature. They were more attuned to the songs of birds
than to the voices of men, more to the slow wood-heart of an oak
than to the cities. Their castle was literally their castle, their defense
against a world growing more hurried, frenetic and larger each day,
more incoherently noisy and meaningless. Orphaned when Michael

was only eighteen, and possessing no other relatives, they clung to each other silently but strongly. They had gone to the same school together; they went to Confession and Mass together. They worked, ate and moved together, the quiet-colored brother and the younger shining brother. It was not expected by their villagers that they appear in the local pub. But it was expected that they have their own friends among the county gentry. However, they were rarely seen and more rarely heard. Sometimes the hamlet would hear Henry calling to his sheep, and the bark of his dog, and sometimes they heard the crack of Michael's gun in the forest beyond the castle. And, they saw the two brothers at Mass, sitting close together as if for protection.

"But they were rigorous in the performance of their spiritual duties," said Monsignor. "There was not a Saturday that they were not at Confession. I don't recall them missing one Sunday Mass. Very often they came through the week, and at many times they were the only communicants there, receiving Holy Communion side by side at the rail. Moreover, in spite of their poverty, they were as generous as possible, tithing themselves severely. The Sisters never appealed to them and came away empty-handed, if it were only a leg of lamb or a loaf of bread, all they could spare on many occasions. And, in that giving, I am certain they went hungry, themselves. It is very necessary for you, my friends, to know how good they were, and how they loved each other and the Church. Henry may have been stupid, but he was noble, as was his brother." Monsignor sighed.

Who knows what Henry, the simple and loving, thought when his brother, Michael, became betrothed to the young and beautiful Dolores? One could be sure, said Monsignor, that he did not cry out or rail against his brother, or curse his fate or run away. He apparently accepted the situation. He was his brother's attendant when the marriage took place in the church where Dolores had been baptized, and her ancestors before her. It was noticed that Henry was very white and suddenly very thin, and that though he smiled there was a look of agony in his eyes. He never returned to the castle. When the young folk came back from a very brief honeymoon in London, Henry had already taken up residence in a shepherd's hut. It was understood, among the three of them, that this was best for all, "though I doubt," said Monsignor, "that there was a word exchanged." Michael and Dolores believed that Henry was delicately leaving the young couple alone, moved by natural reticence.

"A man of intelligence rationalizes his misery after a time," said Monsignor. "He accepts what he has to accept. He expects nothing very marvelous from living in this world. But the simpler man is like a child. He trusts life, implicitly. It cannot be cruel to him; it cannot take from him all that he has. It is kind, it is loving. Suffering is only a dream. He will awake, eventually, from a nightmare and find himself in his mother's arms. Such thoughts are excellent, if they are spiritualized. But they can kill a simple man if he relates them to the objective world."

Henry, to the Monsignor's surprise, appeared one day at the rectory. He sat on a chair and wrung his hands and looked at the priest with the simple and baffled anguish of a lamb that is being tortured. When questioned gently he could only move his lips soundlessly. What was it that troubled him? Henry shook his head, dumbly. All the light that had always appeared to move about him like an aura was quenched. He might have been a peasant, sitting there in the rectory parlor with the ashen light of the dying year on his face. He was looking for help, in bewilderment.

"I was much younger then," said Monsignor, sadly. "I saw before me only a very simple young man who had been hurt in some fashion. I did not see a man who was dying, six months after his brother's wedding. How was it possible to ascribe tremendously deep feeling to a young man whose chief pleasures in life were playing with his dog, hunting with his brother, and wrestling with some young ram in the frisky days of the spring? There he sat in his coarse, homespun britches, with his woolen stockings and thick boots which smelled of sheep-dung. His yellow hair fell in a shock over his forehead; his mouth was half open. The numb misery in his eyes was the misery of a hurt animal—I thought. God forgive me, but I did not know he was suffering because of his love for the Lady Dolores!

I thought it was something else, and I did not know what it was!"

The Monsignor, puzzled, urgently trying to help, talked vaguely to Henry. All men had their wretchednesses; he would not pry. If Henry wanted to speak, he would be heard. But a man had to have courage— Had he anything to say? Henry shook his head. Finally he stood up gravely, shook hands with the priest, went outside and rode away on his horse. "I had failed him," said Monsignor, sighing. "I had given him a stone when he was dying for bread. I gave him generalities, when he wanted to be told that someone knew of his pain, and that God knew more than anyone else what it was, and was ready with consolation."

That night, dazed, tormented, utterly without understanding, without comfort, Henry hanged himself in his hut, attaching the rope to a nail in the rafters.

The Monsignor, after his first incredulous shock, was faced with a problem. Henry was a suicide. If he had killed himself with the full force of his will, in full assent, arrived at coldly and with knowledge, then he could not be given Catholic burial. But Michael, weeping, discussed the situation with the priest. Henry had never been very intelligent; he had never grown mentally beyond the age of twelve, if that. In fact, he had not completed the final forms in school, but had been sent home at the age of thirteen, a hopeless case as his teachers had said. A man had not murdered himself. A boy, without understanding, had left the world, unaware of his great sin. Henry had deeply loved God. He had wanted to return to his Father, Who would give him what men could not.

"And I did not know it was because of my wife, Dolores," said Michael, huskily. "He came to the castle last night, walking in casually. He smiled at me. Then he bent over me and kissed my cheek, took Dolores' hand and kissed it also. He left, without a word of greeting or farewell. I'd not know now if one of the shepherds had not told me of Henry groaning in his sleep and calling desperately for my wife, and weeping even as he slept. Ah, if the scoundrel had only told me so earlier and had not waited until my brother had done himself to death! My brother was crazed; he did not know what he was doing."

So Henry, a man in body but a child in soul, was buried in consecrated ground, near his parents, and all his ancestors, under the mighty oaken trees. Thinking of his bewildered agony, Monsignor could not sorrow over the young man. He could only marvel at the pain of the simple, for which they have no words, and could only pray that Henry now had peace. He said to Michael, as sensibly as possible, "Henry is in God's hands. The future, and life, is still in yours, my lord. Your young wife will have a child in five months. Be as calm as possible with her, for this has shocked her, too.

"I should have known," said Monsignor, with some bitterness. "I am an Englishman, and I did not know the long, dark sorrows of the Irish."

A week after the funeral the young wife visited the priest, arriving in the one shabby carriage her husband could afford. She sat and cried and could not speak for a long time. Then she stammered out that she had never loved Henry at all, that from the first moment Michael had been her love. The marriage had not been forced upon her, as the Father knew. It was only her sense of mischief which had kept her meek when her parents had suggested it. "And do you think, Father," she cried to the priest, "that if my heart had been with Henry I'd have married Michael? Can a woman do such violence to her heart?" She shook her head over and over, her black curls flying about her pale wet cheeks.

The girl sat in her cloak and bonnet and wept bitterly. "It is Michael, now, who is worrying the heart from me. He will not speak; he walks the floor at night. He sighs. He groans. He goes to the churchyard each day. I cannot reach him."

"It did not occur to me," said Monsignor, swishing the brandy in his glass before the fire at Grandmother's house, "to suggest to the child that she assure her husband that she loved him, alone. I thought it was self-evident to Michael. I did not know that the girl was asking me to do something that I believed she had already done. All I could say to her was that time healed all wounds, the most foolish aphorism of them all. She must give Michael time. She must be patient. Above all things, she must think of her child. I spoke to her as if to an English lady, who is always in control of herself. I forgot I was speaking to an Irish girl, shy, uncertain and frightened. The Irish soul is more remote and alone than the English, living more in itself, a prey to moroseness, preferring silence to speech."

The girl had listened quietly, and then she had gone away. "She was not concerned with herself," said Monsignor, "though how was I to know that, being English? She was concerned only about her husband. Henry had killed himself not only because of his own pain but because he believed that Dolores was suffering even more, and that she loved him. By removing his presence, he had thought, he was removing Dolores from misery. Greater love——"

The terrible part of the whole situation was that Michael was as deceived as his brother.

"People," said Monsignor, "talk to each other constantly about the most unimportant things. The world usually sounds like a babbling jungle with the voices of men. But seldom do they speak to each other of what is the most important. If they did so there would be much less sorrow in life and less sin and cruelty and misunderstanding."

Michael had noticed that Dolores had flirted outrageously with Henry, in her innocent and light-hearted way; but then, she had flirted with him, too, and other young men. If Henry had seemed bemused during the time of the festivities at Dolores' home, Michael had been, himself, too bemused to notice it. The brothers had returned to their castle and neither of them had mentioned Dolores to the other, out of their shyness and their pressing debts, which troubled them all their waking hours. Henry looked to his brother as a boy to his father, with admiration and respect for his superior intelligence and ingenuity; he relied implicitly on Michael; to him, Michael could do no wrong, and Henry never questioned him. So when Michael quietly said he must make a journey Henry had not even asked him his destination. Michael, of course, had gone to Dolores' parents and asked for her in marriage, which was the proper thing to do in those days. One did not approach a girl directly. He was accepted, though there was some sad discussion about finances.

Michael came home to announce, as briefly as possible, that Dolores would soon be his wife. He was so full of joy that he did not notice any grief in Henry. As for Henry, he doubtless believed that it was only just that his wonderful brother should marry his own love, even if he was convinced, in his simplicity, that Dolores loved him. Had she not written him gay letters in answer to his own boyish ones?

When Dolores became pregnant she also became pale and listless. Michael did not feel it necessary to inform his brother that he was expecting an heir. After all, there was a crisis about the sheep. Too many lambs had died in the hard winter; many of the sheep were sick with a baffling illness. The tax-rates had been raised by the Sassenagh. The harvest would be small that year. These were the important things to the brothers. Countrymen did not discuss their wives, even to their blood kin, and especially not in those reticent days. Henry saw Dolores seldom; when he saw her the last day, she was in tears, and very white. She had had the smallest of quarrels with Michael that early morning, and when she saw Henry she had cried out in temper, "Oh, and it's wishing I am that I had not married him!" It did not occur to the womanless Henry, who had never loved before and knew nothing about women, that it was the very young Dolores' physical condition which made her hysterical; she was also lonely for her mother, and was frightened, and everything was exaggerated to her. He came to the one conclusion possible for him: that she loved him and had been forced into an unwelcome marriage. If he no longer existed he would not be an impediment to a future happiness between Michael and Dolores. And so he hanged himself that night out of love for the only two people in the world he loved.

"It was simple to understand," said Monsignor. "The fault was with me. I was a man of the cities, of Oxford, of books and sophistication and many complex things. I had not yet learned that people like these live uncomplicated and forthright lives, and that their emotions are direct and turbulent. I was still trying to make Englishmen of these Irish, who are much more honest in their hearts. I would still try to talk with the old peasants in their two-wheeled carts as I had talked with their brothers, knowing and cynical, in the English countryside. No wonder they would look puzzled, or sour, as if I were deliberately mocking them."

After his brother's death Michael, himself, believed that Henry and Dolores had loved each other, that Dolores' parents had forced the marriage upon her because he, Michael, was the older brother with the title, and that he had destroyed two young and loving lives. Had he spoken to Dolores then, or she to him, what happened would never have happened, in terror and anguish. She knew something was fearfully wrong with her husband and she had gone to Monsignor Harrington-Smith, dumbly asking for help, a help he could not give her because he did not understand the situation. She had wanted the priest to go to Michael and tell him, in words she, herself, could not use, that her husband was breaking her heart with his grief, and frightening her, and that she loved him dearly even if she did not know, in her extreme youth, how to comfort him.

So it was that one midnight the youthful priest was awakened by a wild pounding on his door. He hurried downstairs in his nightshirt, for by now he knew that such summons were not trivial and that lives were threatened. He found one of Michael's hairy shepherds, a young lad, on his doorstep, panting. "It's himself, his lordship, who would be hanging himself, too!" cried the shepherd, crumpling his cap in his hands. "Her ladyship—it's herself that wants ye, Faether. Come at once!"

There was a jaunty-cart outside, with a half-tamed horse. The priest hastily pulled on his clothing with trembling hands, and he prayed while he did so. Buttons flew in his haste. The night was cold and overcast; a high pale moon flitted among fleeing clouds, and groundfog concealed the earth in shifting mists. The priest pulled a gray shawl over his shoulders and stumbled out to the jaunty-cart, which smelled of hay and dung and rotten apples, and which possessed two large and uncertain wheels. He sat on the side seat and had to cling for dear life as the shepherd whipped up the cart and it lurched and dipped and soared over the broken road. He was grateful, for the first time, for the shawl an old village woman had knitted for him. The piercing cold of the dank dark night chilled him except for his shoulders and neck and chest, which the shawl protected. The horse snorted and shied; the cart slipped, almost up-set. The black trees hung over the priest's head. Then a wheel fell off, the horse broke away, and the priest was thrown to the ground.

The breath was knocked out of him. Cursing, the young shepherd helped him to his feet and found a stone for him to sit on. "Don't bother about me!" the priest said, angrily. "Go back at once to the Lady Dolores and tell her I am on my way, and if you love your master talk to him. Talk, talk, to him!"

"He's locked in his room," whimpered the shepherd.

"He won't kill himself so long as you talk to him," said the priest. "Don't you understand, you fool, that his soul is in mortal danger? Go on, at once!"

He almost struck the blathering lad in his desperate anxiety. "Go! Tell the Lady Dolores to talk to her husband also! You've got faster legs than I. Run—run as if the devil were after you!"

The priest was afraid that his leg was broken, for it was numb and throbbing. Despairingly, under moonlight as cold as ice, and as shifting as shadows, he rubbed the leg and prayed. He sat alone on the stone; he pulled up his trouser leg; there was an ugly gash, bleeding and deep, on his flesh. He wrapped his handkerchief about it, gasping with pain and despair. Then he cautiously flexed his leg. It was not broken. Still, when he pushed himself to his feet he almost fainted with the pain. Apparently he had torn ligaments. His ankle and knee pounded with fire and agony. The village was far to his left, and if he attempted to reach it for help and a wagon, he would lose time. The castle was nearer, though not to be seen as yet in this forest of great twisted trees and underbrush. "Even if I must crawl, I must get there," he said, grimly, and prayed harder and more fervently than he had ever prayed in his life.

Moving slowly and feebly, sweating an icy sweat in his pain, al-most swooning, feeling the blood dripping down his leg, he moved from tree to tree, gasping, groaning. Thorns grasped at him; when the moon disappeared he collided with trees, knocking his head. He heard owls hooting, and the raucous cries of disturbed rooks, and rustlings in the undergrowth. Thankfully he recalled that there were no snakes in Ireland. Once or twice, without volition, he raised a weak shout for help, and only the owls answered him or some frightened bird. Once or twice he forgot where he was going, where he was, for the pain was worsening and was by now unbearable. He had to drag the leg after him, holding on to trees, to the tops of sturdy bushes. He blinked icy water from his eyes; his head was ringing like a great bell. The shoe on his injured foot felt like a cast of iron, for his flesh was swelling rapidly.

Perhaps it was his pain and his despair that made the moonlight take on a weird cast, shimmering and dancing. He was only thankful that he could see a little better. His forehead was bruised from his collisions with trees. His whole tortured body cried for rest. His leg dragged behind him like a swollen log, smoldering with flame.

He could not see the ground. He was knee-deep in swirling mist. He caught glimpses of floating white shapes in the forest, almost human, formed of the fog. And then he reached a tiny open glade in the forest, filled with the curiously moving moonlight.

A young man was sitting on a log in the glade, smoking (at midnight!) a pipe as casually as if he were home before his fire. A handsome young man, handsomely clad in English hunting costume: pink coat, smart britches, polished boots, and gloves. He had a long head, covered with smooth yellow hair, and a thoughtful, well-bred face. A whip lay across his knees, and he played with it with one hand. His hunting cap was beside him on the log.

The priest blinked, thinking that with each blink the young man would disappear. But he became clearer, instead. I am not dreaming! thought the priest. But what is such a man doing here, in the secret wilds of Ireland, at midnight, smoking a pipe pleasantly, as if it were midday and he waiting for hunting companions? Oh, I am dreaming! My leg has made me delirious.

The young man looked up, smiling pleasantly. "Good evening, or rather, it should be good morning, should it not, Father Harrington-Smith?"

The priest's pale mouth fell open in astonishment. Then he felt a sudden rise of hope. "Is your horse here?" he asked, forgetting his amazement. "I—I have hurt myself. I must go to the castle yonder, immediately."

"Yes, I know," said the young man, meditatively. "That is why I am here."

"Your horse!"

"I suppose," said the young man, as if thinking about it, "that I could produce a horse. To take you back to your rectory. You are badly hurt, are you not?" he added in a solicitous tone.

"What does that matter?" cried the priest, only half hearing him in his extremity. "I must go to the castle at once."

The young man sighed and shook his head. "I am sorry. I am also sorry, though you would not credit it, that I had to command the wheel to fall from that appalling cart. What a vehicle for an English gentleman! Please rest yourself. I am afraid you have torn an artery in your leg. I am sorry about that, too."

I am certainly mad, dreaming or delirious, thought the priest. Staring, he watched the young man rise, and saw his white and glinting smile in the light of a moon that appeared huge and caught in the very branches of the tangled trees. "Please rest yourself," repeated the young man, in a warm tone of sympathy, and in the best of English accents. "Let us talk about the matter."

The priest clung to the tree near him, gasped, closed his eyes for a moment. He saw the redness of agony and exhaustion behind his lids. He opened his eyes to see that the young man was regarding him with gravity. The cold dark forest, the awful moon, swam about the priest as he struggled to keep his consciousness. "In God's name," he groaned, "help me. I have to reach the castle yonder. A young man——"

The stranger's face still smiled, but it was a cold smile. "Michael Cunningham? Yes, I know. He is about to kill himself; hanging. A very disagreeable and unpleasant way to dispatch oneself. But after all, a man's life is his own, is it not?"

"No," said the priest, faintly. "It belongs to God." He struggled to keep himself upright. "Don't you understand, whoever you are? If Michael kills himself, with full knowledge and the assent of his will and soul, he will be forever barred from the presence of God?"

"Do you believe that?" asked the young man, indulgently. "Oh, yes, I had forgotten that you are a priest. My dear fellow! You are a gentleman, of family and culture. You are, in your way, a philosopher, and possess some logic. You are not really superstitious, are you, with all that nonsense about God's eternal anger?"

A sickness such as he had never known before struck the priest, for he thought, I am surely going to collapse. He put his hand on his stomach; he could feel the leaping of his heart. Then, very slowly, his hand dropped.

"How did you know about Michael Cunningham?" he whispered.

The stranger shrugged. "A shepherd came to you, did he not? Perhaps I talked with him, too."

"If you know him, you can let him die, in mortal sin?"

The stranger laughed a little. "My dear fellow, is that any concern of mine? I have some respect for a man's dignity; whatever he chooses to do is entirely his own affair. Yes, I know you are a priest, and priests have peculiar ideas. But again, you are a gentleman, and of a family of gentlemen. It surprises me that you can mouth such idiocies concerning God's anger and 'mortal sin.' Has God taken you into His confidence that you know His thoughts? Do you know the extent of His mercy? Have you considered the life of man, full of misery and pain, and whether it was worth the living? Let Michael Cunningham have the peace he is searching for; is it your affair to keep him from it?"

The priest gulped, and made a feeble gesture with his hand. "Let me pass," he said, in a broken voice. He took a step. It was as if he had come face to face with a sheet of invisible glass that barred his passage. Horrified, he lifted his hand to push it aside, and it was as if he touched stone. Yet it was transparent, and beyond it he saw the stranger, who was looking at him most seriously, and who spoke again.

"You are a young man, for all you are a priest. You have been very vexed, have you not, at the absurd superstitions of the old women and the people of this hamlet? You have admonished them for their belief in ghosts and fairies and the little people, and the return of the dead, and vampires, and their conviction that virtue resides in some objects and evil in others. Excellent. You are quite right. I have often listened to your thoughts, the doubts in the

midst of your prayers. You know the teaching of the Church, that
Satan is absolute spirit, as are his angels. So he cannot annoy or
trouble man with little hoaxes and pranks, such as your foolish people
believe. In fact," the stranger said, contemplatively, "you once considered if Evil could not, in fact, be merely man's perverse nature.
Your superiors were alarmed when you discussed that with them,
and they told you that the greatest triumph of Satan was when he
convinced mankind he did not exist. You accepted their word, by
an act of your will. But you did not truly believe in the actual person of Satan, did you?"

A cold and deathly certainty came to the priest. His lips moved
soundlessly. The moon glared nearer, a sinister white globe.

"Let me pass," said the priest finally, putting his hand to his throat.

The stranger frowned. "I am not preventing you, in this dreadful
state of yours, from going anywhere you wish, my dear sir. You alone
are preventing yourself." He felt in his pocket and drew out a gold
watch, which glittered in the moonlight. "Ah! Michael is adjusting
the rope about his neck. There is some blabbering at the locked door.
His little silly wife, and that shepherd. They are pleading with him.
He will not listen. He cries that he killed his brother, that he is
guilty of murder, and so must die, himself. But those blabberers!"

"Father of lies, a liar from the beginning," said the priest, and
thrust his shoulder against the invisible wall.

"My dear sir! Now you are speaking like one of your peasants! I
thought better of you, Edward Albert Harrington-Smith! Your
intellect has declined in these past months." The stranger threw
back his head and laughed indulgently. Even in the unspeakable
terror of those moments the priest saw how handsome he was, how
at ease, how young. Then he remembered what he had been taught:
that Satan is pure spirit, and can assume any shape he desires at
any time, and any aspect.

"You are Satan," said the priest, and shuddered.

The young man frowned at him haughtily. "My dear Edward!
This is absurd of you. I thought better of your intellect. Satan is
only an abstract."

Michael was about to kill himself, and live forever in a realm that would be without God for eternity. Only a week ago, thought the priest, in his overpowering despair, I considered that as God's mercy is infinite, and though there is surely hell, it is possible that no human soul dwells in it! Only a week ago I thought, again, that Evil is only in man, himself——

"God have mercy!" he cried in a loud and shattered voice. "God have mercy on me! Christ have mercy! Lord have mercy! Christ have mercy——!" He sank to his knees, crossed himself, covered his face with his hands. He moaned as if dying, "Lord have mercy! Christ have mercy! Forgive me! Help me! The most worthless of Your servants, the most detestable! But let me save Michael! Deliver me from Evil—from Evil—from Evil!"

He groveled in his grief and anguish and remorse. His hands fell on the stones and needles and dead leaves of the forest, and they disappeared in the mist. Slowly he raised his tortured head and saw the young man watching him coldly. Slowly, inch by inch, he pushed himself to his feet, bit his lip to keep from shrieking with pain. And never did he take his starting eyes from the stranger. His lips moved in a litany, in the simplest prayer he had ever uttered. He caught the trunk of a tree and pulled himself upright. He took a step. The wall had gone. Still watching the stranger in utter horror and revulsion, he staggered nearer him. Now they were abreast and looking into each other's silent eyes. The stranger stepped back, a single step, and staggering and weaving, the priest passed him, his garments soaked with his own cold sweat.

He went on, dragging step by step. After a little, he glanced fearfully over his shoulder. The stranger was still watching him. Then, suddenly, he was there no longer, and the moonlight was dimmer. From somewhere, near or far, there was a howl as of a wolf. "Deliver me," whispered the priest. "Deliver me. From Evil."

He accepted his pain as his punishment for his urbane sophistication. He rejoiced in his suffering. "But please, dear Lord, do not visit my sin upon Michael. He—that Horror—where is he? Has he gone for Michael's soul? Mary, most tender——"

There was a sudden blankness in his mind, filled with darkness and scarlet flashes. When he could see again he saw the castle on its low rise before him. His exhaustion and pain overcame him again, and he fell to his knees. He heard running footsteps on the stones, the falling of gravel and pebbles. He shivered, and shrank. Then he saw another of Michael's shepherds before him, and the youth, exclaiming in pity and fear, was helping him to his feet.

"Hurry. Let us hurry," whispered the priest. "No, do not mind me. Just let me lean on your shoulder, your arm."

"Sure, and it's hurt you are, Faether——"

"No, no. It is nothing. Just help me, a little."

The shepherd was strong and young; he half carried, half dragged the priest up the rise. Sometimes, panting, he had to rest, so that the priest stood on his own feet, wincing with the savage pain in his leg, and urgently begging for no delay. The castle appeared to move down towards them, gray and crumbling in the moonlight, with only a slit of dim radiance piercing, here and there, its silent bulk, its one remaining tower cutting off the brilliance of stars. The moon floated among her rags of black and rushing clouds, and occasionally disappeared behind them, leaving a wan shine on the black earth. "Hurry, hurry, in God's name," whispered the priest, and the sweating shepherd drew on all his strength. His clothing smelled of sheep-fat and boiled mutton and cabbage; his breath was thick with raw whiskey. At many times the priest had fastidiously closed his nostrils against this stench in the confines of the Confessional. Now he breathed it in deeply, with gratitude, for it was the human smell of a man who was helping him to reach another man on the very edge of hell.

If I do not reach Michael in time, then I dare be a priest no longer, he said to himself, as the pebbles and rubble rattled about them and shifted under their feet. I am not worthy. I have been rejected—if Michael dies. He shut his mind from the unspeakable Evil he had seen in the forest, for at the very thought his mind leapt madly in terror. He knew, as Satan had implied, that the invisible wall had been his own intellectual doubts concerning the absolute, personal quality of Evil. With his acceptance of the frightful truth the wall had disappeared.

He had been in the castle a few times before, but after observing that the brothers were hardly less poor than himself, and that they had been straining their resources to feed him adequately at dinner, he had delicately found a way to avoid invitations. Moreover, the castle was not much more attractive than his small and battered rectory. The always-icy hall, with its mossy flags, its tattered banners, its rattling armor, its faint lantern and dripping stone walls, its echoing roof, its smell of ancient dankness and decay, had always depressed his spirits for days afterwards. Once this hall had blazed with torchlight and the jewels of fair women, and a fire had jumped on the enormous hearth, and there had been the sound of music and the laughter of Irish kings and noblemen and knights, and songs, and the skirling of bagpipes and the wind of dancing. Once minstrels had sat here and told the sagas of ancient and mighty men, and wine had been drunk from gemmed goblets. All this was gone, through the poverty induced by taxes, through loss of fortune, through oppression. The hall was inhabited by mournful ghosts, who cried soundlessly of harps and freedom and the glory of old Ireland.

It was more dismal and gloomy tonight than ever before. The stone stairway led up into darkness. From a high distance came the faint cries of a woman, the pleas of a youth. "I'll tell the Lady Dolores that your Reverence is here," said the shepherd, but the priest shook his head. He had no strength for speech any longer. He could only indicate the stairs with a slight movement of his hand and lean towards them. Blood dripped on the wet flags from his wounded leg. The shepherd led him, protesting, to the stairs, and on his hands and knees, like a desperate penitent, the priest climbed the stones, one by one, his mind swimming in red and black waves. The edges of the steps tortured him afresh; he hardly felt it now. He had only one destination. Ages passed as he climbed, his lips moving in unheard prayer. Then two pairs of hands were helping him up the last steps, and two strong, manly shoulders were supporting him. He looked beyond them to a closed oaken door where Dolores crouched in a pale and sobbing heap in the light of a lantern which swung from the stone wall.

When the girl saw the priest she uttered a broken cry and groveled at his feet, wordlessly praying for help. He pulled in a harsh breath.

He struck the door with his fist. "Michael! In God's Most Holy
Name!" he cried.

There was a sharp silence. Then a muffled and bitter voice sounded
from behind the door. "You could not help him! You would not
save him! My brother! I've sinned against him, and my life is
forfeit."

The priest gasped, over and over, supported by the shepherds. His
eye dropped to the weeping Dolores. He whispered to her, "Let
your woman's loving heart guide you! The tower—it faces the window
of his room. Go up the tower——"

"Father," she sobbed. "The tower is old, falling. There are only
a few steps." She put her hands over her body, as if to protect her
child. "Dark, dark and crumbling—how can I climb?" Her wet
face, streaked with dust, was wild with terror.

"God will be with you," said the priest. "As He was with me."
His strength had returned a little in his extremity. "Go. I am here."

The girl pushed herself to her feet. The lantern showed her di-
sheveled black hair lying on her shoulders, the anguished blue of
her eyes, her white lips, her gray woolen gown swollen over the
outline of her child. "Yes," she whispered. She stumbled away and
went down the stairs, and the priest said to one of the shepherds,
"Go with her to the tower. Help her."

The priest pulled in another breath. He leaned against the door.
"Michael," he said, in a stern and quiet voice. "You have been lying
to yourself. That is sin enough. But you are thinking of a mortal sin;
if you die in it, without absolution, then you will eternally separate
yourself from God——"

"So did my brother," said Michael, wearily. "Go away, you priest."

"Your brother did not die in mortal sin," said the priest, "and you
know that well. He was a child in mind and soul. He did not truly
will his death. You are willing yours. Your parents, your brother,
Our Lord—never will you see them, and always will you be separated
from them, forever."

"I believe nothing," said Michael, in a terrible voice. "Had there
been a God of mercy He should never have let my brother die,
alone and in pain, the child he was——" There was a sound of

weeping. "I took from him his love. I married the girl who loved him. Out of my greed and heedlessness, thinking of none but myself."

"Foolish lies," said the priest. "Lies to yourself." So long as he kept Michael talking he would remain alive. There was a window in the thick stone wall, and there were cracks in the crumbling tower, a few feet away. The priest could see the light of a lantern ascending through those cracks, but so slowly, so slowly. Once the light faltered, fell back. Then it climbed again, inch by inch. He thought of the dark there, the remnants of steps, the close and circling passage, the bats, the cobwebs, the sound of wind rushing through the round and fallen roof, the glimmering of the sinister moon striking against the inner stones, the struggling girl. What if she fell, and died, and her child with her? Oh, God! cried the priest to himself. Have I done wrong? It was a thought—an idea—have I done wrong?

He knew that Michael's room had a huge bay, with a window, so that it faced the tower almost close enough to touch. He envisioned Michael in the room, with the rope about his neck.

"You speak of lies," said Michael, in a low and dying voice. "There are lies that are not spoken. What did you give my brother, to save and comfort him? He came with a broken heart, and you murmured platitudes. His soul was wounded, and you gave him polished phrases."

"Yes," said the priest. "Forgive me. I have sinned before God. But I did not know! But you know, Michael, you know. I sinned in my stupid ignorance, but you wish to sin with the full assent of your will."

"Give me absolution then, before the fact," said Michael, jeering. " 'Forgive me, Father, for I am about to sin.' "

"Open the door, Michael. Let me hear your confession."

"Ah, no, and that I will not be doing! Do you think me a child? You will seize and hold me, and keep me."

"I cannot do that," said the priest. "I've injured my leg." He paused. "And I encountered the devil, himself, in your forest, who tried to prevent me from coming to you."

Michael shouted with laughter. "Is it you who are speaking,

Father? You who spoke of 'superstition'? Who scolded the ould women for their tales of Satanic encounters and the divils howling at night in the forest? Where is your Oxford teaching, Father, and your high-bred disdain for these tales?"

"I was wrong," said the priest. "I saw Satan. He was waiting for your soul. He struck me down, Michael, and I am standing here with an injured leg, and my blood is on your floor." His voice was humble, gasping.

There was a silence. Then Michael's voice was nearer the door. "Oh, and it is so? Tell me, Father, and what was Satan like? He had the horns on him, and the tail, and he breathed fire?" The jeer was louder.

"No," said the priest. The lantern was only five feet, now, below the ruined archway of the high window of the tower. It was faltering below, moving about. "He was not like that at all. He appears to us, Michael, in the forms that may please us most, so that he can the more easily deceive us."

"It is not the Sassenagh speaking, surely?" said Michael, and he laughed his ugly laugh again. "And was it in the likeness of an Oxford don that he appeared to you, Father?"

"No," said the priest, and now he wondered. "He appeared to me in the likeness of the young men I had known as friends in my Oxford days. Yes! That is it!"

"Then how will he appear to me, Father? In the guise of my brother? Then it will be welcoming him, I will." He had lost the accents of his Dublin and London schools. Michael spoke like one of his own people. "D'ye know what I am doing now, Faether? I have just thrown the rope over the rafter. I am climbing the chair. *Confiteor Deo omnipotenti . . . quia peccavi nimis cogitatione, verbo, et opere . . .*"

The priest fell to his knees and clasped his hands and laid his cheek against the locked door. "*Domine, convertere, et eripe animam meam; salvum me fac propter misericordiam tuam . . . !*" The shepherd started to kneel, then uttered a loud cry, and pointed. The priest forced himself to his feet, and looked through the narrow window.

Dolores was standing on the broken and shifting stones of the ruined window sill of the tower, facing her husband's window. Her little hands clutched the sides; she wavered in the moonlight, and appeared like a ghost, herself, in her pale gown, her wind-flying hair.

"Michael! Look!" exclaimed the priest. "Your wife! Dolores, in the window of the tower! She will fall!"

There was an instant's silence, then the rushing of feet, the falling of a chair inside the room. Then a loud and desperate shout that echoed all through the castle.

"Dolores! My love! Dolores! Go down!"

The girl's voice was faint but clear. "No, and that I will not, Michael, unless you come for me and take me down. If you kill yourself, as you have sworn, then I and our child will die with you, for I will throw myself from the tower and we will live in hell forever—together!"

"Dolores!"

The girl said, "You have not known me, that I love you, that you are my heart and life, and that there is no living without you, Michael. But no, Michael, it is you who do not love me, so why should I live? Hang yourself, Michael, and take me with you."

She stood, trembling, catching herself, high above Michael's window. The priest stood at his own window, shaking, praying numbly. The girl looked at the moon. Its strange light glimmered on her face, the dark pits of her eyes, her eerie smile. The wind caught her gray gown and it blew out from her so that she seemed to be sailing outwards with it, and Michael screamed.

Then the wind died, and she was there, still safe, but only precariously so, teetering on the ledge of the window. "What?" she said. "And you have not gone yet, Michael, so I can join you?"

"Dolores," groaned her husband. "My love, my life."

She shook her head. "Not your love. Not your life, Michael. If it were so you would come for me, for I am tired and alone, and I cannot go down these stairs again. I am tired, Michael. It is so easy to die. A step, and I will fall." She put out one small foot, and Michael screamed again. Dolores sobbed, miserably, and leaned forward.

Then there was the shrieking of a rusty lock and the wooden door was flung open, and Michael, with the rope still about his neck, charged out of the room. He did not see the priest, and so knocked him heavily to the stone floor. His footsteps clattered down the stairs. The outer door rocked open, and there was a scrambling on the rubble.

"Dolores! Dolores! Wait! I am coming!"

It was not possible that he could have gotten up those crumbling stairs, the empty spaces, so fast, yet he did. The priest, pulling himself to his feet, leaning against the window, was incredulous when he saw Michael behind the girl, lifting her from the ledge, then holding her, weeping together, in his arms.

"I baptized a fine son for them a few months later," said Monsignor. (Grandmother's great hall clock struck midnight.) "I remained in that parish for five years, and I baptized a beautiful little girl for them, and then another son."

But that was of no importance to Grandmother. She waved her glittering hand impatiently, and cocked her head at Monsignor Harrington-Smith. "And did you truly see the devil, himself, in that forest, Monsignor?" she asked, squinting her green eyes mockingly.

"Yes, I did," he said with quietness. "I had never seen him before, nor have I seen him since. To my knowledge," he added, slowly. "Who knows how often all of us see him? Who can tell when we encounter him? He always speaks in the language we know, and with the pride in our own hearts. If he came to us, hateful and dreadful, this world would be a place of purity rather than of terror and despair and death—for we should avoid him. But he comes to us in the guise that will deceive us most, and sometimes that guise is the appearance of a friend."

The other priests had listened with solemn faces and wide glistening eyes.

"Not always," said Father McGlynn. "It reminds me——"

Monsignor Harrington-Smith became aware of Rose. "Isn't it time for the little girl to be in bed?" he asked.

"Hah!" said Grandmother. "It's little sleeping she does, and I doubt she will sleep this night!"

Rose did, however. But her prayers were very fervent beforehand.

Chapter Three

IT WAS RAINING, OF COURSE, when Rose awakened the next
morning.

Her bedroom was extremely damp and cold, so she hurriedly
washed and dressed and went down to the kitchen, which was her
favorite room. First of all, it was warm, and warmth is not to be despised in England. It was also very large, with red brick walls and
red brick floor, and it had a fireplace which was always roaring and a
black iron stove that was always deliciously fuming. One long wall
was hung completely with copper vessels, from the size just large
enough to boil an egg to one in which major laundry was done—
all graduated neatly. A kitchen maid did nothing but polish those
vessels with vinegar and rottenstone, the instant they were removed
from the fire or stove. There was also, always, a copper teakettle
simmering on the hob, singing away with all its little heart, and
there was a big, brown earthen teapot steaming, good black tea such
as only the British can make and which will put hair on anyone's
chest.

There was also Cook, a fat and lumbering woman with a secret
fondness for children which she hid under a cross expression. She
was invariably good for a small cake baked on top of the stove, round
and thick, made of butter, flour, sugar and condensed milk, and in-
effably delicious. Cook had a heavy hand for the kettle maid and the
scullery maid, and a shouting voice for "the man," a meek little person who did odd jobs around the house. As far as Rose knew from

personal experience, he had no tongue at all, for she never heard him speak. But he did have a huge black mustache that spread out far beyond his cheeks, and which fascinated her. She never did find out what sort of ointment or wax he used to keep that mustache so rigid and in such perfect order and so brilliant. His name was Egbert.

A leaded window, across from the wall that held the kettles, looked out upon Grandmother's vegetable garden. It reached almost from one corner to the other, and touched the ceiling. It had a window seat, with many cushions, and here Rose used to perch, sipping her hot good tea and eating the cake Cook had baked for her, lingering over every drop and every crumb.

So, with anticipation, she took her place on the window seat this morning, sniffing the fragrance of her little baking cake, the smoky odor of the fire, and the rugged scent of tea. The maids were whimpering, and Cook had the aspect of an impending cyclone. Rose knew the symptoms. Grandmother had Her Liver again.

Grandmother's Liver always made a living hell of the household. It had a definite personality for Rose, though she had not the slightest idea about that interesting organ, where it was located, or even if it was attached to Grandmother at all. It lived apart, but imminent, like a brooding bogeyman, and was always attended by Grandmother's oaths, which one could hear right down in the kitchen. "At it again, Her Liver," Cook muttered. She mixed Epsom Salts with some water and ordered Egbert to take it to Grandmother. He shrank. "Go on," said Cook commandingly, but not without some sympathy. "She won't bite you."

"Hah," sniffed the youngest maid, sniggering.

"Cowards, all of you," said Cook, in her Lancashire accent. Egbert looked at the glass in his hand, and his expression was that of one about to burst into tears. "Go *on!*" shouted Cook. "Or she'll be down here, herself!"

That was enough to frighten Egbert even more, if possible, and he darted out of the room with the foaming glass. "And why'n't you take it yerself, Cook?" asked the kettle maid, with some impudence. Cook, who was stirring an iron kettle of soup, lifted her ladle threateningly. "Keep a civil tongue in your head," she admonished the girl. She scowled at Rose. "It's you, is it?"

It was obviously Rose. She discreetly looked away, trusting in Cook's good nature, and regarded the sopping March garden outside, all gray and black and withered stalks under an ominous sky. The rain washed the windows; the fire crackled; hissing water was poured on fresh tea. She heard Grandmother screaming from far up in the house. "It's the drink and the rich food," muttered Cook, who indulged in both, herself.

Then Rose saw a large pan near her, on the window seat. It was filled to the brim with murdered larks, dead little songsters whose lovely voices would never again warble at heaven's gate, quiet little wings that would never rise from warm earth again in a flare of joy and exultation, little claws that would never mark their hieroglyphics in dust again. Rose looked at the three or four dozen of them in the pan, and cried out in repulsion and sorrow, and almost fell from her seat.

"For God's sake," said Cook, angrily. "Wot's wrong with the brat? Speak up; wot's wrong with you?"

Rose could only point, crying, at the larks. Cook shrugged, stared. "Wot of it? Fresh larks, at the market this morning. For a pasty for the Madam, and her guests. A pasty," she repeated, trying to make the child understand. "A big pie. Very good, indeed. Ever so good."

Rose was horrified. She could have accepted murder in time, but not the eating of the fruits of murder. She ran from the window seat and sat on the stool near the fire, crying loudly. She had no words to convey her grief and loathing. She averted her face.

Cook was mystified. "Wot's got inter 'er?" she demanded of the maids. "Not got The Liver too, has she?"

The maids giggled. One of them went to the window seat and removed the pan. "Squeamish, like," she said.

"No worse than chickens, and chickens is the dirtiest fowl, they are," said Cook. "Now, now, stop the whimpers; here's the cake, and very good it is, and fresh tea." But the cake choked Rose and she could not swallow the tea. She went back to her room and cried and did not know why she cried. She only knew she was lonely, and that the wind was howling and the rain lashing at the windows, and that somehow there was no one in all the world except herself, wrapped in a blanket and huddling in a chair for warmth.

She must have slept, for eventually someone was shaking her, and there was Cook with a tray and an uncomfortable smile on her face. "I've brought you some hot broth, mutton and barley," she said. "And a scone or two, and marmalade, and tea. Scones just from the oven, buttered. Now, you'll be a good girl, won't you, and eat it all for Cook?"

Cook sat on the edge of the bed and fed Rose like a baby, and Rose could not offend the good woman. After a little Cook said, "It does no good to cry over things you can't help, Rosie. And the sooner you harden your heart, the less you'll suffer as you go through life. There, now. You've finished the broth. Have a bit of the scone."

"I don't have to eat——" Rose said, imploringly.

"The pie? Certainly not," said Cook, in a sturdy tone. "I'll make a beef-and-kidney little pasty for you, all for yourself. There, now, give us a smile. And if you're a good girl, you can have your dinner right downstairs with me, in the kitchen." This was a favor, indeed, for Cook ate alone, majestically, and not even Grandmother dared disturb her serious meals.

Rose went down to the kitchen with Cook, who had baked the lark-pasty while Rose had slept, and had discreetly hidden it in the pantry. It was jolly there, in the late afternoon, with the fire dancing on the brick wall, the kettle singing, the girls joking, and Cook always threatening meek little Egbert, who came and went with his brushes and pails and polishing-cloths, his small figure wrapped in a blue-and-white-striped apron from neck to ankles. The wind and the rain increased in force, but they only added to the air of warmth and comfort in the kitchen now. The copper vessels shone like gold on the wall, and there was the rich fragrance of cake and soup and a roast wafting through the room. At tea, Rose had jam sandwiches and a slice of cake, and a boiled egg. This was the loveliest place in the world. And she would dine with Cook. Rose reminded her of this frequently, until she groaned with exasperation.

They had a fine dinner together, of beef-and-kidney pie, and the larks were almost forgotten. The kitchen bell jangled on its spring, and Cook glowered at it. "She knows as it's My Dinner," she said, not moving. "She can wait." The bell flew wildly. "Humph," said Cook, buttering another scone. The kettle maid left before dinner; the scullery maid was never permitted in the other parts of the house. She peered through the doorway where she was washing up. "Ain't that her tearing the bell to bits?" she asked.

"It is," said Cook, comfortably.

"Maybe she's got a fit," suggested the girl, with some happiness.

"Not her," said Cook. "It's fits she gives to others. She'll wait till I've done."

But Grandmother did not wait. After about five minutes she charged into the kitchen, wrapped in a red silk robe which gave her hair, on kid curlers, an orange tinge. Rose had never before seen Grandmother without "paint and powder." The Liver, her temper, and her lack of cosmetics made her skin darkly sallow and coarse, and it was sprinkled all over with big gingery freckles. Her pale mouth was writhing with rage, and all hell was in her green eyes.

"And you didna hear me ring, damn you?" she screamed at Cook.

Cook turned slowly on her immense rump, like a liner moving into position. She regarded steaming Grandmother with dispassionate dignity.

"It is My Dinner, Madam," she said, and pointed at the kitchen clock on its shelf. "It was agreed—I think, Madam—when I entered this household, after Lady Humphrey had made me a much better offer, and where my wits were I don't know—it was agreed that My Dinner was not to be disturbed under any circumstances. I'm not one as breaks my word, nor do I expect others to do so." She set her teacup down smartly.

Grandmother paused. Women like Cook were not to be had at the beckoning of a finger. She said, still simmering, but in a lower tone, "It's Elsie's day off, and that you knew, Cook. You could have done me the favor, your damned dinner or no damned dinner. It's nae wonder ye have the backside on you like a lorry horse."

"My anatomy," said Cook, with majesty, "belongs to me. I gave

you no rights to it, Madam, for your uncalled-for comments." Rose
gazed at Cook with admiration, awed at her lofty periods.

"Oh S——," said Grandmother, and she suddenly grinned.

"Wot can I do for you, Madam?" asked Cook. "I'm one as lives
and lets live."

Grandmother snorted. She turned her blue-green glare on Rose.
"It wasna you I wanted, Cook. It was the bairn I was looking for,
and I couldna find her, and I rang the bell. It's a fancy my friends
have taken for her, and they'll be wanting her ladyship's presence.
After dinner," added Grandmother, hastily, no doubt understanding
that Rose had innocently put some curb on her tongue the night before. "And where has her ladyship been?" she demanded of Rose, the
fierce eyes looking like green fire.

"With me, Madam. I invited her to have dinner with me," said
Cook.

"No!" exclaimed Grandmother, marveling, "and you not wanting
the Angel Gabriel at your dinner, if himself should ask!"

Cook lifted her large arm grandly, and poured another cup of tea.

"I makes exceptions, sometimes," she said. "Sometimes," she added.

"Aweel, aweel," said Grandmother, marveling still more. She contemplated Rose thoughtfully. "And have ye nae better dress than
that damned Tartan frock?" she demanded.

"No, Grandmother. Except my Sunday-school blue wool. And it's
only Thursday."

"Put on the damned blue wool," said Grandmother. "Sunday!" she
snorted again. "A shame it is that ye havena proper clothes. I had
twenty frocks at your age."

"I believe," said Cook, "that Leeds do have shops, though they're
closed now. But tomorrow."

Grandmother did not like this hint at all. "You'll be minding your
own business, Cook," she said, curtly. "It's nae your pocket. Mind
you, now," she said to Rose. "At half-past nine."

Though Grandmother was of the school that believed children
should rarely if ever be seen before their twenty-first birthday, she
had no interest in their bedtime. Cook shook her head as Grand-

mother flounced from the room. "It's a good thing, it was, that you napped this afternoon, Rosie," she said.

She permitted Rose to help the scullery maid dry the dishes, and then she took her upstairs to wash her and comb her hair and tie it with a blue ribbon. She buttoned the many back buttons on Rose's fine blue wool frock, which was becoming a little too short. "There's some," she commented, kindly, "that does not like red hair. I fancy it, myself. Tomorrow, I'll curl it proper, with the iron. Too late now."

She led Rose to the door of the drawing-room, admonished her to behave herself, and Rose was on her own again.

Rose recognized some of the priests from the night before, but three were not there tonight. Three strange ones had taken their place.

Rose's old friends greeted her with affection and she was introduced to the three burly strangers. She gathered, later, that one had just arrived from Scotland with gossip and messages, and had dropped in on Grandmother hopeful, as were the others, that he might save her soul. The rich brown burr of him rang heartily in the room, though he was a very old man, and Rose listened to it in her chimney corner. She noticed that the Scots priest laughed much less than did the others, and she thought him ill at first for all his height and his air of ancient vitality. As for Grandmother, she had made a miraculous recovery, her lips very red, her nose very white, and her hair done in an elaborate style. She wore a black velvet dress of more discreet cut than of the night before, for Scotsmen are priggish and even those laymen who indulge in immorality do it as modestly as possible. Grandmother said, "Ah, Faether MacBurne, and ye'll not be disappointing us?"

Father MacBurne was long and lean, with the red, prominent face of the Scot, the curved Semitic nose of the true Celt, and the Celt's fierce eyes. But his hair was very white though thick, and his hands were slightly gnarled. "Very weel, Rose Mary," he said, "but it's nae a sad story like the others."

FATHER MacBURNE AND
THE DOUGHTY CHIEFTAIN

"When I was a bairn," said the priest, "the Scots in the Highlands, the Orkney Islands and the Outer and Inner Hebrides ignored England still, or if forced to acknowledge her existence they did it with bloody dispatch. They wanted nothing to do with the Sassenach, his Parliament, his monarch, his tax-gatherers and his religion. Their fief was still to their vanished kings, and chieftains and clans, and it was a company of valiant Englishmen, indeed, who braved those men in the shadow of their dark hills and before their darker faces. The mace and the dirk were still called into active use, and many an unwary Sassenach was buried in some wild glen together with his tax-papers or his warrants."

The clans, still powerful, had their own laws, which were administered rigidly by local chieftains. It was unusual for any Scotsmen, in those remote places, to resort to city magistrates, except for high crimes calling for ropes or long prison terms or suchlike. But if a man merely fought with his neighbor, as always, he sought out his own chieftain and laid the matter before him. However, if the case concerned murder—and it often did—then sometimes, but only sometimes, it was referred to the city magistrates for disposal via the hangman's rope. It was a terrible thing to be consigned to those granite cities, with the granite statues guarding every intersection, and with a granite sky arched overhead like frozen stone. Your Highlander hated those cities, for he was usually Catholic, and the cities had the odor of Calvin and Knox, and there was no cross permitted on a steeple, not even a Catholic one. And the Scotsman had his own Parliament, as he has today.

Occasionally London was shocked by some unusual amount of blood being shed "up there, among the ruddy Scots," and made inquiries about the matter. But on the whole London preferred to have no part in those affairs. It could be dangerous. And what were a few score Scotsmen more or less? Let well enough alone, said London, wisely, remembering the border raids not so far back in history, and burning hamlets and the mad scream of bagpipes in the black crannies of the hills. London only asked, reasonably, that taxes be paid, and did not press the point too much if returns were languid. The tax-gatherer had learned not to look too closely in hedges where boxes of gold sovereigns might be hidden. He took the man's word for what he "owed." If it seemed somewhat small, in view of the large herds of sheep and the rich meadows and the size of the house, compromise, as always, was the better part of taxation.

The Highlander despised the meek townsman with his books and his bank statements and his eagerness to be legal. Where was the rascal's spirit, then? Where was his blood, his pride? Where was the passion of his soul, the remembrance of his ancestors? All had died in the granite cities. All had died, with liberty. Aye, and he paraded in his larcenous kilts, in the streets, on the holidays, looking brave then, with the bagpipes skirling and his legs stumping, but he was a weak fox for all that, he with the white town-face and the womanish eyes. He was no true son of Scotland. Be damned to him.

The Scotsman, unlike the Irishman—though they are blood-brothers—is rarely sentimental. He is a harsher and bitterer breed, with long cold memory and an unforgiving heart. A feud with an Irishman can frequently be resolved in a burst of good temper and humor, and after a drink or two, especially if a priest intervenes in a spirit of brotherly love and conciliation. But a feud with a Scotsman is for life. He will reluctantly give his word, then keep it, but God help the man who gives a Scotsman his word and does not keep it.

And, if he wants something badly enough, he will get it.

Hence the tale of the Doughty Chieftain.

Douglass MacDougall was the laird of an island so remote that even the inhabitants of the Isle of Skye had seldom heard of it. Very cold, craggy and assaulted by the sea, it was doubted by many that even potatoes, turnips, barley and oats could be grown there, and few believed that cattle or even the hardy sheep could survive in that bitter weather. The race of Somerled had once ruled all the

Islands, and had given birth to the lairds of Lorne, brothers in blood and war and raids on Norway and Sweden. All, then, had called themselves MacDougalls. But later came the clans of Argyll, Campbell, MacLean, MacNaughton and MacDonald, and various others, to make life lively for the outlander and themselves. Robert the Bruce had ranged over the Islands and had done certain bloody things to the lairds of Lorne, and especially to the MacDougalls. The latter were believed by almost everyone to have been pretty well exterminated by Bruce—who went after his countrymen during boring interludes of peace with the Saxon dog. A Scotsman may be one of the most courageous men on earth, but he knows when to retire and lick his wounds, and the few MacDougalls who survived the general slaughter retired to that far isle and thought long and homicidal thoughts. However, reality faced the few families. After a very long time, they thought of asking the help of the great houses of MacLeod and MacNeill, and such, but learned that these had come under the influence of William III and Queen Anne, and were receiving handsome subsidies in return for a cease-fire between all the clans of Scotland, and another cease-fire against England. Protestantism, too, had invaded the ancient Catholic clans, and the MacDougalls were firmly Catholic. There was nothing for it but to hate in the liveliest fashion, fashion songs of war and murder, play the bagpipes stirringly, and, in the hope that the new world would forget their existence, to lie low.

They lay low for centuries, but their hatred did not.

A warrior people do not breed lavishly, for it is hard to stay awake for love after the arm has been busy all day lopping off heads in battle or bashing in skulls with a mace. Too, the warrior has a wide swath of modesty in him, and a fear of women, the latter the result of a simple and primitive perspicacity. None of these things are conducive to large families around the hearth. After centuries following Bruce the inhabitants of Douglass MacDougall's isle numbered some fewer than three thousand darkly Catholic souls, counting even the youngest baby in its cradle and its oldest men. The cattle and the sheep could boast a larger population and breeding rate, even in that fearful climate where the midnight sun could be expected every summer.

Young Father Robert MacBurne had just been ordained in Edinburgh when he was taken by the Bishop to his home. His lordship was by way of being Robert's uncle, oldest brother to Robert's mother, and he was a kindly soul. His manse was poor, bare and cold, with niggardly fires—all he could afford. He eyed Robert with affection, asked about the family, and gossiped a little. He was unnaturally effusive, and Robert began to feel a sensation of nasty premonition. As the Bishop's nephew, he had not exactly hoped for preferred treatment and a parish that would give him luxuries, for he knew that Scotsmen will bend themselves backwards until their heads touch their heels rather than use favoritism where favoritism among other races is the natural thing, and expected. So he began to fear that his uncle was about to assign him to a parish where he would be lucky to get a joint of mutton once a month, and where the old ladies put buttons in the offering plates rather than shillings, or even pennies, and where his church would be about the most poverty-stricken building in the whole county.

The Bishop was short. He was also stout, which was amazing, considering the tiny funds at his disposal and the condition of his larder. Robert was convinced all his life that in some mysterious way the angels must have fed the Bishop while he slept his innocent sleep, or that sheer piety gave him his roundness of face and figure. It could have been nothing else—the angels or the piety. It simply could not have been roast beef and pasties and other luscious things, or even potatoes. The Bishop was also rosy and jolly, the latter unusual for a Scotsman, and he had a high and subtle humor, another trait not customarily found in his countrymen. He was a philosopher and a learned man, possessed of miraculous patience and great gentleness. The gentleness was incredible, considering the state of the Church in Scotland. It was merely a heavenly bonus granted by God to the harassed priests in their Bishop's character. If he could "take a" that like a "mon," then a priest could "take" what he had to, and he always had to.

Robert, incessantly hungry because he was young as well as poor,

was diverted from direful premonitions when he discovered that in
some mystifying way his uncle had been able to secure a leg of
young lamb, potatoes, some sprouts, white bread, and ale in honor
of his nephew's visit, not to mention lemon-cheese tarts which made
a man's mouth water at the mere look of them. (With these the
Bishop, with noble gestures, produced a fourth of a bottle of brandy,
hoarded for just this occasion.) Robert was further astonished at
being offered a glass of Scotland's best whiskey. He was so overcome
with affection, and amazement, that he almost forgot his forebodings.
Then it came to him: he was being fattened like a lamb for the
slaughter. Or, to use another simile, it was the condemned man's final
meal.

The lamb and the condemned man, both simultaneously present
in young Robert, did not mar his appetite, however. He even forgot
to glance apologetically at his uncle's rueful face when he took the
fourth offering of young mutton, after he had first had a monster
bowl of broth stiff with barley, carrots and potatoes, a dish which
would have surfeited anyone, in itself, but a hungry young priest.
"My, my," marveled the Bishop, when Robert had demolished five
tarts, and inhaled several cups of tea rich with cream and sugar.
"It gives an auld heart pleasure to see such an appetite. They'd not
be feedin' ye well, in the Seminary, young Bob?"

Robert, blissful with food, ale, whiskey and brandy and tarts,
sighed dolefully and shook his head. "I've nae had a meal like this
since I was a lad."

And not even then, thought the Bishop, sighing. Nor, he added
to himself, will I hae another, mysel'. It had all cost him three
pounds, which he had been saving for a long time for this night.
They retired to what the Bishop called his library, a mere hole of a
little room solidly walled with books, cold as death, and with a handful of coals on the hearth. A table stood in the center of the room,
and there were two hard chairs in front of the fire, which gave out
practically no heat. Robert, feeling drowsy and stuffed, would have
liked to absorb that fire, but his uncle was now all brisk business. He
was spreading a map on the table, his bald head shining like a
big egg in the light of the one dull lamp, and seeing that map, and

the Bishop's busyness, Robert's premonitions returned in full power and with dismal liveliness.

"Ye'll hae heard of the MacDougalls of auld," said the Bishop, smoothing out the map with small fat hands.

Robert had thought the MacDougalls had been well cleared out by Robert the Bruce and the stronger clans, but his uncle soon disillusioned him. Now, here on this map, if Robert would please come to it, there was a small island. A flyspeck, merely, in the Outer Hebrides, which were no land-masses in themselves. His uncle informed him, with pride, that not even Haakon IV of Norway had been able to land his jarls on that island, because of the valor of the MacDougalls, and, the Bishop added as an afterthought, the general terrain facing the sea. (Robert, much later, suspected the terrain.)

"Catholic, to the mon," said the Bishop, with a happy smile. "There's nae United Free Church there, laddie!"

A Scotsman prefers to have the bad news immediately, rather than to delay it in the hope it will go away if ignored. In other words, Robert said to his uncle, the island needed a priest, and he was to be the victim. The Bishop tried to appear shocked, then he went to one of the chairs and admitted that such was the case. Robert wanted all the bad news in one blow; there was no common sense in cutting off a puppy's tail inch by inch to spare him the pain of one large lop. So the Bishop lopped, after first trying to expound on the beauty, wild and unearthly, of the Hebrides. Robert was not beguiled. He only fixed his uncle with his grim black eye, his hands planted stiffly on his knees.

MacDougall's isle supported itself by sheep-raising and the production of the hardiest wool in existence. ("I can weel onderstand that," remarked Robert.) The wool was much in demand for outer garments, if not for underdrawers. ("Scrape the hide off a mon, nae doot," commented Robert, forgetting the fine meal in his dismay.) It also carried on some brisk fisheries, slate-quarrying, and, best of all, distilling. Robert looked up with a less anguished countenance. The Bishop nodded. "It was their whiskey you had, this night," he said. Robert smiled the slightest of smiles, thinking of a hearty glass of that whiskey each night before dinner, at his own fireside, perhaps with a friend who was at least partly civilized. He then asked about the weather. One knew about the weather in the Hebrides. It was the national boast that a man could get his nose frostbitten, frequently, in mid-July, and everyone had exceptionally high color by reason of being unremittingly chapped. As for their storms—well, they admitted to a man, not without some pride, that God used the Islands as a proving-ground for storms He had in mind for the polar regions. He wanted to discover just how much wind, rain, snow, sleet, gales and general hell any bit of earth could stand without breaking up into chunks.

And MacDougall's isle, suggested Robert, was one of God's favorite spots for testing. The Bishop sat down, as if suddenly tired, and nodded his head. "It hasna disappeared as yet," he said, to which Robert replied that that was damned unfortunate—for him. And who ruled this less than Paradise on earth?

The Bishop hesitated. Why, of course, the laird was Douglass MacDougall. Who else? A fine lad, in his mid-twenties, if somewhat wild, and still unmarried. Robert commented that Douglass probably carried his dirk in his teeth, his two hands being well occupied with more lethal instruments, such as maces and firearms. And, doubtless, he was as unread as any Congo bushman. The Bishop's spirits picked up. No, the lad had taken a short, but effective, medical course in Edinburgh. The reason was obvious to the alarmed Robert. There was no physician on the isle, and in addition to owning and managing the fisheries, the quarries, the cattle and the sheep herds, and keeping general peace and order and acting as magistrate, the young chieftain officiated as obstetrician, bone-setter and general practitioner, midwife and veterinarian. "In a nutshell," admitted the Bishop.

"He'll nae have time, then, for mischief," said Robert, somberly. "It's nae wonder he's never wedded. Nae doot a virgin, by necessity."

There was no sense in being facetious, the Bishop admonished, remembering suddenly that he was a Bishop and this young man, though his nephew, was only a fledgling priest. One had to admire the MacDougall. In addition to his medical studies, he had become exceedingly proficient in the liberal arts, the law, Latin and Greek, and sundry other things. Robert marveled, only half believing.

Then a horrid thought came to him. How did the isle communicate with its sisters in the event of great necessity? It had a telegraph, did it not? It did not, the Bishop confessed. But, there were the fishing boats and sailboats, which every man on the isle could handle—if the weather was not too ferocious nor the seas too high. During at least four months in the year boats from the big ships from Glasgow put in at its one usable cove, bringing necessities and taking away the salt herrings, the wool, the slates, and the thick homespun tweeds. And, at least five months in the year the boats from Mac-Dougall's isle called for the post on the nearest larger isle. "I think," said Robert, "that I'd prefer the Congo." But he said this without much hope. For eight months, then, one had only the MacDougall to turn to in distress or travail. No, said the Bishop, he was wrong. There were six Dominican Sisters there. Robert groaned, and held his head in his hands, and the Bishop looked at him sympathetically.

But it was a sturdy and fairly prosperous place, the Bishop said. The MacDougall was a man for order and thrift and industry, and was no fool. He was also pious—in his way. The kirk was small, but in good order. Things could be much worse, said the Bishop, trying to brighten as Robert sank deeper into gloom. And very healthful. The last priest, who had died two months ago, had lived to be one hundred and ten years old, no remarkable age for Douglass' isle. In fact, to die before one was ninety-five was considered to be dying in early middle age. Robert, unfeelingly, declared that the race was still evidently to the swift and the battle to the strong. More gentle souls perished practically at birth, doubtless. By the way, those Dominican Sisters—— The Bishop hastily changed the subject.

Robert had missed meeting the MacDougall in Edinburgh by two days. The MacDougall had come to the Bishop in search of a pastor, knowing his lordship was to be there to ordain a bevy of young Seminarians. "And how did he know?" asked Robert. "It's nae possible his isle sends up smoke in signals, like the American Indians, and the other isles reply?"

The Bishop laughed merrily. But Robert's relentless eye still burned on his uncle like a black coal. "Aye," said the Bishop, depressed at this. He went on with obviously false enthusiasm about the MacDougall.

"A braw laddie." The MacDougall was several inches over six feet tall, all muscle and extraordinary strength, and remarkably handsome, with eyes as gray as the Atlantic, hair black and curling and lively, a strong heavy nose and a gay but resolute mouth. There was nothing he could not do, or at least there was nothing he would not attempt. "A difference there," Robert remarked forebodingly. The Bishop should have liked to detain him to meet his—er—new pastor, but the MacDougall had been suddenly recalled to his island because of a crisis in lambs and sheep-killing dogs and what not. A telegram from another island had been sent to him. Robert was not interested.

The next day he was on his way to the Outer Hebrides, all the clothes and other objects he possessed in one small bag. The Bishop's ancient housekeeper had put him up a large packet—larger than his own bag by far—containing the remnants of the leg of lamb, some buttered bread and marmalade, a half bottle of whiskey, oat cakes and honeyed scones, not to mention a jar of her best strawberry jam, and the rest of the lemon tartlets, which would serve him well on the cold and draughty third-class carriage on the train "to the end of the world." The Bishop had given his nephew a heavy plaid shawl, which Robert attempted to refuse, knowing how much the old man needed it himself. But the Bishop insisted, stroking the thick folds lovingly. He also gave Robert another treasure: a rosary whose beads were real Oriental pearls, all iridescence, and the crucifix was heavy solid gold, the Corpus carved of mother-of-pearl, exquisitely. These were the only treasures the Bishop had ever possessed, and he insisted that Robert must have them, as he had been saving them for this very day. The shawl smelled overwhelmingly of camphor, but it was a blessing on the train, on his shoulders when he sat up, and covering him almost head to foot like a warm blanket when he lay on the hard bench to sleep, and protecting him completely when he ran out in the bitter rain at lonely stations for a cup of hot tea, carrying his bag of edible supplies.

He had the carriage to himself, for the countryside was busy at this time of the year. Used to solitude, and a solitary by nature as were all Scotsmen, he was not lonely. He prayed, read a sound religious book, ate, slept a little, then surreptitiously took out a reprehensible yellow-backed paper novel in which he steeped and horrified his innocent soul. The racier passages were in French, and it was purely in the interests of relating French to Latin that Robert pored over them carefully, shaking his head the while and deploring modern tastes and the corruption of youth. Despite the shawl, his feet, in their big black boots, were getting numb with cold as the train scuttled north. Houses of dark gray stone lumbered by the carriage windows, and high clipped hedges showing faint green, and brown turbulent burns, and here and there patches of snow just beginning to melt at the edges. This was a wilder, more virile country than England, gloomily lowering under a lowering gray sky, and desolate and forbidding. A dark rain began to fall, mixed with sleet, and trees with lichen-covered trunks pressed close to the carriage, thrashing in a freezing wind. How barren it is, thought Robert dismally, he who was used to dismalness but though on a less outright scale.

Firs, beeches, larches. Did they ever turn green and warm in this wide and brawling countryside? Chunky gray sheep appeared on the meadows, with lambs with black faces, and among them stood the lonely shepherds, wrapped in their plaid shawls from head to foot, and sheep dogs raced about, barking sharply in the icy silence. The shepherds were big men, much bigger than their city cousins, and Robert could see their rugged profiles, as rugged as their hard brown hills. Fierce lines of these hills appeared now in the distance, russet-brown, yellowish or tinged with purple, and once or twice Robert glimpsed the terrible Atlantic, the color of stone but tumultuous, breaking on monstrous black rocks and roaring in the inlets in a rage of white foam. May God forgive him for sending me yon, thought Robert, referring in his thoughts to his uncle, but it was not in a spirit of absolute charity and sincerity.

The train groaned to a jolting stop at an anonymous hamlet and a dozen men and women, thickly clad, bonneted or capped, climbed clumsily into Robert's carriage. A few women curtseyed on seeing him, a man or two lifted his woolen cap, the others stared as bleakly and fiercely as their native Highlands. Robert had spread himself over his bench; he gathered together remnants of lunches and teas, and hid his yellow-backed novel and dutifully opened his breviary. The older ladies remarked to themselves on his very obvious youth and their cold eyes softened a little. One of them said to him in a maternal fashion, "And a fine shawl that be, Faether, made by your mither, no doot?"

The Protestants scowled, but the priest was so obviously boyish in spite of his height and his severe expression that they maintained the scowls with some difficulty.

"Nay, Mistress," said Robert, warming to some human contact and shifting his aching buttocks on the bench. "It was given to me by ma uncle, the Bishop, himself, in Edinburgh."

"I mark him well!" said an elderly gentleman. "He confirmed my youngest!"

"A good mon with his tongue against the Sassenach!" said one of the Protestants, his cragged face flushing with approval.

Robert's thoughts became kinder towards his uncle. He let the ladies examine his shawl, and they approved of the texture but disagreed as to what clan it represented. The gentlemen gave their own opinions. A Royal Stuart; a mon with half an een could see that plain. "Nay, look at that blue thread!" said an old lady with spirit. "Hae I not be weavin' the Tartan, and there's nae blue thread in it!"

"A Presbyterian shawl," said a middle-aged man with the sour wit of his countrymen.

"Aye, nae doot," said another. "It's always the blue, like their noses."

As glares now appeared, and there was some feeling around for stout sticks, Robert changed the subject quickly after a guard came in to light the paraffin lantern that swung from the smoky ceiling. He offered his pouch of tobacco, and the men lit up. Then Robert asked about MacDougall's isle. They stared at him. Weel, there was no sich isle, not even in the Outer, Outer Hebrides. He was mistaken.

"Born in Skye, mesel'," said one man. "Niver heard of MacDougall's isle. They cleared out the MacDougalls many's the year ago."

Robert was at first depressed, then he began to hope. If there was no such isle, then there was no MacDougall and there was no frightful parish with Dominican Sisters in it. But his hopes crashed when a very old gentleman lifted a horny hand.

"Wrong ye are," he said, triumphantly. "It be north by north, and I seen it mesel' when a lad." He stared with pity at Robert. "Ye'll not be goin' there, Faether?"

"That I be," said Robert with wretchedness. "The auld pastor died."

They commiserated with him. The old gentleman enlarged on the subject of MacDougall's isle, and the ladies, even the Protestant ones, said it was a shame and all that for a lad like this to be going yon. "Not so," said the old gentleman, the authority on the MacDougalls. "It aye a Paradise, I heard, but a despotism with the young MacDougall."

"More like the lake of ice in Dante's Inferno," observed Robert. The allusion passed over their heads. They were curious about the MacDougall and his isle. Then they remembered remarks from their childhood. No one could do the MacDougalls in! Robert the Bruce and the rest, not to mention the Sassenach, had tried it, but one could not do the MacDougalls in. If many of them were still alive, then one day we'd hear of them and no doot about it! They had the spirit. Sae sad there was not more of it aboot these decadent days. If the Stone of Scone was ever recovered from the Sassenach's throne in Westminster Abbey it would be taken by a MacDougall! Then Scotia would be free, with her ain king once more.

Robert's new friends left at the next hamlet with the warmest hopes for the end of his journey. The end of his journey, he understood, was also the end of the railroad. His heart was in his boots. He prayed awhile, then found a newspaper from Dundee with decorous headlines relating that two English spinsters had disappeared in Edinburgh three days ago and Scotland Yard was being called in. Miss Mary Joyce and her cousin, Miss Pamela Stone, were ladies of substance in London, and they had been visiting friends in Edinburgh and had gone for a carriage ride alone through the city. The coachman and the carriage had reported back to the friends. The ladies had taken a walk on Princes Street and had vanished into thin air and had never returned. Robert turned the pages listlessly, and then read the Agony Column with deep interest, being a young and imaginative man. This served to divert him until it was time for his breviary again. All was blackness outside his window. The cold grew more intense. Robert took off his boots and rubbed his numbed feet. He wrapped the shawl about them, suddenly blessing his uncle. He ate the last of the cold roast lamb and the remaining tart. There were no more stops for hot tea. He was as chill as death. And the train still screeched and lumbered along. The lantern swayed smokily.

A great bright white moon rose over the hills, flooding the stark countryside with a brilliant illumination. Must be familiar with the same scene on its own, thought the young priest miserably, remarking the silent desolation with only a distant light here and there visible. The train was running closer to the sea now; its pungent odor penetrated the compartment. Once or twice Robert saw crests radiant with icy silver, and heard the booming of the surf. Its boom and thunder became louder moment by moment, until the very walls of the carriage rumbled in answer. He saw lighthouses far out on the sea, flickering. The moon became brighter, almost fierce in its arctic splendor. And the snow patches, though this was May, were larger and whiter. There was a scent of pine and fir, too, poignant, overwhelming.

Then the train, gasping, spent, came abruptly to a halt, and there was a hissing of steam. Robert sat up. A guard came in, lifted his eyebrows politely. "It will be the end," he said.

"Aye, and that it is," said Robert, rising stiffly and staggering a little because his legs were so cold and numb. He flung the shawl about his shoulders, put on his hat, tucked up the last remnants of his journey into his bag, and murmured a prayer. He glanced through the window. The train had stopped at a mere cluster of stony little buildings like huts. One lantern blew against the moon. There was not a soul in sight.

Stumbling to the corridor, Robert halted as if shot. A loud and ear-crushing wail had assaulted him, like all the fiends in hell. A crimson flare lit up the windows of the corridor, and Robert knew they were torches. Now war drums joined the wailing and the sound of tramping feet, and Robert understood that a detachment of very large Highlanders, fully equipped with bagpipes (and doubtless with dirks and maces), were impatiently waiting outside and were serenading an arrival. He wondered who it could be. A laird, perhaps, or a great landowner. It did not occur to him in his boyish humility that this wild music and wilder scarlet light and all these drums were for himself.

The corridor remained empty. The train appeared entirely empty. There was no hail. But the torches flared into a deep crimson and fluttered like flags; the music became more triumphant, more excited. The Highlanders had caught sight of his pale boyish face peering through the corridor window. Now the drums went mad until they rumbled like thunder, and a hoarse and mighty shout went up. By the light of the torches, Robert could now see the Highlanders in full dress, their kilts swirling about the biggest knees he had ever seen in his life; each monolithic face opened in a bellow of greeting; the major-domo tossed his baton, recovered it with a yell. Scotsmen, Robert knew, came in all sizes, but these sizes were immense. Not a man was under six feet tall, and most were much taller, so that their enormous bearskin hats towered to a giant height.

"No, no, it canna be for me," Robert prayed, as the men marched up and down before, not below, the corridor window and the guard beamed at him and ducked his head, and then pulled the bag from his hand, seized his elbow with deference and led him to the door. "Ah, and it's the MacDougall himsel' who's come for you, sir," said the guard, himself amazed that all this savage greeting and uproar could be for one so thin and black and shabby and hardly more than a lad.

"Oh, no," murmured Robert. Then he uttered a cry himself, for he was literally seized by a pair of tremendous hands and lifted down from the steps as though he were a child, and a feeble, frail one at that. The hands set him down, and not short himself, he had to peer

up into a handsome face all gray dancing eyes, big nose and laughing mouth filled with enormous white teeth. "Aye, and it's a welcome
to you this braw nicht, Faether!" said a booming voice, and Robert
knew that it was the MacDougall in full regalia who had handled
him as an infant.

The bagpipes screamed, the drums roared, the torches danced,
and the men marched about their laird and their priest, their knees
pumping high and hard, their heels coming down like earthquakes
on the hard and stony soil. The MacDougall put his Titan's hands
on his hips and surveyed his priest critically, smiling from ear to
ear. "And they wouldna send me a graybeard!" he shouted. "They
sent me a puling laddie with a face like milk! Niver ye mind,
Faether! We'll be fattenin' ye up!" And with this he smote Robert
heartily on the back and then caught him deftly in midflight and
set him gingerly on his feet again.

Robert coughed and strangled and blinked, then when he could
catch his breath he remembered that he was a priest "for a' that,"
and entitled to respect even though this was the MacDougall in
person. "Ye'll keep your hands to yoursel'," he said, with feeble
severity, swallowing his last cough.

The small parade marched about him. The bitterest of winds tore
at his shawl and his hat and trousers; his knees trembled with cold,
his eyes moistened at the flare and glare of the torches, his ears
rang. Never had he seen such a plaid as was now displayed to him
as in acres. His own plaid, allegedly Royal Stuart, paled like the
moon before the sun. It was the most gorgeous plaid he had ever
gazed upon, and he winced. If the MacDougalls did nothing else,
they believed in the wildest colors. Tassels swung from side to
side; boots pounded, shawls danced in the wind like sails. And there
was a rifle slung from every mighty shoulder.

The MacDougall, reproved by his young priest, bowed deeply
from the waist, but not before Robert had seen the glint of deviltry
in those fine eyes. "It's but a welcome for you, Faether," he said.
"And glad we are to see you. Lads!" he cried, and the lads, any of
whom could have posed for a statue of Atlas, stopped abruptly, and

raised a shout that lifted the hair on Robert's skull. Hills roared it back; it even drowned out the yelling sea.

His bag disappeared. Now he dimly saw that he stood very close to the ocean. Black rocks, like miniature mountains, poured with water and foam. Robert's nose and hands promptly lost all sensation. There were boats drawn up in the tiniest of coves, and there, near the boats, Robert saw six Dominican Sisters, tall and grim, their hands folded primly in their sleeves, their coifs glittering in mingled moonlight and torchlight. All, he thought vaguely, well booted for this weather.

He suddenly wanted to lie down somewhere and go to sleep and wake to his little room in the Seminary or in his uncle's manse. He was exhausted. He did not remember climbing into a boat which rocked under him. His head was whirling and aching and he was shuddering and certain he was about to expire of cold. Then the great waves were tossing under him and there were other boats following, and he groaned. The men were singing now, some barbaric ballad concerning the freedom of Scotia and particularly of the MacDougalls.

Though a Scotsman, Robert was no sailor. The smallest lake on a summer day could make his stomach heave. He said to himself, wildly, that it wouldna do for a new priest and his calling if that priest leaned over the side of the boat and expelled remnants of cold lamb and oat cakes and jam. He particularly regretted the last two lemon tarts he had eaten a couple of hours ago. He clung to the side of the boat, praying urgently that he would not be sick. And the MacDougall sat like a giant beside him and smiled at him in the moonlight, and the men sang. The MacDougall, all by himself, sang the choruses.

The terrible ocean was lighted resplendently by the moon, so that the boats appeared to toss in refulgent liquid silver. So intense was the illumination that Robert was forced to close his eyes; it was a nightmare moon that hung in the sky, polished by polar winds, burnished by arctic ice. It faded the stars; it made the whole desolate ocean glitter. Little island after little island came in sight, fell astern and disappeared, and still others lifted themselves blackly, as if made

and carved of basalt, and advanced upon the boats, like crawling
sea monsters or sluggish turtles, and fell back as did the others.

We'll never get there; we'll be lost at sea, thought Robert in despair, and fumbled for his uncle's rosary. He was now so frightened
and undone that he forgot he had a queasy stomach. He listened
to the hearty rowing of the men; the boats pushed into the waves, rose
upon them, glided down into black and shining trenches, rose again
on moon-shining crests.

The MacDougall had been singing alone for some time and now
he was singing a doleful love ballad which boomed back from the
water. He was happy; his voice broke.

> "Or did misfortune's bitter storms
> Around thee blaw, around thee blaw,
> Thy bield should be my bosom,
> To share it a', to share it a'!"

Robert turned his swimming head cautiously and thought with
some spite that the damsel invited to share that bosom would have
yards to choose from, so broad it was, so muscular. In fact, she could
set up a cot on it. But there was no doubting, as the MacDougall,
continuing to offer his lady-love the might of his arm and his sword
and other implements of warfare, sang as a man sings who is in love,
and rejoices in it.

He was apparently a man of singular empathy, for he had noticed
the terror and the misery of his priest, and the efforts he was making
not to disgrace the priesthood, and that he was cold and despairing,
for though Douglass beamed encouragingly on Robert he went on
singing. Now it was Mary O'Argyle, and Robert could not help
thinking that he had an unco fine voice, for all its gigantic echoes.

" 'Twas your eyes, my gentle Mary——!" sang the MacDougall,
and there was actually a tremolo in his throat and his eyes glistened
in the moonlight, as if moistened by tears of passion and devotion.

Gentle Mary! thought the priest. In this God-abandoned place of
wind and ocean and black islands sliding by in lightless silence?
Apparently the crofters went to bed with the sun, and sensible men
they are, the priest remarked to himself. Only blankets and quilts

could console a man for living in such a spot. The boats went on swiftly over the water.

Just when Robert had finally given up hope, the MacDougall halted his singing in the very midst of describing his lady's fairness of countenance and pointed to what appeared to Robert to be a huge mass of rock jutting high up from the argent floor of the ocean.

"MacDougall's isle," he said, proudly, "and all your souls, Faether."

"Not—that?" quavered Robert. "It isna but mountain against the moon."

"MacDougall's isle," repeated Douglass, joyously. He lifted his huge hand as if to smite Robert again, in welcome, but halted it in the air as the priest winced back in fright, waiting to be whisked off into the water. The MacDougall coughed apologetically. "It's me hame, the hame of a' the MacDougalls, and none can land but he that knows the cove and the way." He beamed upon the priest. "Not sae long now, Faether. It's the westlin wind we hae tonight, for a' the moon, and ye'll soon be warm by your ain fire in your ain cot, with a good dinner under your ribs."

Poor Robert shuddered again. "And tomorrow," said the Mac-Dougall, "I'll take ye aboot the isle for your folk to see ye and be proud." He was very good-hearted; he could not see how his folk could possibly be proud of this thin, bony lad who for all his good Scotsman's craggy profile was too narrow of shoulder.

Simultaneously—and this would have surprised them had they known—both Robert and the MacDougall thought of the poor old Bishop far down south in Edinburgh, and their thoughts were less than kind. They brooded darkly on the Bishop, the MacDougall for sending him such a lad and Robert for being sent to MacDougall's isle. It's many the sin I have to expiate, then, thought Robert, and then offered up his real suffering for the sake of the souls in Purgatory, who no doubt would appreciate a breath or two of glacial air, in their present condition. This would freeze the marrow of Satan's bones, himself, Robert reflected, and wondered if he would ever be warm again.

The boats grated on rough sand, and the isle towered over them,

black as midnight, terrible as a fortress, silent as death. Robert made
no protest this time when the MacDougall lifted him gently and
bodily out of the boat and set down his feet on the slipping sand as
carefully as he would have handled a babe. To tell the truth, Robert
would have appreciated being carried so easily to his rectory, and
would have blessed the MacDougall for his mercy. He started violently, for the pipers had begun again, the torches were relit, the
drums thundered. He was going to be piped to his rectory, and for
a moment he wished he were dead and quietly buried in some sweet
spot under a cypress tree.

There was no carriage to carry him, the MacDougall informed
him with that abominable cheerfulness of his. There was not a carriage on the isle, for the streets, half a dozen of them, were too
steep for such, and there was no need. A man needed but a horse, and
there was a fine horse for the Faether, as gentle as a lamb. "And
nae doot it clambers like a goat," said the weary Robert. The Mac-
Dougall thought this a splendid joke and roared, tucked the priest's
arm firmly under his and helped him climb up a rocky little path
that was almost vertical and paved by the moon. The pipers and
the drummers followed without the least difficulty, but Robert stumbled. He wondered about the Dominican Sisters who had come to
welcome him, but stopped wondering when he saw them briskly
and forthrightly lifting their skirts high to their boot-tops and climbing as easily as the men, walking just behind the priest and the
MacDougall and followed by the music-makers. I will never, vowed
Robert vehemently, feel a glow at the sound of drums and bagpipes
again, nay, never in this life!

His first sensation when he climbed up the lip of the hill and was
on fairly level ground, considering, was that he had arrived in a
small world exclusively built of glittering black stone and blazing
silver light. Cobbled roadway, small broad houses, walls, buildings
of all sorts, were of glistening, sparkling, darkest granite; the slates
were dark on the roofs. But the windows shone with lamps in honor
of the arriving priest, and shawled men and women raised a shout of
welcome to which Robert, still staggering from the boat trip, could
not reply except by a lifting of a very tremulous hand. He saw

the spire of his church down the street, brilliant with light, and its sturdy small bulk, and he knew his rectory was nigh, for which he heartily thanked God. He stumbled on the cobbles, but the Mac-Dougall held him firmly, and the pipers piped, the torches threw red shadows on the dark houses, and the drums pealed back from mountain and house front. Robert caught a glimpse of more little narrow streets winding off from this one, each window gay with light. He prayed that no one would enter his rectory with him, no one "see" to him, but that they would be merciful and just let him collapse on his bed or even on the floor.

For all his thinness and youth, he was strong and wiry, but the long day's journey, the intense cold, and, above all, the long boat trip had left him dwindled. His stomach still heaved; the street rocked under him. Then a door was thrown open and red firelight and lamplight streamed out like loving arms to embrace him and he was in his rectory. He looked at the fire, tore his arm from the MacDougall and ran to the fire and stood bowed before it as close as he could get without absolutely charring himself. And this was the month of May, merry May, flowery May, lovely May—the month of the Queen of Heaven!

The pipers kept up their howling outside, and the drums still drummed, but the walls were as thick, almost, as a man's arm is long from elbow to fingertip, which was a blessing Robert was to appreciate later. Consequently, the pipers' valiant music was muted within the little parlor, which was most cosily furnished with rocking chairs and tidies and woolen woven rugs in bright colors, and broad tables and a number of good lamps. And a huge fire, above all. The Sisters came in with the MacDougall, who was bellowing something, and a small plump body with white hair came bouncing into the parlor, all gray calico and white apron.

"Mistress MacDougall!" said the MacDougall in his big, virile voice. "A footbath, hot, for the wee lad, at once. He's fair frozen!"

Mistress MacDougall, elderly and violently rosy, curtseyed to the shivering priest, and bounced back into the tiny kitchen, nodding and beaming. Robert crouched closer to the fire. His stomach had stopped heaving; it was making healthy and plaintive sounds, demanding

supper. Robert glanced over his shoulders and shrank at the sight
of the formidable Sisters, not one who did not tower almost as tall
as himself, and all of whom, if one was to judge from their dour
expressions, had even this early a poor opinion of the new priest.
The Mother Superior, a lady of giant proportions, and very grim,
gazed at him through steel-rimmed half-spectacles and Robert
thought: And there's a one who can make a mince of a man with a
glance.

The MacDougall, who never stopped talking, it seemed, and on
whom the Sisters bestowed wintry but affectionate smiles, helped
the old housekeeper carry in a steaming copper of hot water, then
thrust Robert into a chair before the fire. It did no good to protest; off
came his boots, his long darned black stockings, and then his trouser
legs and underwear were rolled up in a twinkling and his white
thin calves exposed to the unmoved gaze of the Sisters. The Mac-
Dougall seized those calves in one mighty hand and pushed Robert's
feet into the copper. Now Robert bellowed, long and loud, without
restraint. The MacDougall listened approvingly. "It's a braw voice,"
he admitted, and the Sisters, for the first time, looked without grimness at Robert, who was certain the flesh was being melted from his
bones in the hot water. Billows of steam rose to his very nostrils, but
after an agonized moment or two his cold flesh expanded gratefully.

"Weel, we'll be leavin' ye to your good dinner and the fire, laddie,"
said the MacDougall, after he was sure Robert was not going to
bubble in the copper. "It is Mass tomorrow at half after four, for
the men must be at their work, and there is Mass at six for the
women and the bairns. A guid night to ye, then, laddie, and a guid
sleep. It is late een now, eight on the hour."

He strode out, followed by the unspeaking Sisters, and the pipers
started up once more, and the door banged. "Laddie!" thought Robert,
with indignation. And I a priest! He was angry, too, at being called
"wee," he who was above six feet, himself, though not a monster like
that MacDougall. He suddenly yelled, for Mistress MacDougall was
pouring fresh hot water from a kettle into the copper. "Enough,
woman!" he screamed.

Mistress MacDougall set up a table at his side. He had not yet heard her voice, but he knew that his countrywomen were as sparing of words as were his countrymen. Except for the MacDougall, he thought with considerable bitterness. If he's nae talking he's singing, and God knows which is worse, an unfair thought which Robert regretted at once. It came to him that no one but the MacDougall had said a word to him, though the pipers had shouted loud enough. The Mother Superior had not even given him welcome, though she ought, by rights, to have said a few phrases.

Not a talker, himself, Robert still wished for some human communication. He said to his housekeeper, "Ye be a MacDougall, too, Mistress?"

"We a' be MacDougalls, Faether," she answered in her Highland accent. "Every last man and woman and bairn and wean on the isle." She spoke proudly, and busily poured thick mutton soup into a white bowl at Robert's elbow. "But none sae proud and guid and strong as Douglass MacDougall, our laird." Her voice dropped reverently, and for the first time a faint uneasiness came to Robert which as yet had no name. But he plunged his big pewter spoon into his big bowl of soup, which was giving off unbearably delicious odors, and he took up several enormous hot mouthfuls before he would speak again. His feet were warming in the copper; his right shoulder was just slightly steaming from the fire; his thin cheek was very hot. His whole young body rejoiced in all this lamplit comfort. He finished the soup, and saw Mistress MacDougall's bright blue eye shining on him with approval. She then brought a platter of cold mutton, mustard, hot boiled cabbage and potatoes, hot scones and wheat cakes, and a bottle of whiskey. She poured Robert a glass of whiskey, neat, and he took it and smelled it and rolled it about in his glass.

"Best in the world," said Mistress MacDougall, proudly. "It is his lairdship's ain, and made on the isle."

Now, this was illegal, unless the MacDougall had a license from the Sassenach. Robert, without a doubt, guessed that he had no such license, and that if MacDougall's isle were little known it was not simply because of its arctic isolation. There was such a thing as discretion.

"Half after four is an unco early hour for first Mass," he said.

"The MacDougall hae decreed it, for our convenience," said the
housekeeper in a reproving voice. Her face was like a round red
apple, slightly wrinkled, and the bright blue eyes were suddenly
cold. "A guid word to ye, Faether. Dinna cross the MacDougall."

Robert bridled as well as he could with a mouthful of lamb in
his jaws and a big bite of hot buttered scone. "I will cross the Mac-
Dougall," he said, after several swallows, "on a' occasions he needs
it."

The housekeeper folded her hands under her apron. She lifted her
eyes, but not to the crucifix standing over the granite stone mantel
with iron candlesticks upon it.

"It weel be the worst for ye, Faether," she said. "The MacDougall"—and she dropped her voice again in that note Robert had heard
before, to his uneasiness—"he willna brook interference. He is the
laird."

"There is a Laird above him," said Robert. "And He I serve, and
not the MacDougall."

Mistress MacDougall crossed herself dutifully, but her eye sparkled. She studied Robert as one would study a weak calf, the young
priest thought with resentment. She smiled. Nodded. She brought
the teapot, pewter and steaming, and filled an enormous cup with tea
and produced brownish sugar and a pitcher of cream so thick it
hardly touched the sides of the vessel. And there were cakes full of
raisins. Robert forgot his resentment for a moment while sampling
these delights.

"Ye hae a guid appetite, thank God, Faether," said Mistress Mac-
Dougall.

"I'll be needing it here," said Robert, eating a fifth little cake.

"Weel, your clothes—they are nae so warm," said the housekeeper.
"But the MacDougall will hae a care for that. And the vestments. A
prince would want no mair lovely, waiting ye in the vestry."

"I hae me own," said Robert, severely.

Mistress MacDougall shook her head with indulgence. "Ye'll wear
what the MacDougall, the laird, bought in London Town, and not
the puir ones I saw in your bag, Faether."

Robert was immediately determined that he would wear his own, come the MacDougall or hell, itself. He was not a Scotsman for nothing. His uneasiness returned, fumbling around in his mind for a name. "Do ye all love the MacDougall as you, Mistress Mac-Dougall?"

Her face changed to an expression more appropriate for the Communion rail than for a human being.

"Ah, that we do! He is our laird and our master, Faether!"

"Why?"

"Why, Faether? His word is law." Her voice dropped to servility, and Robert's Scots scalp prickled. Scotsmen were the proudest of all men; servility never sounded on their tongues, but servility sounded now on the lips of Mistress MacDougall.

"That is tyranny!" exclaimed Robert, whose countrymen had signed the Declaration of Independence in America, and whose blood ran proud and free through the Carolinas and in the cities of the New World, and all the colonies, and whose ancestors and kin had fought at Bannockburn and with Robert the Bruce and with Bonnie Prince Charlie, and whose heroic sagas resounded around the world.

"Tyranny, Faether?" Mistress MacDougall was puzzled. "We owe sae much to the MacDougall, and his faether, and his faether before him, and all his faethers. He is the Law——"

"And the prophets, too, nae doot," said Robert, whose black eye was glittering. "We'll see aboot this! And Scots ye call yeselves!"

Mistress MacDougall, with a look that did not promise that the young priest would be alive much longer, said nothing more. Silently, with slight gestures, she introduced Robert to his rectory. By this time he had put on his stockings and boots. His bedroom had a small fire, for which he was grateful, for all he was steaming inside and out. His bed was big and billowing with feather mattress and quilts and plump with huge white pillows and blankets. Here the floor was of wood and not of the smooth black granite of his little parlor. The commode held a white pitcher and bowl and a number of coarse white towels, and there was a rocking chair that could have held a giant, and a table on which stood a tall candle as thick about as a man's wrist, and burning cheerily. He had glanced in the kitchen with its stone walls and big fire, and at the larder full as his Bishop's

larder had never been full. And the westlin wind roared at the little
leaded windows and all was snug inside.

Robert looked at the big tester bed and was suddenly overcome
with the desire to get under all those feathers and blankets. He
dismissed Mistress MacDougall, who lived next door with her husband and three sons. He galloped, regrettably, through his prayers,
pulled off his clothing, and fell into the white bosom of his feather
bed and rolled in it luxuriously. For an instant or two he listened to
the wind and then sank into one of the soundest sleeps of his life,
for once unaware of the great white moon peering in his tiny window.

Robert woke to absolute darkness, but to the sound of warning
bells in the pierced iron-colored belfry of his church. He fumbled
for his box of matches, then felt around for the candle and lit it.
Four o'clock, on an icy May morning. The fire had long since died.
He understood that Mistress MacDougall would not be at the rectory
until after six o'clock Mass. He was on his own until then. He had
but half an hour to dress and hurry into his church and prepare.

Reluctantly, for he was still so young, he climbed out of the embrace of his warm bed, and immediately shivered, even under his
flannel nightshirt. He touched the water in the pitcher, wincing. He
hurried through his shaving and bathing. Then he looked for the
clothing he had dropped so hastily last night and wondered, dismally,
how he could wear it in this climate. It had been warm enough even
for Edinburgh, which was never warm. Then he discovered that
while he had slept his underwear had been replaced by garments
which appeared to have been woven of oatmeal, and were as thick
as blankets. He bridled, then decided that comfort was not pro-
scribed by the Church and that it was expected that priests take
reasonable care of themselves as a duty. The undergarments were not
soft, but slightly resembled hairshirts. However, Robert was no
sooner inside them and buttoning them than they became like swans-
down in that chill. His woolen stockings, so lovingly knitted by his
mother, had been replaced by black stockings that were so heavy they
could have stood alone. He pulled them on, rapidly. His toes were

ten minutes after five. He had almost an hour to wait for the next Mass, and he was already savagely hungry. The hearth was neat in the parlor—Mistress MacDougall had apparently not left before he had gone into his bedroom, and then she had taken his old clothing and set out what had been prepared for him—and Robert gritted his teeth. However, she had laid a fire, and he lit it, watching the wood catch under the peaty coal. He would not have his breakfast until twenty to seven, and that would make nearly three long hours from the time of his rising. Then and there Robert resolved that a change would be made, beginning practically at once: women or no women, their bairns or no bairns, the second Mass would be at half-past five and not a second later. Coming down to it, he reflected, he might even insist that the first Mass must be at five. He thought of his big soft bed longingly; he also thought more longingly of breakfast. He no longer felt emotional, which was sinful of him, he decided without too much contrition.

The cold dawn began to filter through his tight little windows, and his hungry stomach clamored. He lit a fire in the kitchen; he lit one in his bedroom. He prayed. He paced. It was time to go into the church again, and this time he marched under the wan light, and thought how stony and gloomy this hamlet was, perched on its mountain ledge. He had now some vague idea of the terrain and he felt sympathy for—what was his name?—who had attempted to land his jarls on this island and had failed. He didna know what he had missed, by the Grace of God, thought Robert, piously.

What he had thought of as a mountain was a large, rough crag, on a shelf of which the hamlet huddled with its meagre, narrow and winding streets. The rest of the island, though hardly flat, and though still almost inaccessible, did have mountain meadows and other tillable land and little lakes and ponds and springs. There was a fringe of fishing vessels tied up below, near the cove, and now as the dawn brightened icily Robert could hear the far hailing of the men, virile and powerful against the bitter air. He peered down and saw the monstrous Atlantic, ashen and turbulent, rushing with crests. And nothing else. Apparently this was the farthermost island. The Bishop had been mistaken; the big ships from Glasgow could never land here; they must stand far out at sea and send in their big flat boats for the salt herrings, the slates, the woolens and the tweeds and whatever else this abandoned spot could produce. How did, in all wonder, the MacDougall and his people truly exist in this watery and stony wilderness? Ah, he, Robert, had it! They produced whiskey in their mountain stills, all illegal, and they smuggled it out! The fine appointments in the church were now explained. And possibly, thought Robert, entering the church again, there was more than whiskey smuggled. Firearms from Norway, without the slightest doubt, to be sold quietly to the other islands and to the mainland, itself. What was it he had heard on the train? "They" could never "do the MacDougalls in." Especially not the MacDougall, and Robert darkly reflected that he was enough for one company of men at least.

The MacDougall, himself, was at the last Mass, among all the awed and respectful women and half-grown children, surrounded by his men. (Did they not work? Or were they his bodyguard?) The MacDougall was piety, itself. He came to the Communion rail and gave Robert a brief and sparkling gray glance, as chill and untamed as the ocean. Robert was slightly unnerved, meeting that glance. It had none of the hearty friendliness of the night before, and when he opened his mouth to receive Communion it was the mouth of a bear.

He was waiting for Robert when the young priest emerged from the church, and his great men stood near him, the rifles slung on their shoulders. But now the MacDougall was as gay as a youth and as affectionate. The Faether would do him the honor of partaking dinner with him that night, and learn more of his parish, and inspect the horse waiting now in the stables of the laird. Robert wanted to refuse. The MacDougall reached out a huge hand and rested it briefly on the priest's shoulder. The lads would call for him that evening. As for the rest of the day, the Faether could inspect the schools and consult with the Mother Superior, Mother M. Dominic, who was by the way of being his, the MacDougall's, second cousin.

Robert looked at the hand on his shoulder without moving, and said nothing. The MacDougall became silent. Robert still stared at the hand. The MacDougall removed it and laughed. "The auld Faether was ma ain faether's cousin," he said.

"I am nae cousin to ye, sir," said Robert. The great bodyguard looked at him in astonishment.

"Sad, that," said the MacDougall. His handsome red lips were smiling and without falsity. "We are a' MacDougalls here."

"Inbreeding," said Robert, coldly.

"Nae mair than the Irish," said the MacDougall. He studied Robert. "There's a wee touch of the Irish in ye, Faether, perhaps?"

"If ye'll excuse me," said Robert, and marched into his house and banged the door after him. He could hear the noise echo back from the great crag that loomed over the hamlet, and he wondered wretchedly if he would ever get used to it. Mistress MacDougall was already bustling in the kitchen and there was a fine odor of oatmeal, baking scones and kippered herring and tea in the air, and Robert, whose cheeks were quite flushed with mingled cold and anger, suddenly was intensely interested. He decided it was "beneath" him to speak of his exchanged clothing. He sat down and ate one of the heartiest, if not the heartiest, breakfasts of his life, and Mistress MacDougall was proud of his appetite. She became garrulous enough to tell him of some of the folk in the hamlet, and the farmers on their rocky acres, and the sheep, but every other sentence fawned on the MacDougall until Robert was sick of it.

"Hae none of ye, man, woman, bairn, sheep-herder, farmer, shop-keeper, any life of your ain?" he demanded.

"But Faether, he is the MacDougall, the laird."

"Sae ye said last night. But he is not your master, Mistress Mac-Dougall, nor the owner of your life."

"If it were not for the MacDougall and his faether and his faethers before him, there'd none be alive at this time," said the old lady in reproof. "If it was not one it was the other, killin' us a'."

"Granted he is a Hero, and his faethers before him, but he is just a man, if your present laird," said Robert.

The thought of the MacDougall being only a man among men shocked the old lady. He was larger than life, she evidently believed.

"And he isna married, and breeding another MacDougall," said
the priest. "Is that his duty to ye a' and his isle?"

Mistress MacDougall colored very vividly, and suddenly changed
the subject, and Robert was intrigued. "He'll be going to Skye or
one of the others, for his bride," he said with satisfaction. "There's
a limit to consanguinity."

"Ye'll hae more tea, Faether?" said Mistress MacDougall with
much haste.

He saw he would get no more out of her. He retired to his bedroom
for prayers, then went to the church again and gave it some more
study. Then there was nothing for it. He would have to meet his
people in the hamlet—and the Sisters, particularly Mother M. Dominic. It was not his fault that he had been indecently displayed
before the Sisters, over his knees, but then they were used to kilts
and saw bare knees all the time. But there was something about
rolled-up trouser legs on a priest, and particularly the legs of underdrawers, which ladies should not see. It was very involved and
very unreasonable, on the face of it, but there was nothing he could
do.

There was not one who did not speak of the MacDougall until
Robert could hardly bear hearing the name again. Even the Sisters
spoke of him more than of anything else. Mother M. Dominic spoke
a little dubiously of some "rare excitement" among the people of
the hamlet and the farms, but what had caused it she did not know.
The children were mum; the men and women were mum. "Mind
ye, Faether," she said, "I dinna trust it, but they will say nothing.
We must think weel; the MacDougall has some surprise for us."

"He must always hae surprises," said Robert in a tone of such
asperity that the old lady lifted her brows in reproof. True it was
that he had astonished them when he had built the kirk for the
"auld Faether," for it was expensive and the men had worked for
months polishing the granite. Was it not a fine kirk? And the
boats had brought the statues and the glass encased in wood from
Italy. There was none finer, said the old lady, but that was expected
of the MacDougall.

"If he is concealing something from ye, Mother, though all else know, then it canna be guid," said Robert, earning another glance of reproof, which was not so rigorous this time, however.

"He hasna told ye, yesel', Faether?" she asked.

"Nay, but I have supper with him this night."

"Then he will tell ye," said the old nun, with such relief that the priest had some direful thoughts. If such a holy woman was harboring doubts and misgivings, then the situation was dangerous. She was so disturbed that she took him on another travel through the school, pointing out the excellence of the tables and the appointments in so distracted a tone that the priest felt his alarm growing.

He felt that there was something sinister about the MacDougall's great men who were waiting for him that cold bright evening when he left the church, though each red and rugged face appeared respectful enough, and each red chapped knee below the kilt bent a little in respect. There would be no pipers tonight, and for this Robert was deeply thankful. Nevertheless, he felt like an honored but well-guarded prisoner when he was led through the streets to what the captain referred to as the MacDougall's Castle. The captain, almost as tall as the MacDougall, himself, looked down at Robert, who had always considered himself uncommonly well grown. I feel squat, he thought, resentfully. Do they breed nothing but giants here?

The escorts' feet rang on the cobbles as if they were shod with iron. Chimneys smoked busily over every slate roof. There was no color at all but for the gardens, which amazingly were filled with scarlet and purple and yellow blooms. But the prevailing color of the hamlet, except for the gardens, was black and gray except for an occasional cream-colored door or one even in sprightly blue. However, the view from every side was magnificent and awe-inspiring, for the ocean was everywhere, lined on distant crests with touches of crimson from the sun in its overpoweringly wide sky, its sky of the palest cold azure. And the west! It was a conflagration, as though the whole world were burning, going up in one vast if silent explosion of red and green and yellow fire, with the eye of doom in the very center, larger than any sun Robert had ever seen before, a red eye which could have held a dozen ordinary suns.

There was not even one other isle in sight. MacDougall's isle stood alone, a black crag against the sunset, the last outpost of man in a holocaust of celestial destruction.

From awe, Robert's mood proceeded to depression and a kind of pervading and nameless fear. Apocalyptic, he thought. How did these people manage to endure such revelations of terror and awesomeness every night? They would have the northern lights, too, as well as the midnight sun in June. They were Catholic; was there still some paganism here, too, some memory of Druids and Thor and all the gods of all the thunders?

"A fine view," he murmured to the captain. But the captain and his men were looking remotely at the sunset, and Robert saw their faces and thought: They may be Catholic and devout, but there are strange shapes in their minds and strange forms casting shadows on their souls, and they are not my own people after all. All at once, and still without cause, his depression lifted, became a kind of exaltation, as he, too, dimly remembered things no longer remembered in this dull and prosy world of modern men, things of vastness and glory and exultant joy which could have been known only by man in the spring of his life, in the morning of his world, things lost but dearly coveted with a passionate nostalgia. The sons of Adam had their memories, but in the elegant cities the memories were overlaid with death, and derided. Here, they lived.

The streets of the hamlet had given way to hedgerows, pungent with the life of May. There was a scent of lilacs and the innocent and carnal earth.

And there was the "castle," with its gravel paths. A black-gray granite house, three stories tall, bulky, forbidding, but lighted at every window, and guarded by two giants in full regalia with their rifles over their shoulders. They saluted smartly as Robert approached with his bodyguard. Four chimneys fumed energetically. The double door of oak, fortified with iron, swung open and there was the granite hall with its iron lanterns and candles, its ancient blowing banners, its enormous fireplace and armor, its thronelike seats of black oak, its bearskin rugs, its coat of arms emblazoned everywhere.

Now the bodyguard left Robert and a tall man in kilts approached him, bowing only a little, and led him into a vast room similar to the hall, with a fire roaring on a hearth that could accommodate six men standing abreast, and hoary portraits on the paneled walls. Here was all the pride of the MacDougalls, pale and painted face, fierce black eyes, long or short curling black hair, plaids, swords, brawny knees, delicate bosoms. Firelight and candlelight: they were part of the past and they were alive. They had never died in the MacDougall, he who resembled those on the walls who were long ago dust.

Now the MacDougall himself entered, blazing with vitality and color, kilted, dirked, bare-headed, his hand extended cordially, palm up to show that he carried no concealed weapon, and he shook hands with heartiness with his guest. "Welcome to this hoose, which has been honored, Faether," he said, "and I hope ye leave a blessing behind."

Robert wanted to say something irascible in the manner of Scotsmen, even when they are on good terms with each other, but he found himself only shaking hands with his host and admiring his handsomeness and height and general air of virile power. Then, of course, he came to himself and said, "Had I had a choice, Douglass? About coming this nicht?"

The MacDougall laughed merrily and called for whiskey, and he pulled a great chair to the fire for the priest, then sat opposite him, his mighty knees red and glowing with chaps and health. He shook his head. "Ah, ye should have known the auld Faether! He was here every Saturday nicht, leaving his blessing! Puir old mon!"

"He died, I think, at the age of well over a hundred?"

"Puir auld mon," repeated the MacDougall, sadly, as if he spoke of a man in his vigorous middle age who had been called, untimely, to his grave.

"Your faether's age when he died?" asked Robert.

The MacDougall's large black eyes saddened even more. "Weel, it was an accident, one might say. He was but sixty. But my granddada—he died but a year ago, and he was one hundred and eight to the day, covered with scars."

"I don't doot that for a moment," said Robert. But the MacDougall, wishing to leave doleful subjects alone, asked Robert how he had found his parish and the good Sisters and all. Robert admitted it was all far better than he had expected, and he asked when summer arrived, which made the MacDougall merry again. He assured the priest that it was practically high summer this very day. Weather fit for a king; wonderful for the lungs; bracing; brisk. The fire roared, but Robert's new thick underwear was not a millimetre too heavy. If this was truly summer, he wondered aloud, what was the winter like? "Put the lungs in ye!" said the MacDougall. Not close like this weather. Far and wide and white, like bells in the ears. Robert could imagine, and he shuddered.

The MacDougall promised him a coat lined with fur for the winter. "No doot I'll sleep in it, too," said Robert. But no, there would be fur rugs for his bed. "Ye'll not freeze," said Douglass with a slight disdain for the city man. He refilled Robert's glass. The whiskey was excellent, and Douglass' eye sparkled with pleasure when Robert praised it. "The auld Faether had a bottle a day, for his blood," said Douglass. This statement would have horrified Robert only twenty-four hours ago, but now he complimented the old priest in his mind for his perspicacity and his attention to his health in this climate. "Ye'll be well supplied from me ain kegs," the MacDougall promised Robert generously. Robert wished to remark that he did not expect to remain here until past the century mark, but in view of his host's hospitality and kindness he prudently restrained the words. They would have been ungracious.

"And now we'll have the sherry for the ladies," said the MacDougall, and smote the bell at his side so that it sounded like a gong.

"The ladies?" said Robert.

"Me future bride, Mary Joyce, and her cousin and chaperone, Pamela Stone," said the MacDougall, with a hint of impatience. "Hae no one told ye of their presence in ma hoose?"

The names rang vaguely in Robert's brain, which was already ringing with the whiskey. He admitted his ignorance.

"Sassenach ladies," said the MacDougall. "Ma guests. Niver did

I think a MacDougall would take a Sassenach bride, but God disposes, is it nae true?"

"True," said Robert. "No one told me."

"Ah, weel," said the MacDougall oddly, and with a little pride that Robert did not immediately understand. "They're not ones to talk, my ain folk."

Then Robert remembered the newspaper from Dundee which he had read on the train and he started so violently that the whiskey in his glass splashed on his hand. "The ladies who disappeared in Edinburgh, with Scotland Yard on their trail!" he exclaimed.

"They didna disappear," said the MacDougall reasonably. "If 'twere so, why would they be here?"

"But their friends, they were visiting!" cried Robert. "They didna know!"

"Do Edinburgh folk know aught?" asked the MacDougall superbly.

Robert stared at him. A horrid thought flitted into his mind. He refused to believe it for a moment. Then he stuttered, "Did the ladies come on their ain?"

"I escorted them," said Douglass, and smote the bell again. "I, and my lads."

"Ye—— No, ye did not!" said Robert, appalled.

"I did," said the MacDougall. "I see we do not have a stupid priest, and thank the guid God for that," he added piously. "I dislike cracking a mon's skull to put a thought in it."

Robert carefully put down his whiskey. He was very pale. "Ye came to the rail to receive Holy Communion," he said. "And ye in mortal sin!"

The MacDougall stared him down, and now he was formidable. "A MacDougall chooses his bride," he said. "It isna for the lass to choose."

"Kidnapping!" said Robert. "A crime. A criminal!"

The MacDougall became even more formidable. "Not sae harsh with the evil words, Faether. I chose my bride, and I brought her here to marry me, and ye'll witness the wedding. Enough?"

"Not enough," said the young priest, clenching his fists on his knees. "I'll nae marry a criminal kidnapper to an unwilling lass."

"She isna unwilling," said Douglass. "What lass would reject the MacDougall and all he is? She is but coy. If, Faether, ye are thinking I hae already taken her by force, clear your un-Christian thoughts away. The lass is as virtuous as the day she was born. The day I saw her——"

Robert's aghast mind could hardly absorb the enormity of the story. Over a week ago the MacDougall had gone to Edinburgh to see the Bishop about a new pastor, and to bring that pastor to his isle. He was enjoying a fine morning of sun and flowers on Princes Street when a carriage drove by, and in that carriage were two handsome young ladies. He immediately fell in love with one who turned out to be Miss Mary Joyce of London Town. The young ladies alighted from their carriage, opened their parasols, and strolled among the flowers, and the MacDougall had followed them and had contrived to introduce himself to them. Robert had no doubt but that his appearance had intrigued the demure young ladies immediately; they told him the names of their friends, who, it transpired, were very distantly related to the MacDougall himself. In fact, he dined with those distant relatives that very night and captivated the visitors. At the very least, Miss Joyce had seemed much "taken." Then and there Douglass decided to marry her, and as time was short his courtship was a little abrupt.

Mary had laughed merrily. Matters were not solved so easily; she was not to be wooed and won, if at all, like a barbarian. Douglass must visit her parents in London, preferably next Christmas, on her twentieth birthday. The very idea of visiting London stupefied the MacDougall, and the very thought of waiting over half a year for his bride enraged him. He could not understand this skittishness, this coyness, this "play-acting." But he would go at once to London, with the girls, and inform Mary's parents that he was marrying her and taking her "hame." Doubtless they would be overwhelmed by this condescension of the MacDougall.

Everyone, the two girls and their host and hostess, thought this all too amusing for words. They did not take Douglass seriously. So Douglass brooded. He returned to the little inn where he was staying and he brooded all night. He called early at the house where the girls were visiting; and the hostess—"nae of my blood; it was her husband, and he but a distant one, tenth removed"—had received him with a coldness even he could not overlook. Her husband had informed the girls of the isle, and Mary had been "shocked to the very heart of her," and so she had asked her hosts to explain to the MacDougall that she was no longer at home to him, and never would be from that day forward.

Douglass had not believed it in the slightest. He haunted Princes Street for the carriage. In the meantime he had visited the Bishop, who had promised him his own nephew. (What perfidy! I didna even know, mesel', then, thought Robert with a bitter thought directed at his uncle.) The ladies did not come to Princes Street, so he haunted adjacent streets.

Then, as he was with some of his men, he came upon an interesting sight.

The girls were in a carriage with their hostess, leaving for the railway station, for they had become bored with Edinburgh. A cart, following them, carried the maid, Agnes, and all the girls' considerable luggage. Later, girls, hostess, maid and luggage formed an island in the center of the hurrying station on this day of dark rain and wind. A Highlander in city clothes came to the hostess with a "message" from her husband in the City, and as it was confidential he drew her to a little distance. The station was very crowded, with trains hooting and spilling steam and soot and passengers scurrying with umbrellas and the lanterns bobbing about. No one heard the maid scream, but the hostess, who had been given a very trivial message indeed, and totally nonexistent, she discovered later, arrived back to the spot where she had left her guests and their luggage, found the guests and luggage had disappeared completely. The maid was screaming of "masked men" who had seized the young ladies and had whisked up all the bags and cases, and had borne them off "as easy as babes." (The masked men lived only in Aggie's heated imagination; she had seen only large men in plain clothes who had thrown the girls over their shoulders and had disappeared into the streams of preoccupied people.)

"I took Pamela Stone with us, also," said the MacDougall to the priest, virtuously. "It wouldna have done for her to travel alone with men, she unchaperoned." The men, moving like the wind, had deposited the young ladies, their encumbrances, and one gentleman to assist them, into a carriage the MacDougall had bought all within the past few minutes for so large a sum, apparently, that the cabbie had disappeared from Edinburgh discreetly. At any rate, he was not seen for months—and this the priest did not discover until much later. His cab, he had said, had been stolen from him while he was occupied with a cup of tea in an inn.

The MacDougall's men and himself had come from the North on their horses. They rode back all the way, with the carriage and the weeping young female prisoners. Pamela had stopped weeping on the third day and had begun to sing, to the MacDougall's pleasure, and he would join her. But Mary had only cried, wrung her hands, "and behaved like daft," said the MacDougall, with indulgence.

"Ye call it daft to object to being kidnapped?" cried Robert in despair.

"A mon chooses his bride," said the MacDougall with amazement that anyone could be so obtuse as not to understand this simple fact.

"And that's a', save for the wedding," said the MacDougall. "Had the auld Faether been here there'd be no talk here of kidnappings and crimes and daftness. We'd be married the day."

Vexed, he smote the bell again and the manservant came in and said the ladies asked to be excused this night from dining with their involuntary host. "They'll nae insult the Faether!" shouted the MacDougall, rising to his immense height. "Bring 'em doon at once, or I'll go mesel' and carry them doon!"

The manservant coughed. The ladies, he explained, enjoying every moment, were Church of England. They did not care for the company of Romans, especially priests.

Robert did not know whether to be angry or relieved. But the MacDougall told the man to deliver his message to the ladies or they'd rue the day. Robert had a vision of him storming the ladies' apartments and bringing them down, one under each arm, like kittens, and as easily. Apparently the ladies thought him quite capable of it—and he was—and in a few moments they arrived, haughtily and silently.

The first to enter was doubtless Miss Pamela Stone, thought the priest, tall and slender and lissome in a bustled dress of blue silk, and with blue silk slippers on her narrow feet. She was all English, from her slim, tearose face, stern pink lips, large, pale blue eyes and smooth golden hair swept to the top of her head, whence it then descended in a cascade of glistening curls to her shoulders. She looked not once at the MacDougall, but gave Robert a glacial glance from under white lids like marble and then half turned away in the very center of the room. Robert disliked her immediately.

The other young lady, doubtless Miss Mary Joyce, was quite different, for which the slightly dizzy Robert was grateful. Smaller, but with the daintiest figure clad in yellow silk, she had an oval, pointed face, tinted warmly with scarlet and olive, and her black and curling hair fell down to her shoulders in a glistening tide from behind her pretty ears. She was winning and beautiful at first sight, with dimples about a rich full mouth, a tilted nose that hinted of Irish blood, and eyes so full and black and shining and so brimming with mischief and joy that Robert was immediately her champion, ready to defend her with his life and rescue her from her direful condition. Her ears sparkled with long gold and diamond ornaments, and there was a ring of diamonds about her soft and girlish throat.

But it was not to her, this charming and delightful girl, that the MacDougall went and bowed before. It was to the proud fair lady, tall and stiff as a young tree and about as yielding. She refused his outstretched hand, but breeding and courtesy impelled her to turn imperially on her heel and stare at the priest, a cold and repelling stare.

"Miss Mary Joyce," said the MacDougall, almost humbly, and with open pride. "And our new priest, Faether MacBurne, who welcomes ye in my hoose."

I do not! thought Robert, vehemently, and he did not know if his outrage came from the thought of the kidnapping or from the

idea that the MacDougall, with all his splendor and glory, should
love such a lass as this—lovely, aye, but like granite, and as kind.

The other girl was surveying all this with eyes glimmering with
mirth, and the dimples deepened entrancingly when Robert was
introduced to her. Miss Pamela Stone. Now, thought Robert, wildly,
when she touched his hand with warm soft fingers, this is a one for
the MacDougall, and not the other who has no heart and no blood.
The girl even curtseyed to him, a trifle mockingly, but she said, in
a voice like a dove, "A good evening to you—Father." Her English
accent did not strike harshly on his ear; it lingered in it, like music.

Mary accepted a chair, without looking at the MacDougall directly,
but Pamela blithely spread her yellow skirts and openly prepared to
enjoy herself on this odd evening. "And how do you find our prison?"
she asked the priest, as she accepted a glass of sherry with an
upward and merry glance at the MacDougall.

Robert did not know what to say. He had not been taught at the
Seminary how a priest should conduct himself in such a situation.
He pondered, his cheeks flushing. "Cold," he said at last.

Pamela laughed. It was a full-throated laugh, without reserve
or demureness. It was the laugh of a woman who loved to live and
who found every day enthralling, even a day like this.

Miss Joyce said nothing. She had refused sherry with the mere
turning aside of her head. Robert had not yet heard her voice. He
was sure that it would be chill and metallic, and he started when she
turned her aristocratic head to him and fixed him with those pale
blue eyes glinting like stone between golden lashes.

"He"—she said, indicating the MacDougall as though he were
a servant, and not looking at him but merely bending the back of
her long white hand in his direction—"is holding us prisoner here
unlawfully and against our will. I hope you can help us, and then
arrange for his punishment."

Her voice was exactly as Robert had expected. He struggled, but
he disliked her with growing strength.

"I shall countenance no unlawfulness in my parish," he said.

He looked at Douglass, who was standing on the hearth and
smiling fatuously at the bride he intended to take, who most obvi-

ously did not intend to take him. In fact, he was listening to her as though she were uttering tender words of grace and kindness.

"Then, rescue us," said Miss Joyce, imperiously, and her tones were the tones one used to an underling fitted only to obey.

Robert flushed brightly. "I am sure the laird will not refuse you passage, if it is your will," he said. He wished to add: "And I pray to the guid God he will not!"

"Oh, it is a holiday," said Pamela. "And Douglass has promised us that we may write letters to our families in London, by the next boat to visit the post island."

Robert was certain that the post would be long in going. He looked at Douglass and frowned in sudden anxiety and anger. "The families of these young ladies dinna know where they are? Are ye so heartless that ye can let them suffer?"

"Ah, not sae heartless, and they know it well," said Douglass, never once taking his eyes from the cold Mary. "They wrote letters with their ain little hands, and they were posted in Dundee."

"He is a liar as well as a criminal who should be hanged," said Mary. "It is true that he permitted me to write to my parents, but he would let me write only that Pamela and I were staying in Dundee with new friends. As for Pamela, she has only a great-grandmother, and no one else, Lady Clarice Stone, and the old lady will be satisfied. He even 'permitted' me," the girl continued, bitterly, "to say in my letter that my parents must not worry. It is possible they received my letter today, and if the police have been looking for us they will now look no longer." She gave Pamela a cool look. "Lady Clarice is senile, Pamela. She will not be concerned, but my parents will wonder how two young ladies could have been so imprudent as to travel to Dundee alone."

"We traveled from London alone," said Pamela, returning the look with one not much kinder than the one given her by her cousin. "Except for that silly maid of yours, Aggie. If she does not return to London, dithering all sorts of mad things, your parents will not be anxious, dear Mary, and I hope our friends in Edinburgh will have intelligence enough to detain the idiot until we have the opportunity to tell our families just where we are and when we intend to return."

For the first time Mary looked straight at the MacDougall, whose fatuousness increased. It was not possible, thought Robert, that those rather protuberant blue eyes of hers actually softened just a little! He leaned forward to see more clearly. Yes, they were softer, though her mouth remained prim and closed. She will make a harsh, demanding wife, thought the priest, and will wither the heart of a man, even the heart of the MacDougall.

"When will Your Highness permit us to leave?" asked Mary in her clipped voice with its undertone of hard struck silver. "Yes, we have asked it before, but now I ask you before a witness."

"When we are married, my dear love," said the MacDougall in softest tones which startled Robert by their depth of emotion. "Then we shall visit your parents together."

"Then I shall never see my parents again," said Mary, without inflection. "They will wonder who our invented friends are in Dundee, when they receive no further letters from us, and I assure you I do not intend to write them again. They will make more inquiries; they will go to Edinburgh, if they are not already there——"

"Not your sweet Mama, my pet," said Pamela, smiling happily. "Hasn't she been an invalid since your last darling brother was born, and bedridden, with three nurses in constant attendance? As for your dear Papa, would he be so rash as to leave his counting-house to search for you furiously, especially as he will have received your letter today, possibly? Do you remember the time your brother Will had an accident on the railway, and nothing was heard of him for two weeks, until it was discovered he was bedded down safely in some farmhouse? Your dear Papa did not rush to his side, nor did he worry over-much, though he cares for Will more than he does for all the rest of you put together." She turned her merry, sparkling face to Robert. "Do not fear, Father, that our families are in distress. Only Mary is. I think."

Mary colored so vividly that Robert knew at once that she had a very bad temper, indeed, a bad augury in an intended wife. He did not like to see a woman's hands clench in rage, but Mary's were clenching now. And in some fashion he knew the rage was directed at Pamela, who had so blithely belittled her before strangers.

Pamela, glancing up sideways at Douglass, lifted her glass. "More sherry, Douglass, if you please," she said. Her voice was seductive, and Robert's head swung to her. He saw her eyes, so black and so shining, and he saw them glisten, and he knew at once that this girl, this charming, merry-hearted and realistic girl, loved the Mac-Dougall, and loved him passionately. He had heard of love-light in one's eyes, but he had never seen it before. He recognized it as one recognizes all true things at once.

But the MacDougall had no thought for her. He refilled the glass, and he looked only at his Mary, who was suddenly looking only at Pamela with a most interesting expression. Mary's face changed. It hardened, tightened. "Is one glass not enough, Pamela?" she asked.

"Never enough," said Pamela. Her fingers had managed to touch the MacDougall's fingers, but they might not have touched him at all, for all he seemed to know.

An elaborate, and obviously false, curve of disgust appeared on Mary's lifted upper lip, and revealed teeth that were entirely too large for a woman and entirely too glowingly wet. Pamela's teeth, showing now in a pert smile at her cousin, were as tiny and bright as pearls in comparison. Mary turned her head on its long neck to Robert again.

"You see our plight," she said. "You must prevail on this man to free us and return us to our families."

"I am in no hurry," said Pamela with a naughty flirt of her thick black lashes at Douglass, who, alas, did not see it at all.

"Shameless!" cried Mary. She clasped her hands and turned again to Robert. "Help us!" she implored.

"I will do all I can," he promised, and did not know his voice was grim and firm.

"How will ye?" asked the MacDougall with genuine interest. "Not one MacDougall will take a message from ye, Faether, to the nearest isle, nor will he take ye, himsel'. Ye cannot bribe a Mac-Dougall. If ye could, the mon would niver dare show his face to his ain folk here again, and that is death to a MacDougall. Nor can ye tell a Sister to send a message in your name, for none would take it for her, though the Sisters are loved and MacDougalls themsel's. Ye could thunder and refuse absolution, but I—I am the MacDougall. Bear your soul in patience, Faether. My Mary and I will be married soon."

And, thought Robert dismally, remembering the softening of Mary's eyes and the faintest softening of her face, and her looks at her sprightly cousin, that will probably be the case. I could wish him a better fate, even gaol.

"I am the magistrate," said the MacDougall, with good temper. "I am the law. Dinna speak to me of God's law, Faether. There was many a mon in the Guid Book who took his wife as I took my Mary, and the marriage was blessed by the Laird, Himsel', Who advised it."

"Hear, hear," said Pamela. "But for one thing, Douglass: I think it best to return Mary."

Fine lassie, thought Robert, smiling in himself. Let Mary take herself off and good riddance to her. She will be a plague in his house if she remains.

Mary clasped her hands to her excellent bosom with a somewhat dramatic gesture and leaned towards Douglass.

"Free us, free us!" she cried. "We will register no complaint against you! Free us!"

"Speak for yourself," murmured Pamela, but only Robert heard.

The MacDougall looked at Mary with his heart in his eyes. Robert wondered at the stupidity of men in love.

"Mary, ask me aught but that," he said.

"Ye must let her go," said Robert, raising his voice wrathfully. "The sooner the better! If I have to row her all the way, mysel'."

This highly amused the MacDougall. "Ye would drown in the first wave, puir Faether," he said. "If ye did not puke your heart out first."

The two girls regarded Robert with deep interest, and he was so mortified that he stood up and said, "I'll not stay in a hoose where I am insulted and my priesthood humiliated and my requests jeered

at. But I warn ye, my laird, that this lass must leave your hoose, and
the sooner the better for all of ye."

"Oh, ye are not leaving, laddie?" said the MacDougall. "We hae
a fine joint tonight, and guid fresh fish, not herring, and the finest
wines."

Robert had already smelled the alluring perfume of the dinner,
but his mind was made up. He said to Mary, formally, "Miss Joyce,
I shall find a way to deliver ye. In the meantime I wish to tell ye
that I willna be a witness to any wedding that is forced, or where
the bride is unwilling." He had a sudden inspiration. "Moreover,
I willna be a witness to the wedding of a Catholic to a woman not
of his Church. I promise ye all this, so he will have to let ye go, and
he knows it."

Mary's head nodded solemnly, but her eyes, fixed on the priest's,
were suddenly glaucous and veiled, and Robert's heart plunged with
misery.

"Oh, Father," said Pamela, and her face had paled a little.
"I have a friend, Catholic, who is married to a Protestant man—there
was no trouble."

"There are restrictions," said Robert, and could not help smiling
at her as if in comfort. "A lass may take instructions and be admitted
to the Church, or if she doesna want that she must only promise
that her children be brought up as Catholics."

Pamela chuckled. "There you are, Mary," she said in a bright
tone. "You have only to refuse all this, and there can be no wedding,
not even by another priest. Be firm, Mary, my dear, be firm, and
all will be well."

Mary nodded, but her eyes shone with sudden hate on her cousin.
"I will remember; I will be firm," she said.

"Please God," said Pamela, and now for the first time Douglass
looked at her and seemed to see her for once. "As for myself, if a
man worshipped a heathen god, all stone and fire, I would say to
him, 'Thy people shall be my people, and thy God my God, and
take me, my darling, wherever you will, to the very end of the
world—if it is your will.'"

Her voice trembled; tears appeared in her eyes. She made a chok-
ing sound, then sprang to her feet and ran from the room.

There was a little silence. The fire roared. The dinner bell
sounded. Mary looked at the MacDougall, and her fair face was
beautiful and there was no question but that the blue eyes were soft
and faintly glazed. But the MacDougall looked at the door through
which Pamela had vanished, and he scratched his head and murmured something to himself.

Robert, praying in his heart fervently, took himself off, pausing
only in the bannered hall to sniff regretfully at the fragrances of
dinner. But he had his pride.

Mistress MacDougall, not expecting him, had left. He had to
satisfy his young appetite with cold lamb and colder vegetables and
tea and bread. But not so strangely he ate almost with happiness.

Robert told the Sisters, the next day, what all the loyal Mac-
Dougalls on the isle already knew. They were shocked to the depths
of their Dominican hearts, not, Robert discovered, at the "crime"
of kidnapping an unwilling young lady, but because of a young lady
who was not Catholic and had no intention of becoming one even if
she married the MacDougall. "There's nae been a Protestant or
heretic among the MacDougalls since there was a MacDougall, Faether," said Mother M. Dominic, almost tearfully. "Is it certain the
laird will have her?"

Robert spoke of law. Mother M. Dominic shook her head. "And
a Sassenach, too," she said, and now her tears were frank.

Robert reproached her for using such a term, but she was not
contrite. He spoke of law again. But the MacDougall was the law,
the nun assured him, and that made matters all the more terrible.
She would go to him at once. She did and reported back to Robert
in as close to a state of hysteria as a Scotswoman can reach.

"I saw the lass, mesel'," she wept. "Walkin' in the garden with
her cousin, the small dark one. She isna a true woman, Faether,
though I had but a glimpse, she so haughty and cold, and not
speaking to the small dark one who saw me and came to me and

smiled like an angel. Why will he not have such a one as this, and not the other?"

"God knows," said Robert, gloomily. He advanced the notion to the old lady that she prevail on some fisherman to deliver a message for her to the nearest large island, where there were Authorities. Mother M. Dominic was shocked afresh. "But the Mac-Dougall is the law!" she exclaimed.

It was useless. What the MacDougall did was right in the eyes of his people, many of whom were servile in their regard for him. He was a high, proud man. He was a despot. He did not appear again at Mass, not even on Sunday, and, of course, he did not come to Confession. Robert wrote him a note.

"You are living in a state of mortal sin, my lord. And well you know it. You have committed a crime, have not confessed it and promised to make amends, and have not received absolution. Therefore, your immortal soul is in terrible danger. You live most dangerously. What if you die without sanctifying Grace? No human being should be more important to you than God. Too, you are a man of overweening pride and you are a tyrant. I will call you a despot, too.

"You will say that all the MacDougalls have been despots, but it would not make it just or pardonable. You will say that you are benevolent, even if a despot, and I will say to you that a benevolent despot is more evil than a cruel one, for the people will rebel against cruelty in time but never—in their greed—against benevolence. Such is the corrupt nature of mankind. You are a man of intelligence and learning, and so your corruption of your people is then the more reprehensible and it is deliberate and done with full knowledge and with the full consent of your will. I need not remind you that he who corrupts his people with gifts and kindnesses, in return for the freedom which God gave them as a birthright, is accursed. He has taken on himself the nature of Satan.

"You must, for your soul's sake, free those young ladies and deliver them to Edinburgh to their friends, as you found them. You must free your people. Is it joy to your heart to see their servility, to have their mindless, unquestioning obedience—because you gift

them and so buy their allegiance? Those who love you truly are not
servile towards you; those who do not truly love you are like serfs under your hand. Is that the love you desire? I have walked among
your people for days, and have talked with them. You say none
would betray you. I say the servile will, for a price, for they are men
not of good will but only of sly and greedy spirit.

"In all things, therefore, you have deeply offended God. Make
your peace with Him."

He underlined the words in which he had said the servile would
betray the MacDougall for a price. If nothing will bring him
to his senses that will, thought Robert, sealing his letter before
giving it to Mistress MacDougall to deliver for him. That proud-
hearted man! thought the young priest, and he thought this with
compassion, and then went into the church to pray for the Mac-
Dougall. He also prayed for Pamela Stone, and that her hopes would
be fulfilled. It did not once occur to him to try to corrupt a man
into betraying the MacDougall, and it would not have occurred
even if he had had any money, which he had not. Benevolent
despotism must cleanse itself, for the people would not cleanse themselves of it.

He did not know until later that what he had written had not
been read scornfully by the MacDougall but with a deep frown
and thoughtfulness.

Then one day, almost June, the MacDougall came to him, himself, greeting him with exuberance and just catching himself before
he clapped the priest on a braced shoulder.

"My Mary will have me, at last, Faether!" he cried.

Robert felt sick and undone. He fumbled for a chair in his parlor
and sat down heavily. He could not speak.

"There are terms," said the MacDougall, and he seemed to fill
the room.

The priest shook his head despairingly. The MacDougall laughed.

"She will marry me before ye, Faether, and will promise about
the bairns. And after we are married she will take instructions."

A soul was not to be despised. "Why not before?" asked Robert.

"I willna wait," said Douglass. "Time for instructions later, we hae decided."

"And the little lass?" asked Robert, more sick than before.

"Pamela?" The MacDougall was silent for a moment or two, then he said, "Had I not loved Mary first, or if I had seen Pamela first, then I should want her, for she hae a great heart and a lovely face." His voice had changed considerably, and Robert glanced up with hope. "But not sae lovely a face as my Mary's," the Mac-Dougall continued.

"There is a Chinese saying," said Robert, praying passionately in his mind. "'A mon who marries a woman for her face is like a mon who buys a hoose for its paint.' The beauty will go, but what of the heart over the years?"

"She hae a proud, high heart," said the MacDougall.

"Like yours," said Robert. "Is that what ye wish?"

The MacDougall chuckled. "I am master of all women."

"There was niver a mon," said Robert, with aged wisdom, "who was ever master of any woman. Aweel. Let me hear the worst."

The MacDougall was silent again, and Robert looked at him alertly. The MacDougall was scratching his poll of thick black curls, and his cheeks were bright red.

"There is a worst, then?" said Robert, hopefully.

The MacDougall's laugh was very loud and very long. But it was false.

"Ye hae heard of Lady Godiva, Faether?" he said when he stopped laughing, and the stopping was very abrupt in the way of all simulated mirth. "Weel, then, my Mary—she of the proud, high heart—thinks to humble me. Ye have said I am a despot, and so thinks my Mary, and she will humble me. So, she will hae me if I walk through the streets of the hamlet at sundown, when a' are at home, men and women and bairns, on the first day of June, in my mother-nakedness, with not even a boot on my feet."

Robert could only stare at him and blink. The MacDougall chuckled again, but this time the sound was a trifle sickly. "I hae no fear that my folk will see me disgraced, Faether, for a' ye have written that some are servile and would betray me for a fistful of pounds. And glad I am ye do not have them!"

"I would betray ye for nothing, nothing at all!" cried Robert, and then was aghast, remembering his threats.

The MacDougall, very serious now, even grave, looked deeply into the young priest's eyes, and his own, gray and fierce, softened. "And it is true," he said. "Ye wouldna betray me if they killed ye to do it. God love ye, Faether."

Robert groaned. He was confused, and he was grief-stricken and wretched.

"Strange," said the MacDougall, "but the little lass, Pamela, told me also, when I told her of my Mary's command, that some of my folk would betray me. But I said to her, 'Nay, it is not so. They will pull their curtains and shut their doors, and not a mon nor woman nor bairn will peep at me, but will hide himself in his hoose as if asleep, and I will walk through the streets with none to see."

"Ye would punish and humble yesel' so?" asked Robert, incredulously.

"Nae more than standing or walking in my chamber at sundown, mother-naked, Faether, alone."

"She would ask this of ye? A woman who professes to love ye?"

"To humble me, the dear lass hae said. It is little enough for my Mary. But after we are married——"

Robert jumped up and cried, "It is nae to prove your love, nor to soften your despotism, which she knows, that she hae asked this silly and shameful thing of ye! It is to gain mastery over ye for life, ye puir fool, to set her foot upon your neck all the days of your life, to laugh in your face for what ye did in your folly! Do ye not see, mon? I hae called you a benevolent despot. But your Mary is a cruel one, and well ye shall rue it until the day ye die, and may God have mercy on your soul!"

The MacDougall's face darkened dangerously.

"Ye do not even love her!" Robert said in his extremity. "I know this, in my heart! Ye are a despot, but benevolent, and ye are also a guid mon. It is not possible for sich as ye to love sich a woman. It is your pride, your ugly pride, that will not be wise and will not understand! Ye hae said ye will marry her, and marry her ye will, if God does not halt it, because when ye make up your foolish mind ye feel less manly if ye change it!"

"Silence!" said the MacDougall, and Robert fell back before the furious thunder of that voice. And then courage returned to him.

"Do what ye will. There is no gainsaying ye, for ye are proud and without wisdom at a'. But I tell ye that if I witness your wedding, as I must as your priest, for ye are Catholic for a' your sins, it will be with a heavy heart and a sadness I hae never known before. But first ye must make your peace with God, in the Confessional, and receive absolution, and do penance, and one of the penances will be that ye free the little lass, Pamela Stone."

The MacDougall had regained his usual good temper. "That I will do, a' of it, and the day after I walk, for my Mary, that day I will hae Pamela taken to Edinburgh." He took up his bonnet and said, "My Mary will visit ye, Faether, before we are married. But it could be ye'd prefer to dine with us?"

"No," said Robert. He had not wanted to weep since he had been ten years old and now he was afraid that he would, right before the MacDougall, unless he left quickly.

The news was all about the hamlet before sundown, and every soul swore by the saints that he would hide himself and would not look. But Robert did not believe them all. He did not believe the servile ones, who would rejoice in seeing the mighty brought low, for all their professed devotion.

Robert thought of going to each of his flock and telling them to hide themselves and not peer at the laird, but all, even the servile ones, would vow and promise. Ye could not trust the servile ones! They would peep, "accidentally" or inadvertently. They would be covered with sorrow, and in their mean hearts they would believe their protestations. Then they would confess their betrayal of their laird, and be so honestly—to them—contrite at the breaking of their promises that the priest would then not be able to do anything but absolve them and inflict penances, and they would march from the Confessional and make a large display of their penances—if they dared do it in public at all—and feel very virtuous, indeed. Who could pierce the dark and devious heart of man? Not even a priest.

Later, forgetting both contrition and betrayal, they would meanly snicker to a wife, a neighbor, a friend. Such was mankind. A servile people, losing awe and respect for their despot, would become a chaotic people, and this isle would suffer, and especially the innocent. It was always the innocent, at the last, who suffered from the cruel and the base.

Robert did not know what to do. He consulted with Mother M. Dominic, who thought exactly as he did, and who had little charity in her heart for mankind. "I hae lived a long life, Faether," she said, "and I hae seen many things, and few there were that were guid. I hae dealt with children for sixty years or more, and it was the rare bairn that lifted my heart and made my soul glad. The MacDougall was one of the few, and ye say he is a despot, and so it is, and my heart is heavy."

Robert knew that cold, proud women were selfish, and that selfish people can love no one but themselves. He had no doubt but that Mary Joyce was fascinated, in spite of her nature, by the Mac-Dougall, but it was a fascination, and even a gratitude, which was based on her own self-love and on her pride that such as the Mac-Dougall could want her and go to such extremities to have her. He appreciated her, therefore, for what she thought she was, and so she could extend her own self-love for a little to the one who had confirmed her opinion of herself. Yes, it was only gratitude and approval; even then, had she not seen Pamela's obvious love for him, and had not her amour-propre been angrily aroused, she would still have rejected him. So, there was spite mixed with her fascination. She could not have borne that at the last the MacDougall might have preferred Pamela to herself. Rumors move fast even in isolated hamlets which only occasionally get newspapers from the outside world. There were claims that Mary Joyce's father had numerous sons, all in his counting-houses, and like many Scotsmen he preferred his sons to his daughter. Mary, with all her airs and graces, was not really an heiress. Her father considered that such a beauty as his Mary should marry well on her own. The MacDougall was no bad catch. He was really rich. A rich girl, the only heir, would long have been claimed by other men had those men been assured of a very substantial dowry. The dowry would not be forthcoming.

So Mary, beautiful but dowerless, could do worse than marry the MacDougall. He adored her. In this hamlet she would be a queen. So, her angry demands to be returned to her "pampering" family had been merely stage-play. Once convinced of the MacDougall's wealth, and once fascinated by his handsomeness and adoration which confirmed her own self-adoration, she had become quite reconciled.

Still, Robert in his misery hoped that she might have some love for him. The thought of a rapacious marriage was too much for him to bear. Miracles had happened before. Mary's keen nature might be changed. He doubted it. If the MacDougall was a despot, and a benevolent one, it was certain that his wife would be even more despotic, and she would be cruel. And greedy. She would spend half her time in London, and be a neglectful wife and mother. To accomplish this, she must first degrade him and make him her slave. There was no other explanation. The future would kill the spirit of the MacDougall.

It was the MacDougall, later, who confessed to Robert that his letter had made him think of his status and his depotism.

A benevolent despot, Robert would think, is bad enough and can become unendurable, but a cruel despot, as Mary Joyce would become when she took the weapon of power from a fatuous husband, would make a hell of this isle. In the meantime, however, the isle was in a ferment of excitement such as it had not experienced since more than twenty years ago when a band of fugitive criminal Norwegians had attempted to land there and force the islanders to hide them from their pursuers. (The islanders had overwhelmed them, neatly trussed them, and had delivered them virtuously to the law at Skye, after a day and night on the ocean in a sailing vessel. If some of the Norwegians became slightly damaged in the process, they had no one to blame but themselves.) Now the isle was to have a lady as well as a laird, and a bonnie lassie she was indeed, with the face and bearing of a queen. Some who had seen Pamela thought her more bonnie, and more like themselves in appearance and in manner, but the MacDougalls were fascinated by Mary's long golden hair and pale face. And it was time for the MacDougall to marry and produce heirs for the sake of the isle and its peace.

On the day before the day on which the MacDougall was to "pamper" his intended bride by walking naked through the few streets of the hamlet Robert considered if he could call any peeping a mortal sin. But the Seminary had not provided, in its rules, for this contingency, so he solemnly told at Mass of Peeping Tom, who had been struck blind when gazing at the "unclad" and virtuous Lady Godiva. Unfortunately, the communicants were more fascinated by the story than the moral lesson. Robert talked of "respect" and "obedience to the wishes of authorities," but only the servile, and therefore potential traitors and mean-hearted, pursed out their lips in plump agreement. Those who loved the MacDougall truly, and therefore did not like his despotism, looked vexed that the pastor should even suggest that they would peep.

Walking through a street of little shops that afternoon, Robert came on Pamela Stone, who was listlessly glancing through the small windows, a parasol tilted over her head, her dark curls flowing from under a flowered bonnet with rosy ribbons, a rosy dress half concealed under a very long black cape which came almost down to her ankles and was embroidered with roses. When she saw Robert she smiled, and her dimples appeared, but a moment later her eyes were glistening with tears.

"I shall be leaving all of you very soon," she said. "I am sorry, Father."

"Sorry to leave this cold spot?" he asked. "Here it be, almost midsummer, and cold as April in Edinburgh."

"I still love it," said Pamela. She breathed deeply of the strong cool air and said, "I feel like a MacDougall, myself! I seem to know the people well."

The tears were like diamonds on her thick lashes in that cold and brilliant sun. "Ah, well," said the girl, trying to smile again, "I shall never forget this island. I shall be here in spirit if not in body. Douglass has sent our letters to our families in London, though my great-grandmother, poor dear one, can hardly be aware that I'm even away. She often confuses me with my dead mother and other female relatives, so she has been spared any anxiety. But—Mary—has written to her parents that she will be married almost immediately to 'a rich and powerful Scots chieftain,' and that all gifts be sent to her here."

She lost no time, thought Robert. He was heartbroken over Pamela's gallantry and tremulous smiles. "Ye'll nae stay for the wedding?" he asked.

"No." Pamela paused, and a sad mischief flashed into her beautiful black eyes. "If I did, Father, I would object at each of the banns! And if that would not be enough, I would object at the altar, itself!"

"I see," said Robert, with gravity. She was quite capable of doing just what she had said, this spirited girl, this passionate and devoted girl. "Ye dinna like your cousin?"

"Mary? Oh, she is very well in her own milieu, in London. I did so want to see Edinburgh," added Pamela, wistfully. "But I could hardly visit it alone, and I detest carrying maids with me. I wanted a companion, and I offered to take Mary, and her mother's maid, Aggie—that fool!—and that is why we are now here. Had I known——"

The generous girl, then, had paid all the expenses of this curious journey, and not Mary, the arrogant and disdainful. "I have left my diamond earrings for her," said Pamela. "My wedding gift." She looked down at her tiny slippered feet, and her throat trembled. "A good day to you, Father. I believe it is tea-time."

She hurried off with fast little steps, her head held up valiantly, and as she passed others on the street they looked at her with involuntary affection and she bowed her head with courteous kindness. It was she, the generous-hearted, the kind, who should be lady of this isle, thought Robert, and he felt a little rebellious towards God. Then he remembered, with contrition, that if men are bent on destroying themselves God cannot interfere. Nevertheless, he went into the church and did some strenuous praying.

The appointed hour for what Robert considered the MacDougall's disgrace was sunset, he remembered. He said to Mistress MacDougall, who was very brisk and hurried in the manse that day: "Sae that none will be tempted, Mistress MacDougall, you and I shall sit here alone with the curtains drawn, by the fire—disna it ever become warm a little?—and then when the MacDougall has passed we shall hae our tea."

Mistress MacDougall's face was a portrait of dismay; her eyes shifted. Robert regarded her with bitter satisfaction. She, like the other servile, always trotted eagerly to obey the MacDougall's slightest edict. (It was strange that the servile, and therefore the destroyers, did so love legality and took extreme pleasure in the letter of the law!)

"My mon, at hame," she murmured.

"Oh, ye will both hide behind your curtains, virtuously? Invite him, then, to hae tea with me, for I havena seen him often."

Mistress MacDougall looked depressed. Then she shook her head. "He is shy, Faether. He'd like to be at hame, waiting for me." Then and there Robert decided that after tomorrow he would replace Mistress MacDougall. There must be a woman of spirit in the hamlet who truly loved Douglass, and must secretly, if not openly, be rebellious towards him in the manner of a true free Scot, an old lady whose blood ran truly in her veins and not treacherously.

He was really frightened, now. Once the servile had seen their laird disgraced, they would flout even the simplest and most rightful laws of morality and self-respect, and the isle would come to the worst grief. Oh, if despots only knew what they did in their benign but too prideful hearts! They knew better, they thought, than their people, what was good for them, and so they attempted to kill the independence born in man. God gave man free will; the despots had no use for it.

Robert had hoped for thunder and lightning and dark skies and sheets of concealing rain for the next day, but it had dawned like a rose and as sweet and warm. One small white cloud over the looming black crag gave Robert a little hope, but it swayed off over the ocean, which was as blue as the eye of a newborn babe. The sunset would have made a poet of an ox. And just as the church bells struck the hour of six Robert firmly drew the curtains over the little leaded windows of the manse, lit a lamp, looked Mistress MacDougall straightly in the eye and sat down with his breviary. She stared only at the fire, her thick red underlip moving in and out with her resentful thoughts.

There was only silence outside, and no sound of footstep, no voice, no movement. The high-minded and those who loved the Mac-Dougall would be staring into their fires also; the servile would be silent, but peeping and gloating. Then Robert heard the smallest quick footsteps on the street—leather—like the footsteps of a child. The MacDougall's feet would make no sound on the cobbles, for they would be bare. What silly child had some silly mother sent abroad on such a portentous day? Robert caught himself in the very act of going to the door and peremptorily ordering the child within until the MacDougall passed, and Mistress MacDougall's eyes gleamed hopefully. Robert went back to his seat before the fire. "Some foolish bairn who slipped away," said Robert. The clock ticked; the fire sang to itself.

Then, half an hour later, the streets were full of excited laughter and loud voices, and Robert ran to the door to find men bending over with mirth and women shrilling vehemently, and laughing also. He called urgently to his sacristan, whom he saw among the villagers, and the old man came at once, laughing so heartily that his face was crimson and tears were streaming from his eyes.

"Mind ye, Faether," he said honestly, after Robert had slapped him vigorously on the back, almost as strongly as the MacDougall's own slapping, "I didna see it with me ain eyes, but some there are who saw it and are telling of it."

"What?" said Robert, with the most awful forebodings. The servile had not wasted a moment to make game of their laird.

And then he listened with astonishment and heard the whole story.

At sunset, precisely, or just as the sun slipped down from behind the crag and began his solitary journey into the western ocean, the MacDougall had appeared alone at the gates of his house, naked as the day he had been born. He had stood there, gazing at the silent and empty street, and then had stepped forth.

What a grand figure he must have appeared, like the marble heroes and gods of ancient Rome, tall and broad and muscular, heroic and splendid in his manhood, and absolutely assured that no eye would look upon him in his nakedness! Robert thought, remembering his own days in Rome and his own awe.

But there were peeping eyes to see and gloat, behind the draperies, at the great laird who had been humbled by a mere woman. The eyes were suddenly dismayed, and they blinked. For the MacDougall had no sooner set his huge feet on the cobbles than "the little lassie, Miss Stone," had darted behind him, had thrown her black cloak with the roses over his shoulders—"and it coming down to the length of a kilt on him," said the sacristan, wiping away his tears of joy and mirth. And then she had taken his hand, firmly and strongly, and in silence—"and he looking doon at her as at an angel suddenly seen with his ain een," and she had walked beside him through the shut and silent streets of the hamlet.

"Nae did they hurry," said the sacristan. "They walked like lovers in the gloaming, the MacDougall with the cape swinging just above his knees, and the wee lassie with her face all lit up with the sunset, and sometimes leaning her head against his shoulder."

Robert could see them with his inner eye, the noble if despotic MacDougall, and the intrepid and understanding girl beside him, and he rejoiced. What revelation had been given to the MacDougall in that moment, what insight? "They walked like lovers in the gloaming." He had not repudiated the girl and her mantle; he had held her hand; he had looked down at the riot of black curls on his shoulder; he had seen her passionate and loving and urgent face, her lovely and womanly face. He had seen love as he had never seen it before, and he had recognized it and had responded to it. He had known it all, in one flash of revelation.

"And so," said old Father MacBurne to the company about Grandmother's fire, "the MacDougall was humbled in his heart, but not as Mary Joyce had intended. He was humbled as we all must be in the presence of unquestioning and unlimited love, which has much of God in it. He saw all that was to be seen, and it is given few men to see in that fashion.

"It was her footsteps which I had mistaken as the footsteps of a bairn on the cobbles, her faithful and following footsteps, the only ones to break the silence."

It was Mary Joyce who was sent off the next day, with all her bags and luggage, not with the husband she had wanted in her arrogance, but only with two fishermen. It was Mary Joyce who was put on the train for Edinburgh. Robert, somewhat sinfully, would sometimes amuse himself with a conjecture about her enraged thoughts, she the rejected, the sent off, the abandoned, the ultimately unwanted, she who had never had anything to give except her barren heart and her ugly pride.

"I am glad to say that the whole isle rejoiced over the wedding of the MacDougall and his lovely bride, who was as fair in her soul as she was fair in her face," said old Robert. "Her husband's Faith became hers, as once she had promised the deaf mon in his ain parlor on the nicht I first saw her, and his folk were her ain folk, and she brought self-respect to the servile, and freedom, through her gentle insistence, to the free. It wasna that the MacDougall was subservient to her. She merely instructed him, and he saw, and may all despots in the world see before it is too late!"

Old Robert sighed. "It is too much to hope. But I mustna complain. I, who did not at first like MacDougall's isle, could never bring mesel' to leave it, and so I remained. I hae baptized the children of the MacDougall, and his children's children, and soon I will baptize his great-grandchild. And the MacDougall and his lady look still as young as the morning, for sich is the air of the isle, and there is nae ache in me and I, too, am as young as the morning, as are they, at least in ma heart."

"But what of the diamond earrings Miss Mary Joyce received from her cousin?" asked Grandmother, avidly, after wiping away a sentimental tear.

"Mary took them away with her," said Father MacBurne. "What could a mon expect but that? It was sae like her."

Chapter Four

LITTLE ROSE WAS SO ENTRANCED by the romantic story of the Doughty Chieftain and his proper bride that she dreamt that night of skirling bagpipes and noble kilted Highlanders and the gray ocean.

She wondered if the MacDougall had a son or a grandson she could someday marry, and she huddled under her eiderdowns in the early morning to dream again.

She kept out of Grandmother's way that day so she would not be forbidden to join the enchanting company at night. There were two new priests arriving, she understood from Cook. Father Mac-Burne had left "with a fistful of pounds" for one of his pet charities, and a message for Rose. She was to be a very good girl, indeed, and God would love her always.

A Father Hughes had listened intently the night before to the story of the MacDougall, so when all the company was about the fire after dinner he said, "I, too, know a story of love, but it is a very strange one, and not to be understood, though since my experience I have heard similar. Who knows if heaven lies about us, not to be seen by our blind eyes, not to be heard with our deaf ears? Would we be frightened like little children? Then God is merciful to conceal almost all from us, lest we die of fear or lose our interest in the life we should live."

Father Hughes was an Englishman, polished and elegant, with fine white hands and an abstracted air. Like all the other priests, he was also old, but he was so vital, and his blue eyes were so young, that one forgot that he was not a young man.

"Yes," he said, "a very strange story of love, indeed, and sometimes I wonder if it was all a dream, for it happened so long ago and it has never been explained to me, nor any explanation advanced."

FATHER HUGHES AND THE GOLDEN DOOR

"I was my old, widowed Aunt Amanda's only nephew," said Father Hughes, with a deeply tender expression on his face. "She had a number of nieces, my cousins, but she disliked them heartily, though they were apparently devoted to her." Father Hughes coughed. "Aunt Amanda was very rich. I was the only one who bore her own family name—Hughes. My cousins were the daughters of Aunt Amanda's sisters, but I was the son of Aunt Amanda's only and beloved brother. She had been like a mother to my father, for she was fifteen years his senior; she had brought him up after their parents had died, and when she was twenty-one, in accordance with their father's will, she was named his full guardian. So, in many ways, there was a filial and maternal relationship between them. My father's two younger sisters—well, Aunt Amanda did not appear to care a great deal for them. She did her best for them, but only out of duty. My father was her pet.

"Aunt Amanda and my father came from an old Covenanter family, and Aunt Amanda was very shocked when my father married an orphaned Catholic girl. She immediately wrote him that she was 'cutting him off.' Not with the proverbial shilling, for the estate had been divided equally among the four, such as it was. She never spoke to my father again, and neither did either of his other two sisters, who servilely did whatever Aunt Amanda did, thus earning her vast contempt. For, you see, Aunt Amanda had married an enormously rich merchant in the City, and she had no children of her own, and my other aunts had married very modestly, and had a number of girls.

"Aunt Amanda had written her brother, James Hughes: 'Certainly, though you have married whom you married, your children will not embrace the Roman Church!' I was the only child, and, of course, I was christened in the Church. Aunt Amanda, I heard, had a small stroke over the matter, but dutifully, as always, she sent the christening robe—which my father, grandfather and all my aunts had worn on that occasion—for me. She did not come to my christening. The robe was returned after I had worn it at that brief time, and Aunt Amanda never answered any of my father's loving letters."

James Hughes was a gentle, dreaming man, who wrote poetry when he should have been studying briefs and such matters in the office where he was a junior barrister. He was a plodding and meticulous worker, and was assigned those dreary research and summing-up affairs which bored his elders madly. He did not mind. He was fond of detail, and it did not occupy all his thoughts. And he continued to write poetry, which was always adamantly rejected by the editors of poetry magazines and other publishers. Apparently it was very bad poetry, indeed, and his son, reading it years later, found it almost embarrassingly naïve and simple. But the man's sweet and innocent heart glimmered on every line.

His wife, Dorothy, was just like him. She was content with their tiny attached house in London, in one of the isolated mews. She was a happy little thing, and thought nothing of money and only of her God, her Church, her husband and her son. If she had one unhappiness it was because she had borne but one child, whom she had named Benedict for her favorite saint. She and her husband clung together like young trees, embracing both body and spirit intimately.

James thought he should do better for his family, so invested his very small fortune in one of the speculative Bubbles which periodically assailed the Islands during those years. He lost it all. So now he had but his salary. He and Dorothy were not too concerned. They lived a dreaming and devoted life apart from the world, after the initial dismay. In many ways, their life together was an idyl. They

read poetry to each other around the fire after tea. James became a
Catholic. It appeared unthinkable to him that the slightest thing
should divide him and Dorothy; he took instructions, and with his
usual single-hearted devotion he entered the Church. If one such as
Dorothy, he reasoned, could be a Catholic, then why should he remain outside the portal?

He had one distress: his estrangement from his sister, Amanda.
He wrote to her weekly, though receiving no reply, until the day of
his death, when his son, Benedict, was ten years old. He had been
killed by a tram, ten minutes after he had left a neighborhood
church and after receiving Holy Communion. A man of utmost virtue, he had made his Confession only the evening before. The priest
assured both wife and son that James had truly died in a state of
Grace. It was possible, the kindly priest hinted, that James had entered heaven at once. His life had always been as pure as milk and
as harmless as spring water.

Dorothy, the good Catholic, was joyous to receive such consolation. But the zest for life had immediately died in the poor woman,
and she was only twenty-eight then. Even when Aunt Amanda came
to the small funeral—James knew so few people well—Dorothy did
not appear to be too aware of her presence, and kept turning her
large dazed eyes on the big, formidable woman as if vaguely, and
only occasionally, conscious of her presence. When Amanda, who
was usually so grimly controlled, suddenly burst into wild sobbing
and tears, Dorothy was dimly alarmed and tried to comfort her,
glancing at others as if questioning why this stranger was weeping.
When someone would say gently, again and again, "Your husband's
sister, dear," Dorothy would nod and murmur, "Of course." But it was
only a polite murmur. It is very possible that to the last Dorothy did
not consciously know Amanda as her sister-in-law, and James' sister.

A month after the funeral Aunt Amanda wrote to Dorothy: "As
I now understand your financial position I will send you a comfortable check the first of each month, and will be responsible for the
education of my brother's son, Benedict." Dorothy read the letter uncertainly then called upstairs: "James, darling, I have received the
most curious letter! Please come down and read it." Silence answered

her, and she shook her head and said to her grief-struck little boy, "Did you hear your father go out, love? He is not upstairs."

Benedict was only ten, and he understood that his mother's mind had suddenly gone, through sorrow and loneliness. Painfully, he composed a stiff letter to his Aunt Amanda, and the paper was blistered with his tears. Aunt Amanda arrived in her glistening victoria four days later—she lived in Grosvenor Square—to find that Dorothy had died in her sleep a few hours before. The birdlike and fragile heart had broken. God, in His mercy, understood that, without James, Dorothy was not truly alive, but only a torn and shattered remnant.

"There are lambs who can withstand the white storms and furies of winter," said Father Hughes, "and come out the sturdier for them, brisk and up-and-doing, as the poet has urged, full of ginger and love for living. But there are the smaller lambs, soft and gentle and bewildered, who die in the first real storm that assaults them. Our Lord, it is said, was particularly tender with them, and sought them out to bring them in from the storm. My mother was one of those lambs, and Our Lord had taken her home. I like to think of my young parents in heaven," added Father Hughes, the firelight shining on his white hair, the web of years thickening over his lean face. "I am so much older than they were. Will they know me?"

Aunt Amanda, apparently, suddenly realized what lambs her brother and his wife had been, and she was full of remorse and grief. After Dorothy's funeral she took small white-faced Benedict home to her mansion, which he had never seen. That night she had placed her hands on his shoulders and had said, "I am a bad, nasty old woman, really detestable. I hope your father can find it in his heart to forgive me." Then she had scowled. "But remember, my young master, not to take advantage of what you may consider a weakness of mine at this moment! You will go, next week, to such-and-such a preparatory school, and a prince of the Blood Royal is there, himself!"

Benedict had said with his father's own softness but firmness, "No, Auntie Amanda. I want to be a priest."

Aunt Amanda threw up her hands in horror, and her large fat face turned purple. She threatened; she vowed. As her husband had been a full-blooded man, she had acquired some rowdy oaths from him, and she roared them out thunderously. But little Benedict was not frightened—at least not too much—and repeated, "I want to be a priest. Papa and Mama knew, and they were happy."

Aunt Amanda slapped his face roundly, burst into sobs, and clutched him to her enormous breast. She had then ordered brandy for herself and a little sweet wine for the boy. They had drunk together in the gigantic and crowded drawing-room of her house, weeping in the firelight.

She was not a lady to give up easily, and Benedict was not a big boy. She cajoled in the days that followed; she described her lonely state with moving self-pity; she embraced, slapped, thrust away, clutched him to her. The boy would obey her or she'd break his spirit! Benedict's spirit remained singularly unbroken. Amanda shouted, "You are as obstinate as your poor father, who had not a brain in his head! Ungrateful young dog!"

On the eighth day she suddenly announced that Benedict would go to a good Jesuit school in London, and that was the end of the matter. For some years. He went up to Oxford, and the row began again. The two now loved each other intensely, as only lonely people can love, and they quarreled almost all the time over Benedict's unswerving decision. Priests came to talk with Amanda; she insulted them, gave them brandy and whiskey, ordered them to have dinner with her, and handed them large quantities of pounds. This was not in the way of a bribe. She merely thought them sensible men who would understand her position, and Benedict's, as her heir. They understood. They also understood that Benedict had a real vocation.

So Benedict went to his chosen Seminary, and Aunt Amanda did not write to him for two months. Then she presented the Seminary, which was very poor, with such an astounding sum that the Bishop, himself, came to see her to express his gratitude and to assure himself, probably, that he was not dreaming and that the cheque was genuine. "It's the money his father should have had, sir," said Aunt Amanda, wiping her eyes and scowling at the same time. "Had I given it to him—the foolish lamb—he'd not have been tramping the street that day, in the fog, but would have been alive now. For he'd have had his own carriage."

Benedict broke it very, very gently to his old aunt that he wanted to be a mission priest. Amanda had another stroke at this, a rather serious one, which served to bring Benedict to her side frequently, a condition that soothed her and made her hope. But when she was walking again, though with a cane, Benedict told her that his decision still stood. She hit him with the cane, and never used it in walking thereafter. "I don't know where God is, to permit this!" she said. "My only living boy, with my father's name!"

Benedict was ordained, and Aunt Amanda was there, and she was in the church when he celebrated his first Mass. She sat upright, extremely fat and tall, and critically watched his every gesture. And tears of mingled joy and sorrow ran down her ruddy cheeks. "Now I can die in peace," she told him, at the rich and bounteous reception she gave in his honor after the Mass, and she knelt for his blessing and her eyes rolled up touchingly. She lived to be ninety-four, and Benedict's Order prospered mightily through her gifts. She left him a magnificent fortune, and she left each of her nieces one thousand pounds apiece. They took him to court, of course, claiming undue influence, but they lost the case.

During the long years that she lived alone, except for servants, in her mansion on Grosvenor Square, Benedict visited her as often as he could, and he wrote several times a week to her. He had long ago, when he was only eleven years old, given up calling her Auntie. He called her Mother. "And no lad ever had a better and more loving and more cosseting," said Father Hughes. "She spoiled me outrageously all her life, and bullied me half to death."

When she was seventy-six and Benedict almost forty, he had just returned from two years in Africa, and he went to Amanda's house at once for the stay which had been granted him. Amanda was not perceptibly older. She was to give a tremendous dinner in his honor the next night. "I do want you to meet a darling old fool," she told Benedict. "Why do they make you wear such an uncomfortable collar? Thank God for no gaiters, though; I really do not know why the poor High Church clergy wear them; silly-looking, I always thought.

Never mind. Now, my darling old fool. Oh, he's several years younger than I am. He's never married. He reminds me of your father. I might remark, here and now, and no offense should be taken, that you have outgrown your father's dreaminess and vapors, and that is all to the good. But Sir Joshua Fielding remains almost exactly like your father. I mentioned he is a bachelor? Yes. And no kin. But nothing concerns him; he drifts through life like that damned woman who fell in love with Sir Lancelot——?"

"The Lady of Shalott," said Benedict, refilling his aunt's brandy glass.

"What a ninny," said Amanda. "She could see the damned man in the mirror, couldn't she? Was it necessary for her to go plunging after him, then dying? By the way, what was the curse on her?"

"I never knew," said Benedict, sitting across from his indomitable aunt and smiling at her fondly. "But I think there is a moral there, that those who dare not look at life should just glimpse it through their mirrors. Reality has a shocking effect on some people, you know. Very unfortunate. I often wonder how they can be so weak."

"Um," said Amanda, with some sourness. "I was never one to stare at mirrors. How was the joint tonight?"

"Excellent. Do we really have to have that stuffy dinner tomorrow, Mother?"

"Yes, indeed. I have invited a number of rich Romans, for your benefit. It won't hurt them to give you a few sovereigns for your Order. Rich people cling to sovereigns like flies to honey. One can understand that. Joshua is a Roman, too, and very good and sweet and generous. He's the Lady of Shalott all over again."

"He refuses to look at life?"

Amanda considered. Then shook her head, baffled. "I don't know, dear Benedict. But how he can look at life, if he does, with such serenity and peacefulness is quite beyond me. He never speaks of religion to anyone. He quotes Shakespeare a great deal, especially Hamlet. What is it he is always saying? Perhaps I am not quoting it exactly: 'There are more things in heaven and earth, Horatio——' There, I can't remember the rest."

Benedict sat up, deeply interested. "Oh? Of course, I remember.

It was not one of my favorite quotations." He paused. "Is Sir Joshua superstitious?"

"Dear me, my child," said Amanda, irritably. "I cannot say about that. How you do go on in irrelevances! What has superstition to do with Sir Joshua, who lives in a world of dreams? I want you to meet him and for you to see what your father would have been like had the sweet lamb lived. It might," added Amanda with a tinge of malice, "give you a start."

Some doddering old man who is possibly senile and has picked up an exotic thought or two in his travels, thought Benedict. He asked, "Has Sir Joshua ever been to India?"

"He's been all over the world, though why I really do not know," said Amanda. "The rest of the world is so not-English, isn't it? Must be very wearing and boring, and one can't trust the water, I've heard, and such sinfulness going on."

Benedict suddenly laughed, remembering D'Israeli's pungent remark on British morality.

"Does he often speak of India?"

"No. Not at all. And he has none of those frightful big brass plates, all carved with symbols and serpents, and strange furniture and hangings, all from India—so fashionable these days. They give me the vapors. Very depressing. One expects cobras to come gliding from under the sofas. No. Joshua's house is just as comfortable and sensible as mine, and in as good taste." Amanda looked about her complacently. Benedict looked about, too, and thought, as he had always thought, how crowded and how tasteless this rich room was, and then he thought how much he loved it as his home.

"I don't think," said Amanda, "that he liked India. But what has India got to do with it, Benedict? How your mind wanders. That comes of the fevers you have been having in heathen places."

Benedict indeed had suffered from various fevers in jungles and in deserts, and he was here at home because his superiors thought he needed considerable time to recover. His superiors were very fond of Amanda now, and increasingly grateful, and she was old.

There was no one at the party even of his own age, and he was not very young any longer. There was not a lady or gentleman present under sixty-five. Most of them were much older. They were all very fat and staid and had round opinions, like Amanda, and they all exuded that serene air which told of large bank accounts and solid investments. They laughed happily and cosily, and were satisfied and content. Sir Joshua Fielding was not like them in the least.

In fact, Sir Joshua resembled, startlingly, a number of old and courtly Monsignori of ancient Italian family whom Benedict had met frequently in Rome. He had their slender and swaying height, their attenuation, their fine and patrician Roman profiles, their bright and mystical eyes, their noble heads, their exquisite manners, their air of detachment and quiet benevolence. Benedict wondered why he had never become a priest, himself, this regal old bachelor whose voice was both soft and resonant, carrying yet calm, and who wore about him, as an almost visible aura, the lofty saintliness of those who are genuinely good and innocent of spirit. And, like the Italian Monsignori, he appeared well aware of reality, in spite of Amanda's fixed opinion of him. This mingling of intrinsic innocence and accepting worldliness was an intriguing blend, and Benedict soon became fascinated merely by watching his subtle face, his slight and graceful gestures, the way he lifted a glass and inclined his head, his sudden sweet smiles, and the laughter, never cruel, which lurked in the corners of his fine mouth. He was the sort of person of whom it is usually said when he is young, "He is not really a child," and of whom it is said when he is old, "He will always be young."

Sir Joshua and Benedict became friends almost at once. He talked of Benedict's life with interest, and he had the marvelous gift of listening and interpreting immediately. While listening, the merry eyes, so youthful and alive, would become soft and grave. And then Benedict suddenly knew, right in the midst of dinner, that in one way his aunt had been correct: Sir Joshua lived for a dream, and lived in it also, quite apart from his mortal life, which he appeared to be enjoying very much, indeed. There was no regret or sadness or yearning in that dream, Benedict saw, no mawkish superstition, no fanatic obsession, no removal from reality.

Benedict began to wonder. Had he loved a girl he had lost, or a virtuous married woman whom he could not have? Certainly, there was a far glow of love in his eyes, but it was the glow of fulfillment and possession and joy. A man did not look like this after he had lost his love.

Benedict began to probe delicately and curiously, for he was only human, when the gentlemen were left alone with their brandy and the ladies had retired to the drawing-room. He had found a seat for himself next to Sir Joshua, who was a general and respected favorite even among those beefy and very earthy men. The mighty chandelier poured down its rainbowed light on the gleaming white tablecloth; the paneled walls glimmered in firelight. The dinner had been excellent. The gentlemen, "Roman" and non-Roman, felt a little constraint at having a priest among them, and quite a youngish one at that. Their elderly lewdness had to be suppressed, and this made them slightly melancholy. So, to give them an opportunity to whisper their innocent naughtiness to each other, Benedict leaned towards Sir Joshua and began his probing in what he thought was a most unobtrusive way. Suddenly Sir Joshua's eyes began to sparkle with paternal amusement, and this made Benedict blush. The older man pulled his chair closer to Benedict's, so that they formed a little island in the midst of gleeful whispers and noisy, abrupt laughter.

The eternal and patient rain of England was falling outside, this early autumn night, and Benedict could hear its mysterious whispering against the shuttered windows. It was a most peaceful sound. It was, as the English said, "a soft night."

"Our friends are being considerate of you," said Sir Joshua. "I am sure you could tell them of more outrageous things than those they are whispering now. They are very good men, you know, my dear boy. The strong, beating heart of England. The strong, lusty heart. I hope it beats forever! I hope the Empire will never disintegrate, as other empires have done all through the past. If that happens, a whole world will be lost to order and character and discipline and freedom. Yes, these are the heart of England. I think it is very kind of them to accept me so whole-heartedly, don't you?"

Benedict was startled. He stared at the aristocratic face smiling at him, and then at the somewhat gross and very much overfed faces of "the heart of England."

"For, you see," said Sir Joshua, removing the ash from his cigar gracefully, "my dear and wonderful father was only a traveler. He carried his pack on his back through three counties every year, walking every foot of the weary way. In the wildest of weather. He was such a little man. A lifetime of privation and hunger and poverty, and the hardest work, had stunted his body. But not his soul. I think he is a saint now, unknown to the Church but not to God. And my mother, to make ends meet, took in sewing and washing. She could not go out to the rich houses to work, for I was a sickly child. I owe my life, for what it is, to her endless and loving care. I was their only child.

"So, you see that my friends are very tolerant, indeed, in accepting me among them, as if I had been born to their wealth and in one of their houses."

Benedict was astonished. He looked at Sir Joshua's excellent broadcloth and fine linen, at his long white hands, so curiously youthful and supple, at his noble features and brilliant eyes. A beautiful ring was on the third finger of his left hand, worn in the manner of a betrothed woman. It sparkled and glowed with a thousand changing lights. It was not an opal, yet it had an opal's restless and shifting colors, its cold yet fiery heart. Benedict found himself looking at that strange ring, even while he thought about what Sir Joshua had told him.

"You are wondering," said Sir Joshua, "how it is that I am now rich and can afford what I have, and my carriage. I did not earn it; not a single penny. You see, my father, in his travels, came to know that the poor women on the farms and in the hamlets and villages longed, as do all women, for some fragrance in their lives, some luxury they could afford which would make them feel cherished. So my father, with my mother's help when he was at home, concocted a smooth oval soap, made of sound if inexpensive materials, and scented quite strongly. It was a sweet and overpowering scent, and seemed to be compounded of roses and lilies and lilac——"

"Fielding's Fragrance!" exclaimed Benedict. "Soaps and sachets!"

"Exactly," said Sir Joshua, smiling. "You know them then."

"Who doesn't?" said Benedict. "The whole world does, and not only the Empire. The soap, sixpence a packet. The sachets, in little satin bags, two for a shilling. The odor," said Benedict, "lasts forever, they say."

Sir Joshua's face subtly changed. "Forever is a long time, thank God," he said, and he looked at the ring on his finger. For a moment or two, or perhaps longer, Benedict lost him completely. The old gentleman seemed to have retreated behind the elegant façade of his body and face, and was now enjoying some deep delight beyond imagination.

"I was about twelve, and ready for work, when my father compounded his first packets of soap and his first sachets," said Sir Joshua, at last. "I helped my parents pour the liquid into a mold my father had made. He had also made his own crude stamping for the soap, and it remains the same today: the name wreathed in buds and flowers and leaves and tendrils. For the first years, until I was eighteen, the products sold modestly but soundly, and my mother gave up her washing and sewing and she and I worked together and my father peddled his other wares, and the soap and sachets, on his rounds. And then fortune came all at once, as it usually does. Large soap companies discovered the soap and sachets, after the women all over the counties refused to buy any others but my father's. Their fame had even come to London, and to Edinburgh.

"My father may have been a saint, but he knew the value of his work. He accepted the most magnificent offer, and continuing royalties: a penny a packet, and two pennies for the sachets, for himself and his heirs, everlastingly.

"Unfortunately, a lifetime of privation ended his life when he was on the very threshold of his new life. My mother, who had suffered with him, died of consumption. I was then twenty-two. I was a millionaire, or rather close to being one. I was not uneducated; my long childhood illnesses had kept me in bed, and I had read incessantly. There is nothing like the boldness of youth! Armed with my fortune, I did what my parents would have me do. I went abroad to the great schools of France and Italy, for, of course, I could not be accepted in England. And when I returned, after several years, I engaged an English gentleman to tutor me, to polish my accent, to make me a gentleman, myself! Snobbish of me, wasn't it?" Sir Joshua laughed gently. "Yes, indeed. And I built the house where I still live, exactly as my parents would have had it, and I live as they dreamed of living. And the Queen enjoys my company. She may be regal, but she is not annoyed by a man's background, if he has other virtues, and her Majesty appears to think I have those virtues."

"I am sure you have," said Benedict, with the warmth of a young man. Then he colored. He was being infernally rude. He had practically forced this fine old man to tell him of his life, and now he was being patronizing into the bargain. He was ashamed of himself. The Italian Monsignori, for all the ancient fame of their families, would not have done this, and they would have looked at Sir Joshua with respect and admiration and would have known him for the great gentleman he was.

"Forgive me for prying," said Benedict. "It is just that my moth— my aunt—seems to be so fond of you, and she particularly mentioned that she wanted us to meet."

"And she has spoken so often of you," said Sir Joshua. "I am glad we have met. I have known Amanda only about two years, for I travel widely. I want to see if there is any spot in this world so beautiful as——"

"As?" said Benedict, when Sir Joshua's eloquent voice stopped abruptly.

"As a place I know," said the old man. "I must tell you of it sometime. And you will be the very first to hear of it." He looked at his ring again.

The gentlemen then rose to join the ladies.

Later, Benedict said cautiously to his aunt, "A wonderful old gentleman, that Sir Joshua Fielding."

"Isn't he?" said Amanda, gratified. "I knew you would like each other at once. And all that money, too. Millions of it. Soap and sachets. The servant girls adore them." She paused and laughed. "I do, also. A little overwhelming, the scent, but such really good soap.

Better than Pears and the imported French, I believe." Her stays creaked, and she said, "I really must go up to bed, my dear. I am not as young as I was. Did Sir Joshua tell you of his immense charities and the yearly fortune he gives to your mutual Church? A fine fellow, dear Joshua."

Just before he fell asleep Benedict remembered the odd words of Sir Joshua: "I want to see if there is any spot in this world as beautiful as—— As a place I know."

There were some souls, Benedict reflected, who are so pure and innocent and noble, so utterly filled with grace, that they are vouchsafed, in ecstasy, some glimpses of heaven. Was Sir Joshua one of them? His face had been the face of a lover, of a man loving, a man beloved, a man who was young.

Benedict paid visits to some priests he knew in London, and to the Bishop. He sounded them out on the subject of Sir Joshua Fielding. Invariably, their faces became full of light and affection. The Bishop could not speak too highly of the old gentleman. "A true son of the Church," he said to Benedict. "A saint. He has told me of his will; he has left everything to the Church, including all royalties after his death. There were several winters when I am afraid we'd have almost starved to death here in London if it had not been for Joshua. He does not wait to be asked; he knows at once when others are in need."

"Would your lordship say he was a mystic?" asked Benedict.

The Bishop stared. "A mystic? No, I hardly think so. We are very dear friends. I should have known. What on earth are you talking about, Benedict?"

"He seems to have a rather mystical expression, sometimes," said the young priest, lamely.

The Bishop smiled. "Yes, I have noticed that, myself. But he is very scholarly, you know, and scholars often assume that expression, distant and thoughtful. Is that it? No, I'd have known if Joshua were a mystic. He is, in fact, a very sensible man, though his house is utterly tasteless, isn't it? He explained it was the sort of house his parents had dreamed of, and so he made it that way. I am sure his taste, which is very fine, does not lead in those ways, but he loved his parents dearly. He has a private gallery of marvelous Old Masters, and a collection of bibelots not to be found anywhere else in London. Objets d'art. That is in another part of the house. A mystic, you said? No, indeed. Sir Joshua is very shrewd about business matters, you can be sure, and he has the best of lawyers who examine the soap company's books annually."

The Bishop laughed. "He has the soundest of investments, which he manages himself. Some rascal or other attempted to cheat him a few years ago, and when Joshua discovered that he made the man smart for it, through the law. He has no mercy for cheats, and detests them more than he does any other criminal. In some ways Joshua can be ruthless, as ruthless as the aristocrat he intrinsically is."

"Did your lordship ever notice that particularly large and beautiful ring he wears, a stone that seems compounded of all the opals in the world?"

"Yes," said the Bishop. "He has asked that he be buried with it."

Benedict thought of that for a moment, then began to tell the Bishop of Sir Joshua's peculiar words on the occasion of Amanda's dinner. But he stopped after the first word or two. Sir Joshua had not asked him to keep the matter confidential. Yet, in some way, he had intimated that he knew Benedict would not be an idle blabber and that he would not betray any trust. If there was anything to be trustful about, thought the young priest.

A few nights later Sir Joshua asked the pleasure of the company of Mrs. Amanda Seldridge and Father Benedict Hughes at dinner in his house. They accepted. But on the day of the dinner Amanda had a slight chill, and her physician ordered her to bed. She insisted that Benedict leave her, however. "He has some remarkable treasures, dear Joshua," she said. "You really must see them, Benedict. And his greenhouse, right in the midst of London! The rarest of flowers. He tends them like a father. He has one flower no one ever saw before. He calls it C'est Egal. Beautiful. Most remarkable."

" 'C'est Egal,' " repeated Benedict. " 'It is all one.' Extraordinary. A rose?"

"No. I simply cannot describe it, child. He never tells where he found it. Perhaps in one of those dark jungle places he has visited in his travels. It is bright gold. When I had a bad chill while you were away he sent me almost a dozen of them. They quite filled the house with the most marvelous scent. Not to be described, truly. And though they were cut flowers they lived for weeks! Just weeks. And then—— Now that is extraordinary." Amanda paused.

"What is?"

"I just remembered. On the last night I saw them, and they were beside my couch, in my bedroom, they were as fresh and scented as on the first day. And when I awoke in the morning they were gone! I asked my nurse about it, and then the servants, and they swore they had not touched them. Yes, extraordinary. But it has a simple explanation; the nurse was very officious. She threw them away while I was asleep, no doubt. Nurses do seem to have an aversion to flowers, don't they? Always taking them away."

" 'Curiouser and curiouser,' " murmured Benedict.

"Alice in Wonderland," said Amanda, proud of her memory.

Feeling somewhat like Alice in Wonderland himself, Benedict went to dinner at the house of Sir Joshua Fielding. He did not know what he expected, but he discovered he was the only guest, and that the great mansion was as disappointingly, if as richly, ugly as his aunt's. All the bad taste and vulgar opulence and crowded bric-a-brac and hideous furniture of the Victorian Age were here. It was the dream of some poor workingman in his most satisfying of fantasies. There was not even the smallest touch of real elegance anywhere, no grace, no charm, no delicacy. Sir Joshua greeted the young priest as warmly as though they had always been friends, expressed his regret over Amanda's illness, and offered whiskey. "I am a true plebeian," said Sir Joshua. "I don't even splash a little soda into my glass. I drink my whiskey neat. And I never touch sherry. I suppose you have wondered how I got my title?"

"No, it didn't occur to me," said Benedict.

"I simply gave a very large amount of money to one of the Queen's favorite charities. Ostentatious of me, wasn't it? But I was sincerely interested in the charity. She was so pleased that she knighted me. And then we became good friends."

He was suddenly grave, then said after a moment's sipping. "She never can forget Prince Albert; she never will. There are some who say that long grief is self-pity. No, I do not think so, Benedict. Do you remember the story of the old man and his wife who were visited by one of the gods, and they treated him so kindly for all he was dressed like a beggar that on the next morning he asked them their dearest wish? They told him that they prayed never to be separated, and so he transformed them into trees, side by side, whose branches mingled together."

He paused, and Benedict thought of his young parents, who had hardly lived except in their dream.

Sir Joshua continued: "There are many who love only once. They are the sort who, once loving God, for instance, never again betray or wound Him, but serve Him with delight and joy and faith all the days of their lives. And there are the people who only love once in the world. Who can say that mortal love is passing, and will be gone? Love, which is the very fiery core of the Godhead, is eternal. A man and woman who truly love each other can never forget, even when reconciled after one of them dies, and sometimes they are never reconciled, though they tell themselves they bow to the will of God. After all, we are human beings. A little more whiskey, Benedict?"

Benedict, accepting, pondered. Had Sir Joshua loved a woman who had died, and did he live with that memory? His words would lead one to think so. If that was correct, then he lived with the thought of her and all his days and nights were permeated with the joy not only of her memory but of the living pulse of her.

"The human heart and soul and flesh are well known to Our Lord," said Sir Joshua, "for does He not possess them, Himself? Who can doubt that He loved His Blessed Mother, and thought about her when He was absent, and then, when He ascended to heaven, did He not remember her? Who can deny this, after a moment's thought? I know it is not a Church dogma as yet, nor even a doctrine or article of Faith, but one of these days it will be infallibly known that God did not forget His Mother, nor cease loving her, for He had been, and is, flesh of her flesh, and heart of her heart. The tradition that she was assumed bodily into heaven will become fully accepted, and then will be a dogma. If He who was begotten from eternity could not forget His Mother, then surely we cannot forget those we love, and look forward eagerly to seeing them again in a far better place than this tumultuous world, this world of sin and wrong and sorrow and evil. To forget them is to insult them, to diminish their memory, to reject their love for us. I am afraid I am speaking in a stately manner, Benedict, but I am of an old generation, you know."

I have seen him only twice, thought Benedict, and he is old enough, almost, to be my grandfather. Does he confide in me because I am a priest?

"I often talked with Amanda about you," said Sir Joshua. "She told me of your parents, and your childhood, and how you grieved for your father and mother. I thought, then, that if I ever met you I should tell you—a very strange story, and a very true one. If," and Sir Joshua smiled, "you were as your infatuated aunt told me you were."

"Am I?" asked Benedict.

Sir Joshua studied him. "I think so," he said, after a moment or two. "But I will be able to know better shortly. What do you think of my thesis?"

Benedict hesitated. "You know we are taught to pray for the dead, and we ask their prayers for us. But we are not supposed to grieve and rebel constantly; we are supposed to be happy that they are safe with God."

"Don't you think that the Blessed Mother was lonely for her Son, and that, perhaps, He was lonely for her, in heaven?"

Benedict said, "As you have pointed out, Our Lord possessed, and still possesses, a human heart and a human soul. So, I should answer 'yes.' Though, of course, there is no time with God; there is only eternity."

"I think our dinner is served," said Sir Joshua. They went into a huge dining-room every bit as ugly and immensely furnished as Amanda's. Benedict thought that the dinner, at the least, would be finely French, with a dash of Italian savor, for one, after all, can carry filial love to extremes. The house was bad enough. But the dinner was exactly like one of Amanda's, and as uninspired. Even the wine was dull.

Sir Joshua, the man of noble profile and patrician graces, relished every morsel of the bloody roast beef, the brussels sprouts, the mashed turnips, the boiled onions and potatoes. He looked with pleasure at the suet pudding, which Benedict, who had a touch of "liver," could not eat. Sir Joshua said, "I've heard about your fevers, Benedict. Perhaps you'd like an apricot or a peach, instead of this delicious pudding?"

"At this time of the year?" said Benedict. "Do you import them from Spain, in silver paper?"

"Oh, no. I grow them in my greenhouse." Sir Joshua touched the bell, and his manservant brought in a dish of opulent apricots and peaches, dewy and cool and fragrant.

"In your greenhouse? In London?" asked Benedict, with incredulity.

"Certainly. They are a dwarf variety, not generally known. I cultured them myself. Do taste them."

Benedict carefully peeled the fruit with the fruit knife, and ate them. He had never tasted such flavor, either in Spain or in Italy or in the Orient. Not only were the fruits refreshing but they were delightful in scent and texture. They were too delicious to spoil even with the best of cheese. A pale rose wine was served with them. "I never tasted wine like this," said Benedict.

"It comes from Chile," said Sir Joshua, pleased at the young man's pleasure.

"I have heard of your greenhouse, Sir Joshua, from my aunt."

"Would you like to visit it after dinner?"

"Indeed, yes."

"And my little gallery of Old Masters?" Joshua laughed a little. "No, I suppose not. You've seen the best in the Vatican and the Louvre and so why should you bother with second-best, which are all I have? I prefer modern artists, however, but they are a little strong for the stomach. You shall see my greenhouse instead."

After dinner Sir Joshua led Benedict through a series of big and gloomy rooms, flickering with firelight. Then they passed down a

GRANDMOTHER AND THE PRIESTS 141

long corridor into an extremely large conservatory. The air was heavy
and warm and damp, and Benedict thought of the jungles. Then he
saw this was no ordinary greenhouse, full of cramped palms, forced
roses, pale gardenias and orchids and other exotic flowers. He was
familiar with all these, but he was not familiar with the flowers in
this conservatory. He walked along the benches and examined them
closely. The atmosphere was burdened with languorous scents. There
were a number of fruit trees, darkly green and thick of leaf, gleaming with tropical and semi-tropical fruits, and there was a feeling
of life here under the many gaslights.

"I searched the whole world for the flowers," said Sir Joshua, and
he named some. "Many of them were very small in their native state,
but careful breeding and grafting—a new art in horticulture—resulted in these large blooms." He stopped before a big single box
filled with dark, rich earth, and Benedict stopped with him.

The box was crowded with blooms, and long stiff leaves. In the
midst of these leaves stood the flowers, large and glowing as if with a
life of their own, and yellow as gold. It seemed to Benedict that they
emitted an aura, fainter than themselves, and quivering. The petals
were as thick as those of a rose, clustered closely together. Not a
single petal was withered or spotted; the stamens appeared smother-
ing in gold-dust. And the scent of them was incredibly sweet, fresh,
and pure.

"C'est Egal," said Benedict, with awe. "My aunt told me." He did
not need to bend to sniff at the flowers, for they were tall. He looked
at them lovingly, and—surely it was his imagination!—they seemed
to bow towards him, as if acknowledging his love and returning it.
And—what imagination could do!—they also seemed to glow brighter,
as if smiling at him.

"C'est Egal," repeated Sir Joshua.

"You found it in some far-off place?" asked Benedict.

"No," said Sir Joshua. "In London, when I was twenty-six years
old. A young girl gave me a single flower, on the street, and these
are the progeny of that flower."

"But, where could she have possibly gotten the flower, Sir Joshua?"

Sir Joshua looked at the flowers bending towards Benedict as if stirred by a breeze, and then he smiled and took the young priest's arm. "Come back into the house and I shall tell you. I created the greenhouse to keep them company." He turned off the lights. A dim green darkness immediately filled the greenhouse, but C'est Egal continued to shine as if illuminated, the brightest pure gold Benedict had ever seen in his life. As the two men passed through the corridor Sir Joshua said, "If the flowers had not—shall we say known you?—I'd not even have dreamed of telling you about them."

What a fanciful old man, thought Benedict. But he glanced behind him, longing for another glimpse of the marvelous flower. When they were in the drawing-room again and sipping brandy, Sir Joshua became very silent and looked at the fire for several long minutes. It was as if he had forgotten Benedict.

Then he said, "I feel I must tell you. I've hardly had time to know you, but yet I feel I must tell you, and I've never told anyone before." He turned his fine head and Benedict saw half of his face in the ruddy firelight, exalted and joyous.

"I was twenty-six," said Sir Joshua. "My parents were dead, and I was very rich because of all their work. I was building this house at the time, this dear, ugly house, and living in rooms at Claridges. Yes, at Claridges. I had returned from France and Italy and Germany, and I had my tutor living with me in my rooms. Sometimes I would become very restless with my memories of my parents, and so I would often leave my hotel and take a tram and then walk the long distance to my old home where my parents and I had lived."

The neighborhood was extremely dreary and deteriorating. It had been just above a slum when Sir Joshua's parents had been there. Now it was a complete slum. Many of the rotting old houses had been demolished, and two streets from his old home a storehouse had been newly built. One could glimpse its gloomy tall outlines above a high brick wall, but only the higher outlines and the dun roof. The area within the wall could be reached only through an iron gate on the street behind. No grass grew within the area, not a tree or a shrub. It was hard-packed clay and gravel. Drays entered through the one gate with goods to be stored, and then sold to retailers.

"Very cheap goods," said Sir Joshua. "Calicoes, ginghams, rattle-trap furniture, bad china, pots and pans, utilities used in quantities by the very poor. The dinginess of the old-brick wall, its lifeless enclosed area, and the hideous storehouse made even the dying slum more depressing. It was a very busy street on weekdays, with the lorries and the horses coming and going, and the children playing on the flags, and the women screaming from littered doorways, and men shouting. It was an evil place, as all poverty and all commerce in those days were evil. It is often said, disdainfully, 'the drunken poor.' But what makes a man drink? He wants to forget, and the poor must have their anodyne as well as the rich. They need it more; they will die to get it, for how can they bear their lives? A man can't live without hope. There was no hope in those streets. I was not drawn there out of affection but only because I wanted to re-member my parents and their neighbors, their friends, so that I should never forget misery and should understand it. I was rich now, but I was determined never to forget, for my soul's sake."

"You have never forgotten," said Benedict.

"No," said Sir Joshua. "I have never forgotten the horror. Or the joy which God gave me there."

On Sundays, even the slum seemed to die. The storehouse was silent, baking in the sun or running with black water, and the clay and gravel with it. The dreadful little houses were quiet; the slum children were washed for a change, and sat meekly and quietly on brushed doorsteps. The whole region stank of coal gas, smoke, dust and offal.

One Sunday, a Sunday as dank and gray as dead wet ashes, Joshua had walked there, along the high and endless brick wall that guarded the storehouse. The city rumbled at a distance. Here, everything was almost soundless. And it was empty. Joshua glanced across the road, and then away. It was then that he saw the young girl walking only a few steps ahead of him. He stopped, in sur-prise. She had not been there a moment ago, and now she was here. She must have stepped across the road at the moment he had glanced away.

He noticed a curious thing almost immediately. Only his own

footsteps rang on the cobbles. The girl walked silently, as if drifting. She was slender, and a little taller than average, and beautifully formed, the shoulders straight, the waist small. She wore a long yellow dress of some material he had never seen before and which he could not identify, but it certainly was not cotton or linen or wool or even silk. It floated about her ankles, and her feet were shod in yellow slippers. It was a cold day, but she did not wear a mantle or a coat, and her head was uncovered. Her hair was extraordinary, of a shining silver-gilt, thick and smooth, and lay on her shoulders and dropped far below her waist.

Joshua was astonished by the silent walking of the girl, her clothing, and her hair. She moved easily and lightly, as if she were some princess walking in her secluded garden. Then he had the most powerful and urgent desire to see her face. As if he had called to her, she turned, smiling, and he was struck still.

He had never seen such a beautiful face, not even on the canvases of the Old Masters on the Continent.

"How can I describe it?" Sir Joshua asked of Benedict, and his voice was the voice of a jubilant young man. "There are really no words. When I tell you that she had eyes the color of lilacs, a nose as delicate as alabaster, a mouth like a rose, and a complexion like a lily, I am really telling you nothing. These are only words. It is like a blind man, blind from birth, who attempts to describe a sunrise. I could only stand and stare at her. I can only say that I fell in love with her at once, and that I never loved again, and will never love anyone but that girl."

"But what was such a girl, dressed like that, on a cold dead Sunday, doing there in those quarters?" asked Benedict.

"She was waiting for me," said Joshua.

"For you!"

"For me. My poor boy. Your eyes are popping. You must put aside your realism for a moment, and merely accept the fact that I was there, and that the girl smiled at me, and that she was waiting for me. She was so obviously waiting that I pulled up my clumsy feet and went to her, my mouth falling as wide open as yours is falling now.

"She was holding a long flower in her hand, the ancestor of those I have called C'est Egal. When I reached the girl I could smell the fragrance of the flower, and see its beautiful glowing heart. I was stupefied, of course. I looked down into her eyes, and she gently put the flower in my hands. Then she said, 'Wait for me. Do not forget me.'

"I've never heard such a voice in my life, never before that day, never since. I have heard the greatest female singers, but they did not have such a voice. I heard what she said, and I was stupefied even more than before, and terribly in love. Then, as I held the flower, she walked about twenty feet ahead of me and touched the ugly brick wall, and for the first time I saw in it a small door. As yellow and shining as the flower I held. The door opened, the girl smiled at me again, then walked through the door and closed it after her.

"Then I could uproot my heavy feet and race to the door. But when I reached it, it was not there at all. There was nothing but the solid brick."

Benedict was silent. His thoughts were confused. Of course, there was a rational explanation. A pretty young girl, walking for her own amusement in that awful place, carrying a flower——

"There was no door," said Sir Joshua. "But I had seen it, and I had seen her walk through it."

The poor old soul is mad, thought Benedict, uneasily, or he dreams.

As if he heard the dissenting thought, Sir Joshua smiled widely. "I am not mad," he said. "I'm not senile, Benedict. I am considered very sensible and realistic. And, I am telling you the truth. 'There are more things in heaven and earth, Horatio——' "

"Yes, I know," said Benedict, with some impatience. "Every—er—mystic or superstitious or sentimental person quotes that at some time in his life, and regularly, I've found."

"You are a priest," said Sir Joshua. "You are taught that the supernatural is as close to us as breathing. You know that the angels are a cloud of witnesses. The Holy Bible speaks very often of these things. And we have Lourdes to remember——"

"You are not saying——!" cried Benedict, shocked and outraged.

"Good heavens, no! How could you think such a thing, Benedict?"

Benedict colored brightly. "I am sorry, Sir Joshua. But you must admit that what you have told me is very extraordinary. Could it possibly have been a dream?"

"I have C'est Egal," said Sir Joshua.

Benedict's mind whirled with thoughts of flower-girls who were very mischievous, and fantasies, and daydreams. He said, "Of course, you never saw her again."

Sir Joshua was amused. "I have seen her many times since then, times too many to count. And I have been inside the golden door."

Benedict stared. His eye then flickered around the great warm and ugly room, at the crush of bric-a-brac, the too-vivid Indian rugs, the rose damask walls, the antlers and mirror over the mantel, the hideous Indian vases filled with gilt rushes and ostrich plumes, the looming furniture and footstools.

The young priest said, cautiously, "And what was inside that golden door, the door through the brick wall which surrounded a dead clay and gravel yard?"

Sir Joshua lit a cigar, after Benedict refused one. A coal appeared at the end, and the old man puffed vigorously. "Ah," he said, "there is nothing as good as a good smoke.

"What was inside the door? I was not admitted for some time. I went every Sunday after that first one to that place. It was nearly a year before my love came to me again, a year of deep misery and longing and hope. She was there as suddenly as she had been there before, between one instant and the next. This time she called me by my name, and put her small white hand on my arm. Lovingly. And she told me her name, which I have never repeated to anyone else, and which I will not tell even you. Then, she went before me, while I was rooted on the flags, and she opened the golden door and closed it behind her."

Benedict wildly thought of devils and demons and possession and wanted to bless himself.

"It was at least six months after that before I saw my love again, on that street, near the wall. She did not smile at me that time. She only said, 'In God's good time, Joshua. You must be patient. And you must pray.'

"Of course, I had never stopped praying. Sometimes it occurred to me to wonder why my love had ever come to me at all, a young man whose fortune came from soap and sachets, and other vulgar things. There was nothing remarkable about me, nothing exceptionally good or virtuous, nothing unusually pious. I attended Sunday Mass, to be sure, as my parents had taught me. It was a duty. I had never given it much thought, that Most Holy Sacrifice. It was just there, something I had accepted from my childhood. Do we not accept this mysterious and beautiful world, the air we breathe, the glories of the sky, the shine of water? These are all mysteries. We accept the sun and the moon and the stars as commonplaces—these majestic and miraculous things from the Hand of God. We are blind men, and deaf. The smallest field flower is a marvel; a bird is a revelation; a wind is tremendous beyond words. But, we accept them, casually and unthinkingly."

As I have always done, thought Benedict, with new humility. But his parents had not accepted them so casually. They had greeted each day as a new miracle, fresh and joyous, and his father had written his stammering poems in pathetic celebration of what he had seen even in the shadow cast by a tree. His parents had had their own glimpses of the Beatific Vision. None had ever come to him. He had been a dutiful and hard-working and devoted priest, moving always among misery and trying to bring light into darkness. He had been obedient; he had prayed with all his heart, and had known peace. But—he had accepted everything as earthily as his aunt, Amanda, had accepted it. They were there. There was work to be done. He, Benedict Hughes, had been a male Martha, concerned with busy matters. He had worked so hard that he had not looked at the stars for years, and had never thought of them. He labored in God's vineyard, but he never caught the fragrance of the grapes. He had suffered meekly, offering up his pain to God for the help of the living and the dead, but he had really never seen the face of God because of the dust of the earth and all the labors he had diligently performed. Yet Christ had paused to admire the lily of the field. He had gone to the Lake of Galilee, so beautiful, so calm, so holy and moving, to deliver the Sermon on the Mount. He had loved the sweet faces of children. He had spoken of the cheeping swallow. He had loved, beyond all imagined love, the charming garden which was the world, the lovely garden He had made. On the night before He had offered up His life for men He had prayed in Gethsemane, the place of olives and cypresses and flowers. His words had been filled with beauty and poetry, for He was Beauty, itself.

No wonder, thought Benedict, that Aunt Amanda had been a little malicious with him and had remarked that he should meet Sir Joshua, who was so like his father! Did she know, herself, how dull he had become, and was she rallying him on it? She had called Sir Joshua "my darling old fool," but there had been a curious glint in her eye when she had said this.

And I have dared to be embarrassed by my father's poetry! thought Benedict. I, who have no poetry at all. He had prided himself on his realism—and realism had closed his eyes with mud.

He looked at Sir Joshua. The old man may have been only dreaming, but what a dream he had had!

"After the second time I had seen my love," said Sir Joshua, "I went to Mass every day and received Holy Communion. In some way it seemed to draw me nearer to her, to bring her closer to me, and to give me a mystical sense of joy—a sense I should have known all my life before then if I had not been so engrossed with work and if I had only taken time. When we receive Holy Communion, we not only receive Our Divine Lord, and His love, but we love others more deeply for that indescribable Grace. We are not only joined to Him, but we are joined in love with those He loves also. I understood, for the very first time, what the Sacrifice of the Mass truly is. The spotless Victim is not only offered up for our sins, but He brings joy to us, and light, and the imminence of heaven. If we do not feel that, then we have felt nothing.

"I did not attend Mass after that as a mere Catholic duty, hardly realizing. I attended out of my love for God, my new love for Him, my new understanding. And so I was peaceful and content to wait. In His good time, as the girl had told me——

"But why a man like me, an ordinary young man, ambitious for learning though I was, ambitious to be as my parents had wanted me to be? I was really nothing at all. My parents had poured a new fortune into my hands. I wanted to please them. But after I had seen my love the second time I knew that I needed to please but One—God.

"And I knew that all my great fortune did not truly belong to me. It belonged to God. I held it in trust for Him; I was His steward. He had given it to me to use in His Name, for the relief of the wretched and despairing, for the enlightenment of those who live in darkness, to help those who spread Faith and courage and assistance. I was, to bring it all down to earth, only God's banker, to pay out the funds which belonged to Him."

He smoked peacefully for a moment or two. "Do you know, Benedict? When I realized these things, and the realization did not come all at once, my very appearance changed. Oh, nothing radical, of course. I had always had some handsomeness, but it was a coarse and common handsomeness. I am not being vain, but only factual. My features did not actually become other features; they merely lost their lustiness, and lightened and quickened. I have, in my long lifetime, seen that change take place in the faces of rosy-cheeked and hearty young girls when they became nuns. I have seen the change take place in the faces of strong and burly young men when they became priests. Not all nuns, not all priests. But so many that it has been remarked upon by others besides myself. Of course, they are holy people, and I am not. But I share a revelation with them, I who was nothing at all. And that is a great mystery."

"You look like an Italian Cardinal I met a few years ago," said Benedict.

"You are very kind, my dear boy.

"But I must tell you the rest. My love came to me more often on that street as I came closer to God. Two years went by, then three. My house was completed. I furnished it. I lived two lives, one concerned only with brief meetings with my love, the other concerned with increasing my fortune, so I could help the Church more and more. Yet, they were a single life; they were like two leaves on a stem.

"Then one Sunday my love said to me, 'Today, you may come with me through the door.'

"She gave me her hand, and I had never touched it before, for she seemed too precious for my touch. It was warm and soft and firm. I had had vague thoughts that if I touched her my hand would touch nothing but air. But her hand seemed as fleshly as my own. She led me to the door, pressed against its golden gleam, and it fell aside and we stepped within together.

"I don't know what I had expected to see, my mind half filled with the memory of the clay and gravel and the storehouse. Strange, but I had not really thought much about it, except that I imagined that in stepping through that door she had simply disappeared from my sight. You can understand, then, with what awe I looked at what was beyond that door.

"Imagine, if you can, an exquisite garden, but a garden that had no boundaries, no walls, no real horizon. It was as wide as the earth, and as endless. It was Eden, before the Fall. Grass was there, and uncountable flowers, among them my C'est Egal, and mighty trees I had never seen before, and fountains and arbors and glens and knolls. The place was full of birdsong, and the wind sounded like a thousand soft harps. But more than anything else was the light, the immutable light, not exactly like the sun, but deeper and more intense. And what peace, what sense of joy, what radiance! And there was no mar anywhere, no blight, no spot, no small ugliness, no dying, not even of the smallest or fullest flower. And, there seemed to be no time at all, but only eternity.

"I don't know how long I stayed. We walked together, serenely, hand in hand. Fragrance was all about us, and sweetness and the tenderest warmth. I have never told you what we had said on the street. I will not tell you what we said to each other in the garden. I will tell you this only: we spoke of our love for each other, but all the rest is my own, except that we also talked of God and His love. There was no lust between us.

"Then time had to take me again, and we went to the door. Before she pushed it she said, 'We will not meet again until you come here to stay. But remember me, and be patient.' Was I sorrowful? A little, perhaps. But how long is a man's life? A few years, a few years of delusion, of waiting. It is a waiting full of peace and faith and joy. I knew, even when I was alone on the street again, that my love was in the garden, waiting for me, and that the waiting would not last forever. But when I go again into that garden, there will be the end of waiting, and only eternity will be there."

The old man sighed and smiled. "I go to the street often, as you can imagine, hoping it will be for the last time. But there is only the brick wall and the gray Sunday silence. Apparently, my time hasn't come as yet. I am growing very old. It can't be much longer, can it?"

Benedict did not answer. He struggled with himself. His common sense told him that he had been hearing a dream, a fairy tale. Harmless, for it had made an ambitious young man almost saintly; harmless, it had brought a somewhat ordinary young man to God. There was nothing actually wrong with all this, and certainly nothing evil. Evil does not lift a man's heart to God; evil does not set a man's feet in the path of justice. Evil does not grow the fruit of joy and charity and love for God on a thorn-tree. Evil does not keep a man chaste and serene all the long years of his life, and urge him to the service of his Lord. Evil does not bring peace.

And, who knew? Benedict shook his thoughts back into a sensible pattern.

"You have told no other priest, except me, of this, Sir Joshua?"

"No. I did not feel it was necessary. But I felt it was necessary to tell you."

"Why?"

"I don't know, Benedict."

"Forgive me, but has it ever occurred to you that you may have been suffering from some illusion?"

Sir Joshua laughed heartily. Then he held out his hand to Benedict. "My love gave me this ring, on the last day I saw her in the garden."

Benedict examined the ring he had marveled at before. He looked into its brilliant and glowing heart, and saw the colors change as the colors of the sky change at sunset. They shifted and shone, blue and gold and scarlet and pearl and rose and fire and flame. They merged

and moved, became limpid and still, then swirled again, as if alive.
The stone was set in a metal that was pale and shining, unlike any
other metal Benedict had ever seen.

"It resembles an opal, slightly," said the young priest. "But it is not
an opal."

"No," said Sir Joshua. He said a moment later, "I've looked all over
the world to find a place as lovely as the garden, for, you see, I am
homesick. If I had found a place which resembled it only a little I'd
have stayed there for at least a while."

"Have you ever wondered why all this—all this—has happened to
you, Sir Joshua?"

"Of course. A thousand times. I am not in the least worthy."

Benedict frowned. "Sir Joshua, you know there is no marriage or
giving in marriage in heaven."

"I know. So Our Lord has said. But we have His promise that we
shall see those we love again. Shall not parents know and love their
child again, and a man his daughter, and a son his mother? Shall He
who loved His Mother and brought her to heaven deny a man that
joy? Shall He who is now surrounded by His saints, whom He knew
on earth, deny that other friends shall meet again and love each other
with a greater love? Shall a man and his wife who loved each other
in God in this world not fall into each other's arms again in rapture
and happiness? God who is love will never deny love, our human
love, for His Son took on our nature and our flesh, and He knows.

"Not only shall we possess God, but also the love we have known
on earth. 'All else besides.' Our treasures wait for us, for He gave
them freely."

"I still don't know why you have told me, Sir Joshua."

The old man looked at him gravely and gently. "Nor do I, Benedict."

"Who is that girl?"

"That I cannot tell you. Do not ask me, Benedict."

Old Amanda was waiting up for Benedict when he returned. He
saw the light under her door, and then heard her booming voice,
"Come in, boy, come in!"

He went in and said severely, "You should be asleep, Mother."

"Nonsense. Hah, what is this? You look disturbed. Did my darling old fool disturb you, child?"

"No. I don't think so. He's a little odd, though."

Amanda grinned wickedly at him. "Do you really want to know why I wished you two to meet? I wanted you to see what you'd not have escaped if your poor, sweet father had lived. He was exactly like Joshua. He'd have made a dreamer of you, too, Benedict, and this is no world for dreamers, though I must admit that Joshua really does very well."

"There are worse things than dreams," said Benedict.

Amanda stared at him, her bold old eyes narrowed. Then she said, quietly, "I'm glad you know that, my dear. I thought you'd forgotten, priest though you are. For, you see, I never had dreams, none at all. Your father had them, and so did your mother, and they were so happy. I've never been truly happy, Benedict. We realists, you and I, may have many virtues, and you above all, but if we lack a dream, then we are more than half blind. No, I have never been happy. And I've been very unhappy, lately, thinking that I had made a complete realist of you, too. You, who can celebrate a Mass! Think of that."

Benedict thought a great deal about that in the days that followed, and as his health improved.

One day he went to the old Bishop and said, "Will your lordship please be frank with me? What is your opinion of me?"

The Bishop did not seem to be surprised. He said, genially, "Benedict, you are an intelligent, worthy, diligent and devoted priest. You have sacrificed your health, and almost your life, in God's service. You have been utterly obedient and steadfast. Nothing has been too much for you. I doubt if you have much in the way of sins, even venial ones. You have served God nobly, and will again serve Him."

"Thank you, my lord. Do you think I love God perfectly?"

The Bishop dismayingly hesitated. Then he said, "What do you think, Benedict?"

"I don't know," said Benedict, with misery. "I suppose I do. Why else should I try to do His work? Why else should I have become a priest?"

"I see," said the Bishop. "Yes, I think, I know, you love God deeply. You had a genuine vocation from the beginning. All of us love God in a different way from others. Just as not all flowers are the same, so love is not the same. There are also degrees of it. Let me put it this way, from what I know of you: you love God, in your own way. But I don't think, in spite of your sacrifices, that you love your fellow-man very much. Do you?"

Benedict was startled. He had not thought of that at all. With shame, he said, "I think I have tried. I have given all of myself that I could. Isn't that love?"

"Not entirely. A man can love God but not his brother. It isn't a new thing even for a very pious man. Do you know what the Protestants say? 'Protestants love man but not God, and Catholics love God but not man.' That is a broad statement, and like all broad statements it is not entirely true. The ideal thing is perfect love for God, and perfect love for our fellows. But, my dear Benedict, it is quite worthy to have the intellectual will to love both, even if we don't have the emotional desire. It is, I believe, enough to will it. God understands more than we know. And, eventually, if one wills love, it will come."

Benedict thought of that, and prayed inwardly for the grace of perfect love for both God and man. Then he said, "Has your lordship seen Sir Joshua Fielding's strange flower which he calls C'est Egal?"

"Oh! Old Joshua! Certainly I've seen that flower. Beautiful, isn't it? He never tells anyone where he found it."

"Has he always been peculiar?"

"Joshua? Dear Benedict, the man really has no eccentricities at all! Feet on the ground, and all that. What makes you think he is— peculiar? I wish we had more rich men in the Church as peculiar as he is! Then hundreds of our priests wouldn't be half starved to death everywhere in the world. He is a saint; I'm convinced of that. We have talked together innumerable times. He is full of sanctifying Grace."

I wish I were, thought Benedict. He did much walking and praying and thinking for the next week or so. Then one morning his aunt said delightedly, "Benedict! While you were tramping about, my dear Joshua brought you four of his lovely flowers, and he has left a letter for you! Do open it and read it to me."

The flowers had been placed in one of Amanda's best crystal vases, and they shone in the Victorian dusk of the drawing-room like living gold. Benedict touched a petal, certain that it would not feel as flowers feel. But it did, indeed. It had an unusual warmth, as if fresh from a hot sun. The flowers blew out fragrance, as if breathing. Benedict opened the letter and read:

"My dear young friend—

"When you receive this letter I shall be gone from your mortal sight forever. No one on this earth will ever see me alive again. I have heard the summons tonight, as my clock struck twelve, and today I enter through the golden door forever. Rejoice with me. Joshua Fielding."

"Good God!" cried Amanda. "What on earth does he mean? Benedict! Where are you going!"

But Benedict was already flying from the house, and the echo of the slamming of the door pursued him down the road in the direction of Sir Joshua's home. A disturbed servant answered his knocking. No, no one had seen Sir Joshua so far today. It was most unusual for him to leave so early in the day. Word had been sent to his club; no one had noticed him there. He had not rung for his breakfast; there had been no sound from his room since he had retired last night. Where had Sir Joshua lived as a young man? The servant stared. Why, he did not know. But wait, Father, please. Sir Joshua was fond of treating the children on a certain road on Sundays; he gave them shillings and pence and brought them toffee, and often sent boxes of new clothes—fancy that, new clothes—for the old people there. The name of the street? "I have it on the tip of my tongue, Father. Just a moment——"

Benedict knew that priests did not seize harmless people by their shoulders and shake them and shout at them, but he forgot that now. He literally shook the name of the slum street from the servant, then went racing off. He found a hack a few streets away, and flung himself on the damp leather seat and promised the man a pound if he would hurry. The horse galloped off, and Benedict clung to the seat as the hack bounced on the cobbles and clattered through the streets.

If I am only on time! thought the young priest desperately. But why he wished to be on time he did not know.

"Here ye are, Parson," said the driver, cheered by the note given him. It was not for him to wonder why a clergyman should be in such a confounded hurry to reach a slum district full of snotty kids, workmen, sinister pubs and screaming, dirty old women in rags. Mission of mercy, as they called it. Benedict flung himself from the vehicle, and raced down the street. It is not a Sunday, he recalled, with some incoherence. The street was alive with noise, racing children, screams, yells, the rumble of drays, the shouts of men, the shrill voices of slatternly women. Ah, there was the long brick wall, and above it the sooty roof and chimneys of the storehouse. A long, long wall, running the length of the street. The flags along it were broken; the houses opposite fumed with crowded life and noise. Strangely, no one was walking near the wall except Benedict, himself, and he was almost running, searching, praying for what, he did not know.

Then he saw Sir Joshua serenely strolling ahead of him, and he stopped and blinked incredulously. He strolled like a young man, swinging his cane, his topper gleaming silkily in the smoky sun. Benedict called hoarsely, "Sir Joshua! Wait!"

The old man turned and smiled at him, not surprised. His face was the face of a happy youth. He touched his hat in salutation, then turned and went on, and Benedict ran behind him. Then he stopped again.

There was a yellow door, narrow and small from this angle, in the brick wall. Joshua put his hand against it and it opened, and he stepped within; the door swung to behind him. He was gone.

Benedict ran to the door. He reached it and pressed his hand to it, panting. It was brilliantly gold, smooth and like metal to the touch. Benedict hurled himself against it with all his strength. It did not move. He beat on it with his fists and shouted, "Sir Joshua! Sir Joshua! Come out!"

A hand was put heavily on his shoulder, and Benedict turned his head and saw a burly workman behind him, his wool cap set low over his eyes, a stinking pipe in his mouth. "What's up, matey?" asked the man. "Not gone daft, be you?"

Benedict cried, "Help me to open this door!"

The man's little eyes stared piglike at him. "What door, Parson?"

Benedict swung about. There was no door at all. The brick wall extended ahead and behind him, for the full street. "There was a door!" exclaimed Benedict. "Here! Didn't you see it, man?"

The other shook his head and squinted at the young priest. He grunted. "Never a door here since the wall was built. Only the gate on the other side. You'd not be out of your head, like, would you, Parson?"

"I saw the door," said Benedict. "It was here." He looked at his hands. There was mortar and brick dust on them, and the sides were bleeding a little with tiny lacerations. "The door," muttered the young priest, stupefied. "I saw it, too."

"Never a door," said the workman. Ruddy bit of business, this, a parson babbling on the street like a chap in his cups. Cautiously, the workman bent his head forward a little to sniff Benedict's breath. The laddie wasn't drunk, but had he gone barmy? He was breathing like a chap with a stroke.

"You'd not like to go inside, Parson?" asked the workman, remembering that the daft should be spoken to calmly. "Through the gate on t'other side?"

"Yes," said Benedict, and he was off again, running down the length of the street, throwing himself around the corner. He was followed by jeers and screams of children and women. He did not hear them. He reached the big iron gate, which was standing open to admit a huge dray, and he rushed through the gate and found himself in a yard exactly as Sir Joshua had described, all blank clay and gravel. He raced along it to reach the point where he had seen the door, followed by the stares and shouts of the workmen about him. And then he saw a knot of men standing above something, muttering and swearing. Benedict halted. He knew exactly what he would see. The knot grew larger, and someone called for a doctor. Slowly, heavily, Benedict approached the men, who parted to let him see what was to be seen.

Sir Joshua was lying, dead, on the gravel and clay, joyously smiling, his open eyes staring at the sky. The great and living gem on his finger was only gray stone now, its fire extinguished, its colors gone forever with the soul who had worn it.

" 'Ow did the toff get here?" the men were asking. "Didn't see him come in the gate. Standing right here, wasn't you, 'Arold? You see him before?"

"Never," said the other, astonished. "Not a sign of 'im. Dead as a flounder he be? One blasted minute he wasn't there, and then he was. Blimey!"

Then the men slowly removed their dusty caps, for Benedict was kneeling beside Sir Joshua and beginning the prayers for the dead.

"I sang the Mass at his funeral," said old Father Hughes to Grandmother's other friends. "I know why he had written me as he did. He wanted me to see the door for myself, and to believe in what he had told me. I believe. But still, I do not understand. Not all. Only a little.

"I do know one thing, however. He had changed my life. I was never a realist again, demanding proof of all things."

He looked at his withered hands, which had beaten so futilely against the golden door, then glanced up at a question. "The inquest? Oh, 'death from natural causes.' But no one was ever found who had seen Joshua alive within the wall; no one had seen him enter through the one gate. No one had seen him fall, and die. As for myself, I was called to testify. I merely said that I had known that Sir Joshua frequently walked in that section of the city, and I had wanted to see him on a matter of importance. I have told no one to this day, except my Bishop, of what I had seen—the golden door through which Sir Joshua had entered, rejoicing."

"But the flowers he had sent you, Father?" asked Grandmother.

"Oh, yes, the flowers." Father Hughes was silent a moment. "When I returned to my aunt's house they had disappeared. The water was there, and the vase, but there were no flowers. Aunt Amanda was enraged. She accused the servants, and I had to put a stop to it, after she had them in tears. There was only a fragrance left, and it stayed for many days, long after Sir Joshua was buried beside his parents. No one ever saw C'est Egal again, and those in his conservatory disappeared also, leaving not one petal behind."

Chapter Five

"You'll be going home tomorrow, Rose," said Cook. Rose stared at her in dismay, not knowing she was a reprehensible child for not wishing to return so soon to her loving parents.

"But Father Lewis has promised us a tale tomorrow!" she said with protests that rang over and over with the insistence of childhood.

"Don't you want to see your dear Mama and Papa tomorrow?" asked Cook, severely.

"No," said Rose.

Cook raised her eyebrows, but Rose only burst into tears. "Why don't you want to go home?" asked Cook curiously.

"I like it here," sobbed Rose.

"With *her?*"

"Grandmother? Oh, she showed me all her butterflies this morning, the gold ones with rubies and emeralds, and her big emerald ring. She said she is saving the ring for me. I don't want to go home!" exclaimed Rose with new sobs. "We haven't anything home like Grandmother's!"

"Probably all for the best," said Cook, philosophically. "But *she* had a letter this morning to send you off. Not that she's shedding any tears. Wot's wrong with you now?" added Cook, as Rose swallowed painfully.

"I have a sore throat," said Rose.

"So, that's how it is," said Cook, who would have delighted modern psychiatrists with her shrewd understanding. "Well, we'll see

wot can be done, though mind you, that throat will be better if you
don't go home tomorrow. You'd not miss one of those tales!"

The sore throat was so bad the next morning that Grandmother
impatiently sent off a telegram to Rose's parents. The telegram was no
sooner off, and unrecallable, than the throat cleared up miraculously.
Grandmother, on being informed of that fact, looked at Rose with
a freckled grin and said, "I didna know ye were so fond of me, lassie.
Aye, you may stay up and listen to Father Lewis, though mind ye,
he's a Welshman, and one knows the Welsh are daft and tell strange
tales."

FATHER IFOR LEWIS AND
THE MEN OF GWENWYNNLYNN

"It began," said Father Lewis, in his soft and lilting Welsh
voice, "when my elderly third cousin, Father Andrew Lewis, wrote
me a very strange letter. He was troubled in his mind. He did not
expound, for we Celts, being a mysterious people, love mysteries by
instinct. But it was obvious that he was indeed troubled, and wanted
my advice. There was some controversy with his Bishop, a brisk man
who liked everything neat and tidy. I believe his mother was an Eng-
lishwoman."

The other priests nodded wisely at this, quite understanding. All
the English liked tidiness and neatness, and in the realm of the
spirit and mysticism things were apt to be above such mundane matters and boredoms.

"Moreover," said Father Lewis, "the Bishop was quite young,
and a Jesuit, and one knows there is no one so brisk and elegant and
down to earth as a young Jesuit. My cousin was none of these, and
the Bishop frightened him half to death with his demands for 'full
explanations, examples, names, details, written clearly and consecu-
tively.'" Father Lewis paused. "There's many a good businessman

lost in a Jesuit. Naturally," he added, "we need such minds, but they do bear down, and country people detest being borne down upon. They know that all the records in the world, and all the briskness, never made an ear of corn ripen faster or a thunderstorm stop its fury on schedule—man's schedule. They have a respect for nature."

"Ah, yes," said the countrymen-priests at Grandmother's.

Father Andrew indeed had a problem. Before he could bring himself, in spite of all his spirit's willingness, to be "full," teeming with examples and details, he wanted the advice, or at least the encouragement, of his kinsman, whom he had guided into the priesthood and who was twenty-two years younger than himself. So Father Ifor went to his aid, in the little Welsh town of Gwenwynnlynn, a town of miners, cupped in the hollow of harsh violet mountains near the sea.

"I had heard of 'wild' Irishmen and 'bleak' Scots," said Father Ifor, with a smiling and gentle glance for his friends around Grandmother's fire. "But the Welsh, though their kinsmen, are somewhat different. Your Welshman is apt to be more combative than the Irishman, less inclined to good humor or a joke, and is even more active than a Scotsman, though that hardly seems possible. He is often bad-tempered, fiercely quick to take insult, dogmatic and intolerant, and would as soon bash you as look at you, if you gave him an offhand expression. Moreover, on the average, he is shorter than his kinsmen, the Irish and the Scots, usually has a thick thatch of red hair, angry blue eyes, a red face, and the distended nostrils of the belligerent man. Such men are frequently adventurers; the Welshman is not usually so; he rarely emigrates. Perhaps he is too engaged in a feud all the time, or has to work too hard in his savage and lonely land to indulge in fantasies of gold beyond the sea. He is inclined, too, to detest wealth—in others—and resent it as a personal insult to him. As for his pride——" Father Ifor shook his head. "God help him. I hear he is making the American press, as of this very minute, resound with his union activities in the coal-bearing regions. One can expect broken heads wherever a Welshman takes up residence."

"My sister," said Father McGlynn, with a reminiscent smile, "married a Welshman. But it was the big hand on her, and he six inches shorter. If there was a black eye, sure and it was on the husband's face."

"It is with good cause that the Englishman calls the Welshman 'the red cock,'" said Father Ifor Lewis. "And Gwenwynnlynn was full of red cocks, and red hens, and a noisier people you never knew. They can out-argue Lucifer, himself, even the children. I have heard it denied, but a violent land, I have seen, breeds a violent people, or perhaps it is that only violent people remain in a violent land. The others discreetly move elsewhere. All Italians are artists because how is it possible to live in so beautiful a country of color and song and exquisite natural form and not be an artist? People are more like their land than some of our 'advanced' scientists would want you to believe.

"My cousin, Andrew, however, was a strange Welshman. He was gentle, simple and good, though in his youthful years he had had the Welshman's red hair and fiery blue eyes and quick temper. The years had leeched away the red hair and the fieriness of the eyes, had bent his small back and made slow his active limbs, but he never lost the gentleness, which, God knows, certainly did not come from his people! However, he did possess the Welshman's resentment of oppression, the privileges of arrogant wealth, and injustice. He believed in fighting evil with good and patience——" Father Lewis paused, looking blandly at his fellow-priests, who had immediately put on pious expressions. He smiled to himself. "Instead of with fists, and the mace and the dirk," added Father Lewis, with a twinkle.

"Ah, well," he said, in his musical voice. "I knew my cousin's hamlet well, having been born there, and visiting him, though not in the past twelve years. Slag, smoking piles of debris from the mines, the acrid smell of coal, the pits, dirt, soot, dust, small and meagre little cottages, blackened tiny gardens, the odor of the sea at night, the dirty rain, and the terrible wall of stark mountains beyond. A very poor hamlet. The Catholic population composed about forty-five per cent of the whole. They were much poorer than their neighbors, and bigotry was everywhere. My cousin's church was falling into ruins; there was no school for the children. But the Anglican church gleamed strongly and the communicants always seemed better dressed. They were not miners. They were shopkeepers. Which reminds me of Napoleon's remark. Ah, well, we need shopkeepers, too, though they have carriages in my cousin's hamlet, and look very English and are pleased if they are mistaken for Englishmen in that God forsaken place. This proves, certainly, that even the Welsh are quite human, though this has been disputed in London."

Father Ifor Lewis bridled a little. "One should always deprecate pride, but a Welshman's pride is an awesome thing. It is not to be despised, for it arises from courage. A Welshman, in the coal hamlets, needs all the courage Our Lord can give him. The mines, of course, were owned by Englishmen—absentee ownership, as it is called.

"Wales is a beautiful if savage country. Mountainous. Stony. Haggard. But so beautiful, if so cold as it faces the wild grayness of the ocean, and so bitter of soul. It has grandeur, and an eerie terror, and an awful, valorous history. Yes, I know it well, for I was born there, and its vision stands in my soul."

The Irishman, said Father Lewis, has clung to the Church through faith and devotion, the Scotsman partly because he despises the Sassenach and will not be dictated to by anyone, but the Welshman has retained his religion, if Catholic, through sheer and angry stubbornness. No one can beguile him. The Irishman will be respectful in the Confessional, the Scotsman reserved and cautious. The Welshman will argue noisily with the priest if opinions collide as to the weight of the sin, and especially over the penance. An Irishman will rarely write to the Bishop complaining about a priest. It is quite usual with a Welshman; he complains all the time. He is absolutely convinced that if he does not fight for himself he will be taken advantage of, even by his priest, who, being Welsh, too, has things to say about the vast amount of alcohol a Welshman can ingest with disastrous results. If alcohol is often direful for the Irishman—the Scotsman is usually not too susceptible, as whiskey is expensive—alcohol is poisonous for a Welshman, as it is for most violent men. And the Welshman drinks, unless he belongs to a Baptist or Methodist sect; even then, he frequently relapses under the sheer pressure of his nature. And his circumstances.

It was with some depression that Father Ifor boarded a train to

Wales, remembering the poverty, the soot, the broken streets, the collapsing little cottages, the half-ruined church and bitter misery of his
cousin's rectory, and the all-pervading atmosphere of angry wretchedness of the hamlet. It had been twelve years since he had seen all
that, and he had devoutly hoped that it would be at least twelve
more. But the old cousin, Andrew, was, like his countrymen, too
proud to wail about his personal troubles, and so if he had asked
Ifor to come he had had an overpowering reason. As the train proceeded into Wales the character of the people in the third-class carriage changed, so that they became progressively shorter, more stocky
or massive, more red of hair and face, more furiously blue of eye,
and more sullen of lip. Their clothing, too, became much poorer and
patched. Father Ifor sighed. He glanced at the big old silver watch
his father had given him on the occasion of his ordination, and he
saw that within an hour he would be in Gwenwynnlynn. He looked
about him at the next station. It had begun to rain, a cold, black,
early summer rain, drizzling and surly. The station was tiny, the
walls of granite, the roof of the thick black slate of the region. But
the people waiting on the platform, to Father Ifor's surprise, appeared
well dressed and contented. A county meeting, perhaps? Then he
saw that they were workingmen and not gentry, and that they wore
wool caps of good material, and their high boots were polished. A
holiday? Father Ifor shook his head. Not even an Anglican one. This
station was the last stop to Gwenwynnlynn and so the men and
women, cheerily boarding the train and talking loudly, were inhabitants of his cousin's village. They had the polished and ruddy skins
of the well-fed, and the bright, quick eyes of those who possessed
well-being of body and soul. A woman or two had a bonnet definitely citified, and two or three girls wore shawls that resembled
woolly lace.

They rushed into the third-class carriages, but Father Ifor noticed
that a few, with importantly set shoulders and lifted red heads, made
for the second-class ones, too. Those who came into the third-class
carriage with Father Ifor either looked at him darkly and explosively
—which marked them as not being Catholics—or touched caps or
curtseyed, which marked them as Catholic. He shifted on the wooden

bench towards the middle-aged man next to him, and said diffidently, "And you'll be from Gwenwynnlynn, perhaps?"

The man swelled out his chest like a cock and removed his cap for a moment. Then he folded his thick arms across his chest. "That we'll be!" he said, with pride. "And it's the finest village in the country! I be a miner, Father, but well paid I am! I live in a cot, but the roof is tight and the walls painted, and there be plenty of ham and beef in the larder! Not as it was. It's when we laid down the laws to the English owners, and asked! They with their millions of pounds! Or perhaps," he added without much conviction, "they was moved to Christian charity and decency." He looked about him with arrogance, and his neighbors smiled and nodded. "It be my opinion it was our firmness when we asked for the better wages and machinery. A man lays down the laws to the Englishman, if he be a man of spirit."

A surly, patched man, middle-aged and stained with coal dust, lifted up a louder voice: "More fool you, man of Gwenwynnlynn. It be we have the same owners, and we has the spirit, too, and they done nothing for us. It's the saint ye have in your Godforsaken hamlet, which I be visiting to see my father, and it was my father who told me."

The well-dressed man removed his cap again, laid it deliberately on his knee, and stared at it. He shrugged. "Well, be it as it may. I think it be the owners, and our spirit——"

"Spirit!" snorted the other. "We be men of spirit, and as for wrestling, it minds me we wrestled the men of Gwenwynnlynn and——"

Father Ifor recognized all the makings of a hearty, and physical, fight developing, and though no one loved to watch a boxing match or a wrestling more than he, he was too interested now in the conversation to permit the fight to develop. Such a fight could lead to a huge brawl among everyone in the coach and there were two or three young women who were obviously pregnant. He said, hastily, to the well-dressed man, "I am Father Ifor Lewis, cousin, third removed, to your own priest. He's asked me to visit him, and seemed troubled. Perhaps you can tell me why; he's an old man——"

The man chuckled richly. "I be Harlock James, at your service,

Father. So your Reverence be the young 'un the old Father tells us of, though it's the city paleness you have, and it gives you the look of age." His face changed and became pious. "The men of Gwenwynn-lynn believe we have a saint among us, by the Grace of God, and we think it is your cousin, Father Andrew."

Father Ifor stared. Mr. James settled himself importantly on the seat, and everyone listened piously.

"He has the heart of a true saint, and the soul, Father, and my father, it was, who told me before he died, and may God rest his soul. Never was Father Andrew's larder filled, and he starved with us. There was no mending the church and the rectory, nor the cots. There was nothing but work," he said, with a touch of bitterness, "in the blasted mines, and dirt, and whining young ones who never had enough to eat, and one glass of beer on a Saturday night. Never an extra shilling to rub against another." He glared at the surly man near him.

"Suffered he did, Father Andrew with us, and bent he became. Not even a bicycle could he afford, to visit the sick and dying in the damned rain and mud and dirt. All on foot. Never complained, he. Never asked. And then he wrote many the letter to the English mine-owners, in many years. They didn't bother their greedy wits to answer. And in the meantime, Father Andrew was with us, and never, but when he was starving, would he take a bite from us when it was offered, and never did he have a glass of beer or the price of it. A saint. And he wrote the letters." Mr. James paused, portentously. "One must have moved the stone heart of an English owner, for men began to come into the hamlet and mend the cots, and there was new machinery for the mines so that the coal dust was not thick the longer, and the church was rebuilt, and a convent, and the four Sisters came to teach in the new school. And two shillings bought what six used to in the market and shops, and every holiday there was a goose and a ham and potatoes at each door, and a carillon of Italy bells for the church, and new cassocks for the Father." He paused, glared at the stupefied priest with triumph. "And a carriage there be for the Father, a little one, with a good horse. The streets were mended with new cobbles. A doctor comes to us, and sets up residence, and we pay nothing! It is all given us. Not a penny will he take, and the pills and syrups be free, too, and he comes in a fine carriage to the cots when he be called, like the Prince of Wales with his beard." Mr. James paused again. "'Twas banking day today, and that's why we all be here. For our wages have gone up, two times."

He looked contemptuously at his surly neighbor. "Aye, I agree. It's the saint we be having, Father Andrew, and will ye tell me why you deserve no saint of your own?"

"Saints," said Father Ifor, hastily, "do not always come where they are deserved." His mind was full of the wildest thoughts. "Have you —have you talked with Father Andrew about this?"

"That we have!" said Mr. James, emphatically. "Does your Reverence take us for idiots?" He blessed himself. "And never a word will he say but to ask us to daily Mass, and penance and good works, and charity."

"Saints always talk that way," said the neighbor. "It's the language they have."

Mr. James ignored him as an inferior who had not deserved a saint, no doubt because of a mass of mortal and venial sins, and therefore not fit to be addressed as a Christian. Another man spoke up, sneeringly. "I be a Methodist, and I gets what you Romans get, too, and if it is a saint you have he's not bothering what church ye belong to."

"Saints," said Father Ifor, again hastily, "come to all men, as Our Lord did. They have no favorites, in the main. And how is my cousin, Father Andrew?"

"A new man!" exclaimed Mr. James. "There's old Granny Burke as does for him, and in he took her orphan grandchild too." His eyes sparkled like hot blue fire. "And tell me this," he said, glaring at both the Methodist and the surly neighbor, "'ow was that kid cured? Bent she was, like an old woman, with twisted legs and shoulders, from her birth when her mother died, and may God rest her soul. Crawled about the street she did, or sat on the high kerb, like a knot, with her little twisted face with the pain in it. And then one morning," and Mr. James' voice dropped reverently, and the others crossed themselves, "she was playing on the street with roses in her face, and nary a twist to her legs and arms, and sings like an angel! And she tells the tale, and we believe it, that one night she saw a man all dressed in light, and he touched her and blessed her, and when she woke up——" Emotion choked him, and a girl sobbed.

"Er," said Father Ifor, stammering, "it was my cousin she saw in the dream?"

Mr. James cleared his throat. "How can a wee one mark the face of a saint in a dream? It was a man in light, and the little lass tells the tale that each day Father Andrew especially blessed her and prayed for her, for it is the good mind she has, and it was not twisted like her body, and she is in school now." He sighed, deeply. "We has gone, the lot of us, to Father Andrew, and kneeled for his blessing, which he gives, but he will not admit he is a saint. In fact, he says he is not, and asks only for prayers and the rest."

"There was a gouging last summer, by one of the men of Gwen-wynnlynn," said the surly stranger, "and it was foul, so your saint has not done you much good, seems."

"Saints," said Father Ifor, loudly, "do not keep themselves to the worthy. It was Our Lord, Himself, who said He came to save sinners, and not the good, who are already saved." He could not restrain a grin, in spite of his confusion. "Could it be that the men of Gwen-wynnlynn were a pack of sinners, more than in any other hamlet?"

The surly stranger guffawed and slapped his patched knee. "That they are. Minds me——"

"I cannot speak for the Romans," said the Methodist, stiffly, "but we observe our duties faithfully, and you'll not find us on the street or in the field, of a Sunday, tossing the ball and fighting and wrestling, and breaking the Sabbath. And drinking," he added, deeply.

"The Sabbath," said Father Ifor, who was, after all, a combative Welshman, "was created for man, and not the reverse. I hope," he said to Mr. James, "that there has been an increase of piety among the communicants, and that daily Mass is not attended solely by the sacristan and the altar boys?"

"It is full to the doors, the church!" shouted Mr. James. "Crowded against the walls! And many's the Baptist and the Methodist there, too, trying to hide his face!" He suddenly smiled. "Ah, you should

see the church, Father! The wonderful new statues. The Blessed
Mother's plaster was faded and breaking, and now there's a new
statue of her, and others, and it's the pride of the village. And the
altar cloths! Irish linen and finest lace. And the vessels! Silver, gold-
plated. And the Monstrance! And the candlesticks, the finest, of solid
silver, and the windows, stained glass, not white glass. Like the
Methodists and Baptists," he added, crushingly.

"We're not for statues and other worldly things," said the Methodist, who appeared a little dejected. Father Ifor said to him, gently,
"One can have beauty in the heart, too, my son." The Methodist
smiled at him with a timidity rare for a Welshman, and a profound
gratitude. "Our Lord," went on Father Ifor, "spoke on the bare hills
and in the fields and in the dusty market place. It is what is in a
man's heart."

Mr. James frowned, and Father Ifor noted this and said, severely,
"It seems that if you—er—have a saint among you, Harlock James, it
has not done you much good in the way of Christian charity. And
tolerance for one's fellow-man, and his ways."

Mr. James' face swelled with the quick fury of the Welshman and
his fists knotted. Father Ifor stared him down, and the others
watched keenly. Mr. James subsided. "I'd not looked for the cousin
of a saint to say that," he said, with heaviness.

"I think," said Father Ifor, "that my cousin has not indicated that
he is a saint, to you or to me. In fact, his letter to me was troubled."

"All saints are troubled when their sainthood is seen," said Mr.
James, in a voice of knowing superiority.

"Then, they should be imitated, and there should be no bragging
of bank accounts," said Father Ifor. "And it should be observed that
what Catholics now have in Gwenwynnlynn the Protestants have
been given, too."

"Only to bring them to the light," said Mr. James, stubbornly.

Father Ifor reflected for some moments. "There can be a reasonable explanation. The owners of the mines are becoming kinder."

"Not in other cots," said Mr. James, proudly. "The same owners,
too."

"My cousin could have been very persuasive."

"That is because he is a saint, Father."

Father Ifor remained silent. Mr. James had begun to annoy him. Of course, it could be explained, all of it, by Father Andrew, and like all Welshmen he was eloquent. But, there was that child—— How had she been restored in an instant?

As if Mr. James had read his thoughts, he said, "There have been other miracles. Mistress Brandiff's cows, and she a widow, were dying, and we knew not why. And then they were healthy, and dropped calves. And there was old Benjamin, blind from a lad. He opened his eyelids one morning." Mr. James paused. "And he saw. And the lapsed ones, they came to Father Andrew and confessed, all of a sudden, and are saints, themselves."

A young woman spoke quickly. "I had nary a child, and I married for ten years, and always losing them in the third month." She blushed and peeped at Father Ifor, for, after all, he was a man and females did not speak of such things to men, not even priests. "And now," she continued, with new resolution, "I have one prettiest."

"And I," said a youngish, middle-aged woman, "I had the cancer." She touched her bosom with a shy, brief touch. "There was no hope, the doctor said. But one morning I awakened, and it was gone!" She paused. "It was the biggest, nastiest lump."

"The Church," said Father Ifor, "does not rely upon miracles to declare a man or woman a saint. It is in the practice of heroic virtues. Many's the miracle which was not a miracle at all. It occurred during nature's own healing processes."

An elderly man suddenly stood up in the swaying carriage and came to Father Ifor. He ceremoniously took off his boot, and then his wool stocking, and the others watched, nodding their heads. He extended a broad pink foot with perfect toes towards Father Ifor. "Look ye on yonder, Father," he said. "I have witnesses. A fire burned more than half my foot away, in the mines. For twenty years I hobbled, and if it had not been for my neighbors, poor as me, my goodwife and I'd have starved, though little they had. And then, one morning, after Mass, I felt a new fire in my foot, and I sat on the kerb and took off my boot and stockings," and he looked about at the others, who nodded again, "there was my foot, as it was as a lad! As it is,

now. That will be your nature's 'own healing processes,' between
one moment and the other, Father? The giving back to me of half
my foot, and three toes?"

"Is it true?" pleaded Father Ifor of the others, and they shouted,
"Aye, it is true!"

"And my husband, who was dying," said a woman, courageously,
"with the priest at his side, with the Last Rites, he opened his eyes,
and sat up and got from his bed. And he with the consumption, and
it is all gone. He is in our fields now, with the barley."

"It is not unknown," said Father Ifor, with some lameness, "that
with the administering of the Last Rites, a person regains——"

The woman shook her head vigorously. "I do not deny, Father,"
she said. "But my husband had been dying for a year, coughing the
blood and heart out of him, and as a skeleton, and then without his
senses, and from one moment to another he was cured."

"Perhaps," said the Methodist, laughing a little, "a curse was removed from the village when Sir Oswold Morgan died."

"Aye, that was a bad man!" said Mr. James. "A man of Satan, himself. A wicked, blasphemous, cruel man. I can believe in a curse,
myself, for the man was a curse."

"A wicked man," chorused the others. "A man without heart or
goodness."

"A baronet lived in your hamlet?" asked Father Ifor, incredulously.

"Aye, that he did. He was born there, and went away, as a bad-
faced, ugly lad, with a curse on his lips for all that his father and
mother were, and a curse on the cotswold. Never was a lad, or man,
hated so much." Mr. James' own face became ugly. "I remember him
well. Full of mischief and the meanness. He came back to gloat on
us, he with his new fine house, and his sneers for Father Andrew,
and his laughing at Father Andrew, and he a baptized Catholic,
himself, though never in the church at Mass."

"How did he become a baronet, with a lot of money?" asked Father Ifor.

"Only God knows," said Mr. James. "It may be he was a thief, or
worse. But a man is drawn back to his home when he is dying, or he

wants to spit on them as is better than he in their souls, and so he came."

"He—disliked—Father Andrew?" said Father Ifor.

"Hated him. Laughed at him on the streets. Shamed him. And where he walked evil came."

"Such as?" said Father Ifor.

But the train had chugged to a stop and they were in Gwenwynn-lynn. Absently, Father Ifor glanced through the window, then was immediately astonished. The black wooden platform was gone, had been replaced by handsomely colored flags in a random pattern. The bleak and sooty banks he had remembered were now a tumble of blowsy summer roses and beds of hardy pansies and clumps of sea-pines. "Aye, and it's handsome now, is it not?" said Mr. James, bursting with pride. "It was the owners!"

"Strange that they did nothing for the other hamlets," said Father Ifor. He looked for his small luggage, but Mr. James had lifted it and was shouldering towards the door. "No cousin of our saint carries his own," he said, marching sturdily. "Aye, but wait, Father, until you see Glenwynnlynn, itself!"

A small neat carriage with a small neat horse and a small neat coachman was waiting. The coachman took Father Ifor's bag, and removed his hat and smiled radiantly. "The Father could not come, Father Ifor," he said. "He's been a little unwell. He's well on to eighty, you know."

"Father Andrew drives about in this?" asked Father Ifor when the horse trotted off and they were rolling over the polished dark stones of the street.

"Aye, but not always. He prefers his bicycle, he says," replied the coachman in the rich voice one uses in speaking of another dearly loved. "His exercise, as he says."

Father Ifor ruminated as they rolled through one clean and winding little street after another, with the small cottages snug under sound slate roofs, crowding together, and the prosperous little shops. But more than all else, the sturdily dressed women and the children with the good boots! An immense fortune had changed Gwenwynn-lynn from dreadful poverty and misery to all this. It was not possible that "the owners" had done this! No, never. Father Ifor knew the owners well. He had been a pit boy, himself.

Then he was vaguely resentful. The people here accepted all that had been done for them so mysteriously with a sort of pride, as if they had been worthier than others. It was their pride that he resented, for he knew they were no different from the inhabitants of the wretched hamlets through which the train had snorted and growled. Their pompous pride! They had their "saint" and their prosperity—they felt they deserved it! That was the intolerable thing.

"How is Father?" he asked the coachman.

"Not so well, Father, and I am sad that it's me to give you the news. I had an old Dada of my own, and when he was old like this, and tired, it was the same look he had, as if thinking thoughts not of this world. Far off, if your Reverence knows what I mean."

There was a great mystery here. Father Ifor had not seen his cousin for twelve years, and they had only intermittently corresponded, though the love between them had always been deep. If Father Andrew was troubled, and he usually the most serene of men, then he was not responding as saints respond, nor would he have so urgently asked his much younger cousin to visit him for "advice." Of course, there had been St. Vincent de Paul, and his working with the poor, and his prying the gentlemen of his own class and nobility loose of their cash in the name of Christian mercy and charity, and for the love of God. However, Father Ifor had always been poor; he was not gentry, not to speak of nobility. And there had never been any rich man in Gwenwynnlynn except for that one—and what was his name? The owners? "Pah," said Father Ifor.

It was known, of course, that saints in the past had frequently performed the miracle of increasing food in times of famine, and had done other equally miraculous things, but Father Ifor doubted that any modern saint could produce the cash to change the hamlet like this. After all, the Bank of England notes could not be counterfeited. Not even by a saint, thought Father Ifor, smiling faintly. He considered his cousin. Father Andrew had several of the heroic virtues, as did all clergymen of all the religions; they had to have them and practice them diligently if they were to endure their own people and work to save their souls. No man became a clergyman as a way of making a living, such as working in the coal mines or in the factories. Father Ifor knew Protestant clergymen and one or two rabbis. They often commiserated together, in an oblique way, knowing that God had bestowed His peculiar Grace upon them, but wondering what obtuseness lived eternally in the deceitful hearts of men, and what hardness of heart. In spite of the prophets; in spite of the Sacrifice on Calvary.

So Father Andrew had a number of the heroic virtues. Was it possible that those virtues had expanded to the dimensions of true saintliness? It was possible. But still—— Father Ifor looked at the wall of lavender mountain, its changing face touched by the red, setting sun. The carriage passed a tiny blue lake, which reflected part of the mountain in a shade of purple and turned the edge of the sun to scarlet fire. Then they were trotting to the street on which Father Andrew's church stood, and the rectory.

The church had been wonderfully restored. Tall and narrow, its slates seemingly washed with crimson water under the dying sun, its cross flaming, it had a look of modest stateliness it had never possessed before. The rectory, too, had been restored. The front garden was filled with flowers. Then Father Ifor saw a knot of respectful men and women loitering near the garden gate. But the shutters facing the street were firmly closed.

The coachman brought up the carriage with a flourish, leapt down lithely, ignoring his fellow villagers, and with a large gesture of importance assisted Father Ifor from the carriage, which irritated the priest a little, for he was in the prime of his life and not decrepit. The men on the street removed their wool caps; the women and girls curtseyed humbly. They gazed at him with marvelous, but annoying, solemnness of face. He tried to smile at them, but it was a little difficult under the circumstances, so he opened the gate and stepped onto the path. Immediately the small throng surged after him. "Wait, there, now!" exclaimed the coachman. "You are not to vex Father. Begone with you all."

"We want only a glimpse of Father Andrew, Tom," said a woman, timidly.

"Glimpse him at Mass tomorrow," said the coachman, closing the gate. Hear, hear, thought Father Andrew, approvingly. He put his hand on the latch of the rectory door, and it opened to let him into the tiny parlor. A snug fire burned on the hearth; there were two comfortable chairs he had not remembered. And a Brussels rug! A ginger cat rose, purring. The coachman deposited the priest's luggage behind the door of the bedroom he had always used, and then said, "You'll do with a wash, Father?"

"Yes. But where is Father Andrew?"

"Here, Ifor," said an old and fragile voice. Father Andrew was huddled against the wall, in the dusk, near the little window that looked out on the back garden. In dismay, Father Ifor thought: He is hiding! But why?

Then Father Andrew came towards him, walking slowly and wearily, and the younger priest saw his face, thin, beaked, exceedingly troubled and sad. But when he smiled the old look of pale exaltation appeared again about his dimmed blue eyes, and he embraced his cousin and said, "Thank God that you could come, Ifor!"

"There, now," said Father Ifor, with a cheer he did not feel. He added, "All will be well."

"I hope so," sighed the old man. He paused, held his cousin off, and said, "They have been feeding you better, I see." His frail hands visibly trembled.

"I eat regularly now," said Father Ifor. But his cousin was looking at the coachman. "Thank you, Tom," he said. "That will be all."

The coachman looked disappointed. He had been waiting for some mysterious ejaculation, some "sign," which he could tell of in the pub tonight. But both priests stood in silence, so he bent his head for Father Andrew's blessing, and he went off, reverently closing the door behind him.

Then Father Andrew said, "Damn it." He spoke with absolute feeling and his old passion.

Father Ifor threw back his Welshman's lion head and roared with laughter and relief. Father Andrew listened to that laughter, and relaxed. He began to chuckle under his breath. He pushed his cousin on the arm. "Off with you, for a wash," he said. "And then we'll

have our supper, and our talk. And God knows," he said, with renewed feeling, "I need it!"

"I've heard much of the story," said Father Ifor. "The villagers, on
the train, so that will spare part of your strength. Are you really a
saint?" he asked, with some mischief.

Father Andrew groaned, and put a hand to his white head, and
laughing again, Father Ifor went into the miniature bedroom where
he had known so many cold mornings and bitter, icy nights. Then
he stared at the dark polished floor, the new poster bed, the large
crucifix on the wall, the comfortable leather chair. He took off his
cassock, then remembered something. His cousin's cassock had been
very sleek, if rumpled, and of the best quality of cloth. His own, in
comparison, was sackcloth. Wondering again, he went to the commode, poured water from the handsome pitcher into the basin,
washed himself vigorously, and dried himself on an excellent linen
towel. He went back into the parlor, where Father Andrew was
gloomily staring at the fire, the ginger cat on his knee. His thin,
veined hand was stroking the animal absently. "It's Mrs. Burke's cat,"
he said, as if in apology, "but the beast has taken a fancy to me. Sit
down, Ifor." He paused. "There'll be brandy in a bottle at the table
near you, and two glasses."

A lamp had been lighted on the mantelpiece, but the shutters had
been firmly closed over the little leaded window. There was a rustling
outside, and Father Andrew's nose twitched irritably. "Have they
no homes or duties?" he asked.

The brandy bottle had been hardly used. The glasses were smooth
and pleasant to the touch. The two priests sipped in appreciative silence. The fire crackled; the cat purred. "I've sent Mrs. Burke off
for the evening," said Father Andrew, "so we could talk in peace.
But there is her grandchild——"

"I heard about it. On the train. If a Welshman can do nothing
else he can talk volubly, and descriptively. Was it really a——"

A dim color had come into Father Andrew's fallen cheeks. He
said, with youthful strength and emphasis, "A miracle? Yes, it was
that. A miracle. As were the rest."

Father Ifor was a little depressed. He had hoped that his cousin could give him a rational explanation for all that he had heard. But the mystery was deepening.

"Then," said Father Ifor, hesitatingly, "there is—er—a saint about?"

"A saint," said Father Andrew. "There's no doubt of it. But blind I was, until it was almost too late. Sir Oswold Morgan."

Father Ifor was stunned. "Wicked. A man of Satan. Blasphemous. Cruel."

"There was the finger of God," said Father Andrew, sighing. "I never saw it, until almost too late. And now the Bishop wants a complete report, and then he will send one of his sharp young priests who will make up his mind if it should be referred to Rome." He paused. "It will be! That I know! The finger of God. And then, we'll have our local saint, and God knows that Wales needs one these days. There is no question that Oswold Morgan will eventually be canonized."

"I heard of him, on the train, and the things I heard——" said Father Ifor.

"That is the trouble," said Father Andrew. He looked at his cousin, and the blue of his youth was shining in his eyes. "Has not the Church always taught that saints are not recognized as such, or acknowledged, by blind men? It is so, now. None was blinder than myself, may God forgive me."

"I heard he hated you, Andrew."

Father Andrew shook his head with sadness. "He hated no one, not even those who hated him. He hated only injustice and poverty and the exploitation of man by man, and man's hardness of heart, and his lack of charity. He hated all sin. For the sinner he had only mercy and kindness. As you have seen, and heard."

He pushed himself wearily to his feet. "Mrs. Burke has laid out our supper. We need only to brew the tea." He studied his cousin. "It is a fine meal. We'll do justice to it, before I tell you more."

They went into the little kitchen, which was warm with a fire, and a kettle steamed on the hob, and the table had been laid with a white linen cloth on which stood platters of ham and beef and tongue and herring, and there were hot breads covered with a prim cloth, and mustard in a little silver pot, and cold brussels sprouts with an appetizing sauce, and sundry other things. Father Ifor was immediately ravenous, and made a mental note that at Confession he should tell that during Grace his mouth watered for the smell of the good food. As a pre-Confession penance he made a ceremony of seating his old cousin, and insisted that he help himself, first. Father Andrew gave him an impish smile, understanding, and turned up the wick of the lamp on the table so that the food could be seen in all its seductive glory, and not a rosy slice of ham ignored nor a cut of meat slighted in dimness. "Eat up," said Father Andrew. "It is all for you, for I take little, to Mrs. Burke's scolding and regret."

Father Ifor ate, putting aside the incredible story of an "evil" man's saintliness. His knife and fork moved rapidly, and sometimes rattled like castanets. Father Andrew, barely touching an edge of ham, and barely breaking off a small piece of bread, was heartened and happy. Ifor had common sense, yet in many ways he was a mystic. It was a comfort to have him in the house, a salve to the soul, for though one knew that God and all His saints and angels, and particularly His Blessed Mother, always heard a prayer and the cries of a man's heart, it did the soul good to have the presence of a human being who spoke aloud in human tones, and in whom one could confide. Ifor was not young, but Father Andrew thought of him as a youth and remembered the day when the lad was only twelve and had come to him and had said, "I will be a priest. Like you. If it be the will of God." A tall lad of twelve, a pit boy, already blackened with coal, already blistered, and three years out of school. Out of the people, themselves, came their strength. Out of their humility and lowliness had come their Saviour. World without end.

They drank their hot, black, sweet tea, slowly and with pleasure. "We will leave all for Mrs. Burke to wash up. To do anything else, though I did it for years until she came to me, she would consider sacrilege, or, more, a reflection on her housekeeping." Father Andrew's sunken cheeks were quite flushed, and he seemed happier.

They returned to the parlor, after giving the cat his share of food, and a saucer of rich yellow cream. Father Andrew produced a bottle of fine port. "The 'saint' seems to have done well by you, too," said Father Ifor, delighted.

"I wanted nothing," said Father Andrew, with sudden gravity. "But it was in his blessed will. For me. Half of his fortune went to help the hamlet, in perpetuity, and the other half to the Church. To refuse what he had given me would have hurt him, and it was little enough I could do for him, considering my blindness and stupidity."

Father Andrew sipped the port. "You will not remember the Morgans, for Sir Oswold was older than you, Ifor, and he had long left Gwenwynnlynn before you were britched. He was the only child of his parents, and his father was a miner, and he was killed in one of Wales' most disastrous mine explosions. Oswold was then but eleven years old, and his mother, to support herself and the lad, went into the mines, herself, for those were the days when women and children worked in the mines, too, and rarely a voice was raised in horror. She would not let Oswold work there, for she wanted him to study, for he would be a priest, he said. I did not know that until——

"What thoughts went through the mind of that lad when his mother came dragging home from the mines, black of face, wounded in the hands, filthy in her poor clothing? He would not have it, no! He would sacrifice what he dearly desired, and go into the mines, and she should stay at home. No, said his devoted mother. Then there was another explosion, and she was killed, and he was alone, a big strapping lad then twelve.

"From his toddling days he had been serious and silent and not interested in those things which other lads love. Though he could out-race and out-throw and out-wrestle any lad his age, and those much older, he had other preferences, and those were books, and, above all, God, and justice and mercy and kindness. He looked about him and saw the misery and desperation of the hamlet, the hunger, the women and children in the mines, the broken men, the soot and slag and ugliness which greed had created. He saw the leaking roofs of the cots, the ignorance, the animal life forced upon his people when they should be recognized as the children of God, and treated honestly and fairly, and not as beasts by the owners in England. Was not a Welshman a man, too, and did he not want a

little song and joy in his life and a few shillings in his pockets, and
a little meat on his gritty table?

"These were the thoughts that set him apart from the other lads,
and so made his face gloomy and somber, and so they called him
ugly-faced and unnatural. He came to the priest before me, who was
not a Welshman, and he laid his just anger before him, and the
priest rebuked him for that anger and spoke of humility and sub-
missiveness and eternity. And Oswold said to him, with new, strange
anger: 'And how is it possible for a man to think like a man when he
is forced to live like an animal, without that animal's security of a
warm shelter the night and food he has earned?' To live as the
miners were living was not living at all, said Oswold. It was a betrayal
of God to ask that His children starve peaceably and not have some
of the fruits of their hard labor. So Oswold left the rectory in his
stern wrath, and the old housekeeper gossiped, and it was said that
Oswold had insulted the priest and turned from his Faith. So, now
he was an apostate, as well as a stranger, and the people hated him,
though the priest reproached them for their lack of charity. The
young Oswold refused Confirmation. If God were against him, too,
he said in his heart, and had no more love for His children than
did their oppressors, then he wanted nothing to do with God. So
thinks the severe and intolerant young mind, especially when it is
stricken sick with woe and grief and pity and righteous anger.

"Oswold went into the mines with a silent, fierce resolution. But
not a woman or child or man there spoke to him, not even the Protestants, who might be expected to side with him against the priest.
He was an outlaw. He bore all insults in the mines with fortitude
and secret charity, and those are heroic virtues. He received the blows
from ignorant and taunting men and did not return them. He knew
the misery which inspired it all, for man will turn upon man in his
despair, and hate the nearest human being because of the horror of
his life. In understanding, Oswold was truly a saint.

"When the priest, dimly beginning to understand, came to a
newly opened mine to pray for the safety of the workers, Oswold
stood apart with a cold proud face, his lip curling, and this further
infuriated the people. The priest tried to talk with him, and he would

not. The priest wrote him letters, and he never came. I have seen the letters, which Oswold kept. His anger was not against the priest, but against God. And, as he worked, he thought more and more. He slept in a mere ruined shelter. What he could spare he would stealthily slip into the hands of children, a copper or two. If a Christmas goose mysteriously appeared at the door of the priest, or that of a starving widow with children, no one dreamed that Oswold had gone hungry for a long time to provide it, he with the 'ugly, dark face,' and the 'blasphemy,' and his apartness. Nor should I have known of it if I had not seen a letter from the priest, in which that regretful old man expressed his suspicions, and begged the youth to come to him. But Oswold would not, for he was a stubborn young Welshman and he could not forgive God for all this desolation and death and ruin and suffering.

"Then when he was about fifteen, Oswold disappeared. But he wrote to the priest in the fine and careful hand in which he had schooled himself, and it was the letter of a man not a youth. I found it in one of the old priest's books, lying forgotten and moldering in yonder case. And it said, 'I shall not return until I can deliver my people from the cruelty of those who oppress them and from the indifference of God. I beg of you that you forgive my rash words, but not the words themselves, and only the intemperance of them. If it is possible for you, Father, pray for me, though I shall not pray for myself! I am alone, as all men are alone.'

"When I read that letter," said Father Andrew, "I knew. But that was three years ago and too much time had passed, and it was almost too late.

"It would take many days, Ifor, to tell you what Oswold did when he left Gwenwynnlynn, in the darkness of the night, with four shillings in his pocket, and all that he had in the world on his emaciated body. In his youth coal was mined painfully with hand and pick and shovel. Labor was cheap. Who cared to invent any machine that would lighten that labor? Who cared about the men, women and children who periodically died in the mines, or spent short lives gasping out, in consumption, the dust they had inhaled, after years in the mines? They did not complain; therefore, they had nothing to

complain about! The miners in Newcastle, England, had better hours
and better wages, for Englishmen so near to London will often
shout. But London, to the Welsh, was on another world. It was to
the Newcastle mines that Oswold went, and he studied, and read,
and watched, and thought, and it came to him, suddenly and brilliantly, what a machine could do to save the flesh and blood of
man.

"He invented that machine. The owners would have none of it,
none of it. But there were miners' unions gathering strength in England, and so Oswold went to them, and they demanded the machinery. Oh, there were riots and strikes and threats and the police, but
the unions were almost as stubborn as Welshmen. By this time, in
England, no women or little children were permitted to work in the
mines, and men were beginning to understand that they had a right
to live as well as the gentry and the nobility, as well as the Anglican
clergy, as well as the gentlemen farmers and the owners of blooded
horses. The next step, for Oswold, was to appeal to the despised
bourgeoisie of England, the merchants and large shopkeepers and
the factory owners, for the industrial revolution was gaining great
power in England now. 'It is to that mighty middle class of England
that all men of good will should bow in honor,' Oswold told me three
years ago. For they had no traditions of arrogance and gentility
and family and titles, and they were not intellectuals who talk and
do not act. They had their own grudges against the upper classes
which despised them, and they were near enough to the workers—
for nearly all had been poor in the beginning, and oppressed—to
feel sympathy and outrage and fellowship. So grudges and charity,
for once, joined hands in behalf of the suffering, and there are times,
Ifor, when I wonder if grudges are all evil. One must remember
the American Revolution——

"Oswold, with his drawings and his eloquence, soon interested the
manufacturers, who had the satisfaction of the support of the unions
in addition. They faced a sudden and formidable situation, for contrary to what the average man believes, the 'idle' and 'luxurious' are
keenly aware of anything which will threaten a single penny they
own. They may be adulterers and even much worse, and may lie in

the suns to which they eternally flee when cold is on the land, and they may seem indifferent to the events of the world, but let the slightest suggestion arise which concerns their investments and they are resolute men of ruthless purpose. Nations may fall; despots may rise; thousands be massacred, and they pursue serene ways of pleasure—provided that these catastrophes do not affect their purses.

"And so it was that the mine-owners gave it to the workers that machinery would replace them and throw them out of work and into destitution.

"But they did not know Oswold. He had his facts at hand. He recalled to those newspapers who would publish what he said—and let no one boast of a free press, Ifor!—that the same controversy had arisen at the time of the invention of the sewing machine, and the locomotive, and the steam engine. 'Rather than taking work from men, they produced work for men, on a tremendous scale,' he said. 'They also increased the comfort of man and enlarged his mind and freed him from the grossest labor.' The newspapers not agreeable to Oswold attacked him as the enemy of the workingman, and it is not the least odd that these newspapers were the ones whose owners despised the workingman and all he represented. Such sudden virtue became incongruous even to the most unthinking. The manufacturers made Oswold's machines, and paid him the magnificent royalties he demanded.

"He had other inventions, too, which would insure more safety in the mines. They were expensive; now even the newspapers which had supported him paused. So Oswold and the unions fought alone, and they won. It will never be truly safe to work in a mine, but the greatest dangers could be eliminated, and is not a man worthy of his life?

"Oswold became a very rich man, and he was knighted, as Her Majesty declared it, for services to his countrymen. He did not marry, for he was a celibate at heart. And now he was sixty-two years old, and all his struggles had spent him. He remembered Gwenwynnlynn and he returned here to die, in the sight of remembered mountains, in the sight of the graveyard where his parents and grandparents and their ancestors before them had been buried. And in sight of the church whose old priest, now dead, had not understood in the beginning. He saw Gwenwynnlynn as it was, and he determined to change it, and he did, for in the heart of every saint there is the deepest love for God and His children. You see, my dear Ifor, he had forced the sale of the coal mines of Gwenwynnlynn to himself. But no one knew it. Not even I, until three years ago, when Oswold was already dying."

The hard cold rain made the fire splutter on the hearth, and Father Andrew threw more coal upon it and used the poker to advantage. He looked at "young" Ifor, who was thoughtfully staring into his glass of port.

"Slowly," said Father Andrew, "Oswold tried to buy the other mines, but he could not, for however rich a man is he cannot do everything alone, and he had sworn his friends to silence about what he had already done. Those friends were the poor leaders of the unions, struggling everywhere, and they loved him devotedly and gave him their word. He had no other friends. Saints rarely have friends; they are usually hated and derided, for they love, and love is always rejected by hard-hearted men. One only has to consider Our Lord—and the state of the world, which does not improve measurably. Who is interested in a newspaper story of a man's charity and sacrifice? But let a member of the Royal Family commit the smallest indiscretion, or the heads of the Continent's royal families, or let a new style be introduced, or a murder of impressive proportions be committed, or an actress be drawn into a grand affair by a 'notable personage,' and the people seethe with silly excitement and talk of nothing else in their pubs and on the street. Oswold had no fear that what he had done would be mentioned to any extent in the newspapers. He had murdered no one, he had taken no notorious mistress, he had scandalized no one, he had not engaged in breeding the horses which could be expected to win at the Derby, he had done nothing shameful, nothing evil. Therefore, why should space be given him anywhere in the newspapers?"

"And he came back to Gwenwynnlynn," said Ifor, refilling their glasses. "He was spent; he was tired. But he had been hated here."

"He wished to make what he called 'a modern hamlet,' so that others could see and follow. They will, eventually. They may not do it today, nor tomorrow. But they will do it. What has been done for Gwenwynnlynn will be known; it will take a little time, but it will be known. Oswold had his offices in London. He left proof that it was possible not only to maintain former income by installing better conditions, but to increase it! And no rich man can forever remain aloof from such possibilities."

"But no one knew here, Andrew? Why is that?"

The old priest sighed. "Saints do not advertise themselves; good men do not seek out a name in the world. I did not know.

"Oswold built a house for himself in Gwenwynnlynn, he who had no wife and no children. He told me, but so much later, that he had never had a house before, and he wanted one now. It is the instinct of man, his instinct for shelter when he is sick and old, or when he is young and has a family of children. But—he had not forgiven God."

"And you consider him a saint?"

Father Andrew smiled. "Once, when I was a child, I read a story of a man who wept for His people, and mourned for them. He is Our Lord. And then I read another story of a man who also wept for his people and their sufferings, and upbraided God for them, and he helped his people, though they did not know it. And when he died and was confronted by the Judge, the Judge asked, 'Who is there who will defend this man?' And a multitude arose and cried out, 'He delivered us from pain, out of his love and mercy, and he led us into peace, though our eyes were blind in those days.' And the Judge said, 'You have done good, My blessed servant, for when you sheltered the least of these and fed them and clothed them, you did it unto Me.'"

A howling summer gale thrummed in the chimney. The ginger cat jumped into Ifor's lap, and he stroked it absently. He remembered again the hatred and contempt of the cotswold for Oswold Morgan, that bitter and loving man, and he felt humble.

"The men of Gwenwynnlynn did not know him, as I did not know him," said Father Andrew. "Their lads threw stones at his windows and broke them. For, he had the hard cold face on him, and he would not speak, and wandered over his acres alone. He read and he studied. And he did not pray. He remembered his mother and his father.

"I'd not have known at all, even in the beginning, when he was here, if I had not gone on my rounds, hoping that we could build a school for our children. The Sisters were here, but there was no school. I went to Oswold's grand house, and he opened the door for me, himself. I took up my courage, and asked him for money, and he said, 'I give no money to the Church.' I said to him, 'God has not left you. You have left Him,' and he uttered a jeering curse and shut the door in my face.

"But a week later the Sisters received a fine piece of land near the little convent they have, and it was written to them from London that an anonymous donor had given them the land. More, they need have no worries for the school. It would be built for them at once. And so it was, a school to make the hamlet gasp in pride and joy. That was but the beginning. But you have heard that from the men of Gwenwynnlynn, on the train. Tomorrow, I will take you into the church, before Mass, and you must assist me, and I will show you what Oswold Morgan did for it."

"And how did you finally know?" asked Ifor, with passionate interest.

"God reveals things suddenly, so all may know at once, or in His mysterious ways He reveals them but to a few, and slowly, so that their stupid blind minds, such as my own, will learn. For man is stubborn in his stupidity, and prefers his prejudices to the truth.

"My first suspicion came about one Sunday afternoon, warm and sunny and balmy for Wales, after my dinner. I went on foot, for I had not even a bicycle then, to visit the sick and old and dying. And on one street I saw Oswold's fine carriage, with its two black horses, and he was in it, his hands on his cane. He was watching some children playing, the children he had rescued from starvation and disease and premature work. He did not speak; he did not smile. He only looked, and I paused, and it was as if someone had touched my cassock and said, 'See what you must see.'

"The children played, and the coachman sat on his high seat, and

Oswold sat on his cushions, his hair shining in the sun from under his fine silk hat. Then bit by bit the children came nearer the carriage, and they began to glance at the unsmiling man who sat there, and they came closer, without speaking. Then they were not playing any longer. They leaned against the carriage and they stared solemnly up at that withdrawn and bitter face, and he looked back at them, and it was as if an exchange was made, for suddenly a very little girl took off the red ribbon on her plait and reached out and put it in Oswold's hand. He smoothed it, nodded, and then drove off. The children played again, and I stood and thought. A little thing, but momentous. The children had seen his love for them, though their wiser elders had never seen anything. He had drawn them with that love, as a fire draws a cold man.

"And on that very night I went to the home of a miner who was dying of the consumption, as was told you by his wife on the train. He was unconscious. All were kneeling about him. We had prayed the Litany for the Dying. I was saying, as the man was gasping his last breath, 'I commend you, dear brother, to Almighty God, and I entrust you to Him Who created you, so that by your death——' When suddenly the dying man blinked his eyes, color surged into his cheeks, and he sat up and looked about him and shouted—indeed, he who was dying shouted—'What is this?' And he looked at his weeping wife and children and his friends and at me, and was astounded.

"You can imagine the rejoicing when he threw aside his blanket, laughed and demanded food at once! But I had heard lonely footsteps in the dark on the street and I rushed to the door, old as I am, and stared up the road. There was a bright thread of moon in the sky—and I saw Oswold Morgan walking slowly, tapping his cane on the cobbles, his head bent. I went after him, and though I am so old I ran like a young man, and I took his arm. He frowned at me in his dark way, and I said, 'He who was dying is well——' And he pulled his arm from my hand and said, 'Is it mad you are, old Father?' and went on his way."

Father Andrew shook his head. "He did not know, certainly. But later, much later, he told me that he always walked like that, late at night, arguing with God why He permitted suffering and sadness and the pain of the innocent. He did not know, either, that he was blind. He did not know he was praying! He did not know he was asking mercy for those in the shuttered houses he passed, and that his whole soul was prostrated in his desperate prayer, and with faith. For a man who argues with God, and cries for mercy for others, is a man who believes, let him say what he will. He is love, and God never is silent before the cry of selfless love, but always does He answer it, Ifor, in one way or another."

The two priests filled their pipes with tobacco; the ginger cat purred. The little clock on the mantelpiece struck nine sweet notes. The wind beat in the chimney like a restless heart, and the rain smacked at the windows, even through the shutters.

"And so it happened," said Father Andrew, after his pipe was drawing well and he had removed his slippers so the soles of his old feet would warm on the fender, "that each time a miracle occurred Oswold Morgan was passing in the night. I knew this, myself. Four times I saw him with my own eyes, and on other times I made the most prudent inquiries, in the most casual manner. Had anyone, I asked, seen Oswold Morgan that day, and the happy people would stare at me impatiently and say, 'What is that to us? Yes, now you mind me, I saw him passing. It is good he did not know of this miracle you have done, Father, for he would have cursed us instead!'

"And that was when I became frightened at last, for God knows I am no saint, and it was the first I had recalled—though there may have been other occasions—that I was being addressed as one of the blessed. I said to my people, 'I did not do this thing, nor was it done through me. God can perform miracles through His chosen, and He has not chosen me!'

"But all I said, in patience, and then in vexation, and then in warning of sin, went unheeded. I, Andrew Lewis, a lowly priest, an unworthy man, and a sinner, was no saint! But someone unknown was, and though I resisted, I came to know who it was, though he did not know it, himself.

"There are ways of making inquiries discreetly. It took a long time, through the Bishop and his friends in London, to discover who had made a joyous place of this hamlet. But the Bishop was pledged to secrecy, and he asked me to come to see him in Cardiff, and so I went, and he told me. It was Oswold's determination that the hamlet not know their benefactor; if it became generally known, he had warned his solicitors and others, he would withdraw at once, and leave Gwenwynnlynn forever.

"I had my terrible predicament at home. The people knelt for my blessing, which I always gave. But when they address me as a holy saint, then I must protest. You saw them at my gate, to-night——"

"But Oswold Morgan is dead now," said Ifor. "You can tell them."

Father Andrew shook his head. "It is not easy to decide. Let me tell you.

"One afternoon I went to see Oswold Morgan again, determined to look on that strange cold face, and praying that some enlightenment be given me. I found him sick, and close to death, attended by only one woman, old and a widow, who would consent to be near him. For, you see, the people say he is 'of the devil.' I sent the old woman away, then words I had not intended came to my lips, and I said, 'I know you, Oswold Morgan, and I am blind no longer.'

"He looked at me, from his bed, his great poster bed covered with finest blankets, and he asked me what he had asked me before, 'Is it mad you are, old Father?' So uninvited I sat near him, and we looked eye to eye for a long time, and he was the first to turn away, sullenly. I saw how feeble he was, and sick, and close to dying. I said to him, 'Come home, my son, for your Father is waiting. He has been with you always, and you did not know.' "

Father Andrew stroked the hot bowl of his pipe. "Oswold did not speak for a long time; he must have slept a little, in his weakness. Then suddenly his eyes opened, and like a child he said, 'Bless me, Father, for I have sinned.'

"I heard his Confession. I came to him day after day, and he told me all that I have told you. He confessed his good as one would confess his sins, and he would smile at me, briefly and darkly. But still he did not know that his very passing a house of the dying or sick or crippled, and his intercession ceaselessly for them, had cured them.

I did not tell him. God would tell him on the proper occasion.

"Then one afternoon when I was preparing to visit him I had the impulse to take the Host to him, and the holy oils. It came like a command to me, and tears rushed into my eyes. 'Oh, no,' I said in my heart, for the doctor had told me that Oswold was improving, that his great heart was rallying lately. But still I obeyed that silent command, and I went to him on the bicycle I had mysteriously found near the door one morning, and when the people saw me, and saw what was in my hand, they removed their hats, and wondered who was dying.

"It was as I feared. My friend was dying, and he was alone. Dumbly, for he had no breath, he watched me prepare the table near him with a white cloth. Dumbly he stared at the crucifix I placed there, and the lighted candles, and the bottle of holy water, and the dish of other water in which I washed my hands. I wiped them on a towel. We were alone. I said, 'Peace to this house—— You shall sprinkle me with hyssop, O Lord, and I shall be clean; You shall wash me, and I shall be whiter than snow.'" Father Andrew paused. He pulled out a huge handkerchief and blew his nose. "May God spare me," he whispered, "from having to administer again to such a one I know now I most dearly loved and knew, and honored."

"But, it was a privilege," said Ifor. He was still a trifle dubious.

Father Andrew nodded. "But my heart is human, after all. I blessed Oswold; I prayed, as a priest must pray. I anointed him. Alone, I prayed the Litany for the Dying. And then for the first time those dying eyes brightened, and Oswold whispered, 'I asked only one favor of God: that you would know and come to me, today.'

"To administer the Sacrament of Extreme Unction to a saint is a Grace not given to many," said Father Andrew, with some bewilderment. "Why did He give that Grace to me, in this small forgotten place, in that lonely house? But let me continue. I had just said, 'Go forth from this world, O Christian soul,' when Oswold, with a smile of incredible beatitude, murmured like a contented and weary child, and fell asleep. There was no struggle, not one last gasping or groaning. He died in the utmost peace, and in the dying he turned his head expectantly, and smiled again, as if recognizing someone he loved who had come for him.

"I stayed with him for a while, and prayed, and saw his joyous peace in death as he had never known it in life. And then I closed his eyes and folded his hands and left him alone. I—I sent a telegram to the Bishop that night. And the Bishop replied that Oswold Morgan be given Christian burial, and that I would have information shortly.

"There was no one at the funeral but myself and the pallbearers, whom I had pressed into reluctant service, and the sacristan and the Sisters. There was none there whom his intercessions had cured, none who ate because of him, though starving before——"

"But, they did not know," said Ifor, gently.

"True," said Father Andrew. "You see how human I am, that I can mention that? Within a week three important solicitors arrived here from London, bearing documents and Oswold's will. I have told you the contents. But they gave me a letter from him, which he had written for me before he died. He had asked me, as his deepest wish, that I never reveal to the men of Gwenwynnlynn how he had helped them to some happiness and comfort and had saved so many of their lives, and had mended their homes and their streets and their church, and had given them their school, and endless other joys. To the last, as I have said, he did not know that his intercessions had also brought greater miracles to them.

"And so, I have kept his secret from them, and all the other secrets. But I have written the Bishop, and so he has asked me for full reports of the miracles, and the heroic virtues, far beyond the ordinary, which Oswold Morgan practiced. In the meantime, I am in a quandary. My vexation grows daily at being treated as a saint who has done wonders. And I must keep Oswold's last request."

Ifor puffed at his pipe. He had a pragmatic turn of mind. "It is not stated in the will that the people are not to know, or that if they are told of how Morgan benefited them the will will become null and void?"

"Ifor!" exclaimed Father Andrew, a little scandalized. "No. It was not so stated in the will, of course. But his letter to me——"

"Was the request of a great man who did not know he was—

er—a saint," said Ifor. "But, as he is doubtless in heaven, and now
eager to receive prayers and to intercede for miserable sinners, you
must ignore that merely mortal letter. However, it is in the hands
of the Bishop, and finally, of Rome. In the meantime, Andrew, you
can do your share by slowly informing your flock of what Oswold
Morgan has done for them, and will continue to do for them through
his will. It will shock them, no doubt," said Ifor, with some relish.
"But men need shocking regularly, I've discovered. Men do not
easily take to their hearts others whom they have hated, for then
they are shamed and that is intolerable. And it is harder for Welshmen than most."

He took a little more port and looked at his old cousin's downcast
face. "Look at it this way, too. When the Bishop's sharp young priest
comes to Gwenwynnlynn, and the people do not know about Oswold,
the priest will receive the most scandalous reports, and that will
probably end the matter. And what an injustice to your friend, the
saint!"

"Ifor," said Andrew, after a few moments. "What a mind you
have! You are quite right!"

Ifor had considerable mischief in him. He said, "And have there
been any miracles since Oswold died?"

Andrew considered. Finally he said, "I am not absolutely sure of
that. It has been nearly three years——"

"The finger of God," murmured Ifor. "If there have been no miracles, authentic ones, for three years—— Ah, well, let the Bishop
decide." His mischief made his eyes sparkle. "It is possible, after all,
that you are the saint, Andrew!"

The hard summer rain had diminished when Ifor was alone again,
preparing for bed. But a cold blue lightning pierced the shutters
of the window. It was hard, considering what he had heard tonight,
for him to concentrate on his prayers. Then, just as he was about
to fall asleep, his right shoulder irritated him. Again. A very slight
irritation which had appeared some weeks ago. It was hardly an
itch; it was hardly an ache. Had he been sleepy he would not have
noticed it at all. There was the faintest of prickles to it now, which

might be only his imagination. He reached under his nightshirt and touched the spot, and it was as he remembered: the very smallest of rising in his skin. He had not touched it deliberately for some time. It appeared a little larger than before to his finger. The prickle, if it was one, was not in the slight elevation after all. It was nearby. Annoyed, Ifor lighted his lamp again, removed his nightshirt, stood before the mirror over the commode, and peered over his broad shoulder at the spot.

It was considerably larger than he had remembered, an intensely black spot right near his shoulder blade. And just below it, a smaller one, about one-sixteenth of an inch in diameter, whereas the other, to his surprise, had increased to about one-quarter of an inch. Tentatively, he pressed them both. The larger one was sore, only a little sore, but the irritation was not imaginary.

The savage blue lighting quickened through the shutters, then there was a smashing crash immediately afterwards. The room hummed. Ifor murmured a prayer. He put on his nightshirt again. Then he remembered something which gave him an extraordinary sense of relief. A few years ago he had acquired some warts on his hands, and then a crop had appeared behind his right shoulder and another crop on the side of his face. "Eat some mushrooms," said the doctor, sagely, understanding that warts are a mystery and come and go at times by the most ridiculous hocus-pocus. So Ifor had eaten some mushrooms, confident of the doctor's sagacity, and the warts had disappeared except for two small darkish ones near the shoulder blade. He had not thought of the matter for years. Apparently two had remained after all, and had become black. Black. The relief drained away. There was something ominous about the word, some vague connection—— He went to bed and in the midst of the storm he fell asleep.

He had forgotten the whole matter when he awakened at dawn.

During the next few days he lived serenely and contentedly, realizing that he must have been tired before he came to the hamlet, for he felt a pleasant languor before going to bed. The people of the wild and heroic country, the fiercely azure lakes, the stark mountains and rusty outcroppings, the rapid little streams, the soft

and musical voices, all aroused his old memories and day by day
he became more and more a Welshman, even to developing an
irascibility he thought he had overcome. His voice acquired the old
accents. He assisted at Mass; he became a familiar sight to the men,
who pulled their caps, and to the women, who curtseyed, and to
the children, who smiled at him shyly. He was able to relieve Andrew
at Mass some mornings, and though the old man protested, it was
evident that his mortal flesh was very weary. And the church, narrow
and small, was like a gem—because of Oswold Morgan.

He met the doctor, who lived in a small new house near a rill,
and he and Andrew confided the contents of Oswold's letter to Andrew. The doctor, Catholic himself, agreed with Ifor that the request
should now be ignored, for the sake of both Oswold and the villagers.
"God did not intend His saints to be ignored," he said. He told
Ifor of the miraculous cure of Mary, the little granddaughter of
old Mrs. Burke. "An absolute, authentic miracle," he said. "I examined the child myself when I first came here. Not even the best
of surgery could have helped her, nor the best of drugs, even opium,
relieved her periodic bouts of pain. You have seen the little lass
yourself, Father? Well, and then. Is she not a picture of health
and liveliness? There, too, is another matter which is distressing
Father Lewis. He cannot, in all honesty, continue to let Sir Oswold
go unknown, and the villagers will continue to regard him as a saint,
and vex him, to the hurt of their own souls and perhaps his, unless
the truth comes out. I will help you, myself," he added, as he showed
the younger priest his fine surgery. "When my patients come in, I
will say: 'You owe this cure, or this help, to Sir Oswold, who paid
me, and who continues to pay me through his will, and you must
thank him in your prayers!'" The doctor's red Welsh face looked
roguish. "Ah, and I've long wanted to say it, but Sir Oswold asked
me not to, and now I can."

"A fox," said Father Andrew to his cousin, a little later, but fondly.
"His stipend is enormous. He was well known in Cardiff, and is
known well to the Bishop, and that will be a help when the sharp
young priest arrives. How Oswold persuaded him to come here, and,

mind you, I do not deprecate it, though—— I do not know, Ifor. That must have been a miracle in itself."

That Sunday after Holy Eucharist, Father Andrew stood in his pulpit and said simply to his parishioners, "It is a lovely church we have, and there is no more beautiful, for all its smallness, in Cardiff. For this we must thank, in our prayers, he who did this for us, Sir Oswold Morgan, who loved us, we who so little deserved his love."

The doctor had already spread the story to his patients and they had incredulously, and with sullen and human resentment and expressions of disbelief, communicated it to friends and relatives. What! Old Oswold, with the ugly face of him, the blasphemous man, the man who lay buried in their churchyard but who, by the terms of his will, had desired no monument? They had hated him; as human beings, they hugged their hatred to themselves; they would not willingly relinquish it. "The doctor's aye an ass," they said in their pubs. "It's the joke he has with us." Ah, a joke. Eagerly, it was accepted, and with sighs of relief. "He will have a joke," said the doctor's gardener. "I mind me——" He was heard out, happily. And then Father Andrew made his stunning announcement on Sunday, and, as a priest, he would not lie.

Father Andrew, sighing, saw wondering, stupefied and blank faces. These were bad enough. But the indignant faces made his heart burn. Indignant. Because the owners had been proved to be no Christians at all, in their lack of charity, in their hate, in their stupidity! Resentment flushed brows already flushed with wind and sun. Vexation glittered balefully in proud eyes.

"If they dared," said Father Andrew to Ifor, as they ate their dinner, "they would desecrate his grave, some of them. They are that angry. Oswold was one of them; he dared to become rich and so become apart from them. His work, his imagination, his genius: all these were as nothing to them. They preferred to think the vilest things of him in connection with his money. He had been born in this village—therefore, their silly reasoning continues—he cannot have been of importance. But the worst crime he committed was helping them, raising them from mere animal living to manhood.

No, people have not changed since the first Good Friday. They still would love to mangle and destroy those who help them."

Old Mrs. Burke said sharply, for she was a privileged character: "And perhaps they are right, Fathers, and I beg your pardon for it. It may be that they know in the hearts of them that they deserve nothing, so why should they get something, with no merit of their own?"

"A philosopher in elderly petticoats," said Ifor, then quickly complimented the old lady on the juiciness of the joint. "Mrs. Burke, I think you have uttered a profound truth."

She tossed her head with pleasure, but Father Andrew, Ifor reflected, would have to spoil it. "I mind me," said the old priest, "that you were one, Mrs. Burke, who said it was sacrilege to bury Sir Oswold in the consecrated churchyard."

But Mrs. Burke was femininely ready for him, and she said with sturdiness, "I did not know he had been the instrument for a miracle for the little lass, Father."

"Oh? They are now ascribing miracles to Sir Oswold?"

Mrs. Burke was exasperated. "Father! A man who gives to his people what Sir Oswold has given must be a saint, and if there is miracles about, then he must be the cause of them, and there is miracles." She sighed in disappointment, thinking of her lost prestige of being housekeeper to a saint. Then she brightened, and her old sparkling eye fixed itself on Father Andrew. "And could it be, Father, that it was you who told him his duty, and he did it, and then——"

Father Andrew groaned and lifted his hand. "Mrs. Burke," he said slowly and loudly, "I did not even visit the poor gentleman until he was on his deathbed, and never did we talk together, until then. And that was long after he made a little heaven of what had been a little hell, and long after the miracles."

In some way the people transferred their resentment towards Sir Oswold to the two priests, and on the next three days only the sacristan and the altar boys and the Sisters were on hand at Mass. "That will show them," they said in the pubs, but what it was that would be shown was not quite clear. The doctor, too, was avoided, sharing in the general resentment. On Sunday, however, the church was filled again, not out of forgiveness, but out of obligation, teaching and habit. So it was with some involuntary sternness that Father Andrew prayed, *"Bonum est confidere in Domino, quam confidere in homine."* (It is better to trust in the Lord than to confide in man.)

Those who had been cured began to speak of the great ability of the doctor, and this led to confusion, for the doctor was on the side of the immediate objects of displeasure, the priests. Then, very slowly, the church began to be revisited for lonely prayers, and there were more people at the daily Mass. But the Welsh, as Father Ifor constantly said, were stubborn. Let them stop hating themselves, in their own good time, for being stupid and un-Christian, and let them start forgiving themselves, again in their own good time, and "they'll come around." Father Andrew hoped so, dubiously, but he was overjoyed when he heard his first Confession, "after the uproar," and the penitent said, "I am guilty of lack of charity in that I hated Oswold Morgan, who roofed my house and built the good school for my children."

"I am guilty—I am guilty—I am guilty." The refrain increased, with growing fervor. And then one day Sir Oswold's lonely, unmarked grave, except for a tiny wooden cross which Father Andrew had put upon it, was heaped with late summer flowers, and the people were happy again, having forgiven themselves.

In the meantime Father Ifor helped Father Andrew to collect his notes and write out his report to the Bishop. They did this after tea, and as quickly as possible, as there had been a somewhat impatient letter from the Bishop. And Father Ifor had to end his holiday soon, which had been extended after supplication and explanation.

The first cold from the dark gray ocean and the somber mountains was already on the land when Father Ifor told his cousin that he must leave the next Monday. Father Andrew's face became dejected. "And I have worked you so hard, lad," he said, "so very hard. In spite of the good food, you have lost flesh, and there is a tiredness in your eyes, and a paleness about your mouth." The old man looked more keenly, then was alarmed. "You must visit Dr. Brecon, for my own heart's comfort."

Father Ifor protested, but to ease his cousin's alarm he went with him to Dr. Brecon's surgery that afternoon. The surgery, as usual, was full, but a priest came first, and so Ifor did not have to wait. "Well, and well," said Dr. Brecon, "have we more trouble on our hands?" But he looked with sharpening interest at Ifor.

"It is nonsense," said Ifor. "I am in the best of health. I am here only to please Father Andrew."

The doctor sounded and thumped and examined, with new and shining instruments which intrigued the younger priest. "In good order," said the doctor, at last. "Heart, lungs, stomach, bowels. For a man of your age, Father, you are doing well. Put on your shirt." Then he said, quickly, "What's this, what's this?" And he took the priest by his bare shoulder and pulled him nearer to the window.

"Two warts I had, from a large crop of years ago," said Ifor impatiently. But the doctor took a magnifying glass and in deep silence examined the warts. Still in a grave silence, he reached under Ifor's armpit and probed with his fingers. Then he sat down, hard.

"What is wrong?" asked Ifor.

But the doctor went to his waiting room and summoned Father Andrew, who came in full of trepidation at the sight of the doctor's face. "There'll be something wrong with Ifor?" he asked, and his voice broke.

The doctor opened his mouth, then closed it. He looked at his hands as if he hated them.

"We are men," said Father Andrew. Father Ifor, watching the doctor, put on his cassock, slowly. "What is it?" said Father Andrew.

"The very worst," said the doctor, and his fox-like face twisted with pain. "It could not be worse. Melanoma. And, it has already metastasized. There is a—growth—under the armpit, an ugly lump."

"What does it mean?" Father Andrew whispered. Father Ifor buttoned his cassock. His fingers were trembling a little. Black. Now he knew, and remembered.

"There are times," said Dr. Brecon, "that I wish I had had common sense and had become a miner, myself. Sit down, Father Andrew, do." He glanced at Father Ifor. He said, desperately, "After all, you are priests and you know that life and death——" His voice stopped.

"Ifor is all that is left of my family. He is all I have," said Father

Andrew, and all at once he was no longer a priest but a terrified old man, lonely and sad. "What is this melan——"

Father Ifor spoke for the first time, and gently. "Black cancer is the popular term for it, Andrew."

"Go then, please, Father," said the doctor, who had lost his courage.

Ifor took his cousin's arm and looked down into the watering blue eyes. "There is no cure for it, Andrew. It means—death. It has spread. It means I am soon going to die. Andrew?" But Father Andrew had put his worn and spotted hands over his face, and the bent shoulders were heaving.

"We are priests," said Ifor, pleadingly. "We know death as close as a brother. We know it is our portal into eternal life, and to the Beatific Vision."

"There will be pain?" asked Father Andrew from behind his fingers, through which drops of tears were running.

"Yes," said Dr. Brecon. "But it is not a slow thing, not," he said, in a lower voice, "in the condition it is now."

"Have we ever feared pain?" asked Ifor of his cousin. But he was a man, after all, and there was a twisting nausea in his bowels, and a human fear. "God's will be done," he said, and he was afraid as he had never been afraid before, not even when he had been caught in the mines by an explosion and had been rescued only in the very nick of time.

Dr. Brecon went to his medical cabinets and he shook out a handful of very small gray tablets and put them in a little bottle. He handed them mutely to Ifor. "Morphine?" said the priest, and the doctor nodded.

"I do not have pain yet."

"You will," said the doctor, sadly. He hesitated. "May I look a little more closely?" It was to divert Andrew rather than anything else which made Ifor consent. The doctor found more lymph glands invaded, and small lumps here and there. "Yes, pain," he said, in the flat voice of a man who dares not express his emotions. "Very soon. I suggest you ask your Bishop to relieve you of your duties, Father. I will give you a paper to send him." He sat down at his desk, relieved not to see the two priests at this task, and wrote rapidly.

"A mistake, perhaps?" implored Father Andrew, when the doctor had finished. Dr. Brecon shook his head.

"Father, I studied in Edinburgh, and I saw many such. There is no error. But if Father Ifor would like to have another consultation in Cardiff, or London, I can arrange it."

Father Andrew, at this slight reprieve, was all tremblings. And so Father Ifor, who wrote first to his Bishop, then went to Harley Street in London, and was gone for four days. But before he returned to Gwenwynnlynn he visited his Bishop.

When he arrived at Andrew's rectory he was smiling, and Andrew clasped his hands and cried, "It was a mistake?"

Ifor embraced him and said, quietly and firmly, "No. Dr. Brecon was right. I have the report of two Harley Street men. It is even worse than he had told us. But, we are men, and more than that, we are priests. But I have good news for you, in a way. I am being permitted by my Bishop to remain with you until——" Then he could not speak, for old Andrew's face was stricken and he was very still.

"Until you die," whispered the older priest.

"How many of us are permitted to remain with those we love and are dear to us until we die?" asked Ifor, and tried not to think of the sleepless nights he had passed, and his heavy weariness, and the throbbing in the lumps.

"There can be no operation?" Father Andrew pleaded.

"Not with this, Andrew. They can cut out the—the blackness— but it reappears very quickly. And it spreads. There is no cure. But we could pray that someday there will be a cure for this disease. Andrew? Do not look so. I am only a man, if I am a priest, and I have a man's fears. See, I am here with you again, and you must comfort me and help me——" He stopped, for suddenly Andrew's face was radiant and his eyes were shining.

"I know!" cried Andrew. "How is it possible that I am still stupid? I will ask Oswold to intercede for you, so that there will be a miracle!"

He clapped his hands like a delighted child. Father Ifor was depressed. He sat down, overcome with his tiredness. He was not worthy of the intercession of a saint; priests accepted God's will. And Oswold had not been acknowledged as a saint, except by Father Andrew and a few in this lost little hamlet. But he said, kindly, "If it will give you some—peace—Andrew. You must expect nothing, however."

"There has been no miracle since his death that I can concede as a miracle!" cried Father Andrew. "That is already in our reports, which we have not yet sent to my Bishop. Perhaps it is God's will— the finger of God—that there should be another and incontrovertible one!"

"One must not tempt God," said Ifor.

Andrew was vividly outraged. "Is prayer tempting Him, devout, humble prayer, that He assure us, his priests, that Oswold is one of His blessed ones, a saint?"

"In this case, I am afraid, yes," said Ifor. "We have wanted Oswold to be acknowledged as a saint, and declared blessed, and canonized. We are Welshmen, and we are eloquent, and we can plead a good case. That, alone, would arouse suspicion."

"Your reports from Harley Street, and Dr. Brecon's report!" said Andrew, not listening. "Let me put them away safely. And then, Ifor," he said, with a young man's passion, "you must go with me into the church and I will pray to Oswold to intercede, to cure you by the Grace and merits of Our Divine Lord!"

Ifor thought of the learned Devil's Advocate in Rome, who would dexterously question the "sainthood" of Oswold Morgan, and look askance on two simple priests who were apparently hoping that one of their countrymen would receive the great accolade of the Church. Ifor, the Welshman whose pride had never really been crushed, thought of the ridicule that would come to Wales. He could see himself and Andrew, who was almost doddering and senile, in Rome, and the Archbishops there, and the Cardinals, and the questions, questions, questions. He shivered.

"Do not do this, Andrew," he begged. For to a Welshman death is preferable to humiliation. And he thought of the "sharp young priest" in Cardiff, who was probably not even a Welshman, who would smile in a superior fashion at two lowly Order priests with obscure parishes, and would imply that they wished to make them-

selves "singular," with a miracle of their own. Ifor winced. Then
he was relieved. There would be no miracle for himself, certainly,
and so he would never be questioned. "Very well, Andrew," he said
fondly, "let us go into the church, and let us pray as we always pray,
that God's will be done only."

They went into the church, and Father Andrew hurried like a
child, pulling at Ifor's hand.

It was a cold bright day and every window in the little church—
each window very high and very narrow—glowed like a multi-
colored gem. They had the aspect of the illuminations on vellum
of the medieval monks rather than of glass, for there was depth to
them and living color. They stood, vivid and intense, in the rough
gray stone walls, like ardent prayers made visible. The walls rose
narrowly to a rude groin-roof, from which hung the golden chains
of ancient chandeliers, fitted for a multitude of candles. The Stations
of the Cross, which Ifor had often knelt before, appeared alive,
so delicate and fine and pure and precise were the mosaics. The
people spoke of the statues of the Blessed Virgin Mary and of St.
Joseph as "stone," but they were of the finest Carrara marble,
exquisitely executed, as were the panels of the altars. But inevitably
the eye was drawn to the great high altar, surmounted by an enormous crucifix evidently of ebony and ivory so that one was certain,
when abstracted for a moment or two, that there stood the actual
original cross and He who was on it was of flesh. It drew the eye
away from high silver candelabra glimmering with tall white candles.
It drew the eye from everything but itself.

Someday, thought Ifor, as he knelt beside his old cousin, this
will be a shrine, a place that must not be missed, whether or not
Oswold Morgan was a saint—which Ifor could still not quite accept.
Certainly there had been forbidding saints and irascible saints and
saints who castigated with eloquent tongues, and saints full of holy
anger, and saints who were not loved or even liked in their lifetimes,
but surely none had been so dark and surly as Oswold Morgan, so
universally hated except for an old priest and a doctor—well, yes,
there were the children, but Father Andrew was a romantic and he
could possibly have read in that episode of the silent children and the
gift of the ribbon something which was not really there. Perhaps

Oswold had been in the habit, in his isolation, of tossing coppers to
the little rascals in the streets—out of sheer human rebelliousness
against the universal dislike that surrounded him—and so the children had merely gone to the carriage in greedy expectation. A whole
hamlet could not hate a man so thoroughly, one and all, if he had
any saintly qualities discernible to a keen eye. Yes, he had done
much for the hamlet, but that may have been a perverted revenge.
So shrewd and clever and intelligent a man, capable of amassing a
fortune through inventive genius, must have known that someday his
benefactors would discover who he was, and then would suffer in
their souls for their lack of charity. That would nourish a revengeful
soul exceedingly! And he had taken care—note that, dear old Andrew, deep in your fervent prayers now—that the request that his
name never be known to those he had helped had not been included
in his will! Eventually, he had wanted to be known, even if it were
only after his death, and he had wanted his revenge, not only on the
hamlet, but on the Church. Was he laughing in——? Where was Oswold Morgan this hour?

Half ashamed of his thoughts, when he should be praying, Ifor
glanced at Father Andrew, who was gazing at the mighty crucifix,
his lips moving, his rosary hanging from his hands, the beads slipping
one by one through his fingers. His tired eyes were bright and clear
and believing; the ardor of his love for God made a light shine on
his features. Here, thought Ifor, is a saint if there ever was one,
and perhaps we need look no further.

But still—— There were strange things, not to be explained. To
attribute the cure of the dying and the crippled to the works of
Satan, to deceive the people, was to stand with the Pharisees and
cry, "He has a devil!" And it was quite notorious that when Satan
and his angels created a sensation they never chose a little hidden
spot far from the regular paths of men. They liked panoply and
amazement and trumpets; the saints did what they did almost in
stealth, asking nothing except that men love God. And certainly
the beautifying of a church containing the Holy Eucharist would
hardly be on their program of deceit! But still——

Ifor brought his thoughts sternly back to his prayers. He submitted
himself to the will of God, but he thought of the ignominy of a

painful, screaming death. If only, he prayed, that it is Your will that I die in the silence of the night, with only Andrew beside me! Or even alone, in Your Presence, with Your Most Holy Name on my lips. The proud Welshman, thinking of the nearness and agony of his death, was still proud, and he was afraid that in his dying he would forget that he was a priest and be only as other men.

Then he heard a stern voice within him, "A Pharisee?"

He struck his breast with his clenched fist and prayed for forgiveness. He was sweating lightly even in the chill of the church, and he could feel the ominous throbbing in his cancerous glands, a throbbing like little drums. He could also feel that draining within him, quickening day by day, almost hour by hour, the draining away of his life into the sands of death. His whole human body started, as it started so often now, in primeval alarm, aware of its awful peril, aware of the steady approach of its enemy. The body knew, long before the soul. The enemy was not far away; Ifor could hear its footsteps in the throbbing of his flesh. The body instinctively cried for flight, but it had no place to go but the grave.

The sweat became heavy on Ifor's forehead and between his shoulder blades, where death had already set his seal. It is natural for me to be afraid, he said to himself, as he had said to others so many times before. Did not Our Lord, Himself, know human agony and human recoil from death in Gethsemane? Ah, it was easier to say that to others than to one's self!

He felt a touch on his shoulder, and Andrew, smiling, whispered to him softly that he must visit old Mrs. Forde, but that Ifor should stay, if he wished. Ifor, weak with his fear and his slow dying, nodded, and Andrew left him. He could hear Andrew's rustling tread and movement on the stones, and he pressed his feverish forehead on the top of the pew before him, grateful for the coolness as he knelt.

Finally, he lifted his head. He could not tell himself that he was at peace; this numbness of mind and soul was not peace. It was not even resignation. There was no one else in the church but himself. He looked at the flickering candles on the altar, sighed, glanced away, then looked again.

He had not heard that man come in, that man standing before the rail and gazing up at the great crucifix. He must have entered when Ifor and Andrew had been praying side by side, and had seated himself in the foremost pew, and then, having completed his prayers, was examining the altar. A stranger, then. Andrew had never seen him before, this tall stooped man in a very dark gray city suit, his white head glimmering a little in the scented light, the curve of his cane hanging on his arm. His back was to Ifor, and the excellent tailoring of his clothes was evident to Ifor's faintly curious gaze. Then the man knelt at the Communion rail and clasped his hands and dropped his head. For what was this stranger praying? And coming to it, what was such a man doing here, in this lonely hamlet? There were no grand houses or inns where such as he would remain, and visit. An owner, then, from England? Peculiar that he should come, for owners sent their agents, and it was the rare one who ever appeared even in the best of the mining districts, and Gwenwynn-lynn was not one of the richest mines.

Or, he was a stranger who had heard of this beautiful, narrow little church, and had come to it as to a shrine?

The stranger rose, looked at the crucifix again, genuflected. Then, very slowly, as if in deep thought, he moved up the aisle towards Ifor, who pretended to be absorbed in untangling his rosary. It was not good manners to stare at strangers, and especially not for a priest. Those who came to pray were deserving of their privacy.

The slow footsteps came firmly up the aisle, then they stopped. Ifor, through the corner of his eye, saw finely polished boots, the end of the ebony cane, and the excellent tweed of the trousers. The man wanted to speak to him, to exchange at least a smile. So Ifor, after a moment or two, looked up.

He saw a dark, withdrawn face with the bluest eyes he had ever seen—a grave face and melancholy eyes. The nose was strong and belligerent, the chin massive and cleft. The wide thin mouth was serious and unsmiling. Then, as Ifor helplessly continued to stare, the stranger smiled, and instantly the gravity and sternness were gone and the manly face was sweet and kind.

Ifor involuntarily began to rise, but the man kindly shook his

head. Then he looked steadily into Ifor's eyes and smiled again. It
was a smile of brotherhood and understanding. Then he left Ifor's
side and went up the aisle into the far sunshine of the open door,
and was gone.

Ah, well, thought Ifor in surprise. He stayed for a few moments
longer, then left the church. The street outside was almost empty,
except for a few distant playing children, for mothers were preparing tea, and it was not time for the men to be leaving the mines.
Ifor went into the rectory. Mrs. Burke was laying the cloth in the
kitchen for the priests' tea, and the kettle was humming on the hob.
The old woman smiled at him with an anxious, maternal smile, for
all knew, now, that Father Andrew's younger cousin was very ill,
indeed. Ifor knew that the doctor had not told, but he suspected
that Andrew had asked his parishioners for their prayers.

"Well, now, it's refreshed you look, Father Ifor," she said, "and
I do hope you have some appetite for the good tea."

Ifor began to smile, then stopped. "Coming to it," he said, in fresh
surprise, "I feel uncommonly hungry, Mistress Burke." He examined
his sensations; why, certainly, his stomach was not turning, as was
usual these days, at the fragrance of kippers heating in their pan
and at the sight of a little platter of pink ham. In fact, he actually
was hungry! "I'll have a wash," he said, "and then Father Andrew
will be here, and I'm looking forward to that tea!"

He went into his room, and it was only when he had closed the
door that he became aware, with shocking astonishment, that the
throbbing in his glands had stopped, and that a sudden and
incredible sense of well-being, as of new blood, was pouring all
through his body. He felt like a young man, or at least like a vigorous
middle-aged man, again. He had not felt like this for all these weeks;
no, not for a year, or even two years. Quiet, he said to a heart that
quickened in its own amazement, there are possibly recessions. This
must be one.

He unbuttoned his cassock. Then his fingers stopped. Where had
the summer gone, or had it gone and he not noticed? The bright
light of the evening sun had never seemed so pure and sharp, or it
had never seemed so for a long time. The early autumn flowers

flooded their scent into the little room; had they been this way before and he had not known it? All of life, suddenly, became quicker, closer, keener, and so very dear, and so filled with peace.

It had been so long since he had felt anticipation and eagerness, yet they were rising in him now, an exultant tide. His fingers shook while he unbuttoned his shirt and removed his collar. "Thank You, dear Blessed Lord," he said, "that You have heard my prayers and have given me Your peace and blessing, in these, my last days. To have this is more than a whole lifetime is worth, and I shall never forget."

He flung the shirt from him and looked into the mirror above the commode, and astonishment again struck him forcibly, for there was color in his cheeks again and his eyes were sparkling. He touched his cheeks and forehead, slowly, wonderingly. They were cool and fresh to his touch. Then, very slowly, his hand dropped and he was staring at himself in the mirror and his eyes were widening and his mouth was falling open.

He stood so for a long time, then he swung about and looked at his shoulder in the mirror. The evil black spots had vanished; where they had had their awful being were two faint rosy smudges, as if fingers had been pressed on the healthy flesh for a little. But even as Ifor watched, the smudges faded, and the skin was smooth and fair.

"No!" whispered Ifor. "Oh, it is not possible!"

He stumbled to his bed, and fell on his knees, and spread his arms upon the wool coverlet and wept.

He did not hear the knocking on his door, for tears and prayers had been incoherently mingled together in a great storm of thanksgiving and adoration, and humility and shame and contrition.

"Ifor!" exclaimed Andrew, in fright. "What is it?"

Ifor got to his feet and he seized Andrew by his arms, and his face was still streaming with tears. "Tell me!" he cried. "Tell me of the face of Oswold Morgan, and the look of him!"

Andrew stared blankly. "Tell me," pleaded Ifor. "For I think I have seen him."

"Ifor, Ifor," stammered the old priest. "Oswold—he was tall and bent, with a dark face, thick black brows, blue eyes like a lake, the chin of a stern man, a grave face, a white head, a thin, serious mouth—— Ifor, what is that you have said?"

Ifor was silent and he panted a little. Then he said, humbly, "It was he I saw, in the church, when I was alone. It was his intercession —your prayers——" He drew a deep breath. "Look!" he cried, in an exalted voice, and turned about so Andrew could see his back. "Look, it is all gone, the swellings, the pain—— Andrew, your Oswold is indeed a saint——. I was given a vision of him—— Andrew!"

"Yes," said Father Ifor to the absorbed faces around the fire, "that was ten years ago, and for a man of my age I am very well, indeed. Each year I am examined by three competent physicians, for Rome is prudent. The reports go in that I am free of melanoma, and continue to be free. Father Andrew and I were called to Rome for questioning. The Devil's Advocate was stern with us, and sometimes hectoring. And so he was to Dr. Brecon. He was less so to the fine doctors from Harley Street, who confessed the truth and said they 'had no explanation,' and distastefully admitted that it was a miracle.

"Rome does not move quickly in these matters. It may be many years hence, but one day, if not in my own lifetime, there will be a new saint announced among the company of the blessed to whom prayers may be directed and his intercession pleaded. He was known to men as Sir Oswold Morgan, but to God he was known as His servant, Oswold of Gwenwynnlynn, who practiced the heroic virtues as only a saint can practice them, and who loved his fellow-man with all his heart, and continues, to this day, to answer the prayers of those who seek his intercession with faith and pity, with fear and hope, and with trust in the mercy of the infinite God."

Ifor smiled. "While Rome prudently continues the prudent course, the men of Gwenwynnlynn are already revering their saint, and I, who am their priest since my cousin died eight years ago, can hardly rebuke them when they cover Oswold Morgan's grave with flowers, and kneel beside it to pray, though there is no fine monument upon it. And few strangers to know where he lies, except those who love him. The men of Gwenwynnlynn."

Chapter Six

THAT NIGHT LITTLE ROSE, in tears, prayed most heartily to "Saint" Oswold Morgan of Wales that she could remain at Grandmother's for some time more. For a new priest had arrived to try to bring Grandmother back to the Sacraments. He had said to the company after Father Lewis had finished his tale of Oswold Morgan, "Ah, it is faith that indeed moves mountains, though how many men know it? But strange it is that doubt often increases faith, as they say the fire tempers the fine blades of Toledo so that no man knows the secret so well as they. Doubt is of Satan, it is said, and well do I know it, and he is the testing fire."

"Sometimes, I am thinking," said Grandmother, dryly, "that he burns all in the fire while he's at it, and there's nothing left."

Father Timothy Donahue pondered on that, puffing at his pipe. "If that be so, then the faith in the beginning was nothing, a dry reed ready for the burning. But if it has juices in it——"

Father Donahue was tall but not so tall as his Irish colleagues, but taller than the Welshmen and the Englishmen. He had strong but gentle black eyes, alive and keen for all his age. "If it has juices in it," he repeated. "But I should not be proud, I'm knowing, but humble, for faith is of God and cannot be commanded but only bestowed."

He shivered a little and Rose was immediately entranced. Then the dreadful thought returned that she must go home tomorrow and miss this promising tale. So she spent at least half an hour imploring

Oswold Morgan for his intercession with that vague but mighty God of all these holy men. (She thought of Him as stern and forbidding and sharp with the whip and not to be turned aside and not to give mercy except reluctantly, for so she had been taught at home. But Oswold Morgan, she was certain, had access to that severe Ear, and so she implored him.) Try as she would, no disabling illness came to her help.

At breakfast that morning Cook beamed at her, then considering the beam unseemly, looked strict. "It seems," she announced, "that *she* has had a letter from your Mama and Papa asking her to keep you awhile. Something's come up."

Regrettably, Rose rejoiced. So, there had been another row and she could stay. Her prayers to Sir Oswold had been heard.

FATHER DONAHUE AND
THE SHADOW OF DOUBT

"I would be going now to the village of Carne on the west coast of Ireland," said Father Donahue, "and it was joy I was feeling and gratitude, for I would be having my own parish, and I should be no curate any longer in Dublin, bullied by the irritable old priests. Ah, it's irritable I am now, myself, after all these years of the rheumatism and the obstinacy of my people, God love them, but I was young in those days and I told myself, in the innocence of my heart, that I'd be no bullying priest, shouting at the spalpeens in the Confessional for a venial sin, and roaring hell-fire at the old women who hid their coppers and cared nothing for the missions, and making the poor good Sisters tremble in their boots at a confessed hurrying at the prayers. I'd not be bellowing at the men for an extra beer they drank in the pubs on a Saturday night, they with their hard work and their harder hands on the plow in all the hours the good Lord sent.

"No, it was the saint I'd be, and they'd be calling me good Father Timothy. There's not a young priest who does not dream of saint-hood, which," added Father Donahue with a quelling look at the younger priests around the fire, "is a fine dream, a heroic one, but at-tained very rarely, my boyos. St. Patrick was a saint," he added more kindly, "but not an Irish one, and there's many a lesson there to be learned.

"I was twenty-four years old, and raw from the bullying, but now I'd have my own parish. Old Father McGowan says to me when I left, 'So, it's from under my thumb you are running, lad, and there's joy in your foolish face. But here you have been under my wing, and now Our Lord has called you out into the cold, and may the saints help you!' He laughed uncommonly sour, I thought, and I packed my little bag and was glad to go. He says to me when he shook my hand, 'And pay my respects to Father Sullivan of Larney, which would be the other village, fifteen miles to the east, and a blessed man he is, and ask him to remember me in his prayers.' "

Father Donahue had not the slightest intention of calling upon another "old priest" in Larney or anywhere else on the high-hearted day he left the rectory in Dublin, a day or two before the first Sunday of Advent. He was certain that Father Sullivan was not only old, but unlearned, and that he mumbled Latin with only a casual understanding of it. There was no reason to believe he was not very irritable also, and had absolutely no faith in young priests going to their first parishes without a guide. However, a great snowstorm blew up in a twinkling, and the train bogged down in Larney station, and the wild white winds whipped through a man's clothing and turned his blood to ice. There would be a delay of several hours, Father Donahue was told. He counted the shillings and pence in his pocket, and the one-pound note, and decided that Father Sullivan, "an irritable one," would at least offer a man, even a young priest, a drink of good Irish whiskey and treat him to a substantial if flavorless dinner. After all, he could not remain in the little station without freezing to death, and the engine was rolling up its eyes in an expiring expression and letting off its steam feebly. Let them build up the fires and clear the tracks a little, and he, the young

priest, would be sheltered at a fire with a drink in his hand and
a dinner waiting at a warm table.

Consultation with high authorities (one old man) at the station
convinced Father Donahue that the train would not be leaving for
at least four hours, and so he asked directions and plowed off vigorously through the snow to Father Sullivan's rectory. He had been
born in a little Irish village and had lived there until he had gone
to the Seminary, but he had forgotten, God have mercy on him, how
dreary and sad and woeful a little Irish village could look near
sunset on a snowy twilight. Silence. Harsh whiteness. Lashing gales
like frozen whips. Chimneys fuming smoke. Never a soul to be seen.
If a dog barked the sound echoed and re-echoed against white hills
and from the roofs of the thatched cottages. An eerie mauve light
over everything, and in the low carvings of the snowbanks. Bleak
and twisted trees. Forsaken, forsaken. For the first time Father Donahue thought of the village of Carne, which was probably no more
cheerful than this, and his high young heart began to drop with
alarming speed. How was it that he had forgotten? He glanced at
the west; there was a blood-like smear in the gray clouds, and
above it a tiny ice-green lake of air, enough to freeze the heart out
of a man.

But the rectory, tiny though it was, was warm and full of lamplight, if it did smell, as all rectories seemed to smell, of wax and
paraffin and turpentine and what could only be the odor of sanctity.
(The latter had been sadly missing at the two rectories where he
had lived in Dublin, for both the old priests had had irascible tempers
and little patience. "And no wonder," said Father Donahue, sadly,
as he meditated on that long-past winter twilight and his four years
in Dublin, and the bare larders.)

Father Sullivan was a small, rotund man with sparkling black
eyes, a sweet and lavish smile, and a head of remarkably thick
white hair curling all over his forehead and ears and far down
his nape. He had a complexion like that of a cherub, and his plump
hand was warm and hearty. His profile was craggy, yet it was a benign cragginess. He was delighted to see "Faether McGowan's lad,"
and had prayed only that morning that the lad would find time to

call upon him. The old priest was very happy, genial and full of hospitality. Better still, the fire in his minute parlor was very hot, his whiskey lifted one's spirits, and there was a fine stew, he promised, simmering in the kitchen, rich with lamb and sliced potatoes and onions, and a suet dumpling or two, and dark sweet tea.

He was the same age as Father McGowan, and as he refilled the young priest's glass with the burnished whiskey he poured questions on "the lad." How was darlin' Tom, and his old ailin' sister who kept the house for him, and how was Dublin, and how were the people recovering since the Famine? "I was a little lofty at first, with this old simple priest," said Father Donahue, "this old priest who talked like a child of the Famine, as if he'd not suffered from it, himself. Yet, as he babbled, it was wisdom I saw in the big black eyes and an understanding in the quick smile. And it's confessing I am, here and now, that these interested me less than the fragrance of the stew bubbling in the kitchen and the rich smell of the dumplings bobbing in the boiling water nearby. The whiskey, it was, then ran to my cold toes, and I hoped that the train would not be starting that night and I could sleep by this fire, on the hearth, wrapped in a blanket or two."

The young priest was surprised that his host could speak of Father McGowan as "darlin' Tom," that shouting, formidable old man who was a terror in his parish. So in some bemusement he accepted another little glass of whiskey, and did not notice Father Sullivan's sigh when the older priest held the bottle to the light. Fortunately for what was left in the bottle, Father Sullivan's housekeeper, a somber old lady, asked them irritably if they intended not to have their tea this night, and they went into the kitchen and fed themselves heartily. The housekeeper, Father Sullivan's cousin, of whom he was apparently frightened half to death, kept up a monologue about young men's appetites and what would there be on the table tomorrow except oatmeal, which was bad for Father Sullivan's stomach. The younger priest did not let this funereal monologue deter him, for he had heard the same wailings in Dublin, and the old ladies, with the Grace of God, invariably managed to feed their charges, if not sumptuously. But it vexed him, in his youth, that

the old ladies appeared to have no reverence for the clergy but
regarded them as simple children who must be protected from the
appetites of visiting priests, intransigent parishioners, and, always,
"the Bishop." The monologue inevitably ended with "the Bishop,"
and it did this night, along with the dumplings. But as the two surfeited priests returned to the parlor the old lady shouted after Father
Sullivan, "And you'll not be forgetting the letter to the Bishop this
night, and I'll take it to the post!"

"My, my," murmured Father Sullivan, drowsily, as he toasted his
woolen toes on the fender and listened to the storm, "it's a tartar she
is, my cousin, and what it is she is wanting me to write the Bishop
I do not know. It's forgotten, I have."

"The old cousins and aunts detest the Bishops, I'm thinking,"
said Father Donahue, also drowsily.

"And the Bishops pick up their robes and run from the sight
of them," said the host, chuckling. "Ah, and what would we do
without them, Tim?"

Father Donahue stayed the night, curled on the settle near the
fire, heaped with blankets and shawls, having been assured by
the old cousin that the train would not be leaving until morning.
How she knew, Father Donahue did not question; he knew these
old ladies who had second sight. He thought them ignorant souls,
but he invariably listened to them, more or less meekly.

"Old Agnes has taken a fancy to you, my boyo," said Father
Sullivan after Mass the next morning. Father Donahue doubted
this, remembering Agnes' scowls and reprimands. But as he was
leaving the house for the station Agnes shouted to him, "And call
for Jack, if you'll be needing him, and mind you not to forget!"

"It's second sight she says she has," said Father Sullivan, shaking
hands with his guest, "and though the Bishop frowns it's long he's
been from the country, he sitting in Dublin." He paused. Then he
repeated, twinkling, " 'Mind you not to forget!' "

"I won't," promised Father Timothy Donahue, brave again in
the bright white morning. He set out briskly for the station, and
it did not surprise him to learn that the train in truth had not left the
night before but was building up a fine head of steam just this

very minute and screaming to go to Carne. As if, thought the young
priest, it was my fault for the delay.

The distance to Carne was only fifteen miles, but the train
stopped at every paddock, it seemed, and at every farm gate. So
Tim Donahue had ample time to reflect on his new parish, which
he was deeply afraid resembled Larney. He was not disappointed
in his premonitions. Carne was even smaller, and within sight
and sound of the howling black sea, and was much colder even
than Larney, and apparently harbored less substantial citizens, if
possible.

Two old men in woolen leggings, or gaiters, and wearing thick
old brown caps, met him at the station, scrubbed and brushed and
very shabby, with patched elbows. "It'll not look like much, Carne,
Faether," said one of them kindly, "but it's the good hearts we have,
and the rectory's tight, and so is the ould church." He had seen the
young priest's expression of dismay, and he patted Father Tim's
arm like a grandfather. "Not like Dublin, I'll be thinking, but we
love the good Faethers here and it's not saucy we are in the Confessional." Father Tim was a little heartened by this as they led
him to a jaunty-cart, heaped blankets on him, and drove him off at
a spanking pace. "The ould Faether could not meet ye," shouted the
other old man over the clatter of hoofs on black wet cobblestones.
"It's the rheumatism he has."

And no doubt I'll be having the rheumatism soon, too, thought
Father Tim, gloomily, shuddering even under all the blankets,
which smelled highly of horse, and flinching when the icy wind
struck his cheeks. Snow had fallen here, too, and the dark hills
behind the village were streaked with it, like pallid veins, and
Carne huddled under a white quilt of it. The main street (there
were but four other streets besides) was narrow, unkempt, lined
with tiny little shops whose windows were sightless with steam,
and there was a goodly sprinkling of pubs between. This will be
a drinking village, thought Father Tim, recalling the trim pubs of
Dublin. There was an inn, also, with a board creaking in the wind,
and it was brave with red and blue and white and announced that

it was "The Dashing Falcon." Birds do not dash, thought the priest, to divert his forebodings, but it has a lively sound.

The old men informed him that the "ould Faether" would be leaving tomorrow, that the good Sisters had smarted up the rectory and were waiting there to greet him—Father Tim shivered—all four of them. His housekeeper did not live on the premises; she was a widow with five children, and she "did" for the priest daily, including Sunday dinner, and left at sundown. This cheered Father Tim a little; he had been the only son in a large family of girls and female cousins and aunts, and on the occasions when he had been a curate the housekeepers had bullied him like the dragons they were and regarded him as a mere slip of a lad in need not only of maternal attentions concerning mufflers and warm socks but of guidance. One of them had known more theology than a local, much-esteemed solicitor, who prided himself on his knowledge, and she was given, in odd moments, to arguing obscure points of doctrine with the curate.

The "ould Faether" had discreetly locked himself in his little bedroom to escape the nuns and the housekeeper who "did" for him, on the plea of worse rheumatic pains today. He did not emerge until he heard masculine voices, and knew that his relief was at hand. He then crept painfully from the bedroom into the little parlor, which seemed stuffed with people, so small it was, and he greeted Father Tim with sincere expressions of joy. "A stout boyo," he said, nodding, his weary old eyes brightening, and Father Tim had the distinct impression that he would need to be "stout" in Carne.

The tiny rectory was indeed "tight," so tight that the parlor steamed with the heat of the red peat fire and the heat exuded by the welcoming committee. Father Tim had a confused glimpse of brick walls painted a leprous white—this done only yesterday by himself, said one of the old men proudly—and they still smelled pungently of whitewash. The few chairs were black but sturdy, and so was the one table with its unfragrant paraffin lamp, which was burning smokily against the dull dimness of the winter day.

"Lovely, lovely," murmured the "ould Faether," who was obviously dying for a quiet drink to ease his pains, a drink he dared not take in the faces of the nuns, all of whom stood high in their habits except for the Sister Superior. She was one of the smallest ladies Father Tim had ever seen, with the face of a pink-cheeked angel, the loveliest of gentle blue eyes, and the most tender of rose-tipped mouths. So Father Tim, surveying her, knew that she had a temper like a holocaust, a nature carved from solid iron, and an obstinacy to make a donkey envious. She appeared to be about thirty, and therefore she was somewhere in her late sixties or early seventies and had never known a pain or twinge in her life. She gave him the sweetest and most submissive of smiles, and he heard her, in his mind, saying quite clearly: "There'll be no nonsense from you, Faether, and no interfering in our affairs, so mind you know your place from the beginning. I know you lads: full of zeal and briskness, but we'll tame you!"

Indeed! Father Tim replied to her coldly in his mind, in his best Dublin manner. She gave him a radiant smile, quite knowing what he had said, and he was certain that St. Cecelia had never possessed such radiance, and his heart sank. There was such a saintly smugness about her, brightened with triumph. She had quite accurately understood that here was a lad who had spent most of his life under the firm thumb of womenfolk and knew when not to cross them, and she was pleased.

Finally the nuns departed, after receiving Father Tim's blessing, and they moved off in a tight group, already teeming with remarks they would make when alone together. Tim had not the slightest doubt that the Sister Superior would comfort them with assurances that he would be no bother to them "with his interfering."

"A lovely soul," sighed the "ould Faether" of Sister Mary Grace. "Such piety, such devotion, and"—he paused to reflect—"such energy." He looked at Father Tim and cackled. "A saint, boyo, a saint."

"So I've seen," said Father Tim. The old priest clapped him on the shoulder to cheer him, but he shook his head reminiscently. "I'll be advising you not to cross her. It's owning the school she thinks she does, and she's the magistrate, she thinks, of the village, and there's not a soul that does not become half the size at the sight of her. Ah, but now for a good drink to warm the cockles of our hearts."

The snow came down in large wet patches. The two priests had a big if tasteless dinner. Mrs. Casey loved loaded platters, for she always took the leavings for her brood of little children, and so she heaped up the mashed potatoes and the turnips and the thick bread and the boiled beef, and kept a sharp eye out that the priests did not overstuff themselves.

After a reasonable nap following dinner, the old priest took the younger one out for a view of the village. There was a bicycle, which was church property. They both walked today. The villagers had much business on the main street, and always seemed to be clotted in the path of the priests, so Father Tim knew he was on inspection and was being weighed in very scrupulous balances. This made him uncomfortable, and stiff when introductions were made to a few of the more important citizens and citizenesses. He knew these inspections of "new" priests, for he had engaged in them as a boy with his family, and he also knew that there was very little charity in these inspections. Especially among the elderly ladies, who ought, properly, to be home on this cold and nasty day taking care of their rheumatic joints.

His parish, of course, was not just Carne but the countryside about it. "Ah, and it's a lovely sight on Christmas Eve, just before Midnight Mass," said the old priest, a little wistfully. They returned for tea, and then the old priest took the younger into the minute church, very tidy, very poor, and with colorful if appallingly bad and cheap statues. There was not one that could not be bought for three or four pounds in one of the religious shops in Dublin, in far back-streets. But the high altar glowed with tall white candles, if the holders were only pewter, and the crucifix was quite passable if a little gaudy. There was only one stained-glass window; the others were of plain glass.

This told Father Tim more of the financial state of Carne than anything else. An Irishman may be half starved and live in a shanty, half frozen, but he did love to see his church "have the finest." Father Tim felt deep compassion for the people of Carne. The villagers "lived out of each other's pockets," he was informed sadly, and sold various items to the small farmers who surrounded them.

The farmers were not exactly prosperous, either. In short, Carne was very similar to Father Tim's childhood village, the memory of which never failed to depress him, and he could not help thinking of the rectory in Dublin with some regret.

The old priest left the next morning with unseemly alacrity, Father Tim thought, for all his expressions of reluctance. (Father Tim had not slept well on the makeshift pallet in the parlor. He had heard the howling black sea so loudly that it had appeared about to engulf the rectory.) So, in the afternoon he was alone with Mrs. Casey, busy with her blacklead on every available iron article from the fireplace to the iron-and-brick stove in the kitchen. The smell of the blacklead mixed with the smells of paraffin, turpentine, whitewash and wax, and it all gave Father Tim a headache, so he went into the church to pray for patience and for relief for his homesickness, and for strength to do his duty. In retrospect, old Father McGowan in Dublin lost his irritability and became a benign saint, a man of monumental charity and sweetness.

The church was crowded at Mass the next morning. Of course, the season of Advent could account for some of these pious assisters at Mass, but Father Tim doubted it. The parishioners watched him with falcon eyes for the slightest slowness or fumbling. He sighed. Every Irishman was really a priest at heart, and God help his pastor if he did not come up to expectations. The old ladies, of course, were the worst. They were, in the spirits of them, Sister Mary Graces. The Sister Superior was the most vigilant of them all, and though the church was frightfully cold, young Father Tim found himself sweating. The altar boys' faces expressed nothing but worship and awe, and they were exactingly polite, but Father Tim knew altar boys! He had been one, himself. These lads would duly make their reports to parents about the new priest. It was with a personal desperation that Father Tim prayed, "*Ad Te, Domine, levavi animam meam: Deus meus, in te confido; non erubescam, neque irrideant me inimici mei. Etenim universi qui te exspectant non confundentur.*" The organ did more than wheeze; it grunted at the entrance hymn. It grunted very loud; the communicants nodded with satisfaction. The choir, all three of them, had bad colds. The offerings came to exactly two pounds, three shillings, and tenpence. Remembering his home village, Father Tim was somewhat cheered. This was a fine offering, in view of what Carne was.

Sister Mary Grace put him through a brisk rundown on parish matters the next afternoon. Without raising the sweetest voice he had ever heard she let him know that things were well under control —due to her vigilance and authority. Father Tim sat very straight and tall in his chair, and knew that he was not in the least impressing this saintly lady, who let him see, but most courteously, the edge of her temper when he made what to her appeared to be foolish queries. She was about to take her leave, then whirled on him quickly, so quickly indeed that he was startled.

"It is about time the divil will be making his appearance," she told him.

"What?" cried Father Tim, in confusion.

"Every twenty years," she told him factually. "Be prepared, Faether."

"Oh, come now!" he exclaimed. "And in this season of Advent!"

She shook her head reprovingly at him. "Always, at the holiest seasons, Faether."

He looked into the eyes so like an Irish dawn, and saw she was not joking. He thought. He remembered the tales of boyhood. Satan had a bad habit, indeed, of presenting himself at the worst times, to the confusion of the faithful.

"Hum," said Father Tim, who had received many lectures on the subject of superstition. "And what will he be looking like, Sister?"

She folded her arms neatly, and considered. "Who knows?" she murmured, with mystery.

"And you'll have seen him, once, perhaps, Sister?"

She nodded, with more mystery. "When the ould Faether first came."

Father Tim was left to ruminate whether new priests brought Satan along as a matter of course to a parish, an idea that was not complimentary. Then he shook himself. It was about time that remote Irish villages were brought up to date and discarded forbidden superstitions. He would speak of that next Sunday. He sat before

his lonely little fire that night after tea and prepared his sermon in
his mind. Mrs. Casey came in to say good night to him; she carried
a black string bag on her arm, of considerable bulk, but Father Tim
was more discreet than to ask her what it contained. It had, however, a smell of black pudding, which he had had for tea. Well,
after all, a laborer was worthy of his hire, and the major part of
the hire of poor women like Mrs. Casey was the leftovers from the
priests' tables, and who could question that in view of the five father-
less children?

Father Tim was rereading the *Imitation of Christ* for the fifth
time, an exercise he had imposed on himself during the season of
Advent. Each time that he read it he found more than he had found
before, so he read, occasionally rose to trim the wick of the lamp
and toss a few pieces of peat on the fire. The wind was very noisy
tonight, and the sea joined in. It was lonely, but it was peaceful.
The little clock on the mantelpiece ticked away. Snow was falling
again. Bed, tonight, under half a ton of blankets, would be welcome.

The only thing was that he did not feel sleepy, as he usually did
at this hour. He murmured a few preparatory prayers, turned another page. The sea shouted under his very window, he thought,
the black and ugly sea. The clock ticked.

There was a sudden loud banging, as of a loose shutter in the
wind, or rather, it sounded like a pistol shot. Father Tim put down
his book and pipe, and went searching. The little house had exactly four windows, and all were shuttered tight. The one door was
firmly latched. After this inspection, Father Tim said aloud, "Nonsense." The fire burned furiously. Was there really a change in the
air, a very subtle change? "Nonsense!" He must remember to rep-
rimand Sister Mary Grace, even if she was Sister Superior. Did
she make it a habit of spreading superstition among the poor people?
It did not seem likely; she was a woman who exuded common sense.
Yet, she had said——

Father Tim said his prayers, and retired. It was very black and
cold in his little lair of a bedroom. No wonder rheumatism was rife
in the village, with the dankness. He got up and opened the bedroom door so that some of the last heat from the parlor could enter.

The shot sounded again, louder than before, somewhat like the noise of a medium-bore cannon. Trees snapping in the cold? But it was not very frosty in spite of the snow. Did demons, Father Tim asked himself with humor, always announce their coming with firearms? If so, then their inventiveness had become very crude. The young priest went back to bed, yawning this time, and fell into deep sleep, the sleep of the youthful just, the faithful.

He did not like Sister Mary Grace, for he was afraid of her. But in the next days he acquired respect. She had the village fully regimented. In fact, she was a drill sergeant. There were no loose ends anywhere, no messes to reorganize, no confusions. The people came faithfully to Confession, and always, in the background, hovered the form of Sister Mary Grace. She lines them up in platoons, no doubt, thought Father Tim, and drags them from sickbeds. There was little sin in Carne, he discovered. Part of this was due to poverty. But then, when was poverty any ally of virtue? Usually the reverse. The men gathered in the pubs and drank their beer and argued, and sometimes fought and got drunk on something more potent than beer, but Sunday morning inevitably dawned as pure as the first dawn of Creation, and the church was filled.

And everywhere the women and children, and even the men, said, "Sister Mary will have attended to the matter, Faether." She did. One of these days, thought the young priest with foreboding, she'll be calling on me to put me through the catechism. He avoided the saintly old lady with the face of a blooming young girl. She left notes with Mrs. Casey for him, calling attention to some oversight or making firm suggestions. She was beginning to be a goad in his side. He began to ponder on writing the Bishop, himself. But he had no doubt that Sister Mary Grace had already intimidated the Bishop, so it was no use.

He could find nothing wrong with the woman. That was the trouble.

The season was the season for prayer, for preparation for the birth of the promised Saviour, and it was a season of joy. The little shops teemed with farmers' wives shopping for gifts. A brighter light shone in the eyes of expectant children. The horses moved faster. Even the old men had a sprightly air about them. The Sisters were preparing the crèche. Christmas carols were practiced in the little school under the sound of Sister Mary Grace's ruler. And the snow sifted down at twilight, soft as an unuttered prayer, and as beautiful and patient. If it had not been for the ever-present roaring of the unappeased sea Father Tim would have been content.

The people of Carne were healthy, except for the pervading rheumatism. They also lived to remarkably old ages, even for the Irish, who considered eighty to be mere middle age. There were very few midnight alarums for the Last Rites, and practically no funerals. Baptisms there were, galore. And a few very hasty but very necessary marriages, under quiet circumstances, due to the season. Then the young people went happily back to perform, legitimately, the rites they had been performing illegitimately. No one pointed fingers, which spoke of charity. Father Tim was able now to find familiar faces in groups, and to speak to almost all the villagers by their Christian names. He even permitted himself to believe that he was liked, and he was not wrong. Usually little hamlets were always suspicious of a priest for the first year, and kept him under strict surveillance. Mrs. Casey assured him that he met with Sister Mary Grace's tacit approval, and she thought that he should smile with pleasure. "Ah, but she and the ould Faether had their rare fights," she said, with wistful relish. Father Tim was faster on his feet than the old priest, and so managed to avoid the Sister Superior dexterously, most of the time. Yes, she was indeed a saint. He'd have preferred a woman not quite so saintly, and not on the job all the time. It was not that Sister Grace lacked humor; she was full of jokes. The village loved her and quailed when she bore down on any inhabitants with her habit flying and a look not quite so saintly in her magnificent blue eyes. "She should run for mayor, that she should," said Father Tim to Mrs. Casey, who first giggled, and then looked reproving.

Father Tim shopped in the village for Christmas gifts. He bought his mother a Belleek pitcher, which she would greet with pride and joy. He bought his sisters trinkets. And he bought old Father McGowan in Dublin six fine linen handkerchiefs, and was amazed at himself. The postmistress carefully stamped everything and sent the packages off.

All at once it was the day before Christmas. Not a thing had been overlooked, thanks to Sister Mary Grace. There were no last-minute scrambles, no sudden utterances of despair. No emergencies. It was splendid, but a little dull. Father Tim wished he might be able to drop in casually at the little school, to listen to the last practicing of carols or the rehearsing of the choir, but he was afraid of Sister Mary Grace. He knew by instinct that she did not care for casual droppings-in. It's asking for an appointment I should be doing, thought the young priest dismally, or a ticket, perhaps. He thought again of writing to the Bishop that Sister Mary Grace's great talents were being wasted in little Carne. She should be the Reverend Mother in some enormous convent, preferably three thousand miles away, in America, for instance, which was a mission country.

The last post before Christmas delivered a letter from old Father Sullivan in Larney, wishing his young brother in Christ the joys of the season. Father Sullivan promised to visit Father Tim shortly, after the holidays, and this lifted the heart of the regimented young man. He discovered that he was indeed lonely. Father Sullivan had a few old friends in a village just south of Carne, a mere hour's trundling on a bicycle.

Then it was Christmas Eve, and there was the fine fragrance of an onion stuffing being prepared in the kitchen by Mrs. Casey, in readiness for the fat goose contributed by a farmer. There was also the scent of mincemeat and citron and broth, and the baking of oat cakes. "You'll be spoiling me, Mrs. Casey," said Father Tim, deftly stealing a little tart. His vestments had been repaired and patched and mended where necessary and he looked at them proudly, white as snow, and glistening. His mother had bought them for him, secondhand, only a year ago.

Father Tim's young heart sang with reverence and joy and gratitude this night in his first own house, in his own parish, and about to celebrate the great Mass of rejoicing in his own church. He even could feel some affection for Sister Mary Grace and her army discipline. He was not tired, though he had been hearing Confessions all afternoon. There were always some boys and girls who, overcome with the joyousness of the air in the village, had been doing some quiet celebrations of their own, and had belatedly discovered they were in a state of serious sin. Father Tim never failed to marvel at the forgetfulness of humanity, which never forgot forbidden delights and invariably forgot virtue. Even within arm-reach, as it were, of Sister Mary Grace, at that. *And where they find the places she is not is beyond me,* he would think.

Midnight Mass was especially affecting to him, for he had been born on the stroke of midnight, at the very moment thousands of choirs were chanting angelic joy. So, with a light step he entered the church to the entrance hymn: "The Lord has said to me, You are my Son, and this day have I begotten you. . . . Why have the Gentiles raged, and the people planned vain things? Glory be to the Father . . ."

Never was a Mass more heroic, more stately, in that tiny church, with the sea seemingly clamoring at the door and the wind sweeping the eaves. Everything was perfect. The choir had recovered from its bad colds. There was no sniffling in the church, no uncouth stumblings. The people rose, knelt, sat as a man. Blissful, his heart trembling with thanksgiving, Father Tim crossed himself with the Sacred Host. He received the Host, and fell into profound contemplation. *"Quid retribuam Domino pro omnibus quae retribuit mihi? Calicem salutaris accipiam, et nomen Domini invocabo. Laudans invocabo Dominum, et ab inimicis meis salvus ero."* The candles flamed. This was not a little country church; it was a vast cathedral.

It was then, at this most sacred moment, that the most dreadful thing happened. For, clearly in the young priest's mind, there was said, with calm coldness, "What is this blasphemy?"

He was so shocked that he slightly reeled. His whole body turned bitterly cold, and began to tremble. He lifted his head, dazed. The voice said, "Do you believe that the great Lord of endless universes actually condescended to notice your earth, this meanest of all mean specks of dust, and was born of a Jewish maiden nineteen hundred odd years ago—to save these wretched creatures bowing and crossing with you? Blasphemy! Blasphemy!"

Sister Mary Grace looked up from her clasped hands alertly, all her instincts alarmed. And what was wrong with the young priest? He should be crossing himself with the chalice now and chanting, *"Sanguis Domini nostri Jesu Christi custodiat animam meam in vitam aeternam. Amen."* But he was standing dazedly with the chalice in his hand, his back to his people, and it was as if he had been struck to stone there and could not move. The organ rumbled; the choir waited. And still he did not move. One of the altar boys glanced up, wonderingly.

"Blasphemy," repeated the calm and dreadful voice in the priest's mind. "You teach it is the great sin to despair of God's mercy or presume on it. How much more blasphemous it is to teach that He is even aware of your existence, He, Lord of ten hundred billion suns and their planets about them. You would drink of His blood and eat of His flesh, you, an ignorant man among ignorant children?"

With an enormous effort, and by mechanical means of habit, Father Tim crossed himself with the chalice, and hardly murmured: *"Sanguis Domini nostri Jesu Christi custodiat animam meam in vitam aeternam. Amen."*

"Blasphemy," said the voice. "Do you truly believe that what you are is immortal? You have seen the animals of the field die, and men on their beds, and was there a difference, a gleam at all, that an actual soul had just left its human body? No, there was not. You are not even blasphemous, for there is Nothing to blaspheme. Fool! Acknowledge your folly, and depart in the remnants of what dignity is left to you."

The organ coughed tentatively; the choir cleared its throat. Sister Mary Grace felt a thrill of deep fear as Father Tim turned feebly and yet rigidly on his heel, and she saw his blind white face and dark staring eyes. But he was whispering, audible only to those in the first pews: *"Misereatus vestri omnipotens Deus, et, dimissis peccatis vestris, perducat vos ad vitam aeternam. Amen."*

Sister Mary Grace pressed her clasped hands to her breast in heightened fear. She tried to see a single shifting light in those blank eyes, but not even the candles illuminated them. It was as if the priest were seeing into some awful pit and could not prevent himself.

The calm voice was murmuring derisively, "But there is no God to forgive! To invoke Him is to invoke the mindless wind, which is violent but without sentience."

If ever Father Tim had had doubt before, he would at this moment have been able to say quietly in himself, "Go and let me be." It would have been an old struggle once again, and again overcome. But he was an untrained soldier on the battlefield, for he had never doubted and had never been wounded before.

In some manner he was able to proceed by mere instinct and remembrance, but there was nothing in him now but black silence and a deathly cold. There was no voice, no shaft of light, no joy, no bliss, no reverence. There was nothing where once had shone a flame. There was a dull deafening in his ear, so that even his own voice sounded far off, like an echo, and the choir was only a distant and impertinent mutter. Somewhere within him there was a vast upheaval, as if something dear beyond all life had been thrown down and shattered, beyond all recall and beyond the help of prayer.

The candles dazzled his eyes and misted them. He genuflected when he must, and moved when he must. His mouth was filled with raw acid. Who were those before him who rose and fell and bent their heads like marionettes, like silly things on strings? What were they to him, and to any God? If there was a God?

He must speak, and he spoke, languidly, heavy with a weariness he had never known, aware of weakness but held by it. And then there was a hiatus in his mind which he could never fill again all the rest of his life. He simply was unable to remember what happened, or if anything happened at all.

His next really sharp memory was of finding himself in his chair before his own fire, and Mrs. Casey's hand swam into view containing a glass of liquor. He waved it aside; his body was drenched with icy sweat, and shuddering in it. His vestments—he had at some time removed them, but he did not remember. Opposite him sat the Sister Superior, Sister Mary Grace. She was very pale. Her bloom was gone, and it was an old face that was turned on him, with white lips and webbed cheeks.

He could not speak. Mrs. Casey spoke soothingly for him. "Ah, and what a hard thing it is, in a strange church, among strangers, and on your own! Do have a sip, Faether."

"Let him be," said the nun, quietly, then added with more kindness, "Yes, and wearing it is. A cup of hot tea would be better then, Mrs. Casey."

Mrs. Casey went to the kitchen, sadly shaking her head. Sister Mary Grace leaned towards the young priest and murmured, "Faether? It is not sick you are?"

He groaned. He felt very numb and detached. He said, "Was it a fool I made of myself?"

"No, not that, Faether. It was all perfect, that it was." It was an old voice that was speaking now, no longer brisk and authoritative. "Did you have a chill?"

He appeared to be considering that, but he was not thinking. He nodded his head and said, "Yes. A chill." (How could he possibly celebrate Mass in the morning? How could he possibly eat, sleep and drink again? Live again? God have mercy on me! he said in himself, and it was as if something stirred in him and he heard the calm, cold voice again: "What God?"

He had put his lean young hands over his face and felt very sick and broken. Then he had a wild thought: he would get on his bicycle, and he would ride away at once, and never would anyone who had known him see him again. "Only honest disillusionment," said the voice. "But honest it is. Go then, and do not return, in all honor, for you are no hypocrite."

"And would you have me send for Faether Dolan's young curate?" asked Sister Mary Grace, anxiously. "For the morning? From Murtagh's Woods?" (This was the village five miles away, and Father Tim now knew Father Dolan and his new curate well.)

He hesitated. Then his natural Irish strength returned to him, and his common sense. He must think about this thing which had come to him. He had not given it a name yet, nor did he think it had a being except in his own imaginings. In the meantime, he would conduct himself properly. His numbed body and mind sat in heavy listlessness together.

"Thank you, Sister," he said. "I had a chill. It is over now."

Mrs. Casey returned with the hot sweet tea, thick with cream, and he drank it slowly and stared at the fire, which did not warm him. When he looked up again—and it seemed a long time had passed—Sister Mary Grace had left him and Mrs. Casey sat in the chair. "I do not like your color, Faether," she said, "but there are the little ones waiting me at home——"

"And it's a cold, black night," said Father Tim, rousing himself a little. A cold, black night, he repeated in himself. "Go, then, Mrs. Casey."

"I'll be in, in the morning," said Mrs. Casey. Go, go! he shouted in himself at her. I must be alone! She stood up, gave him several hesitant glances, then left.

He thought that when he was alone he would be able to think clearly and surely. But instead it was as if his soul had been frozen, and all its thoughts, and that it lay a thousand miles under thick green ice on another planet. He could feel only that evil stirring in himself, that alert and watchful stirring which had nothing to do with him, and was apart from him. It was, he was to say later, like a dry rustling of something that would not sleep or be quiet, but slid about the ruins of the great thing that had been shattered in his heart.

It was Christmas morning, and he did not pray, for he could not pray. Or, rather, he would not attempt it, for a now-deadly fear of alerting the horror in himself. So long as it only twisted about the ruins and did not speak, he was not too threatened. He went to bed and did not blow out his candle, but stared at the cold brick wall until it was time to rise for Mass.

The word had gone about, through Sister Mary Grace, that the young Faether "was not himself," and that any mistakes or fumblings must be overlooked. They were, but not without some sad headshakings and murmurings later.

"I must have eaten part of Mrs. Casey's good Christmas dinner," said old Father Tim now to Grandmother's friends. "But I do not remember it. I remember only that I wrote a desperate letter to Father Sullivan in Larney, and begged him to come to see me at the first possible moment, as I needed him as much as life, itself. Mrs. Casey posted it."

Mrs. Casey was no sooner out of the rectory, with her loaded, black string bag, than he vomited, not once but many times, he who had no memory of ever vomiting before in his strong young life. The retching tore him apart. Staggering, crimson-faced, he fell on his bed and must have dozed. But he would not let himself think. The horror was still rustling about the ruins within him, and he dared not arouse it. He dared have no dialogue with it.

If there is no God, how can I live? he said only once to himself, for the thing stirred eagerly and he deafened his ear to its voice. He would wait for Father Sullivan, who would have the letter tomorrow. And how soon would he come, that old priest who had insisted that he be called if necessary?

Father Sullivan arrived two days of hell later. ("I know what hell is now," said Father Tim to his friends. "It is the total absence of God. It is a hell beyond endurance—this separation of the soul from God.")

Father Tim could have wept with agonized relief when Father Sullivan arrived, all white curls and cherubic face and craggy, benign profile. He clasped the younger priest's hands and studied his face with an expression of fatherly concern. He told "the lad" that he was so distressed over the letter that he had begged Father Dolan to send his curate to the Larney parish for a day or two so that he could visit Father Tim. In the meantime, he was staying in Murtagh's Woods with Father Dolan.

They sat before the peat fire and Father Tim began to talk, at first stammeringly, then with wild, loud words of despair, and with wide, disordered gestures. He spoke as if in the Confessional.

"I accuse myself of blasphemy, of all the dark sins that infest the mind of man!" he cried. "But I do not call it blasphemy, for how can it be blasphemy if there is no God? Father, I never—doubted—not one moment in my life, from the time I could toddle until this Christmas Eve. But the doubt must have been there, festering. I am an honest man, Father. I cannot continue to be a hypocrite, but yet I must until I either stop doubting or—go away."

Father Sullivan did not reply for a little while. He had listened gravely; he was graver now. He knocked out the dottle in his pipe, refilled the pipe, lit it, then puffed slowly and thoughtfully. Then he looked directly at Father Tim.

"It is not wrong to doubt," he said. "The saints have all doubted."

"So I learned," said Father Tim, rubbing his white cheek with his knuckles. "But though they fell they rose again, stumbling on. I cannot even rise."

"There is no virtue, I am thinking, in never having doubted," said the old priest. "Lack of opportunity is not a grace, either in chastity or faith. The opportunity must come, and it always comes unexpected, lad. The mind must reject; the soul must reject doubt."

"Tell me!" cried Father Tim. He paused, and there were tears in his eyes. "For how can a man live without God, a priest or a shepherd or a woodsman or a farmer, or a banker or a king?"

Father Sullivan smiled coldly. "They do, that they do," he said. "More live without God than with Him. It is the child who thinks that the world is full of faith. The man knows it is not."

Father Tim stared at him in bewildered silence, not understanding.

"Nor must you believe," said the old priest, with derision, "that faithless men are unhappy, that the marks of their doubt, and their rejection, lie like smallpox pits on their faces. I have met many of them. Many of them. And most of them are the happiest of men, for they believe only in themselves and are dependent only on their own strength."

Father Tim moistened his paper-dry lips. He could not look away from the pink and tranquil face near him. Then he said, faintly, "I am not so young nor inexperienced, Father, that I do not know that the world is full of faithless men, and that they do not suffer from their doubt. But—afterwards?"

"You are talking, I think, of after death?" Father Sullivan's lip lifted. "But why should the thought of eternity distress the faithless man? He does not believe in eternity, in the life of the soul. He believes that when he dies he is as dead as his dog."

"But, after death," mumbled the young priest. The cold sweat was on him again.

Father Sullivan said carefully, "You know, I am thinking that the Church is not explicit about the condition of the soul after death, unless the soul is saintly and so goes at once to heaven. There have been thousands of conjectures. We know there is Purgatory, but what its environment is—that we do not know. We are taught of hell, and more has been written of that than of heaven, and we believe it is the eternal separation of the soul from God, which is agony unbelievable."

He looked at Father Tim, and there was a strange intensity in his eyes, which were no longer beaming.

"But," stammered Father Tim, "if there is no God, and no heaven, there is no hell."

Strong hardness came into the voice of Father Sullivan. "There is surely hell," he said. "There is surely hell. A man can believe in that and not believe in God, for he can say to himself, 'God is dead.'"

Father Tim shivered, and the raw acid taste was in his mouth again, and vaguely, as if in deep twilight, he saw the great ruins that lay in himself, shattered and dead, thrown down and destroyed.

He said, with weakness, "But, if there is no God, and all religion is mummery—ah, and you'll think it a childish question!—why or how are we here, two men before a fire, priests, talking as we are talking?"

"It is said by the faithless men throughout the ages, and many of the wise also, that it is blind chance and accident. Or delusion. I have no arguments. Faith is a grace; we cannot will it for ourselves. That is the teaching of the Church. It is a gift of God. If it has gone from you, then the grace has been withdrawn."

"But why?" cried the young priest.

"I do not know," said Father Sullivan, brutally. He looked through the tiny window, staring out at the cold and snowy day. Then he said in a brisker voice, "But, in your arguments—and they are yours, not mine—if there is no God there is no grace, there is no faith. So, there is no 'why.'"

Father Tim stared at him again, and he saw that the old priest was smiling oddly and he was—it was not possible!—contemptuous. Father Tim shrank in his chair, and Father Sullivan, murmuring something, threw more peat upon the fire. It blazed at once. Its red light illuminated the old man.

"You think I am contemptible," said Father Tim, his heart breaking.

"I have contempt for a man who does not know his own mind, but must be faithful and full of prayers one day, and full of doubt and rejection the next." Father Sullivan spoke with slow emphasis, and with a cruel gleam in his eye.

A different voice entirely spoke within Tim, a voice he had never heard before. It was measured and tender. "Have you not heard the cry to God: 'I believe! Help Thou mine unbelief'? That is man's cry from his birth to his death; it is the cry of all mankind. You are not alone. Christ understands. Did He not, Himself, ask His Father, while He was on the cross, why He had been abandoned? It was His human nature that was crying."

Yes, yes! whispered Tim in his heart. He smiled a little, tremulously. He looked at Father Sullivan, who was watchful, and yes, surely contemptuous. It was odd that he should also look somewhat disturbed. The sudden light in the young priest's eyes died.

Father Sullivan said, "If there is God He surely respects more a man who honestly and openly doubts, and who has not received the gift of faith, than He does the hypocrite. Did He not denounce the hypocrites, Himself?"

The coldness and darkness and silence took Father Tim again.

"Tell me what I should do," he begged. The fire did not warm him. It burst into flame and roared in the chimney, but it did not warm him.

"Be an honest man. And go away," said Father Sullivan, with the utmost harshness. "Do you think God, whom you doubt, will have a man at His high altar who doubts as you doubt? If nothing else, you must have respect for what you have been taught, and the multitudes who live by it. They are wrong, you are thinking; it is all mummery, you are thinking. To you, that is the present truth. You are a fine, big lad. You could leave this hour, with a letter for your Bishop for the post, and be on the docks in two hours for the next ship to America. A strong and healthy lad like you." He sighed. "And you will forget in the new country, and it is rich, they say, and an honest man with some learning can make his fortune."

"What are you saying?" cried Father Tim, grasping the arms of his chair.

"The truth," said Father Sullivan. "And it's the truth you are knowing in your heart."

"My soul," said Father Tim.

Father Sullivan lifted his eyes impatiently. "Have you not said you do not believe in the soul?"

He stood up. "Think on it," he said. "The train leaves for the harbor in one hour. Write your letter to the Bishop. You must not be seen in your running—which is an honest running. Go quietly."

Father Tim was still young, and he was wounded and bleeding, and Father Sullivan had not helped him as he had wished to be helped, nor comforted him, so he cried like a young boy, "You hate me!"

"I hate all fools," said Father Sullivan, and he picked up his coat and hat and fastened his buttons. "But who else lives in this world? Still, it's a honest man that I prefer." He took out his heavy silver watch and studied it. "There is but fifty minutes."

"And you—you are telling me I should do this?"

"I do not command," said Father Sullivan, coldly. "I only suggest."

He ambled towards the door and stood with his plump hand on the latch.

In one last crushed appeal, Father Tim said, "You would have me desert—all this—leave my flock, run——"

"Dear boy, you have already deserted; you have already left your flock; you have run since Christmas Eve."

"Your blessing, at least," said Father Tim, and in his childlike despair he fell on his knees. Father Sullivan looked at him bitterly. "I have no blessing for you, boyo." And he went out.

Father Tim slowly struggled to his feet. His heart was beating wildly; he was half mad with despair and terrible sorrow and misery and bewilderment. Mrs. Casey was shopping. She would not return for an hour. Father Tim then thought of Sister Mary Grace, the old woman who served God with youth and ardor. She would help him, as Father Sullivan had not helped him.

"That foolish old woman?" asked the cold, calm voice. "An old woman like an old soldier, with a hard hand, and no knowledge. You, a priest, would go to such a one?"

"No," said Father Tim, in anguish. He looked at the clock on the mantelpiece. The village was quiet, the men at work, the women shopping for their families, or caring at home for their children. Feverishly, Father Tim ran into his room and wrote an abject (but honest) letter to his Bishop. Then he counted his money. He had five pounds. Was it enough for his passage? Surely not. But he had heard of strong young men working their passage. A savage and disordered uproar had taken his mind, like a storm, through which his thoughts feebly probed and directed him. He threw his few bits of clothing into his bag. He opened his wardrobe door to search the wardrobe. How had his white vestments gotten there? He must have taken them off in the house. He saw his mother's face, worn, smiling, full of love and faith. He cried out and buried his face in the vestments, and it was as if he had died at last.

If he had not seen those vestments, which rebuked him, which made him remember his mother, who had bought them with such pride and faith and love, he would have gone. He would have been on the train. He would have fled forever, into the hell of exile from God. But the sight of the vestments overcame him. He sat down on the cold floor and held the vestments to his cheek and he wept, and he said over and over, aloud, and loudly, "God have mercy on me, a sinner! God, Almighty Father, give me Your Grace again——"

He held the vestments in his arms as a man holds a life belt, and clung to them. His tears ran down his face and dripped upon his chest and then fell on his hands.

He heard a loud knocking on his door, and he thought: It is Father Sullivan again, and he derided me and gave me no comfort,

and he is said to be a wise man of understanding and kindness.
And yet—— The knocking became imperative, so he wiped his eyes
and got to his feet and went to the door to confront Father Sullivan
and say some bitter words to the man of whom he had asked the
waters of consolation and hope, and instead had been given Dead
Sea fruit.

But it was Father Dolan of Murtagh's Woods on the threshold,
panting and red from his bicycle ride. He smiled at the sight of
the young priest, then his smile left his face. He came quickly, for
an old man, into the parlor, and said at once, "And what is it, lad,
what is it?"

Father Tim bent his head and weakly walked back to the fire
and collapsed into his chair. "Ah, then, it is true. There is something wrong," said Father Dolan. "Am I in time, my son?"

The clock had moved a half hour. Tim could not speak. The
priest waited with loving patience, seeing Father Tim's haggard face
and the agony in his eyes. Then he said, gently, "Yes, it is true. And
that is why poor old Jack asked me to come to you, at once, in his
letter I had from him this morning. A matter of 'extreme urgency,'
he said. Tell me."

But Father Tim had sat up suddenly. "What is this you are saying?" he exclaimed. "Father Sullivan left me not half an hour ago!
He was in this room. He——"

"That is not possible," said Father Dolan, who was a large bear
of a man, with a big and comfortable face. "He broke his leg the
day before Christmas, and sent for my curate, who has been there
since. It was not Father Sullivan you saw, Tim, but a stranger. But
who was he?"

"Who was he?" repeated Father Tim, stupidly. Then he clenched
the arms of his chair. "But I know him! I stayed with him in Larney!
I could not be mistaken! He said he came in answer to my letter!"

"Then the angels conveyed him," said Father Dolan, seeing the
younger man's distraction, and trying to ease it with a joke. "And
what did the angel in the guise of Father Sullivan say to you? Or
Father Sullivan supported by the angel, with his broken leg?"

Father Tim turned as white as death. But he said, looking into

Father Dolan's eyes, "He told me to leave the Church, my flock, and to run, and to write my Bishop that I was running."

Father Dolan was shocked, but he said, quietly and kindly enough, "Tell me."

And so Father Tim told him. Mrs. Casey came into the house with her bags of supplies, but seeing the priests talking so absorbedly, she moved like a shadow into the kitchen. She put the kettle on, and got out the oat cakes and the marmalade. She knew Father Dolan, and what a fine man he was, with his understanding, and his strength for all he was so old. The poor young Faether needed such a man in his strange misery.

"So," said Father Dolan, soberly, "it was not old Jack, who will be on his back for months, God love him. But, who was it?"

They looked at each other in silence, and there was a sudden chill in the room.

Father Dolan then spoke slowly. "I admonish my flock for superstition. All can be explained, I have told them, naturally. But, I have never truly believed it. Heaven—and hell—are closer to us than we suspect."

"Then," said Father Tim, "it was—a demon." The evil rustling in him had gone. The shattered column was high and bright and white in him again. There was no cold, calm voice any longer.

Father Dolan nodded vigorously, then blew his nose. "It was, it was! And God's mercy saved you, for truly in your heart you did believe. Doubt comes to us all, many times. Do not think it will not come to you again, my son. It surely will. But God has been good to you. He has let you look on the face of the Destroyer, for he knew the child you were, who was not yet armed. He would not let the enemy take you, in your innocence. The next time you will be armed, and will have to fight, for evil does not give up so easily. It will be a stronger testing, then."

"Then, it was not an illusion? I did not dream it?"

Father Dolan hesitated. Superstition must always be rooted out. Then he was flooded with surety, and he said, "It was not an illusion. You did not dream it. Ah, and look at the fine tea Mrs. Casey has brought us, and shall we not enjoy it?"

Father Tim had a fleeting but joyous thought that a tea was a homely comfort after confrontation by the eternal Adversary. But God's love came in a good tea as well as in an ecstatic revelation.

He and Father Dolan enjoyed their tea heartily. While doing so Father Tim said, "Sister Mary Grace had her anxieties. It is truth that she said, that Satan would be near; he comes every twenty years or so, with a young priest in his innocence and arrogance, who believes he knows more than old ladies worn in the service to God. I must go to her tomorrow, and tell her, and beg her pardon."

"You must not!" said Father Dolan, helping himself to another cake and marmalade. "I know these old nuns. It's on my own neck they are, forever carping and finding fault. Do not puff them up. I have known Sister Mary Grace a long time; a lovely, wonderful Sister, a true daughter of God. But it does not do to let a woman know she was right all the time!" He chuckled. "There are some things which must be kept discreetly from women, even saints like Sister Mary Grace."

Chapter Seven

IT WAS INEVITABLE, OF COURSE, that Rose had to return home to her parents, who greeted her fondly and were in a state of high euphoria about each other. Rose did not trust these states, but regarded them with the wise detachment of childhood. It was a summer that was unusually cold and dreary, and in consequence the tempers of Rose's parents did not remain blissful. However, they never reached the state where it was necessary to ship Rose "off again to the old devil."

"The old devil" was enjoying herself mightily among her kinfolk in Ireland, and then after a hearty row with some of her older sisters she took herself off to the Mediterranean in high spirits. She sent one postcard to Rose's parents: "Am enjoying myself here. Pity you will never visit this lovely place. But you would not appreciate it, I'm sure." This so aroused Rose's Mama's anger that she vowed that never again would she speak to her mother-in-law, nor give that lady the pleasure of "little Rose's" visits in the future. Rose was so distressed that the dreary summer seemed part and parcel of her. She even longed for Grandmother's old parrot, and his way of catching a little girl's hair in his beak and pulling with glee.

The lonely child had few playmates, for she found their boisterous games disagreeable, their rude humor infantile, and their native cruelty too much for a sensitive little girl to endure. They reminded her of Grandmother in some respects, and once she asked her mother: "Do some people not grow up, Mama?" Mama said, "Of course they don't. They die young."

"Grandmother didn't," said Rose, reflectively. This so amused
Mama that the remark became a family joke, or at least as much of
a joke as the grim Covenanters could appreciate. One of the uncles
referred to his mother thereafter as "the auld child," to distinguish
her from the real children of the family.

It was years later that Rose found that indeed "some people do
not grow up." Grandmother was one of them, for which Rose in
many ways was thankful. Grandmother might be unlovable to her
family, but to those tired and weary men who visited her in her
house she was a benefactor.

A drearier autumn followed the dim and dreary summer at last,
and Rose was off to school to worse miseries under the eye of Miss
Brothers. When she should have been learning her sums she was
thinking of the strange tales she had heard at Grandmother's. Then
she began to ask Sir Oswold Morgan, and all the other saints of
which she had heard, to deliver her and return her to the splendor
of Grandmother's house, the comforting cakes of Cook, and, above
all, the kind and holy men about the fire.

But it was November before Mama's and Papa's tempers were
sufficiently irascible at the weather to provoke them into another row.
For a day or two the row was only sullen, and Rose began to fear
that it never would reach the explosive state, and she would never
again see Grandmother's house. She recalled, too, that Mama had
said that she would never go there on another visit.

On the last day of November, a particularly vile day, the simmering tempers of Rose's parents broke into flames. It was sad that little
Rose rejoiced, and eagerly watched and waited for the moment when
Mama would drag her luggage from the small closet under the stairs.
She came home from school one day, wet and wan, to find her luggage already packed, her best blue velvet coat laid out (with the
white fur at the wrists) and her new umbrella. Mama's eyes were
sparkling with anticipatory wrath, and Rose, looking at the luggage,
did not mind the smack she received for "coming in all wet like a
drowned puppy." She did not even mind the injustice. She was
going to Grandmother's again.

It was as if she had never been away, except that Grandmother had new dresses to show an awed little girl, and some fine new jewelry she had bought in Biarritz. She said to Rose, "So they're at it again?" referring to Rose's parents. Rose said, happily, "Yes. Are any Romans here yet, Grandmother?"

There were, for dinner. Grandmother had apparently accepted the fact that Rose would be present about the fire, or at least she did not notice her small granddaughter in the chimney corner. She was much "taken" by a youngish priest, an Irishman with an elegant English accent, who had a tale to tell and one which Rose was never to forget, though she forgot many others over the years.

FATHER PADRAIC BRANT AND THE PALE

"There is nothing which raises the spirits of a priest to what one hopes is holy gratitude than being elevated to the Monsignori," said Father Brant, speaking in his precise English voice, just a trifle over-accented. (He had studied for a year at Oxford, and the other priests, understanding, ignored the accent politely. He saw this, and smiled a little, ruefully.) He went on: "Nevertheless, as priests are only human, it is a hard struggle, sometimes, to keep from indulging in a feeling of purely human exultation tinged with pride. One has been recognized, after all, as somewhat superior to the run-of-the-mill priests. The Church, knowing this, has a wise and ancient way of calling on the Monsignori at unexpected, and often inconvenient, moments, and sending them into highways and byways and humble vineyards to 'help' a hard-pressed old pastor, and hear Confessions, and celebrate Mass in less than notable parishes. After a few such experiences in the practice of humility, a young Monsignor comes to realize that his duties embrace harder service to God and His children, and that his elevation means simply that, and not a personal honor. He has just been called to heavier labor, for which he has been prepared by the Grace of God in being given a better physical constitution and a better mind, not through his own merits, but only by the merits of Our Lord.

"But shortly after my elevation I did not realize that in its entirety. My parents in Sligo did not have the means to enable them to travel to London, but they sent me their happy blessings and expressions of joy. The Bishop in London, an old man and an old friend, kindly granted me a holiday so I could visit my parents. 'And no side,' he said, winking. The Bishop had a lot of wisdom; I remember blushing. It was twenty years ago.

"It was a joyous reunion, with my parents, and all my brothers and sisters and scores of uncles, aunts, cousins and in-laws, and all their collateral relatives. They were so proud of me. I found myself becoming a little pompous, but they appeared to expect that, so I became even more pompous. My English accent increased, and my delicate ways. They were awed, and not resentful. If my Dada had kicked me briskly it would have done a lot of good, but what humble Irish father of a Monsignor would remember that that Monsignor was the fruit of his own loins, a squawler in the cradle, the once-wearer of very damp nappies, a screaming toddler and a nasty little boy? Such remembrances, in the presence of the Edge of the Purple, would be sacrilege to such a father, who was probably, in the sight of God, much worthier than his son. So, nothing was too good for me at the old, battered homestead on the few meagre acres, and the female relatives cut into the household money to serve me dainties, and the male relatives were lavish with the best Irish whiskey and the kegs of beer. The men of the village strutted about proudly, and talked of the next village, which could not boast a Monsignor. As I was naturally priggish, and had, up to then, an unsuspected reservoir of snobbery, or 'side,' as the Bishop had called it, I became an elegant English Gentleman. In fact, so elegant was I that the English landlord, visiting his mansion a few miles away, invited me to dinner! Though my family, naturally, detested the Sassenagh, they were overwhelmed by the invitation, and there is another evidence of the paradoxical quality of human nature. 'It is possible,' I said, in my gentlemanly accents to my parents, 'that I may give him A Word.'

"I am afraid," said Monsignor Brant, "that I forgot all about A Word when I arrived at the mansion, for the Englishman talked only of guns and shooting, which interested me, and the results of the Famine some decades ago which had killed so many of my people and had cut down the revenues of the landlords. Moreover, I was over-whelmed by the grandeur of his house, the lordliness of his servants, and the excellent table and wines. He had sent a carriage for me, and the carriage carried me home, and it was only then that I remembered that I had given no Word at all. Worse, I remembered that the Englishman, kindly, quizzically, had said to me, 'Brant? Brant? Isn't that an English name, and not Irish?' I had replied, 'I really do not know,' and had sipped at my gold-and-crystal glass with the most delicate air.

"So I must go back a bit. A childless great-uncle, who had gone to London and made his fortune in the importing, and selling, of Irish blankets, tweeds, and sundry other goods—a shrewd trader, that—had taken a fancy to me in my early childhood. He was a widower and childless. He was convinced I resembled him closely, and as men love themselves so heartily and with such devotion, he extended his self-love to me. He persuaded my parents to let me live with him in London. He would send me to Oxford! He would make a gentleman of me. More, he hinted that I would probably be his sole heir. All this dazzled my poor parents, who had such a brood to feed and shelter and clothe in a time that was still struggling to overcome the effects of the Famine. They could not pack fast enough for me, and so I went to live in Uncle Padraic Brant's comfortable, bourgeois house in London. It was not a fine section, for it was occupied by lower-middle-class tradesmen and some mediocre doctors and barristers, but in comparison with my old home it was the pur-lieus of Buckingham Palace. Uncle Padraic (for whom I had been named by my clever if simple parents) had a servant, too, an old lady with a hard eye and a hard hand, who did not like children, and I was then but nine years old.

"I could not go to the best public schools, of course; Uncle Pad-raic's fortune, though comfortable by Irish standards, was not ex-actly magnificent. Moreover, he was a 'nobody.' But he did send me

to the best public school he could afford, being somewhat of a snob,
himself, and it was my first experience with a school whose teachers
were not Sisters and which was not under the direction of a priest.
In short, it was a secular school. Uncle Padraic was severely crit-
icized for this by his pastor, but he was a stubborn man. 'Let the boyo
have his experiences, Father,' he would say. 'It's no harm they'll be
doing a good Catholic lad.'

"Perhaps it did do me some good," said Monsignor Brant, thoughtfully, "though not for some years, and in a reverse fashion. My
classmates tried to ape the snobbishness, aloofness and gentility of
what they respectfully called 'their betters,' and their efforts were so
successful in this direction that they became obnoxious and vulgar.
For, as we know, nothing is so vulgar as an oaf who exaggerates gentility, and thus parodies it. 'Their betters,' however, would soon put
them in their places once they entered society. But that was in the future. They, and I, had not yet learned that true gentility is simple, un-
pretentious, and kind.

"When I was fourteen Uncle Padraic sent me to a school, newly
opened, run by the Jesuit Fathers, who tried to knock a little sense
into me. I am afraid it did not do a great deal of good. 'And where
does the name "Brant" come from?' a young priest asked me. 'It
is not a good Irish name.' I had 'passed,' more or less, as an English
lad, or at the very least as a Scots-Irish lad, among my former classmates, though it had not been an entirely conscious deliberation on
my part. I had simply decided that gentlemen avoid trouble at all
cost, and controversy, which true gentlemen do not avoid at all. I
had not discussed religion with my former classmates, who were all
High Church, and I am afraid I had allowed them—in my pursuit
of gentility and refinement—to believe I was 'Chapel.' A Methodist
or Baptist, say. This was their assumption, and I had not enlightened
them.

"Half of the Jesuit Fathers were Irish; the others were Englishmen.
I became a favorite of the English, perhaps because some guilt
in them, only half known to them, themselves, had drawn them to
me sympathetically. If the Church is not regarded with immense
esteem in England today, regardless of the Norfolks, she was regarded

with deep contempt, fear and loathing among the English in the days of my boyhood. A Catholic—English, Scots or Irish—could hardly hope to 'rise in the world,' as they called it then, and I mean socially, for even Catholics of fortune and title were not invited to the better parties and events of their peers.

"Only those who are, or have been, without the Pale can understand what this can mean," said Monsignor Brant, with some bitterness. "It is especially hard for proud young boys, and I was proud. Young people want the esteem of classmates; this desire is rooted in human nature. To be despised, to be ignored, to be pushed aside by a gesture or a shoulder or a cold glance, wounds beyond imagining. And wounds for life. A man is a man, and those who regard him as less than a man, and challenge his humanity, for reasons solely of race or position or color, challenge God, Himself, Who was born of an oppressed, small people, of a Maiden despised of the Romans and of the grand gentlemen in Jersusalem, who, though of their own blood, thought themselves much more cultured and civilized than the wretched people of Nazareth, and preferred to forget that thousands of their fellow-Jews knew neither Greek nor Latin, and could not discourse on the latest philosopher or the most refined way to set a dinner table, and could not, above all, chatter knowingly of the cultures of the world.

"No other species in all the world hates its own as does mankind. A wolf is respected by his fellow-wolves, for his wolfhood, and so this is with all the others, except man. It is notable, and one of the grimmest of all jokes, that it is only the stupid, half-witted sheep which reject one of their own kind if his wool is black rather than the prevailing dirty-yellow. It is a commentary on mankind, which has more than just one resemblance to sheep.

"At any rate," said Monsignor Brant, after reflecting a little, "I was sensitive, as all boys are sensitive, and I did not want to be despised and rejected, and I did not want to remember that Our Lord had been despised and rejected, too, of all men. I wanted to be charming, innocently happy, accepted by my peers. If by permitting my peers to believe a lie which I had not uttered, myself, and if by that permitting I was graciously accepted into hockey games and other sports and amusements, and was not looked on scornfully, I was content. I am afraid that I became hysterical when Uncle Padraic sent me to the Jesuit Fathers' school, for now I was openly branded for what I was—a pariah in Protestant English society. My former classmates ignored me on the street. Isolation enveloped me, the sad, degrading and contemptible isolation of the Pale. For a few months I became physically ill, and cried at night.

"I could not become, for a long time, a member of the community in which I found myself. Even here, in the Jesuit Fathers' school, there was snobbery and aspirations to a silly 'refinement.' The Catholic English boys kept themselves apart, more or less, from the Irish Catholic boys. Or, at the very best, they tried to 'tame' them, as they called it. 'One should show the Protestants that not all Catholics are simple or uncouth or unlettered,' an older boy said to me, he thinking I was English, myself. 'We have A Duty to our Holy Religion.' On this specious rock we rested our battered scruples, and became more English than the English, with overtones of the High (Established) Church in our manner, accents and general behavior. This was all the result of our sin of pride, and it is Lucifer's mightiest weapon.

"When I was sixteen we were addressed by a visiting Jesuit Father who spoke on vocations for the priesthood. I had been considering vocations of an entirely different kind, and had been meditating on the law or medicine. Law, in those days, was regarded as the profession with the greater prestige, though I was more drawn to medicine. I like to believe that unknown to myself, in those days, I wanted in my dark, young lad's heart to serve humanity. But the Jesuit Father was two important things: he was gentlemanly and very elegant and spoke like a Fine Englishman, and he was eloquent and dedicated. The Church, he said, needed not only humble parish priests, who were, after all, he conceded with a gentle smile, the salt of the earth, but she needed Men of Culture and great intellect. (The Father's name was Burnham, and he was English.) There was a sudden and tremendous release in me, and I do not like to think of the full meaning of that release, which seemed to promise me freedom from the Pale and at the same time service to suffering humanity. It was this dubious release which inspired me to speak up and blurt out that I thought I had a vocation.

"Strange to say," said Monsignor Brant, "it appeared that I did have! Under all that fraud and hypocrisy and mournful longing to be accepted and not despised must have lain a quivering human soul that really panted to serve. My teachers questioned me for hours; if some of the wiser looked a little doubtful or thoughtful at first, I ignored them. Meeting some considerable resistance from them, I was inspired with ardor and vehemence. At any rate, I was finally accepted to attend the Seminary. My original exaltation was severely tested, for the Church will not have a heart divided. But I was dogged, and the more resistance the more ardor and devotion, until, finally, long before I was ordained I was, in all the recesses of my soul, a priest. For that most awesome Grace of God I can never express, fully, my gratitude.

"My parents were wild with joy, though Uncle Padraic managed to restrain his enthusiasm, and once called me 'a damn young idiot.' I loved Uncle Padraic, but I had loved his fortune more. Now, I loved only God. During those years in the Seminary I knew the first peace I had known in my life, the first true dedication.

"Well, I was ordained. Did I mention how I became a Franciscan priest? I had deeply admired the English Jesuit Fathers, and some of the Irish ones, but the finger of God directed me to the Franciscans, and how that was I suppose I will never know. Some of the Jesuit Fathers were disappointed at my choice, but the older and wiser ones nodded their heads and all their original doubt of me disappeared.

"I was assigned to one of the poorest and meanest of parishes, in the West Side of London. At first, I felt a little rebellious. I was a learned, intelligent and educated young priest, and here I was, curé of souls, in a parish whose richest man dealt in harnesses and other horsy goods, and whose poorest were prostitutes, occasional laborers, charwomen, street-sweepers, drunkards, wife-beaters, and the physically and mentally diseased. Violence was the customary thing, and vice the customary amusement. Did I say I was a 'little' rebellious? That is an English understatement! I am sure that I spent more time on my knees than I did standing, praying for humility and consolation and help. I prayed to St. Francis almost constantly. There were times when I wondered how I could have chosen such an Order. But again, that was the Grace of God.

"In time I was given another parish. Without pride I can now tell you, my friends, that my Bishop was pleased with what I had done in that awful parish, though I am sure it was only through the intercession of St. Francis of Assisi and the Grace of God. Each parish was better than the last. And finally—I was a Monsignor, and I went to Ireland to visit my parents.

"It was all that adulation of the humble—and the relatives—that undid me. I preened. My name was Brant, and not Murphy. I was very young, and though a priest, I was also dreadfully human. I basked. I walked with elegant strides. My English accent—for I had spent a year at Oxford at Uncle Padraic's insistent request, to test me, as he said, hopefully—became extraordinary. On the last day in Ireland the old parish priest, who had a really devilish twinkle in his eye, presented me with a blackthorn shillelagh. I looked into his wise old eyes, and I was embarrassed. Had I really been that silly, that obvious? Nevertheless, I tucked the gift into the bottom of my handsome luggage—presented to me on my elevation by very old Uncle Padraic—and took the boat to Liverpool, and there picked up the train for Manchester and London. It is sad to remember that when I was on the boat I furtively threw overside the large brown package of food my mother had prepared for me, though I kept the bottle of the best Irish whiskey an uncle had given me. I had a moment's regret that it was not Scotch.

"The train was crowded—that is, the third class, and the first—for liners had come in from America. I had thought to indulge myself in the first class, but there was not a seat in the carriage. As for the third class—that was unthinkable. I was a Monsignor now. I soothed my conscience with the observation that there was no room in the third class, either. So I found a second-class carriage which was not too crowded. I had neglected some reading, so I looked for a compartment that was not seething. Amazingly, I found one that was totally empty, and I disposed of my luggage in the rack, and settled down with a book, very learned, on the life of St. Francis. It was also stupefyingly dull. I had assigned myself this book as a spiritual exercise. I had had the vague thought that I needed it.

"Suddenly the door of the compartment opened. I thought the intruder to be a very young priest like myself, and then I saw he was an Anglican Catholic. He stared at me, then impatiently tossed his bag onto the rack, and chose a seat opposite me, and near the corridor, so he could be as far from me as possible. He was not a Bishop; he was only an Anglican priest. He probably had a country parish. He was a vicar, and, I observed to myself, smarting, he possibly had a frightful time with the tithes and the old ladies who were penurious, and the matrons with marriageable daughters who no doubt pursued him relentlessly if he was still unmarried, and the coarse country gentlemen with their horses and their sealed purses, and the spinsters who oversaw everything and were arrogant, and the country gentry to whom he had to defer and placate and plead with for funds, and the rich old widows who put buttons in the plate. So, benevolently, I pitied him.

"And, of course, he despised me as a Roman. In turn, I despised him as a harried mere Anglican priest, under the thumb of his lordship, the Bishop. His clothing was far better than mine; he wore gaiters, too, modest ones. He also had a fine cane. I suddenly thought of the shillelagh in my luggage. His cane had a silver top, beautifully scrolled. He made a point of putting it close to his knee. He opened a London newspaper and affected to be immediately engrossed in it.

"Yes, he was as young as I, and both of us had a considerable distance to go before we would be even twenty-seven. He was as tall as I, and as thin, and as elegant. He had a long, thin, flushed face, a long thin nose, and protuberant blue eyes, and a thin, impatient mouth. His young hands were as smooth as a girl's, and his fair hair was smooth, also. After a little, it suddenly occurred to me that physically we could have been brothers! The only thing that separated us was our habits.

"The train did not move. There were whistles and shriekings

and clankings, but the train had some minutes to spare before moving on.

"Now, Englishmen are amazingly shy. Once this shyness is breached, they are the friendliest and most considerate of men. But the breaching is a formidable thing, and not often accomplished.

"I worked on charitable thoughts as the newspaper rustled busily, and I saw only the thin black knees, the gaiters and the polished black boots. I was not very successful. What a silly prig, I said to myself, for after all, I was Irish in spite of my name, and the Irish are friendly folk. He reminded me of my classmates in the public school, and suddenly I felt degraded again, and rejected. And, as I am Irish, my temper began to rise. A miserable Anglican priest, bullied by the women in his parish, fawning on the gentry, placating matrons with daughters, pretending to an interest in horses and dogs! What a life was this!

"In turning the newspaper, he dropped it inadvertently, and bent to retrieve it. When he raised his long and narrow head our eyes met. Did he see my anger, my eager contempt? Or, did he see, at last, that we were two young men together? And, did he think I was English, and had he seen our resemblance to each other?

"It could have been all these things. It could have also been that we were lonely and unsure of ourselves. For he gave the most tentative of smiles, ready to erase it as an error of mine if I did not respond. I gave him the same sort of smile. He indicated the newspaper. 'Beastly people, the Russians,' he said. 'There's been still another pogrom. Quite uncivilized!'

" 'Quite,' I agreed, with my Oxford accent. He looked surprised, then pleased.

" 'One never knows,' he said, darkly, 'with such people. Barbarians, really.'

" 'One never knows,' I repeated.

" 'Quite un-English,' he said.

" 'Quite,' I said.

"He paused, and we looked at each other, warily. Then he said, 'I am Father Francis Cutledge, Old Riding, Sussex.'

"'I am Monsignor Brant,' I said, with a little hateful pride, 'of London.'

"'Brant,' he said, musingly. His face brightened. 'Are you a relative of Sir William Brant? Devonshire?'

"I smiled. I am afraid it was a rather superior smile. 'No,' I answered.

"Now he was certain that not only was I an Englishman but I came of A Family, probably much better than Sir William's. He folded the paper carefully on his knee. He was prepared to chat, to be tolerant. After all, we were English Gentlemen, though I was unfortunately a 'Roman.'

"'Er,' he said, shyly, 'my father was—er—a Roman.'

"I was interested. 'Truly?'

"He nodded. 'And—so was my mother. A convert.' He looked slightly depressed.

"'And you became an Anglo-Catholic?' I said.

"He studied me. Then he lifted his proud young head. 'One has to go where one's conscience, and convictions, call.'

"'Quite,' I said.

"Being an Englishman, he revealed no other secrets. He looked at the paper again, and repeated, 'Beastly people, the Russians. Intolerant. Ignorant. And dangerous.'

"'The Eastern Question,' I assented, using one of the passwords of Oxford.

"He beamed, and his face was the face of a boy.

"'One likes to remember,' he said, 'that in England such cruelty and barbarity and intolerance are unknown. One likes to remember that we have no Pales here.'

"'Not visible, anyway,' I said. 'Not too obtrusive.' I could not help that little smack.

"'But we are the people of the Magna Charta,' he said, flushing a trifle. 'We are not barbarians. In politics, in dealing with the Empire, we are tolerant of all people.'

"'Exigency,' I said. 'The Empire would collapse if—we—were intolerant. Even the subject, the colonial, people would not put up with too much overt arrogance and bad treatment. After all, they are men, too.'

" 'Exigency?' he said, in amazement. 'I never thought we English were exigent.'

" 'Indeed, yes,' I said. 'After all, I have spent most of my life in London, you know.'

"So I was a Londoner, into the bargain. I probably knew many of the nobility. I probably had relatives engaged in high finance and politics. One had to remember the Norfolks. The poor boy looked a little downcast, and I am afraid that I felt no surge of Christian charity. I was thinking of the Famine that had killed so many countless people of my own race, with no help coming from the English. I was thinking of the English landlords, and the tax-gatherers, those most detestable of men. And, I thought of Cromwell, who had driven Irish men, women and children into the sea, and who had called them 'lice and nits.' My heart began to burn.

" 'But all in all,' said the other man, 'we are an Example to the World. The only civilized section of America is Boston, for instance, where live the descendants of English families.'

"I though of the old Mother Superior of a convent in Boston who, not many decades ago, had been trampled upon, to her death, by a mob of Bostonians, in her own convent, and the assault upon her nuns, and the violation of the altar, and the scattering of the Host and Its desecration. 'Ah, yes, Boston,' I murmured. I thought of the hate and contempt and disgust visited on Irish Catholic immigrants to Boston, the drawing-aside of skirts, the attacks on priests in the very streets, the frightened children in the little parochial schools, the basest labor which my countrymen had to accept in that Hub of Culture exported from England, the open insults inflicted, the scorn and derision. The Pale. Suddenly my heart burned for another reason than racial or religious: the hatred of man for man, the monstrous, inexcusable cruelty of man for his brother. My soul was filled with righteousness. And, it was then that God tested not only me, but the Anglican priest, Vicar Cutledge, who was also as stupidly righteous.

"The door of the compartment opened and we saw a very strange man peeping in on us timidly. He could hardly have been more than thirty, but he appeared much older, for he had a fine luxuriant beard, silky and black and slightly curling. He was tall and emaciated, and clothed very oddly, indeed, in black trousers which came only to his knees. From there, down to his peculiar boots, he wore white cotton stockings. He had on a long black coat to his knees, and even below, which flapped about him. He had a curious black hat. But what finally struck our attention were the large black eyes, shining and glimmering, the excessive whiteness of the skin beyond the beard, the delicate nose with sharp nostrils.

"All this would have been shocking enough to delicate Englishmen who had no prejudices. But the man exuded a most foreign odor, compounded of mothballs, alien food, and an un-British air. He had no gloves. His long white hands had a faint and constant tremor. He carried luggage that had a most exotic design on it.

" 'Please?' he said to our staring faces. 'Iss—it is nott——?'

"We were so stunned by this strange apparition that we said nothing. Then Vicar Cutledge instinctively moved from his far seat and planked himself right beside me! Newspaper, cane and all. We drew together, against this foreigner.

"He sidled through the door, starting as it slid to behind him, for the train had begun to move. He sat down as far from us as possible, no doubt feeling our animosity to a stranger, our instinctive, childish animosity. He looked at us for a long moment, we long-nosed, fair-haired, face-flushed young men. Then, pleadingly, he extended a piece of cardboard to us. 'Iss?' he murmured. Vicar Cutledge moved distastefully. I forced myself to glance at the cardboard. 'Ticket,' I said, loudly. 'Very well.'

"He pondered on that a moment, translating it into his own language. Then he nodded brightly and treated us to a radiant smile which showed excellent teeth, a most un-British expression. 'Goot,' he said, proudly. He was so proud that he could hardly contain himself. 'Englissh,' he said. 'Englissh. Like German, no?'

" 'No,' Vicar Cutledge said, coldly.

"Now, both of us were educated young men, and we knew German and French. We could have spoken to the stranger in German. But we did not. Almost knee to knee we huddled together. We British. We unprejudiced, tolerant, Empire-building people. Vicar Cutledge's cane caressed my knee.

"The stranger obviously did not understand that he had been rebuked, not only as a vulgar person who began a conversation without the minuet of propriety in a public carriage, but because he was also a foreigner. Vicar Cutledge hastily handed me a section of his newspaper, and I let the book about St. Francis fall to my side. We both buried ourselves in the pages. The train moved along the dreary gray walls of Liverpool, then began to clatter on its short journey to Manchester.

" 'Iss right? Mant-chest-arr?' said the stranger, anxiously, to our newspaper-covered faces.

" 'Manchester,' I said, sharply.

" 'Goot,' he murmured.

"We read. I was acutely conscious of the foreigner's presence, and his odor, which became a little intolerable in the close compartment. But we were both so afraid of moving—which would have given the foreigner an opportunity to talk to us or make a comment—that we endured the closeness and sweated. He kept his hat on, I noticed, after a furtive glance at him from the edge of the newspaper. What on earth was he? What was he doing in England?

" 'Peculiar—er—people coming to England, now,' murmured the Vicar to me.

" 'Quite,' I answered.

" 'A question was raised in the House, recently,' murmured the Vicar.

" 'Understandable,' said I, and may God forgive me.

" 'He is going only to Manchester,' said the Vicar. 'We go on to London.'

" 'Be grateful for small things,' I said, in my ugly, priggish voice. I had a warm fellow-feeling for the Vicar.

"The volume of St. Francis sharply nudged my thigh. Pettishly, I pushed it aside. I read the editorial in *The Times* concerning Russia's latest pogrom and thought of my Irish ancestors. 'Beastly,' I remarked to the Vicar, pointing to the editorial. 'One Should Do Things about This.'

" 'Quate,' he said, having deftly picked up my accent.

" 'We are civilized people in the world, now. I trust,' I said.

" 'Indeed,' said the Vicar.

"Unknown to us matching accent to accent, the stranger had moved right across to face us. He reached out and gently touched my knee. I started, let the paper drop a little. He was smiling, and pointed to my collar, and then to the Vicar's.

" 'Iss—iss?' he tried, helplessly struggling for the word.

" 'Priests,' said the Vicar, in the loud and rejecting voice used for foreigners.

"I did not like that. I did not consider him a 'priest.' I pointed to myself. 'Monsignor,' I said to the stranger with his great black eyes, his liquid, pleading eyes, and his alien beard.

"He smiled again, radiantly. He fought for words in his small English vocabulary. Then his eyes shone. He pointed at me with delight. 'Iss—'Igh—priest?' He indicated my Edge of Purple.

" 'Monsignor,' said the Vicar, chillily. 'Not a Bishop!'

"He had relegated me to a low class. I gave him one of my own chill looks.

" 'The next elevation,' I began.

"He gave me a superior smile.

"I was not High Church. I was not really recognized; I should never be recognized. In England. I was without the Pale. I was suddenly sick with anger, and remembrance, and furious that I should be angered.

"We stared bleakly at each other, the Vicar and I. We served the same God, and we looked at each other with superior distaste. The stranger was momentarily forgotten.

"The stranger said, in his wavering, guttural voice, 'Iss—men of Gott—Holy Iss Nam.'

" 'Priests,' said the Vicar.

" 'I am a Monsignor. Of the Holy Catholic Church,' said I.

" 'Men of Gott—Holy Iss Nam,' said the stranger, delighted.

"We could not understand his delight. We gave each other another bleak glance.

" 'Holy Catholic Church,' said the Vicar to me. 'On what authority——?'

" 'The Apostolic Succession,' I said. 'You do not have it. Yours is a religion formulated by man. Ours is the Church, founded by Our Lord.'

" 'There can be some controversy there,' said the Vicar, knowingly. 'We claim——'

"The stranger nudged me again. 'Iss—man, you—a boy. Gott——'

" 'Many are called but few are chosen,' said the Vicar, vigorously.

" 'Chote-sen?' said the stranger, bewildered.

"I was feeling a little less hostility to the stranger. I pointed at myself. (After all, the Vicar had used the King James Version of the Holy Bible.) I made a beckoning motion, pointing upwards clearly, then pointing to myself. The stranger looked bewildered again. Impatiently, I pointed outside the window, to the sky, then again to myself.

" 'Ahhhhh!' said the stranger, nodding, and making a rich sound. He folded his hands together.

"At least, I thought, he had some reverence for the clergy. But why had I not spoken in German—if he understood German? However, that reverence! I warmed to him a little.

" 'Holy Iss Nam,' said the stranger, and bent his head.

" 'Holy is His Name. The Holy of Holies.' The stranger understood.

"Then the Vicar leaned towards me and whispered, 'Not a heathen, apparently.'

"I had not forgotten I was without the Pale. But, as a cultured gentleman I could not show my displeasure, and as a priest I should be as meek and humble as my Lord. I struggled mightily with myself. And I said—and may God forgive me—'Not from the benighted, at least.'

" 'But these foreigners,' murmured the Vicar.

"We were again brothers, in snobbery, products of public schools.

" 'Ah, yes,' I sighed.

"The stranger was looking at me intently, with that beaming, brilliant smile of his. " 'In England,' he said. 'Iss in England——' He struggled for the right word. He fought for it. Then, desperately, he made a gesture of beating, of pounding, of cutting of a throat.

" 'No,' I said, understanding all the gestures.

" 'What does he mean?' asked the Vicar.

"I took some pleasure in my answer. 'He means we don't kill people here, in England, if they are different from us.'

" 'Certainly not!' said the Vicar, shocked. 'We are civilized people! But these foreigners! How can we make him understand that, outcast though he is, a foreigner, and peculiar, and not English, he is safe?'

"Safe, I thought. Where, in God's name, is it safe for a man to live? Safe from his enemy, his fellow-man?

"The stranger had subsided into himself. His hatted head was bent, his hands folded. He was murmuring strange words, rocking back and forth in his seat. My skin began to prickle with an awful warning. And then the train pulled into Manchester station.

"There was a crowd outside, eager, searching at all windows. Running back and forth, shouting to each other, pointing. Not for me. Not for the Vicar. I felt very lonely, and very young.

"Then the eager, searching faces were at our window, and joy lighted them. They raised their voices in loud exultation.

" 'Rabbi! Rabbi!' they cried, and pointed at the stranger with joy.

"The stranger rose, and waved his hand at his welcomers. He lifted his oddly designed luggage. He smiled at us, then pointed to the sky, then to himself.

"He said to us, gently and sweetly, pointing at himself, 'Iss—Russia. Pogrom. Iss coming to England. Rabbi.' He searched our confounded faces, and his own saddened and there were tears in his eyes. 'Iss—wife—kilt.' He made a stepping gesture from the floor, three times, to his thigh. 'Iss—child.' He held up three fingers. 'Kilt.' I knew a little Hebrew, and knew what he said when he said it: 'The Lord giveth and the Lord taketh away. Blessed be the Name of the Lord.'

"'What did he say?' asked the Vicar, whose face was dark red now.

"I did not answer.

"The rabbi watched us. Then he raised his hand, blessing us. 'Iss men of Gott. Goot men.'

"He left the train and we sat there and we did not meet each other's eyes. The rabbi was absorbed by his joyous people, who embraced him, and kissed him on his cheeks. He stood taller than all of them, radiant, happy. Free.

"Then the Vicar spoke, in a low voice. 'Not good. We. Not good at all.'

"'Not good at all,' I repeated. I looked at the Vicar. 'I am not an Englishman, either,' I said. 'I am an Irishman.'

"The Vicar extended his hand. And I shook it. In silence we completed our journey to London. We trundled along, in our desperate, guilty silence.

"We rode in silence, in the Pale of our inhumanity. A brother had spoken to us, a man of God, like ourselves, and we had rejected him. We had despised him. We had despised each other, and taunted each other.

"And so it will be, forever," said Monsignor Brant, "until man learns that no man is beyond the Pale of God. Let us know that, before we die. Before we die."

Chapter Eight

Rose, THAT NIGHT, remembered that she had once, when walking with her mother, seen a dusky-skinned man in a long coat and a turban. Curious children followed him, snickering among themselves and pointing.

"Now, Mama," said Rose to her husband many years later, "may not have been the gentlest of souls. But there was one thing she would never put up with, and that was insulting a man, or belittling him, or treating him contemptuously, because of his race or his color. 'He is as God made him,' she would say, 'and who are we to question God and ask Him why He had not created all men of one color only, and as alike as peas in a pod? And if he has a different religion from us, that is his affair, and between himself and his God. If his religion is not good, then it is up to us to show him his error, but not to persecute him for that error.' And so, when I went to bed that night I told Sir Oswold—I was still so afraid of God—that never in my life would I despise anyone for being what he was, so long as he was not a wicked man. I felt very virtuous as I fell asleep. It's not a matter of virtue at all, but human decency and understanding. At any rate, I remembered that about Mama, after Father Brant's story."

The next night Rose met a short, very fat old priest with a jolly face and cheeks the color of ripe pears, and eyes like blue grapes in the sun. He laughed a great deal; he appeared to enjoy life mightily. Moreover, he made instant friends with the parrot, a creature who destested everyone. The parrot, however, became quite maudlin over Father Ludwin, and insisted not only on giving him a prized monkey-nut but stood watchfully to see that the priest ate it. Father Ludwin did so. He carefully kept his face polite, though his mouth puckered. He said to them all about the fire, "You never tell your host that you do not care for a particular dish. Animals are especially sensitive when they offer a delicacy."

"What hae we here? A new St. Francis of Assisi?" chuckled Grandmother.

Father Ludwin chuckled in return. "A kind thought," he said. "Once I remember that a dog gave me a bit of rotten partridge. I took castor oil after that tidbit. And that reminds me of the 'demon lady' and her dogs. It was long ago, near Glasgow. Ah, what dogs she had. But I must tell you," and he sat down and smiled.

FATHER ALFRED LUDWIN AND
THE DEMON LADY

"I was a very downy priest, indeed, when I was sent to a largish hamlet not too far from Glasgow. It was my first parish. The hamlet, I discovered approvingly, was brisk, hard-working, responsible and independent, with a scattering of Protestants, mostly the large landowners who lived on their property and did a great deal, in brotherly love and mutual assistance with Catholics, to increase the general prosperity. In fact, I have nowhere found so Christian a kindness and understanding in my other parishes, where the Catholics and the local Protestants were customarily at each other's throats.

"The hamlet had already developed a machine-woven type of tweed which amazingly simulated the tweed woven on home looms. Moreover, it was less harsh and had less tendency to stand away from the body as if it had a dour life of its own and it would be—er—damned if it conformed to the confines of any figure. Consequently the tweed was much in demand in the Isles and the colonies and even in America, where gentlemen and ladies prefer not to itch violently, in tweeds, when the temperature rises slightly above freezing. This tweed was more pliant and complaisant and agreeable, woven in a spirit of intelligent compromise. The factory weaving it employed many men, and some women, at good wages, and had enlightened ideas as to the relationship between employers and workers. The product was cheaper than the usual Scottish tweed, for Glasgow was close at hand for shipping abroad.

"The hamlet had three good schools, one High Church, one grammar and one parochial. So cordial were all relationships that the Anglican priest, a Presbyterian minister, and myself took turns visiting the schools to deliver kindly talks to the pupils. I confess that my own were often couched in the loftiest language, which the children politely received, if with some bewilderment. But then, as I have said, I was young and downy, and convinced that I must never miss an opportunity to Enlighten and Edify the Young Mind, as the saying was then. I am afraid that I frequently bored the young people to death, but they had been rigidly trained in courtesy.

"While we were all so very cordial it was understood that none of us—Catholic, Anglican or Presbyterian—must encroach on the other's territory. It was an unspoken and gentlemanly agreement, but firm, I discovered. We sallied forth to the schools only when invited, and we visited each other only when invited. My dreams of a personal Apostolate began to wither. And then I discovered that my hands would be quite full enough with my own people. For my parish was near the edge of the hamlet, and quite rural, and the farmers were more prosperous than the majority of farmers in other places. The prosperity gave them much independence of mind, and there is nothing more independent than a Scotsman with a bank account and a private little hoard somewhere in the house, and a large joint of beef or mutton on a Sunday, or a large fat fowl. My countrymen are by nature cantankerous and inclined to irritability, and endlessly looking for what they call 'discussions' but which are really arguments, frequently bloody. They were, of course, all lawyers, for, as it has been said before, every Scotsman is either a lawyer or a deacon, or a wee minister.

"My people were all three of them, and they were all, without exception, bluenoses. This is not extraordinary among Scotsmen. While not averse, occasionally, to straying up the garden path, they don't enjoy it very much, and they hate it among their neighbors. The most fanatic of the bluenoses, naturally, were men who had dallied more frequently than others. And their wives, who were never deceived, hated the gay girls and ladies who threatened the warmth of the hearth, but, more than that, the shillings and gold pieces in the tea caddy or under the sugar or in the mattress. A Scotswoman will forgive a husbandly stroll, if not too flagrant, but she'll sit grimly on the family private hoard to be certain no part of it ends up in a trollop's skirt pocket. Adultery to a Scotswoman, I am afraid, is less a violation of one of the Commandments than a violation of the shillings and pounds in their hiding places. Perhaps this accounts for the fact that prostitution is a little less rife among Scots gay ladies than in other races. The lady of the house is usually the Keeper of the Purse.

"So, while I discovered sober husbands who sometimes found business in Glasgow, I found no girls in any quantity who were too beguiled by the hard and reluctant springtime to 'forget themselves' for a romp in the buttercup fields. They, too, were hard-headed. Love has always had a rough time in competition with savings, in Scotland. 'Throwing her cap over the windmill' rarely netted a buxom girl any cash, and there was always the danger of not getting a virtuous husband in the hamlet, for men do talk, you know, even Scotsmen. So virtue in Scotland is never too endangered, the virtue of chastity, of course.

"My parish was not too sure of me in the beginning, and I certainly was not too sure of myself. After all, it was whispered, my mother was a Sassenach, and I had spent more time in England than in Scotland. (How they found out these things I do not know, but a Scotsman, though he would deny it, is a vigorous gossip, especially in the hamlets.) They were afraid, too, that when I discovered the prosperity abounding everywhere I'd begin talking severely of tithes, and there is nothing a Scotsman hates more than a tithe, which makes him think of the English tax-gatherers. At least, that is what he says. But I knew, instinctively, that the whisper had gone about: 'Hae a watch on the new pastor. He's but a lad, and lads are improvident.' So, while I was eloquent in my pulpit on the needs of the Church and foreign missions and perhaps another school, and the propagation of the Faith, I was uncomfortably aware that the women's purses were tight-shut and the men had buttoned down their pockets. I was vexed, at first, for these were fat people. Later, I used more devious means to obtain cash. Did I say devious? I was wrong. I had to learn brutal tactics. But that is another story.

"There was a landowner of impressive property on the outskirts of my parish. My women parishioners immediately informed me, on my arrival, that the landowner, a Scotswoman like themselves, was a 'besom,' which is not a complimentary term and can be used to indicate a bad-tempered woman, a girl who laughed and danced too much, a prostitute, or a lady of openly questioned virtue. This particular landowner was the latter. She was Jezebel incarnate, a lady of such vices and such mischief as to make my people wonder why Satan did not appear in a cloud of fire over the mansion and carry off the poor female in flames and with a stench of brimstone."

A Catholic lady? Father Ludwin asked at once. Aweel, if ye hae a mind broad as the Atlantic. Earlier she had come with her husband to attend Mass every Sunday, and showered (disapproval here) gold coins and banknotes in the plates, and could be seen at Confession every Saturday. "A fair fanatic," one of the ladies assured Father Ludwin, "and always with the nuns about her. But," they added darkly, "it was nae for long. Not mair than six months. It was her that drove the old priest to an early grave, and it's nae wonder, with her carryings-on, after her husband died. She wouldna see him after that, nor the good Sisters." And then, not more than a month after her husband had died, she had launched on a career of great wickedness. "Full of mortal sin, an' a' that, Father. Mortal sins a penny a dozen."

The lady's husband, through a series of deaths, had inherited the broad lands, the moors, the fine meadows, the glorious house, the cattle and the sheep, the fat fields, and the title. It was unexpected.

He had been only fourth in line for the title, and a barrister in Glasgow, and his lady, though poor, had been gentry in her own right, in Glasgow. Oh, there had been great doings in the mansion on its small hill, among the vast old trees, before young Lord McLeod had—died! All the local gentry had been constantly invited, and there were fiddles and dancing, and many came from Glasgow to spend weeks. It had ended when George, Lord McLeod had—died. It was some time before Father Alfred's young ear heard something peculiar in the intonation of "died." He was too puzzled before.

What was the "mortal sin"? The ladies cast down their eyes and delicately referred the priest to their husbands. Their husbands, though cautious, were more explicit. Mortal sin—constant adultery among the local gentry. No Sunday Masses attended any longer. No Easter duty. No more frolics on the green on Whitsuntide, to which everybody had been invited. Blasphemy. Curses on the "auld Faether" when he presumed to attempt to visit her. "It's a hard face she'll have on her now," the new pastor was informed. "A face like the divil, himself, all wild-like, and furious."

"Children?" asked Father Alfred. There were knowing smiles and shakings of heads. Aweel, now, the lord and his lady had been married but a little time. And nae doot her master, Satan, had informed her of methods to avoid the contretemps of a bastard in spite of her beddings-down with the local gentry every night. "One mon is always after another. She'll nae see too much of one; she must hae changes for her diviltry and amusement."

Her age? The women shrugged. The older spitefully guessed it as at least thirty. The younger generously reckoned it was much younger, perhaps not more than twenty-three. Appearance? The older women shrugged and talked of demon-faces. The younger wistfully suggested incredible beauty. "She'll hae that, Faether, for who else could draw the men to a living divil in human flesh?" She was rarely seen any longer. But always, every night, the mansion was aglitter with lights and alive with laughter and music. And then, at midnight, when decent folk were abed, the lights would finally go off. Father Alfred mused who was moving around, or awake, to see lights go off at midnight.

Servants? Aye, that. Three auld women from Glasgow, and Protestants who never had a civil word nor stopped to speak in the shops or on the streets. Tall, silent women in pony-carts, who ignored the most pleasant of greetings. "Divils, theyselves, Faether, nae doot." There were gardeners by the day, from the hamlet, who were paid well, and never saw the mistress. They affected to be much frightened, but the pastor decided this was pretense or the wages too high.

Lady McLeod slept all day, long after her lovers had left, and she arose only when the sun went down. It was rumored that she walked within her high walls, alone, wringing her hands and weeping, before her guests arrived. She walked, and walked always, in the forests, in the glades. And the gardeners reported eerie wailings and cries. Lady Martha, no doubt, was accosted by devils in her solitary walks, and received her daily orders from them. "And she never attends Mass, not even on Easter Sunday?" asked Father Alfred. Heavy shakings of heads. One farmer, more informed than others, suggested Black Masses, and blessed himself, shuddering.

Father Alfred was young. And avidly curious. He called it concern about a Christian soul that apparently was quite damned. Or, possibly, mad. But what had driven her mad, then?

The fanatic bluenoses talked quite openly to the priest of setting fire to the mansion and driving out the "divils." Arson, said the priest sternly, was not approved by the public authorities. Then, he had some inspirations. He would make queries elsewhere. He had now become curious as to how and why the young lord had "died." Was Lady Martha another Lady Macbeth?

He went to the Chief Constable, who was not Catholic. Father Alfred had had enough, for now, of talk of Satan, Black Masses and devils in the green woods and copses and in the fat fields. He had seen the holdings from very afar, rolling gently, vividly vernal, and he had seen the distant wide, high walls which hid the great "hoose," and the shut gates, and had heard the constant howling and snarling of many watchdogs prowling the territory within the gates. The menacing sound had come to him on the winds from the west, an ugly clamor as of jackals.

The Chief Constable was a thin, sinewy and "black" man, with a sharp grin. He was much older than Father Alfred, but even the downy priest was not as unsophisticated. So Father Alfred had to press his lips tightly together to keep from smiling when the other man immediately informed him, with a worldly gesture, that he was no "believer," but "belonged to the agnostic school." The priest doubted very much that Mr. Marshall could define agnosticism, but he gave Mr. Marshall the expected, and delightedly received, admonishing frown, feeling himself considerable of a hypocrite while doing so. He must be very careful not to let the Chief Constable suspect for an instant that the young priest knew him for a most unworldly man, if competent in his duties.

"And what will be your business, sir?" asked the Chief Constable, unable to keep from his "agnostic" voice the inevitable reverence for and the secret envy of the Scotsman of the clergy.

The priest looked about the brown and dusty office reflectively. "It will be the matter of a certain lady," he said. "A lapsed Catholic, perhaps. Lady Martha McLeod."

"Ah, that one!" exclaimed the Chief Constable keenly. "A rum business, there. I hope ye hae no listened to the folly of your own congregation, and their tales."

"Tell me, yourself, please," said Father Alfred. He paused. "I prefer to come to authentic sources and not to listen to rumor."

The Chief Constable expanded, regarded him with favor, glanced about his office, puffed, and became pompous. Nevertheless, he told a meticulous story, free of wandering details.

The young lord had taken over the estates and had brought his young lady to the mansion. "Ah, there will be a rare beauty, that one," said the Chief Constable. "Lovely as a rose in bloom. Nae wonder the lassies aboot detested her on sight, and their mithers, and the unmarried spinsters. Her age? Not more than twenty-two, even now, and it may be less."

George, Lord McLeod had been a shy and retiring young man, in his middle twenties, a little shorter than his beautiful wife, fair, thin, delicate of feature and hand and voice. Though indubitably a Scotsman, and a lover of the countryside for all he had been a city man, he had some characteristics that offended both the local

gentry and the people of the hamlet in general. He would kill nothing, no matter the necessity. The estate had been overgrown from
neglect. "The auld laird had been doting," said the Chief Constable,
and the gardeners had taken advantage, and had engaged in open
poaching, which they called hunting, in broad twilight after their
day's work was done.

The "pesties," too, had flourished. Weasels, rabbits gnawing on
young trees, foxes, squirrels—all. And cuckoos decimating the broods
of the song birds, and rooks in such quantities in the great oaks and
larches that they were a curse to all the farmers in the neighborhood.
But the young lord would permit no shooting of any of them, no
hunting whatsoever. He had been known to say that God had blessed
animals before He had created and blessed man, and that the earth
was as much their home as it was the home of fallen man. Many
had been the arguments between him and the old priest, whose own
tiny garden was being destroyed by the "pesties." Man, said the old
priest, had been given dominion over all the earth and all the animals. "But not to kill them wantonly," said the young lord, with
obstinacy. "Only man destroys his own species. The fox, the wolf,
are more moral than man, for they commit no mortal sins." Sometimes the old priest shouted; the young lord was invariably respectful,
but stubborn. He was also a vegetarian. When he and the young
lady had guests there would be fish on the table, and good egg-
dishes, but nary a joint, a roast or a fowl. He ate sparingly, refused
the fish, ate the eggs, and consumed abnormal amounts of vegetables.

There were many deer on the great estate, and the servants reported that the young lord would go out in very early morning to
watch them, and the birds, and the "pesties," through field glasses.
When the hard winters came there was food scattered about for all.
It was no wonder, then, that the animals appeared to love him and
would graze on the very lawn near his windows or gambol on the
broad windowsills and build their nests near the wide oaken doors.
Their voices filled all the land with a clamor of sound, which George,
Lord McLeod found delightful, far more delightful than the voices
of his fellow-men, whom he appeared to fear a little.

It was young Lady McLeod who engaged in festivities, and who invited the guests. Gay, charming and vivacious ("There must be French blood, aboot," said the Chief Constable, sighing), she became a favorite in almost no time. It was noted that she adored her husband, and that the adoration was returned. In the very midst of a lawn party they would inconspicuously seek each other out for a handclasp, for a smile, and, behind some shrubbery, for a quick kiss. But then, they had been married only a few months and so they could be forgiven for the "display."

Though George would do no hunting, and showed no interest in horses and sports, he was a general favorite, for he was kind, gentle, thoughtful and full of charity. He was also very pious. His young wife possessed these traits, also. The old priest, an obstinate man himself who therefore naturally disliked obstinacy, occasionally fumed at George concerning some of his more unorthodox opinions regarding the lower animals, but had no other complaint. The young lord rebuilt the church "from top to bottom," imported fine Italian bells, and built a new little rectory from the ground up, with a gas stove and gaslights! He paid the salary of the old priest's elderly sister, who kept his house. He put more fireplaces in the convent, and kept the coalbins filled, and showered fine linen handkerchiefs on the Sisters and other acceptable gifts, and renovated the parish school. There was nothing that the old priest could even hint of that was not almost immediately done, and done lavishly.

But it was reported that Lord McLeod—"and even meself, I thought it blasphemy," said the Chief Constable—firmly believed that all animals, even the "pesties," had souls, souls unlike those of men, but souls for all that. "Look at St. Francis," he would say. "He called the birds his brothers and sisters. He was not using fancy; he was speaking a fact." The animals were totally innocent; only man was evil; only man could fall into serious sin. And did not Jesus love innocence above all things, He so innocent Himself?

The old lord had had a gun-room, filled with every conceivable kind of lethal shooting weapon. George, being a thrifty Scotsman, had the butler, who was an ardent hunter and gunsman himself, keep the guns in fine repair, and oiled. George often hinted that he would sell out the guns one of these days, a remark that shocked the old butler, who had been with the old lord, also. This was all brought out during the inquest——

"The inquest?" asked Father Alfred, sharply.

"Aye. But I was coming to that, sir," said the Chief Constable, with some reproof.

"Was there some suspicion that Lord McLeod was murdered?" asked the priest, who was a devotee of Sherlock Holmes. The Chief Constable observed him for a few minutes, then he said, "But I was coming to that, sir." Father Alfred sat on the edge of his chair, impatiently.

The gun-room was always kept locked, and George kept the key and gave it to the butler only when necessary for the guns to be oiled and cleaned and the room dusted. No one else ever entered the room.

The servants, and young Lady McLeod, discreetly did not tell George that there was much illegal hunting, and poaching, on their property during the autumn months. But somehow, he found out. Perhaps he had discovered a wounded deer, or a dead bird with shot in its breast. He expressed the first rage his wife and servants had ever heard from him. The grounds were posted and penalties listed. Carrying a large club, which everyone doubted he would use even on the most flagrant of poachers, he being such a gentle young man, he would walk for miles each day over his property, and some- times at night, with a lantern, looking for any rascal who would dare defy the posting and dare to kill. Lady McLeod, who always remarked that her husband was of a delicate constitution, approved of the day-walking, and often accompanied her lord. But the night- searches alarmed and then terrified her. Yet the hamlet was a peace- ful one; there had not been a single prisoner in the gaol for over five years, and those who had occasionally occupied it before had been men who had looked upon the wine until it was too red, indeed.

So Lady McLeod knew that George was in no danger from any poacher or hunter at night, they being so much more clever in the forests than he, a city man. But she did fear that he would stumble over some rock, or fall into the deep brook that ran through the property, or have his head knocked off by some overhanging branch.

Or, that he would be lost in the darkness. She would go with him on the few nights he ventured out with his club and lantern, but this ended when the doctor discovered she was "in an interesting condition."

"But I thought there were no children," said Father Alfred.

Indeed and there were not, said the Chief Constable, grimly. The poor young lady had lost her child, a fact not generally known.

Ah, there were such parties at the mansion and such dancing! The young lord and his wife were having a secret celebration, and everyone was curious, and no one was told. It was evident that they were overjoyed at the very thought of a child. The doctor testified to this fact at the inquest. Father Alfred, who loved tales of inquests, moved farther to the edge of his chair.

Last September, early in the month, almost a year ago, George and his wife were sitting together before the fire, he reading, she with her embroidery. They heard a distant shot. George sped out of his chair like a bullet, himself. The old butler had heard the shot— and never had anyone come so close to the mansion as this—and he hurried to his master, who was already pulling on his jacket, his lighted lantern and club on the table beside him. It was a dark and moonless night. His lordship might have an accident in the darkness. The butler and Lady McLeod pleaded with George, but as usual he was obstinate. He would confront the poacher; he would seize him by the scruff of the neck and haul him to the magistrate. He was all fire and resolution, this small, fair and gentle man, his face flushed with anger. "There'll be no murder on my land," he said. "Stand aside, Andrew."

The very thought of George seizing a poacher and dragging him some miles to the magistrate made even the alarmed young lady smile, and the butler smiled. He would not listen to their arguments. He even shouted. This brought Cook, herself, from the upper regions, with her hands under her apron. She was a sensible woman, but George would not listen to her either. He ran out of the house, shouting his threats. Lady McLeod, in her condition and fear, burst into tears. Cook made tea for her and tried to console her. The butler opened a fresh box of biscuits, and stirred up the fire. The master would find no one. He would be home shortly. But the young lady pulled aside the draperies and looked at the black sky and wept about her lord's inadequacies in dealing with rough terrain. So Cook and the butler remained with her, plying her with tea, and finally, as an hour became almost two hours, with brandy. And they testified to this at the inquest. They had not left the poor girl for a moment.

The clock in the vaulted hall struck midnight. The butler gave Lady McLeod more brandy; Cook pressed her back into the chair. The girl was insisting on going to look for George, herself. She implored her servants to go with her, a shocking thought, in the darkness. And an early autumn wind had arisen, loud and authoritative at the doors and windows, and rain was now falling heavily. There was no doubt that George had gotten himself thoroughly lost and that he was wandering, somewhere, in the dark and cold and wind and rain. Lady McLeod had every window lighted. She commanded the old butler to pace on the lawns, waving a lantern. (He was the only man in the house now.) At three in the morning, overcome with exhaustion, fright, and brandy, the young lady fell asleep in her chair. At five, the butler, drenched and battered, went into the hamlet to gather up men willing to search for the young lord.

Many were willing, including the few policemen. They began to search the forests and every inch of the estate for the young lord, beginning at the very gray dawning. Somewhere, they were certain, he was lying helpless, probably with a broken leg, for there were bad patches of rock and broken ground on the terrain. They shouted in the windy twilight of the morning, rain lashing their faces and putting out their lanterns. They wandered, searched and called for hours. It was nearly noon before they found George, Lord McLeod. In deep brush. Dead. Shot. A pistol from his own gun-room was in his hand and there was no sign about that any other person had been in the vicinity.

The bullet, a single one, had entered his right temple, and his face showed powder burns. He had been killed at almost immediate range. The police and the searchers had already trampled up the ground and had scattered fallen leaves. One of the policemen, the constable, had then gone ahead to "warn" the young lady of the death of her husband. The rest of the men began the dolorous march back to the mansion, carrying George's soaked and bloody body. When they arrived they discovered that her ladyship, on being informed, had uttered one terrible cry and had collapsed, and a servant was already dashing for the doctor in a pony-cart. She had lost her child a few hours later, and did not emerge from her stupor for twenty-four hours. Her only relative was an aunt in Glasgow, and a telegram had been sent. George had only distant cousins, all female, scattered throughout Scotland. They all eventually arrived. The mansion teemed with them, with the old priest and the Sisters, and the multitude of George's friends among the gentry in the vicinity.

It was reported at the inquest that Lady McLeod had said, when awakening from her stupor: "Who would kill my George, my darling, so cruelly, so mercilessly?"

She had been very calm and very pale, and she had said to the Chief Constable and the priest, as she lay in her bed, "Who would murder my George, and why?"

They hurriedly assured her it had been a terrible accident, but she had shook her head and repeated over and over, "Murder, murder, murder."

She never cried after that, but her soft and lovely face became fixed and wild. She came quietly to the inquest and insisted that her husband had been murdered. George could not bear even to look at a pistol or any other firearm, and much less would he touch one. He had run out of the house only with his club and pathetic lantern, to catch the poacher and bring him to justice. He had, she said, been deliberately lured to his death, for everyone knew his habits and his hatred for hunters and poachers.

It was the butler who had discovered that a pistol, a rather ancient one, was missing from the gun-room, and he had reported this to the Chief Constable. No, he had not had the key, but the gun-room was unlocked. He had found all this to be true a few hours after George had been brought home dead. The key to the gun-room was found in George's pocket.

There could be only one conclusion at the inquest: Death by misadventure. George, unknown to his butler, cook and wife, had stopped impulsively at the door of the gun-room and had taken out a pistol and had forgotten to lock the door afterwards in his haste. He had then gone struggling about in the darkness, threatening and shouting, and had fallen and the gun had gone off and killed him.

"Murder," said Lady McLeod, steadfastly, looking at the jurors. "George would never have taken a gun under any circumstances. He never even thought of them. You have heard this from the lips of Andrew, himself. The key in George's pocket means nothing. He always kept it on him, for fear it would be found by the gardeners, or some careless person. He would have preferred to kill himself than to kill another, even in self-defense. George was murdered."

She sat in the box, wild-faced but quiet-voiced, her gloved hands clenched together, her black widow's veil falling over her shoulders. "Murder," she repeated. All thought of her disastrous state, the loss of both husband and child, and looked at each other uneasily, with one thought: that she had become mad.

"But I didna think that mesel'," said the Chief Constable. "Lady McLeod's face was wild, indeed, but quiet, and she spoke with absolute authority, as if she knew, beyond any shadow of a doubt."

So the Chief Constable had questioned her gently. Had Lord McLeod any enemies? No, none that she knew of. A male relative to inherit the title, estates and money? No. Had he aroused hostility in the hamlet, or perhaps even in Glasgow? No, all had loved George. She answered each probing question clearly and without trembling. On what, then, did she base her dreadful suspicions that he had been murdered? She told the jury.

Before recovering consciousness on that terrible day she had "seen" George. He had come to her with blood on his face and neck, and he had been white and stiff. He had told her that he had been murdered, coldly and deliberately, in the forest, but he did not know, as yet, his murderer. She, his wife, must find that murderer and bring him to justice.

"Now," said the Chief Constable, "it is known that we Scots are fey, and Lady McLeod was a Scotswoman, for all she had had an English education." The jury listened to her seriously. The Chief Constable had resumed his questions. Not a juryman doubted that

she had indeed seen the ghost of her husband and that she had
heard his message that he had been murdered. But these were modern days. So the verdict of death by misadventure had been reluctantly given. Lady McLeod stood up, looked slowly at the jury, and
had left the room.

It did not end there. Lady McLeod summoned Scotland Yard,
itself. An Inspector had come, had inspected the site of the murder,
had questioned everyone concerned, had consulted with the Chief
Constable and the jurors, the servants and the butler. He listened
thoroughly to the tales of George's eccentricities concerning animals,
and his indictments of his fellow-men for their wanton cruelty
against the innocent. Could such a man, finding a killed animal,
have lost his head and turned on the discovered hunter, who had
then shot him in self-defense? The Chief Constable considered this
question. No. It was not possible. His lordship could never have
threatened anyone with a pistol, not to mention using one. Besides,
the butler and cook had testified that he had taken up only his club
and lantern and had then run into the night. They had heard the
door slam after him, seconds later. He could not have stopped at
the gun-room and seized the pistol, even if he had been the sort of
man to do such a thing or even think of it. The guns had been
cleaned two weeks earlier, and the door of the gun-room locked by
the butler, himself, who had then delivered the key to his master.
There was no possibility that the room had remained unlocked. So,
only one man had had access to that room in two weeks and that
man was George, Lord McLeod, who never entered the room.

"The only evidence," admitted the Chief Constable to the Inspector, "that his lordship had been murdered was Lady McLeod's insistence that she had seen her husband's ghost and that he had told
her."

The Inspector did not believe in ghosts. He studied and restudied
the evidence, reading for hours. He sighed, shook his head. Death
by misadventure. He went to the mansion and repeated this to her
ladyship. And she had said, "Murder, murder, murder."

Her conviction of this was so fixed that she discharged all the
servants, including the old butler, and had engaged three grim

women from Glasgow and had employed gardeners who did not live on the premises. Somewhere, she believed, lurked George's murderer, perhaps a servant, perhaps a workman, perhaps one of the gentry, their friends.

Then, astonishingly, with her husband "hardly cold in his grave," as the hamlet said with shock, she resumed her parties and her festivities, and the mansion was lighted to midnight, and there was dancing, and fiddlers. And, always a man, a different one, who remained behind in her ladyship's bed. A scandal. For the first time whispers went about that her ladyship knew more about her husband's death than she had admitted. Her insistence that George had been murdered, her summoning of Scotland Yard, had been "a blind," to divert suspicion from herself. The Inspector, in Glasgow, heard of these rumors and quietly paid several more visits to the Chief Constable. Unknown to Lady McLeod, he had her whole life investigated, and her husband's former life. Nothing came of it. And the scandalous doings at the mansion continued, and increased in fervor and gaiety.

"And that is all?" said Father Alfred.

"All," said the Chief Constable, firmly.

"And what do you think?" said the priest.

The man filled his pipe slowly and carefully, struck a wooden match and lighted the pipe. "And what do I think?" he said, musingly. "I think his lordship was murdered."

"By Lady McLeod, or someone she had hired to do the job?"

"Nay, nay," said the officer, emphatically. "Not Lady McLeod, and ye'll be doin' well, sir, not to listen to the women. 'Demon lady!' Ach, they are soft in the head. And jealous and mean and gloatin', always lookin' for scandal. Niver was a pretty lass that the women were not down on her, with the lies and the tales."

The Chief Constable glared challengingly at the priest. "It's the agnostic I am," he said, "and I dinna believe in—things. But I do believe that the young laird's soul did come to her ladyship and tell her the truth, that he was murdered in cold blood."

Father Alfred was no "agnostic" himself, and he was decidedly fey in spite of the Church's admonitions against "superstition." The

Church, after all, did acknowledge apparitions, though with certain strictures.

"But why should anyone murder Lord McLeod?"

The Chief Constable shrugged, looked darkly at the priest. "That I dinna know. But for certain, he was murdered. I hae seen the truth on her ladyship's puir lovely face, and in her eyes. She didna lie."

Father Alfred was sure of that, himself. He also was afraid for Lady McLeod, who had "fallen away" from the Church, had cursed the old priest who had wanted only to comfort her, and who had riotous festivities at the mansion almost every night, and who was an adulteress. So Father Alfred went to his Anglican colleague, who said he had arrived in this hamlet three months after his lordship's death, and therefore knew nothing. Father Alfred went to the Presbyterian minister. "Aye," said Mr. Russell, "I believe his lordship was murdered, and sae do we a'," he added. "Her ladyship?" He shrugged. "It's nae in a mon's power to know a woman. I hae niver seen her. And what would be your interest, if I may ask?"

"Her soul," said Father Alfred, sadly.

What a sorrowful story, he thought, later, but not without some excitement, which he sternly interpreted as a love for justice and the saving of Lady McLeod's soul, which was now blackened with many mortal sins. Was she a murderess? Father Alfred delicately approached the nuns, who overwhelmed him with indignant denials, especially the old Sister Superior who had once been Lady McLeod's confidante. "Your language, Sister," Father Alfred murmured to the old lady, who had become vehement and hostile.

"I'll nae hae a word spoken against the puir lassie," cried the Sister Superior, "for all she willna see me now! It's her heart that is broken. Mad? It is possible. It is your prayers she is needing, Faether, and nae your curiosity," she added, with some shrewdness which made the young priest blush. So Father Alfred, followed by the sparkling eyes of the Sister Superior, went into the small neat church and prayed for Lady McLeod's soul. After his supper that night, he reread his favorite book concerning Sherlock Holmes. This was another occasion of "the locked door," without doubt. But, what was he thinking? Scotland Yard, itself, had affirmed the verdict of death by misadventure.

The next day was soft and golden in its autumnal hinting. Father Alfred thought of Umbria as he stood in his little garden and saw the wide and gilded light. How sharp were the scents of mowed grass, of ripening fruit, of harvests!

He brought out his bicycle, and tied a prudent bag to the handles, containing a small but sturdy club, a large flannel cloth and sundry tidbits from his own larder. His short but muscular legs moved rapidly and within a short time, though he was covered with dust, he arrived at the high walls of McLeod House. He leaned the bicycle against the granite structure and surveyed the enemy territory. The walls were topped by formidable iron spikes at least a foot high, and Father Alfred suspected that broken glass was sprinkled between them. While he was reconnoitering slowly he heard a rushing sound and then the insane howling and barking of dogs on the other side. Father Alfred knew all about dogs, and he said aloud, but absently, "Quiet, there." He was not in the least astonished when the howling and barking subsided to confused whimpers, and questioning murmurs.

He found a place where two spikes were missing, and he studied the wall. Easy! Tying his bag to his coat, he found apertures for his feet and began to climb the wall; the dogs on the other side questioned him. "I know what I am doing," he admonished them, and they murmured respectfully in reply. "Just be patient," he said. The dogs yelped a little. He climbed carefully, studying the mortar and the stones. His head rose above the wall and the dogs were ecstatic. "Nice lads," he said to them. "Just be patient." As he had suspected, there was shattered glass on the top, and he removed it with his thick flannel cloth. The spaces between the spikes: would they be sufficient for his plump buttocks? He decided it would be a tight fit, but when was the world not a tight fit for everybody? He swung his legs over the wall and sat on the top of it, like a short, stout cherub. The dogs below laughed and smiled at him; big dogs, black and gray and shaggy. He opened his bag again and tossed down bits of meat and fowl and scones, with jam, and a few bones, and watched them scramble with joy. Not one dog was smaller than a good-sized wolf.

He loved all animals. He knew that food was a mere introduction to them, and that afterwards they wanted more information. So he waited until the dogs swirled below him again. "It's just," he said reasonably, "that I've come on an errand. I hope you understand, laddies?"

"Certainly," said the oldest dog, who now spoke for all. Father Alfred barked back in subdued tones. The oldest dog gave an order, and all the animals, at least fifteen of them, lay on their bellies and fixed their eyes on Father Alfred seriously. "I think we'll wait awhile, for the mistress," said Father Alfred, addressing the leader.

"It is only courteous," responded the old dog. "After all, we have a duty to do."

"And so do I," said Father Alfred. He looked about him. Never had he seen such beauty before. Green lawns, like ruffled silk, rolled away from the walls and mounted in a stately fashion to a long, low, gray mansion, almost smothered in oaks and larches. Here and there flower beds flamed with red autumnal flowers, and here and there a tree was almost strangled in scarlet vines. Beyond the house the land dropped away to kitchen gardens and arbors. Bees hummed in their extreme hurry; a bird or two questioned the young priest. The silence was wide and sunlit, and full of peace. The distant windows glowed with gold.

"A person could be happy here," said Father Alfred to the old dog.

"Indeed," he responded. "We are happy. All, but the mistress."

"For whom we must wait," said Father Alfred, tentatively.

"For whom we must wait," said the old dog, quietly.

"Ah, well," sighed the priest. "I understand your position. But these stones are infernally uncomfortable."

The old dog snuffled in sympathy, and his companions snuffled also. But the old dog was firm; there was no moving him. He was apologetic. But one must stick to one's responsibilities. How else could the world survive?

"Quite right," said the young priest.

He heard a sudden shout of female laughter. The dogs got to their feet immediately, and stood at attention. The oldest moved off majestically to where a girl was standing in the shade of an enormous oak.

"Why are you barking at my silly dogs?" she asked, in a fresh young voice.

"We were not barking; we were talking," said Father Alfred.

"Pardon me," said the girl, with mockery. "It sounded uncommonly like barking."

"Then you do not understand animals," said Father Alfred. "They all have a language of their own, and it is our stupidity that we have never taken time to learn it."

"Well, well," said the girl. "What have we here? Another St. Francis?"

"Not at all. But I've lived with dogs all my life, and sometimes their conversation is very interesting."

Father Alfred peered at the slim figure under the deep shade of the trees. The old dog said, "We must have patience."

"I have all the time in the world," Father Alfred responded.

"What are you two talking about now?" asked the slim, vague figure.

"We are having patience with you," said Father Alfred. He wished the girl would emerge from the blue-black shade so that he could see her clearly.

"Indeed," said the voice, somewhat coldly.

"For instance," said the priest. "I'd like to see you and talk with you. I don't care for lurkers."

"Neither do I," said the shadow. "What are you doing, lurking on my wall?"

"Waiting to talk to you."

"I don't talk with priests."

"Very unfortunate. For you, Lady McLeod. I assume you are she?"

"Yes. And who are you? The nappy-priest who has just come?"

Father Alfred considered this affront gravely. "I am twenty-two years old," he said. "Hardly an infant."

"Elderly," the shadow agreed. There was a silence. The old dog looked back and up at the priest, imploring more patience. The priest nodded. The bees hummed. The birds asked each other what was going on. The wind loitered softly.

"Aren't you going to invite me to descend?" asked Father Alfred. "Why don't you?"

"Your dogs have a duty. Unless you give them the word they'd be honor-bound to tear me to pieces if I jumped down."

The girl was silent a little. Then she said in a queer, soft voice, "You do know about animals, don't you?"

"God's darling creatures," said Father Alfred. "He must have a great sense of humor, and fantasy, and joy. After all, He made the raucous parrot with its ridiculous colors. He gave dogs a sense of honor and humor. He gave dignity to the cats, and He gave laughter to the rooks. He decked the caterpillar with the rainbow, and gave whimsy to the robin. He told the noble elephant about monogamy and faithfulness, and informed the tiger how to use his stripes to protect him from enemies. He explained safe mating principles to the hedgehog, and taught the eagle how to train her young. He——" Father Alfred stopped, for he had heard a sound of weeping.

"You sound like George," said the young female voice, smothered in sobbing.

"Perhaps," said the priest, "George wanted me to come to you."

"I think," said the oldest dog, "that she will give me the order to let you down. I apologize——"

"No apology is needed," replied the priest. "I understand perfectly."

The girl said to the oldest dog, "Down."

"You see?" said the oldest dog to the priest, and lay on his belly. The other dogs obeyed his word.

The priest carefully climbed down the inner wall. The dogs wagged their tails and watched his progress. The oldest dog trotted to him and kissed his hand meekly. "Fine laddie," said the priest, rubbing him behind the ears. "I wish men were as good."

"Do stop that barking," said the girl, and she emerged from the shadows. "It isn't quite clerical."

She stood before Father Alfred, considerably taller than he, and slender; much too slender in her light blue dress which swept the

grass. She was like a blue flower, swayed by the wind. Her golden
hair lay unbrushed on her shoulders, like a cape; her eyes were blue
in the tight pale face with its beautiful white lips and sharp little
nose. There was about her an aura of restlessness and agony. Then
her face became convulsed; it took the priest a moment or two to
understand that she was trying to smile at him and that she was not
just grimacing.

"How do you do?" she asked, primly.

Father Alfred rubbed his buttocks. "I seem to have missed brushing off all the glass," he said.

The girl contemplated him a moment or two, then laughed aloud
freely, and the dogs rose up as a man and laughed with her. Father
Alfred touched the sore spot, then examined his finger. There was
no blood. So he laughed also.

"Why didn't you ring the bell?" asked Lady McLeod.

"If I had done so, would you have let me in?"

"Of course not," she agreed. She examined him carefully with her
eyes. "You don't look very formidable." She hesitated. "Would you
like some tea?"

"I'd be delighted," said the priest. "Strong, of course."

She led the way towards the house, and he could see how very
thin she was as the blue dress blew about her. The wind lifted her
long golden hair, and revealed the haggard outline of her white
cheeks, the marks of gray agony about her lovely mouth. So this was
the "demon lady" of the hamlet, this suffering girl, this tormented,
lost girl. The dogs followed, commenting among themselves. The
oldest trotted at Father Alfred's side, touching his hand occasionally
with a cold nose. "It is very sad," said the dog.

"I can see that," said the young priest.

"But what should trouble mankind, which rules the earth?" asked
the dog.

"I trust," replied the priest, "that you will be spared the knowledge."

"Are you two talking again?" The girl glanced over her shoulder.
"We have just made some sorrowful comments," said the priest.

"George," said Lady McLeod, going on again with her head bent, "always talked with animals. Just as you do. Do you really talk?"

"Yes, certainly we do," said the priest.

The grass was like velvet under the sole of one's shoe. The wind was full of spice. The sun was a blessing, and a promise. The long gray mansion lay under its blue tangle of shadow, and the door was open, and a harsh woman stood on the threshold.

"Maggie," said Lady McLeod, "tea in the morning-room, and oat cakes with strawberry jam, and some slices of pound cake."

"I didna hear the bell," said Maggie, staring with affront at the priest.

"I didn't ring it. I climbed over the wall," said Father Alfred, with a human desire to discomfit the woman.

"Over——" she began, and then stared at the affectionate dogs. Lady McLeod led the way through the stone-vaulted hall with its stained-glass windows and to a sunny room beyond, fresh with prints and gay with hand-woven carpets. The oldest dog had followed as a matter of course, and then lay down over the priest's boots and contemplated him with gratitude. "I hope you can help her," he said. "But, what is the trouble?"

"God has blessed you," said the priest. "You will never know, for you are not a murderer."

"She has the kindest heart," said the dog, after considering a moment. "She would never injure any living thing."

"That I know. Now," said the priest.

"I should like to know what you two are rumbling about," said Lady McLeod, who had seated herself at a little distance.

The priest studied her candidly. "We have just informed each other of the goodness of our hostess," he said.

The girl's mouth opened slightly, then closed in its pale carving of silence.

The tea was brought by the stiff and haughty Maggie, who departed with a clatter of heels. Lady McLeod filled a fragile cup for Father Alfred, then, after a little hesitation, she filled one for herself.

"Why did you come?" she murmured.

"For one reason only: to know you, to find out if I could help you."

The girl put down the silver pot and stared at it. "No one can help me but myself," she said. When the priest did not answer she looked at him quickly, with a blaze of blue eye.

"You know all about it!" she cried.

"I know what I have heard," he said.

"George was murdered!" she cried again.

"I think so, too," said the priest. "I want to help you discover the murderer, and bring him to justice."

The girl put down her cup and lay back in her chair, a flaccid figure of exhaustion, mute and despairing.

"I have tried for a year," she whispered. "Almost every night."

"Through mortal sin?" said the priest.

She opened her eyes at him, wide and brilliant. "I have committed no wrong," she said, slowly and quietly, "except the deadly sin of hatred, and the sin of anger. I still commit them. I shall never have peace until I find George's murderer."

The priest looked down into the cup. He believed her. Then, she had not committed adultery, in spite of all the tales.

"And when I find him," she said, very softly, "I shall kill him, with my own two hands. There'll be no judge or jurors; there'll be no hanging. I shall kill him, myself."

She put her hands over her face, hands as fragile as porcelain, and almost as transparent. "You never knew George. No one knew him, except me. He was a saint."

"And a saint wants you to find his murderer? And kill him, yourself?" The priest was greatly alarmed.

The girl dropped her hands. She shook her head. "No. He wants me to find the murderer, and deliver him to justice. But, the law's delay! He could escape."

"He will not escape the justice of God," said Father Alfred.

The girl was silent, but her white mouth twisted in mockery. "Tell me about it," the priest pleaded. "I know the story; I know the verdict at the inquest. I know to what you testified, that your husband appeared to you after death——"

The girl's head dropped on her breast. "I saw George again," she murmured. "He still did not know his murderer. And, he could not forgive, and so he is not at peace. I do not know if he is in Purgatory; he did not tell me. But he is not at peace. He is afraid for me. He is afraid that eventually his murderer will—that I will come to love him, and marry him. George's murderer. And so, a few months ago, George told me that no workman of the hamlet, and no servant, had killed him, and had plunged him, unconfessed, into death and into eternity. It was one of our friends. Here, close by, within sight and hearing."

"Oh, it could be illusion," said the priest. "You have suffered so much."

The girl shook her head so that her yellow hair flew like a whirlwind about her.

"You do not know!" she cried. "Since the moment we came here there have been the men——! The young, unmarried men! Many of them, trying in one form or another to make love to me! Look at me now, old and white, but still they come!"

The priest looked at the young pale face, fixed now and furious, but still incredibly beautiful.

"They knew I'd never divorce George, and could not," said the girl, in a low and muttering voice. "So, one of them decided to kill him, to leave me free, so that I could marry again. Someone, it must be, who wants me, and wants George's money, someone who is not too rich, someone who is unmarried. So, I have my dinners and my dancing, and each time I search out a different man, and I give him all he wants to drink, and more, then I whisper for him to stay. And he stays, when the others are gone, drunk, in his cups. And then I talk to him, gently, lovingly, saying I did not love George, and that I love him. Can you not understand?" she cried desperately. "One of these nights a man will confess, when he is drunk enough, and with the promise of my bed before him, and marriage! He will tell me he did it for me!"

Frightfully disturbed, the priest stood up and began to pace the floor, thinking. The girl watched him, clenching and unclenching her hands. The dog watched him, anxiously.

Father Alfred finally stopped in front of the girl. "Has it ever occurred to you, my lady," he said, sternly, "that there is always the morning, and that the man will remember what he has confessed? A man who has killed once will kill again. He can only die once. You are in awful danger."

The girl laughed loudly. The dog trembled. Father Alfred did not move. "Danger!" she cried. "Do you think I'd let him live until morning? I'll kill him immediately! I am not afraid of guns, as George was!"

"You will then become a murderer, yourself," said the priest. "Then, you will never see your husband again. You will never know God, or possess Him. Do you think your husband wants that for you?"

"I will kill," said the girl, quietly. "I will kill the man who murdered my dear George, and killed my own life. There'll be no trial for him."

She looked suddenly and fiercely into the priest's eyes. "There has been no man who has already confessed to you?"

"If such had occurred, I could not tell you," said Father Alfred.

She smiled strangely, and nodded. "Then, he has not confessed."

She stood up. The priest did not move. "Does Holy Mother Church mean nothing to you, Lady McLeod?"

"Nothing means anything to me, not even God, so long as George's murderer is free and safe."

"You have indeed committed a mortal sin," said the priest. "You have murdered already in your heart."

She lifted her hands restlessly, then dropped them. She smiled, and it was a smile not quite sane. "When I have killed him, Father, I will confess to you, and you will absolve me."

The priest did not answer. He picked up his hat and looked at it. He said, "I should like you to promise me something, my lady."

"No," she said.

"I should like you to promise me," said the priest, "that when, and if, you discover this man you will tell me and the Chief Constable and leave it in our hands."

"No," said Lady McLeod.

The old dog looked anxious and accompanied him to the gate. "Is there a way I can help you?" he asked.

The priest looked down at him seriously. "I do not know," he said. "I really do not know. In the meantime, I will pray."

The dark autumn came, and the thunder of the winds, and the sky was low and murky. The winter came, with snow and gales, and long icicles hung from the roofs. In a few weeks it would be Christmas. The children skated on ponds and practiced carols, and Father Alfred quarreled with the organist, who disliked Plainsong and wanted more flamboyant music for the holy days. The nuns were fractious, having bad colds, and Father Alfred was depressed.

No one had confessed murder to him in the Confessional. Father Alfred now knew his parish very well. The gentry who were Catholic were coming to Confession more regularly as the holy days approached. But no man confessed murder. Father Alfred singled out those young, unmarried men among the gentry who had not come to Confession at all, and wondered, night after night. He saw them at Mass, but not at Confession. He considered each one, carefully, particularly those who did not come to the Communion rail. And then he practically came to the conclusion that there was no murderer at all, except in Lady McLeod's disturbed mind, and in the mind of the Chief Constable, and that Lord McLeod had indeed died the death of misadventure. So Father Alfred prayed for the soul of the young man, dead in his youth and love, and put his "ghost" out of his thoughts.

There were only twelve young men, unmarried, in their late twenties or early thirties, among the Catholic gentry families, the county families. Father Alfred had been invited to the homes of their parents, or older sisters, or aunts, for family dinners. It had been a horrible idea to him that any of these fine young men could have murdered, and the priest was becoming ashamed of himself more and more each time he was invited to their homes. There were some older bachelors, precise and womanish, whom the priest discounted as having ever shown any interest in the human female at all. An uneasy thought came to him that there were gentry in the county who were not Catholic, and would therefore never come to him for Confession. If one was a murderer he might never be discovered. In some manner the priest managed to gain some invitations to these gentry, through his Anglican colleague. His hosts and hostesses, and their young, unmarried sons, were the souls of serenity and teeming with good works, and had no objection to a "Roman." A lesser number of the gentry were Presbyterians, and Father Alfred, in three months, had contrived to meet these also, if a son, unmarried and youngish, was on the premises. He had never met any finer people.

A few days before Christmas he was called to give the Last Rites to a very old man. A snowstorm was beginning and he pedaled industriously on his bicycle to get home soon. He found the Chief Constable in his warm and tiny parlor, whistling merrily to his lovebirds in their gilt cage. "Aha," said the officer, grinning, "I could have saved ye all the trouble if you had asked me, but you did not. The Inspector and mesel' were there before ye." He laughed amiably at the priest's abashed expression. "Great minds," said the Chief Constable at last, and generously, "run in the same channels. There's not a lad that was not scrutinized and investigated. But you had the good dinners, did ye not, and it's the fair favorite you are in the county now."

He chuckled, and shook his head. "And what's this tale I hear of ye talking with the dogs? Aha. All gets out in the town. There's some who say you are fey and some as says you are soft in the brain. Are ye still reading Sherlock Holmes, eh?"

The young priest colored violently, and lost his temper. "It was you who said that Lord McLeod was murdered!" he exclaimed.

"And so he was," said the Chief Constable, soothingly. "But I thought in your rambles you may have come across something. Eh?"

"No," said Father Alfred. "Tea?"

"Ye hae nothing stronger?" asked the officer with a wink.

Father Alfred got out his precious bottle of old brandy and two small glasses. The two men sat in front of the fire, and thought. Then the Chief Constable said thoughtfully, "My cat. She's fair fey, hersel'. And what did the dogs tell you, young sir?"

Father Alfred peered at him suspiciously, but the officer was truly interested, so the priest said, "They're worried about their mistress. See here, I don't think I really can talk to the dogs——?"

But the Chief Constable shook his head vigorously. "I talk with me cat, and she's a wise one. When I think it over, later, I think I am mad. But I am not. Nor are you." He paused. "So the dogs are worried about the lassie. So am I." He looked at Father Alfred. "She'll be getting a bullet, hersel', if she goes on like that."

"Like what?" asked the priest, astonished.

The Chief Constable winked again, seriously. He held up two fingers. "I have been a policeman for longer than you hae lived, laddie, and I'm nae fool, if I say it mesel'. Nor is the Inspector. We know what she's up to, and, it seems, so does your highness."

Father Alfred was so distracted that he refilled the two glasses. The Chief Constable held up three fingers now. "Three of us," he said. "It's a wonder how you got in the mansion, so mild you look, and young, and pink in the face. And plumpish. But I've heard the tale."

He stood up and stretched. Then he was not smiling. He said, "I am the Chief Constable, and all know my job. The Inspector is not here. But there has been talk of your sidlin' aboot. A fair mystery it is to all policemen how the talk travels, with nae sign of human communication. Young sir, keep to your church and your auld folk and the young ones. Leave the investigations to me." He shook a lean finger in the priest's face. "I had a lad your age; killed in India. It will be nae pleasure to me to find a bullet in you, some dark morning, when you've been prowlin'."

"I don't 'prowl,'" said the priest, with angry dignity.

The Chief Constable sighed, shook his head, and departed.

All the anxieties and worries returned to harass Father Alfred. He had written several times to Lady McLeod, begging her to see him, and she had not replied. He did not go again to the mansion, for that would have put a severe strain on the dogs' courtesy. One did not do that to friends. He heard fresh stories of the goings-on at the mansion, each one more scandalous, and finally he was obliged to warn his flock of the serious sin of scandalizing for the sake of scandalizing, and out of lack of Christian charity.

The mansion was dark on Christmas Eve and there was no party. A considerable portion of the Protestants in the hamlet disdained to celebrate Christmas, a matter over which Father Alfred and his Anglican colleague shook dismal heads. But New Year's was a different affair to all canny Scots, for gifts were not required except the one of a bit of dried herring on entering a house. The young year rolled on, and it was wretched February, with dark and streaming skies, loud and battering winds, and long, cold nights.

On one particularly bad day, the priest encountered the grim Maggie in a fish shop. She refused to recognize him at first, for all his smiles. Then he sidled up to her and said in a low voice, "How is Lady McLeod? I have been worrying about her."

The woman snorted, seemed about to say something, then closed her big gray mouth tightly. The priest waited. She shrugged. "Daft she is," she said, and for one instant the priest saw dread and pity in the hard little eyes. "It'll nae be long——" She turned away abruptly and marched from the shop.

Father Alfred could not sleep that night. Shortly before midnight he pulled a coat over his nightshirt, went out and stared in the direction of the mansion. He could see the far gleam of many lights, raying out against the low and gloomy sky. It had stopped raining, but the air was heavy and dull, with a feeling of the pestilential. The priest, sighing, returned to his low fire, waiting for drowsiness. Then, shivering a little, he did fall asleep, and the last ember winked out.

He began to dream. He dreamed that there was a hard knocking on the door, and a crying, but when he went to it and opened it there was no one there, not even a shadow. He dreamed that he went back to the fire. And the knocking began again, thunderous, and he started awake, the sound loud in his ears, and the feeble crying. But when he ran to the door he recalled his dream of the knocking, which probably had no existence at all except in his sleeping brain. If it had not been for the dim whimpering on the doorstep he would not even have opened the door, though his hand was already on the handle. It sounded like a desperate child crying, or a dying man. He flung open the door.

The great gray-and-black shaggy dog of the mansion was there, the master of the dogs, the leader. When he saw the priest he rose on his hind legs and flung himself on the priest's chest, as if imploring, and the priest instinctively caught him in his arms and held him tight. Then he was filled with a sense of disaster. The lamplight outside, faint though it was, showed that the dog's paws and legs were dripping with blood. "Poor laddie!" cried the priest, and holding him as if he were a wounded brother, he drew him into the house for examination. The dog resisted, whining, his fierce eyes rolling with entreaties, his tongue lolling.

The priest examined one of the front paws while the dog's whimpers became frantic. He saw at once what had happened. The brave animal had actually managed to scale the high granite wall about the mansion; the brave heart had ignored the stabbing glass on the top. And then he had leapt down the other side and had come racing for the priest.

Father Alfred did not question how the dog had known where to find him, or why he had come. He said, loudly and calmly, "Yes, yes, I'll come at once. Be quiet, friend. I must dress a little, and then get my bicycle." "Come, come quick!" whimpered the dog. "She is in terrible danger!" "I know," said the priest, his heart pounding, as he pulled on his trousers and then his boots, and then his coat.

He ran to the door, with the dog beside him, then halted, looking about the room. The poker! It was heavy, short and broad. He went out to the shed and got his bicycle, and the two, the man on the light vehicle, and the dog, rushed side by side to the mansion, like two silent and desperate shadows under the ominous sky.

There was not a soul about, not even one of the policemen. There was no time to look for any of them, Father Alfred knew, but how he knew he did not know. He used what breath he had for prayers. And the dog ran as silently as death beside him, fleeter even than himself in spite of the bloody paws, the torn and wounded paws. The priest looked down at the dog, and said, "I will need you. You are better than an army."

They reached the wall. The dog ran along it, however, to a gate, and waited, panting loudly in the dark silence. It was almost too black to see anything, but the dog's eyes were gleaming and vivid, as is the way with animals at night. Father Alfred tried the high iron gate, but it was locked. So he began to climb it, the poker dangling awkwardly in the pocket of his coat. It was harder to climb, actually, than the wall itself. The priest heard a scrabbling sound below him, and he called down softly, "No, wait. I'll open the gate for you, if I can." He was dripping with sweat halfway up. He could see the upper windows of the mansion, and all was dark. He gave a single thought as to why the other dogs were not howling, and then he knew. The leader had ordered their silence. When he reached the top he could hear the crowded breathing of them, and see the glimmer of their eyes below. Now he had a time with the spikes, but at least there was no glass. He tore his coat, his sleeves, his trousers, getting over the spikes, and one of his hands had begun to bleed.

Then he was over and climbing quickly down. If only he had a lantern! He had to feel in the deep darkness around the lock. Ah, it was a cunning bolt, not a lock, and a bolt that could be reached only from the inside. He pulled it back with all his strength, for it was thick and strong, and the gate creaked open a little. The big dog was at it in an instant, thrusting it wide open with his mighty shoulders. Then he was racing towards the house with the dogs at his heels, and among them, stumbling, raced Father Alfred, with the poker swinging in his hand.

The mansion was totally dark, except for a long vertical sliver of light between draperies on the first floor. Father Alfred ran to it, tried to see within the room. He caught a glimpse of a white wall, the edge of a portrait, a rosy shadow of the fire. He tried the window, and it was locked. He ran to the door, and it was locked, also. Then he went back to the window and shattered the glass with the poker.

There were two thunderous sounds and a whine near his ear, and then the howling of a dog, which had apparently been hit. A gun, then. Father Alfred scrambled over the low sill of the window and was about to drop into the room when he heard another sound. The opening of the outer door, and then a faint stream of light, and in that light the shadow of a man. "Get him!" he shouted, wildly, to his friend the big dog, and the dog flew like a huge moth to the man, and there was a desperate scream. Father Alfred, satisfied, dropped into the rich room.

Lady McLeod, in a long white gown of silk and lace, lay face-

down on the red carpet of the room, motionless, her golden head
dropped between her outflung arms. Groaning, the priest ran to her
and bent over her, and fearfully turned her about. Her face was
livid, her eyes staring and rolled up, her tongue partly protruding
from her open mouth. There were purple splashes about her throat.
She had been strangled. Praying, the priest felt for her pulse, though
without hope. It was just perceptible. She was still alive. He raised
his voice in a loud shout for help, and then he drew a deep breath
and pressed his mouth to that of the girl and blew his breath into her
throat. Vaguely he was aware of voices, screams, lights, the yelping
of dogs, but all his attention was on the girl. He pressed her ribs in,
released them, and blew his breath of life into her. He caught
flashes, through the corner of his eye, of whirling skirts and cries for
the police. He heard a door banging, then the rattle of harness, then
the pounding of hoofs. Someone, he thought with detachment, has
finally gone for help.

In and out, breath upon breath, pressure slowly but firmly on the
delicate ribs. He had learned this method at school; it had saved
many lads fished from pond and stream. He concentrated all his effort, all his silent prayers, all the extreme exactitude of which he was
capable, to saving this life. Were the ribs beginning to contract and
expand a little, on their own? He did not stop to see. He breathed
in and out. And he prayed mentally.

Then the cold and swollen lips under his began to warm and stir.
He gave himself a swift glance at the girl's face now. The ashen
color was being replaced by a whiter and clearer shade. The staring
eyes were closed, and the golden lashes were fluttering. The priest
continued his ministrations, until the girl started convulsively and
strained for breath of her own, and caught it, and expelled it. She
did this several times, and then the priest knew she would live. He
tried to rise. The room swung about him, and he fainted.

From far off, after a long time, he heard a voice say, "It's all over,
laddie! Here, drink this." There was a cold glass at his lips, and he
obediently drank the brandy. "A brave laddie," said the Chief Constable's voice, and another man answered, "Aye, and he's a' that, sir."
Another masculine voice said, "Don't drown him or strangle him with

that, Bob. Let him swallow slowly." Father Alfred swallowed slowly and gratefully, his eyes still closed, for a heavy weight seemed to be lying on them. He did not know where he was and it was not until he had swallowed all the brandy that he could remark to himself, "What is all this? Where am I?"

He opened his eyes painfully to a glare of many lamps. The room —what room?—appeared to be seething with men and women, though actually there were only the Chief Constable, three policemen, the doctor, and two of the servants. Then the priest recalled everything, and tried to sit up. He was lying, he noticed vaguely, on some long couch covered with green velvet.

He tried to cry out, to speak. The Chief Constable put his hand on his shoulder, and Father Alfred fell back, weakly. "Her ladyship is in her bed," said the Chief Constable, "with one of her women with her (who is a nurse), and under a drug. She'll be as right as rain, laddie, before another day is up. And it was you that saved her life!" he added, admiringly. "How did ye get on to it, at last?"

"I didn't," said the priest in a croaking voice. "The dog came for me, and told me." He started. "The poor, brave dog! Where is he?"

The doctor said, "Bound up nicely, and sleeping, I trust, in his kennel. So he came for you, did he? Because he could not get into the house himself, and knew himself helpless against a gun. And there's some that calls them dumb animals!"

"The man?" asked the priest, after a moment, and with fear. The Chief Constable's face darkened with hate and rage. "The dog was holding him like death, with the help of the others, when we came. It's young Laurance Highland."

The priest could have wept. Laurance Highland, only son, only child, of Sir William and Lady Highland, the child of their middle age. The Highlands, vigorously practicing Catholics, devout people, good people, kindly and simple and charitable people. They so loved their son, the handsome, gay, laughing son, twenty-six years old, who had never injured a living thing in his life, not even a fox or rabbit, until the night he had killed Lord McLeod, for love of his wife.

The priest had to hear it all, even while he told himself over and over, I'd never have believed it! He was the only one I never really suspected. Not Laurance, who in a state of mortal sin had received Holy Communion piously every Sunday, and who had confessed in the Confessional only to the lightest of the venial sins. Why had he done this? To direct any suspicion anyone might have had of him, if anyone had suspected at all?

Apparently not even Lady McLeod had suspected him very much, for so she had whispered when they had gotten her into her bed. But he was unmarried, and young. He had also treated her with respect and deference and kindness, unlike the others who were actively wooing her. However, on this night, she had confronted him as she had confronted others, with drink, then with soft words, then with pretended love. And he had responded, and almost with pride had told her the truth, thinking that for what he had done she would fall into his arms! Into his drunken, groping arms, with exclamations of love!

They had been alone in the drawing-room, after all the guests had gone and the women were asleep high in their rooms under the roof. Lady McLeod, laughing, and with hate and murder in her heart, had disentangled herself with some excuse, and had run to the gun-room for the very pistol which had blown out the life of her husband. She had returned here, to find Laurance sprawled sleepily, but smilingly, on the green velvet couch. And she had told him that she was going to kill him.

He had, apparently, pretended to be sleepier and drunker than he actually was, for he had let his face become empty and slack and had raised himself a little on the couch, looking directly at the gun pointed at him. He was slender and athletic; from that half-reclining position he had hurled his body like a missile at the girl, and she had staggered back under the impact and had dropped the gun. He had then seized her by the throat, in his terror for what he had revealed, and had begun to strangle her thoroughly to death when Father Alfred had smashed the window. He caught a glimpse of the priest's head, dropped the girl to the floor, picked up the gun, and had fired. Believing that he had hit the priest, because of the sharp howl of the dog, he had run to the door, and had been seized by the great dog.

"He has confessed it all, and is now in gaol," said the Chief Constable. "And he will be hanged. There's nae fight in him any longer, now that his parents know, may God have mercy on the puir souls."

"But how could the dog, that big brute, have known, and have gotten over the wall so quickly, and brought the priest?" asked the doctor, marveling. "It's not possible, of course, but the dog must have known, watching his mistress through the window, that she was in danger, long before Laurance had confessed, pridefully, to her in his drunkenness, long before she had gone for the gun, long before Laurance had taken her by the throat. It's not possible——"

"It's a' that," said the Chief Constable, with solemnity. "We hae the evidence."

The doctor shook his head again, marveling. "We shall never know," he said.

"It is an evil thing to call an animal a brute," said the other. With pity, he gave Father Alfred another drink of brandy, then, on second thought, gave one to himself and one to the doctor, and, after a pause, to his three men. They let the priest sip alone for a while, and wondered at his thoughts. He was thinking of how good the Highlands had been to him. It was they who had built the parochial school in the time of the "auld Faether." It was they who were so generous for the missions. It was they—— Tears filled the young priest's eyes. He had never loved any woman but his mother, his three sisters, and one old aunt. In the abstract, he knew that men sometimes killed for a woman; he had never encountered the actuality before. Yet, though Laurance had killed for Lady McLeod, he had attempted to kill her also. The lust to murder, then, was stronger than love.

Man was utterly dark in his soul, vile in his thoughts, treacherous of speech and action, more beastly than any poor beast, not to be trusted. Yet One had died for him; One had considered him worth saving.

"Lord, have mercy on us. Christ, have mercy on us—Lord, have mercy," whispered the young priest, while the tears ran down his face and he bent his head and clasped his hands.

He came the next day to see Lady McLeod, ringing the gate-bell and being admitted at once by the policeman on guard. But first he went to see his friend in the kennel, and was greeted by the bandaged one with love, laughter and pride. "We saved her," he said. "We two." The priest kissed the large shaggy head and rubbed the rough ears. "No, you did," he said. Then he went to call on her ladyship, who was sitting up in her bed, her throat bandaged.

Her eyes began to brim with tears when she saw him and she held out her hand to him, and the woman with her discreetly left the room. But Father Alfred did not take the offered hand. He did not listen to the painfully whispered words of gratitude. He waited until she had finished. And then he looked into her eyes, sternly.

She bowed her head and clasped her hands, and whispered, "Bless me, Father, for I have sinned. I accuse myself of attempted murder——"

She made her full, if halting, confession, and then a perfect Act of Contrition. And the priest absolved her of her sins.

"Still," said Father Alfred to his friends about the fire, "had she not done what she did the murderer would never have been caught. She was a brave woman. But, as St. Paul has said, we see through dark glasses now—— She married one of George's friends two years later, and they had four fine children."

"And the good dog?" asked Grandmother.

"Oh, Lady McLeod gave him to me, in her gratitude, and we were fast friends until he died of a great age, in my arms. I never had a better or more understanding friend. And I sometimes wonder—— It is possible that George, Lord McLeod was right, after all."

Chapter Nine

THE NEXT NIGHT FATHER WEIR, a tall lean Scotsman, said, "I often think of the tale of Father MacBurne and the Doughty Chieftain, of which he told us last year. He was a despot, if I remember, that chieftain, but a benevolent one. One wonders which is worse. A benevolent despot believes that he is wiser than his people; a cruel despot despises them. Yet, in their effects, they are the same.

"I once knew a cruel despot, and he was, of course, the unhappiest of men, for it is not in the nature of man, unless he is a devil—and there be so many devils!—to oppress his fellows.

"Ian MacVicar was a cruel despot, but he was a man with a soul, and so he was desperately unhappy. He was also proud and disdainful. He had little love in his life. But I must tell you of him."

FATHER THOMAS WEIR AND THE PROBLEM OF VIRTUE

"I was a very young and naïve priest, and shy indeed, when I was sent to my first parish in the Highlands," said Father Weir. "I hae a bad chest then, and it was thought it would do me good in the country air near the sea. My mother filled my valise with heavy woolens she had knitted and woven, and sent me off with two

pairs of thick socks on my feet, and two pullovers on my chest. I was
as thin as an eel, but my clothing fattened me. I smelled of cam-
phorated oil, for my mother, God rest her soul, was a believer in it,
and so I was sent off drenched in it under a layer of red flannel—
also on my chest. I remember my face well, over all that, pinched
and flushed, my eyes trembling with shyness.

"I was all atremble, too, at the thought of a parish of my own,
with no superior to rescue me. My parish was poor; all Scottish
parishes were poor in those days. There were thirty Catholic families
in a hamlet of some six hundred others. The others were Scots Presbyterians. Their occupation was sheep, and trading, and fighting
for amusement, and drinking, when the puir souls could afford it,
for the nights were long and cold and there was not even a Punch
and Judy there or a pantomime to bring merriment to the folk. Oh,
but there were some braw fights on a Saturday; all things served,
particularly religion. But Sunday was a death, spent in the kirk or
sleeping or recovering from the raw whiskey festivities of the night
before.

"The Scotsman, if a Catholic, does not approach his religion in
the spirit of joy and fulfillment as does his Irish brother. He is as
dour as his Presbyterian neighbor, and so I knew I was in for it,
my father having been a Highlander. When he beats his breast at
Mass he does a hearty job of it, not the little tap of the Englishman.
It sets him to coughing for the rest of the celebration. The choir
groans; it does nae chant. The Highlander, in the Confessional, is
scrupulosity itself, to the point of eccentricity. I think few Scots
Catholics are in hell; they would bore the devil, himself, with a
constant recitation of their sins."

The hamlet was even worse than the boyish priest had expected
in his more depressed moments. It hung almost on the lip of a great
cliff, and all the houses were of dull gray stone with thatched or
slate roofs, and all the tiny cobbled streets, five of them, circled
tightly about each other. To the right of the hamlet the brown and
heathery hills rose, gloomy and harsh, and here the sheep grazed.
Even in summer, when Father Weir arrived, it was very cold, the
sun rarely shone, the sky massed itself over the hamlet in heavy dun

blankets. The odor of the sea and the pines never left the harsh and blowing air, and added their own particular somberness to the locality. The prevailing colors were black, gray and brown, not to be lightened by the little flower gardens struggling to survive in that weather. The only center of gaiety was the pub, uninspiringly named "The Thistle." All in all, it was far bleaker than any hamlet in Scotland which Father Weir had ever seen. It was very clean and very, very poor. It was also fierce.

The "wee kirk," named, of course, St. Andrew's, was so small as to appear toylike, and clean and bleak inside. Even the high altar was bleak, and the crucifix had been cleaned so often that all the gilt had disappeared and only bare wood remained. The statues were tiny, the homespun linens rough if starched within an inch of their coarse lives. The floor was stone, the wooden pews narrow and incredibly uncomfortable, the kneelers unpadded, as was the Communion rail. There was but one stained-glass window. This one, however, was strangely beautiful and expensive. "Squire MacVicar hae done that," said the priest's off-and-on housekeeper, a fat middle-aged lady who was co-owner of the local pub with her husband. For a moment the priest was cheered. A parishioner rich enough to present the kirk with a window like that not only had taste but was pious and kind-hearted. The housekeeper ruined his hopes by observing that the Squire was not Catholic.

"Then, why hae he done it, Mrs. Logan?"

The housekeeper shrugged and did not answer. Being Scots, himself, the priest knew that he would receive no more information from this source. He might be able, within a year or two, to discover why the Squire had been so generous and so tolerant, but he doubted it. Three were more likely, picked up from many sources in fragments.

The rectory consisted of one fairly large room which was to serve as parlor and study, a bedroom hardly large enough for a sheep dog to turn about it, and a kitchen with brick walls and a large fireplace on which all the cooking was done. The fireplace was the only source of heat for the whole miniature cottage, and so if he was not to freeze to death promptly the priest would have to permit the kitchen door to be open at all times. This did not make for confidential chats in the parlor, and Father Tom suspected that Mrs. Logan would have her ear cocked all the time. There was nothing a woman loved more than to hear something spicy and juicy, preferably scandalous. The Scots might be reticent about solid information but they were gossips.

The walls of the cottage—that is, the two rooms outside the kitchen—were of grim dark wood, which were not lightened when the young priest hung his large crucifix where a fireplace ought to have been, and his rather bad daguerreotypes of his parents and a very bad and crude lithograph of the Sacred Heart of Jesus. The furniture of the parlor consisted of one uncushioned settee (near where the fireplace ought to have been), two straight chairs as still as a frozen Scotsman, and a bare wooden table. There was also a rickety bookcase, with a few moldering books, mostly in Latin. Father Tom put his own collection of books beside these relics, and tried to feel less depressed.

His family was poor, even for Edinburgh folk, but they had at least indulged themselves in some comforts, such as fat feather beds. The young priest discovered that the bed in his rectory was made of planks of wood on which a straw mattress, prickly and thin, had been laid. The blankets felt like haircloth. He immediately sat down and wrote his mother to send his old feather bed and some blankets. He had another thought; he searched for sheets. There weren't any. So he added sheets to his list. Towels? Three brown articles resembling sackcloth, so he added towels to the list; he hoped his mother would not be too alarmed for her lamb, so he wrote, "It is not a rich hamlet, and I do like plenty of linens and little comforts." He hoped his mother would include some of her cakes and that his father, who was a thoughtful man and a past Highlander, would send a bottle of whiskey. He would need it on the raw nights.

His reticent parishioners did not call on him the first night, but Mrs. Logan informed him that they had "seen to" the larder in his honor. Brightening, for he had an excellent appetite, the young priest examined the larder. It contained a smallish ham, a joint of mutton, a bag of brownish oat flour, three glasses of marmalade, a sack of potatoes, another of turnips, and a box of slightly wilted brussels sprouts. There was also a goodly sacking of the perpetual oatmeal, a box of very dry and stiff kippers, a dozen eggs and one fresh fowl, a tin of cheap tea, and a big lump of butter. The parishioners, Mrs. Logan informed the priest with pride, would keep him in groceries—with some prodding from herself—and he "wouldna starve." Thankfully, thinking of his stipend, the priest expressed his gratitude. Then he noticed two fat and handsome bottles of the best Highland whiskey. "Ah, that," said Mrs. Logan, with more pride. It was a gift from Squire MacVicar, who didna touch the stuff himself, he being a teetotaler; he had bought it from the pub at a handsome price.

Squire MacVicar was taking on exciting and delightful qualities. He would, said the young man, call on the Squire almost immediately. Mrs. Logan shook her head. "I wouldna do that, Faether," she said. "He doesna like priests and Catholics." Then why? Mrs. Logan shrugged again, tolerantly. Now the Squire was mysterious, and like all Scots the priest loved mysteries.

"He's a hard man, but a saint," said Mrs. Logan, with unusual loquacity. A Scots Presbyterian saint was a unique idea, and the priest pondered on it while he ate his plain but plentiful meal of oat cakes, tea, a slice of ham, marmalade and a bit of seed cake which Mrs. Logan had contributed to the general welfare of the priesthood.

Ten people, all very old men and women and too aged to be very curious, came to Vespers that long evening. If they saw their new priest they gave no sign of it. The priest returned to his cottage. It rained coldly and heavily that night. And the rain came in along the eaves and about the ancient windows and left puddles on the flagged floors.

"There's nae much ye can do aboot it, Faether," said Mrs. Logan resignedly. "The cottage is very auld."

"Why havena the men repaired it?" asked Father Tom, forgetting his self-deprecatory shyness in his indignation.

"Aye, Faether, they have. But it's an auld hoose. It doesna leak, the roof, but only in the westlin wind."

Father Tom thought of himself in this cottage all through the howling north winters, with the westlin wind. He had no doubt

that winter winds blew steadily from the west in this latitude, with
a touch of polar ice added. Mrs. Logan, who had a very snug house
indeed, herself, informed him that the men "hae been sae busy" with
the sheep and the lambing. Father Tom, feeling unusually in command of a situation, because of this fine new indignation he was ex-
periencing, said, "It's nonsense you say, Mistress Logan. The lambs
are all mutton now." The men had had plenty of time before he came
to mend the roof. He knew what had detained them: the cost. He,
Father Weir, had A Chest, and he wouldna die for a' them, because
of a pound or two. The warmth in his cheeks and his body did not
diminish and he almost strode to the little tool-house behind the
church, searching for a ladder. He found it, brought it to the cottage
and climbed it and inspected the steep roof. Ah, just as he had
thought! Many thick slates were missing, at least fifteen of them, in
strategic places. He examined the others; sound. His father built
houses from the ground up, and he had taught his son the art of
laying slate as well as mortaring brick walls.

He went down the ladder briskly. It was a fine morning, cold,
clear and brilliant, with a touch of autumn in the air—and a cold
clear wind blowing sharply. There had been twenty people at Mass,
most of them old, but he had said a number of Masses when he
and one altar boy and the sacristan had been entirely alone. He
literally marched into the kitchen and demanded a barrow and asked
where the slate dealer had his shop. Mrs. Logan, who had confided
only last night that the new priest was "aye young and no bother,
and I'll manage," was taken aback by Father Tom's doughtiness,
which was really only as thick as the pastry on a tart.

It seemed that the gentleman who sold slates, bricks, stones and
mortars had his shop down Bannoch Road, on which the kirk and
the rectory stood. "Take the left turning, Faether," said Mrs. Logan,
rather shocked to see the priest trundling a barrow through the
streets. Father Tom set out, the barrow making a wonderful rumbling
on the cobbles. There were very few people on the street; the men
were at work, the women about their houses, the children helping
or playing in the small gardens. Yet Father Tom had the peculiar
idea that every stiff lace curtain quivered as he passed each house,

and he was quite right. The Presbyterians were startled and shook their heads. The Catholics were embarrassed and curious. The bleak and bare little street was filled with the cold sunlight, and there was a nasty wind whisking about. Father Tom was grateful for his mother's two pullovers under his habit, and even for the red flannel—saturated with camphor—on his chest. It came to him suddenly that despite the rain last night, and the chill today, he hadn't coughed since his arrival. He was quite preoccupied at this sign of improvement, so preoccupied in fact that the barrow unseeingly crashed into a bicycle on the road and an alarming cry rose.

Father Tom stopped instantly. He had been staring at his white hands, while he trundled, thankful for the new strength in them, and so he had not been watching. A bicycle now lay on its side on the high kerb and a very small young man, in black, was sitting beside it, having been tossed there at the collision. His black hat had been knocked from his head, and he was now brushing it off with his elbow and regarding its state with dismay.

"I'm very—very s-sorry!" exclaimed Father Tom, who frequently stuttered, especially when encountering strangers. "I didna see you——" He went to the small man's rescue, and was greeted by one of the sweetest smiles he had ever seen in his life. The stranger appeared to be about his own age, twenty-two, but much smaller, and even much frailer. He had fine reddish hair, large shy blue eyes, a gentle mouth and the big nose of the true Highlander.

"Nay, it wasna your fault, sir," he said, kindly, as Father Tom agitatedly swept him off with his handkerchief. "I take it ye are the new priest?"

"Weel, yes," said Father Tom, blushing. The other young man was blushing, also. "Could ye be one o' my parishioners?" asked Father Tom.

The other young man blushed even brighter, and, exactly like Father Tom, he stammered. "Nay, nay—it is to say—it is—— I am the minister!" he said on a fast burst, as if about to choke.

They stared at each other in their intense shyness, their faces deeply red. Then they laughed, at first faintly, then with relief at recognizing a brother. They shook hands timidly. "Bruce Gregor," said the minister. "Not MacGregor!" He paused, and the youthful pink face became very firm. "Not the Clan o' MacGregor!"

His vehemence startled Father Tom. "Oh?" he murmured. "Not —not the Clan o' MacGregor."

"Not!" said the minister, folding his short thin arms firmly over his chest and casting a defiant look up into the priest's higher face.

"I—I see," said Father Tom, dubiously.

The minister's arms unfolded, his face became crimson, his mouth trembled, and he shook a finger at the young priest. "I'd nae be a MacGregor to save me soul!" he said, and did not stammer now. His blue eyes flashed with passion, then seemed to become moist and all the sudden fire went out of him.

"The Clan o' MacGregor—it—it is a Catholic clan," said Father Tom, shrinking a little as he thought he had been insulted.

The minister started, then the moisture increased in his eyes. He stammered painfully, "It isna—it—it isna that, laddie! No, not that. It's ma father-in-law. A MacGregor."

Father Tom was so surprised his mouth fell open. He had thought the minister to be fresh from a Seminary, and less than twenty. Yet, he was married.

"Your father-in-law—he is Catholic, Mr. Gregor?"

"Not that. I fear he hasna God. He willna come to the kirk at a', since I married my Betsy." He stopped, in miserable confusion.

"Dear me," said Father Tom, aching with sympathy.

The minister tried to smile. He blew his nose on an immaculate handkerchief which was just as darned as the young priest's own handkerchiefs.

"I wouldna care if it wasna for Betsy, his one lass," said the minister. "It is the sore heart she has, and she but seventeen." He colored brightly again and looked aside. "And with a wee wean coming, too."

"Dear me," repeated Father Tom.

"Oh, but I'll not be keeping you, sir," said the small minister, ashamed of his brief passion. He looked at the barrow.

"Slates," said Father Tom. "The hoose leaks."

Mr. Gregor sadly shook his head. "As ours," he said. "Pots and pans in the bedroom." He thought he had said something slightly indecent to this celibate brother, and his blush came readily again.

"And there's nae a one to mend yours?" said Father Tom, who had had a vague impression that most ministers were "comfortable."

"None," said the minister. "It's sae hard, the noo, since Betsy and I were married. There's nae other kirk in the place, and though they come there's little in the plate—the noo. It's a' his fault; he rules the dam—the place. And there's no leaving here yet; my first congregation. Good Squire MacVicar!"

"Ah!" said Father Tom. "The one that's put the window in my kirk? And he hae give me the fine whiskey, too!"

The minister nodded. "It's his way to make a mock of me." Bruce smiled miserably. "Ask the braw auld lad to put the roof on your hoose and he'll send his men aknocking before the sun's up tomorrow. Not that he loves you, but for a mock."

Father Tom was musing in astonishment. Then he looked at the barrow. "Fifteen slates," he said. "How many do you need, Mr. Gregor?"

"Aboot the same. And where will ye get the men to do the work?"

"I'll do it, mesel'."

"You?" The minister was all one amazement. Father Tom could not help lifting his chin with pride.

"It's nae hard. My Dada taught me."

A slight touch of envy shadowed Mr. Gregor's boyish voice. "A man of parts, is it? Weel, a good morning to you, sir, and perhaps ye'll have tea with Betsy and me on Sunday?"

"I hae a big ham," said Father Tom. "I'll come, if I may bring some ham. It may spoil, for one."

The young minister looked hungry at once. He got on his bicycle. "My Betsy makes a fine gooseberry tart," he boasted. "We'll be expecting you." He paused. "Auld Bob, there, he'll be cheating you if you don't mind. Haggle him doon."

Every curtain on the street was twitching. The cold sun blazed on polished little windows, and wisps of smoke rose from stone chimneys against a sky fiercely scoured blue by the northern wind. The trundling of the barrow echoed in that shining silence. Father Tom reached Auld Bob's place at the turn on Bannoch Road, which was the end of the village too. Heaps of slate, piles of lumber and mounds of brick lay on the packed earth, and there was a scent of sawdust in the air and a stench of horse manure. Two horses, in fact, were tethered close by, and Auld Bob, himself, was sitting smoking his pipe in a rocking chair, awaiting customers. He was fat, broad and tall, with white hair and a large white mustache, and he wore a thick tweed jacket and a tweed cap. He had very small and very sharp blue eyes, which he opened in amazement at the sight of the young priest with his barrow. Then he stood up, surlily, pulled his cap reluctantly, and stood back on his heels.

"Ye'll be the new Roman," he said, without any other salutation.

Father Tom always winced away from brusqueness, and always blushed at a rude remark. He winced and blushed now. "That I will be," he said. Suddenly, without any reason he knew of, he straightened his back. "I'm come for slates. Thirty of them."

"Slates?" said Auld Bob, as if he had never heard the word before.

"Slates," said Father Tom. "It's them over there, if ye'll look."

The broad and weathered face of the older man darkened, but Father Tom looked him firmly in the eye. "Slates," said Auld Bob, hurriedly, and stamped off to a pile of them and stood waiting. He puffed with violence on his pipe and a blue cloud half obscured his face.

Father Tom dropped his barrow and examined the slates critically. He shook his head. "Not fit for a doll's hoose," he said, rubbing his finger along one edge. "Crumble in the first snow. Hae ye no better?"

"Are ye insulting me slates?" demanded Auld Bob.

"I am, that," said Father Tom, dumfounded at his new self. "If ye hae no better I'll go elsewhere."

Auld Bob muttered something which Father Tom suspected was a profound obscenity. Then he stamped over to another pile. "And will your lordship condescend to look upon these?" he asked.

"His lordship" took his time examining the better slates. They were quite good. But Father Tom was a Scotsman and he flexed his mental muscles and prepared for combat. "Not sae good as in Edinburgh," he said.

"And how would your lordship know that?"

"His lordship knows all aboot slates."

"Aweel!" said Auld Bob. "I doot it."

"Thirty slates," said Father Tom. "That would be six shillings for the lot."

"Are ye mad?" cried Auld Bob. "I——"

"Paid that wholesale," said Father Tom, with an assumption of weariness. "And ye quarried them ye-sel', too, without doot."

Auld Bob put his hands akimbo on his thick hips and said menacingly, "If ye were not a wee minister or such I'd brain ye, laddie!"

The two stared inimically at each other. Then Auld Bob said, "Ten shillings."

"Six, and be quick aboot it or it will be five."

"Nine!" shouted Auld Bob, turning purple.

"Five," said Father Tom.

They compromised on seven, and Auld Bob bitterly loaded the thick slates in the barrow. He tried one of the handles and was immediately happy at the weight. The "Roman" would have a job trundling that along the cobbles! Break his damn back. Father Tom counted out the seven shillings from his meagre store.

"Ye're worse than a Jew," said Auld Bob. "At the haggling."

"God pity a poor Jew who haggles with a Scotsman," said Father Tom, sternly. "Ye hae Jews in this hamlet, then?"

"Not a one! I hae never seen one."

Father Tom nodded. "It is always the stupid who parrot the stupid. A good morning to you, and mind your tongue in the future."

He was so astounded at this new self he had discovered only today that he did not hear Auld Bob's imprecations that followed him. He mused on his new self all the strenuous way home. Had God given him a new grace? He was still too young to know that he had become strong on encountering Bruce Gregor, who was even younger, more vulnerable, more shy and timid than himself, and in greater need of protection and sympathy. He was sweating profusely when he trundled the barrow to the cottage and set down the handles. He wiped his face, fanned himself with his elderly hat, and looked up at the roof. Two hours' work at the most. He had totally forgotten that he had A Chest. He went into the house for his meal, a fine slice of ham newly baked, mashed potatoes, mashed turnips, oat cakes and butter and tea. He ate with a new heartiness and Mrs. Logan gave him a maternal smile of approval. Then she sighed.

"And who will ye be getting to put the slates on, Faether?"

Father Tom took a large draught of tea. "Mesel'," he said.

"Ye-sel'!"

"Aye."

Mrs. Logan was scandalized. "Ye'll be jesting, Faether!"

"I'll not be jesting," he said. "I can do a good job. My Dada taught me."

Mrs. Logan threw up her hands. "But Faether! The scandal!"

"There is nothing scandalous aboot honest work, Mistress Logan," said Father Tom. He drew a deep breath. "And I'll be damned if I live under a roof that leaks." He was freshly amazed at himself, and at his profanity. He rose severely to his full height, which was very tall indeed.

"Our Lord did nae ask the great ones in the cities to do His work," he said. "And He was a carpenter, Himsel'."

He was pleasantly tired and went for a nap in his tiny cell of a bedroom and slept more deeply and sweetly than he had ever remembered. When he awoke there were four old gentlemen waiting to see him to discuss kirk matters, and to brief him about the hamlet. He gave them some of Squire MacVicar's whiskey, to their delight and shy pleasure, and drank a tot himself. He could not recall having felt so vigorous since his early boyhood.

"That Squire MacVicar," said one old gentleman, shaking his head proudly. "He is a fair one. A saint."

Now Father Tom could satisfy his curiosity. Squire MacVicar had the finest sheep in the country, and many flocks of them, and employed many shepherds. He was also the landlord of half the hamlet. He owned the rich meadows three miles distant, and had a revenue from the pubs of six villages. He was also "invested," which Father Tom took, rightly, to mean that he had property and money and bonds in Edinburgh, his original home. He had come here when a young man because he, too, had had A Chest. Now he was practically lord of the hamlet and its vicinity, and was lordly in appearance, too.

He had founded and set up a fine free school, and had been, until very recently—the old gentleman coughed—almost the entire support of his kirk. He kept his houses "up," and had established a fund for the support of the old folk, another for the sick and temporarily indigent, and supplied all the hamlet's geese on Christmas and all its hams or young lamb for Easter Sunday. He made no difference between Presbyterians and Catholics. Though it must be admitted, another old gentleman said, that he had no love for those he called "Romans." Quite the contrary. But he was a just man, merciful, provident and charitable, though with a temper when crossed. "If there was ever a man without sin, Faether," said an old gentleman, "that one be Squire MacVicar." The Squire did not smoke or drink; he lived plainly in a house "doon the road" not distinguishable from its neighbors except for its large garden, and its furniture and curtains. His life was austere, almost rigorous. He paid uncommonly large wages, and expected and received good work in return. He was "down" on the sinful, the slothful, the heavy drinkers and smokers. He demanded that others live as purely as he did, except for the Catholics, whom he had long ago decided were residents of the Outer Darkness. Nevertheless, he "did" for the Catholics as he "did" for "his ain folk." Just. Firm. Severe. Blameless. All the old gentlemen agreed.

"And his lady?" asked Father Tom, with an innocent face.

They shook their heads. The poor lady died ten years ago. There was a housekeeper in the house, and there was a gardener for the garden and jobs outside.

"And nae bairns?" said Father Tom, more innocent than ever.

Only one child. The old gentlemen did not move in their stiff chairs but they subtly seemed to draw together as if in defense of the Squire. Betsy MacVicar, a lovely lass, but she had not married well.

"Sad, that," said Father Tom, encouragingly, and deftly refilling the glasses. The old gentlemen exchanged eloquent glances, and sipped the whiskey and did not speak for a little. Then the most

loquacious, his ancient face flushed with the whiskey, spoke. The
daughter of Squire MacVicar had married the wee minister of the
Presbyterian kirk. They had run off together to Gretna Green, when
the Squire had refused his consent.

"And what had he against the minister?" asked Father Tom.

They all looked at each other uneasily. Well, it seems that the
Squire had not liked the minister from the very beginning, when
he had come here less than two years ago. "A soft lad," the Squire
had called him, and the Squire did not like soft lads. Moreover, the
minister was "sae poor," with no private means, and he could never
bring himself to "speak up" even to the most cantankerous of his
congregation. (And when a Scotsman is cantankerous, thought
Father Tom, he can make the devil, himself, nod enviously.) The
wee minister did not come of gentry, as did Squire MacVicar, who
had inherited considerable money. His father had a poor shoe shop
in Glasgow, and he was a Borderlander, which meant, of course,
that there was more than a suspicion of Sassenach blood in the
family. The wee minister protested that he was pure Highlander,
and it was only misfortune which had sent his parents to Glasgow,
but the Squire did not believe him and so the hamlet did not believe
him, either. It was evident that what the Squire disliked all his
neighbors disliked automatically.

Even before the marriage the Squire had attempted to have Mr.
Gregor removed. But the authorities in Edinburgh were as adamant
as himself, and every bit as stubborn. The hamlet was small, and
Mr. Gregor was a young man of impeccable character, said the authorities, sternly. It was his first parish, and the authorities intimated
bluntly that if he survived this hamlet he would survive anywhere.
In short, they had not too high an opinion of the Squire and the
hamlet, which was very cruel of them. (Father Tom took a sudden
liking for "the authorities" in Edinburgh, whoever they might be.)

So, under all these circumstances, said the old gentlemen, the
Squire was not to be blamed for withdrawing support from the Presbyterian kirk, and the congregation gave as little as possible for the
support of the kirk and the wee minister and Betsy. She had made

her bed, had Betsy, and she could lie in it. The old gentlemen nodded solemnly.

Father Tom was very young and very gentle; he felt almost the first wrath of his life against Squire MacVicar. Had he not met Mr. Gregor that morning he might have been as censorious as these old folk, and would have spoken of disobedience to parents and such like. But he had met Mr. Gregor, and in those moments he had felt a fraternal fondness for him and a vague desire to help him in some way.

The Squire had intended to build a new manse for the minister, but when he had met Mr. Gregor he immediately withdrew his offer. His money would not go to house a lad without visible character and family and funds. The Squire was of the Clan of MacGregor on his mother's side. Father Tom lifted his head alertly. His father had been a true Highlander, with a vague relationship to the Clan, himself. Father Tom felt his thin cheeks beginning to burn warmly with excitement.

"The Squire's mother, then, was Catholic?" he said.

The old gentlemen looked vague. Well, now, they had never known the Squire's parents. He was not very young when he had come here. He had been thirty at least. After he had established himself in the hamlet, which had taken five years, he had gone to Edinburgh for a wife and had brought his lady home. "A lovely lass, like Betsy," said one old gentleman. "And little more than half his age. He was fair to die when she died." The Squire, who had doted on Betsy before his wife's death—his only child—had become obsessed with her afterwards. There was nothing too good for Betsy. She had gone to school, a fine school, in Edinburgh, and had lived with the Squire's sister-in-law, her aunt, a widow of much wealth, herself. The Squire had brought the lass home when she had done with her school, and had intended to take her abroad two months later. Then she had fallen in love with the wee minister, and they had married in great haste. The Squire, said the old gentlemen, had been quite mad for a while. Then he had begun his revenge against his daughter and her husband.

"Sich a good man," said Father Tom, with irony.

But the old gentlemen took him seriously, and nodded in chorus, and said "Aye" in chorus. Had he been a Catholic he would inevitably have been called a saint, and probably canonized in the future. Sad that he wasna Catholic.

"I think," said Father Tom, dropping his Scots caution, "that the Church will survive, not having him as a communicant."

This startled and confused three of the old gentlemen, but the fourth looked at the young priest shrewdly. Not sae soft as he seemed, but what did he mean by that sly remark? There was a nasty look in his eye, too. The old gentleman began to smile. He liked a lad with spirit, and he had thought, originally, that the young priest sadly lacked that commendable virtue.

Had the Squire liked the minister before Mr. Gregor? the priest asked. The old men again exchanged uneasy glances. Well, no. The Squire had not liked that one, nor the one before him. Nor the other. He had fair broken their spirits, too, but it was their fault, not the Squire's. Weak lads. Feckless. No character. Father Tom nodded grimly to himself. He was beginning to have a very good idea of the Squire.

There were no Sisters in the hamlet. The Catholic children attended the Squire's good free school, and none of the Protestant children were permitted to jibe at them. The priest, of course, was expected to teach the children their catechism. In time, and with the growth of Catholic families, the Sisters would come. Father Tom hoped, a little unkindly, that this would not happen too soon. Sisters invariably took over a parish and dominated it.

Then one old gentleman said that the Squire had actually offered the "auld Faether" a convent for nuns, but for some reason the "auld Faether" had politely refused. This aroused Father Tom's interest; however, the old gentleman had no explanation.

Father Tom wondered what the priest of the nearest hamlet which had enough Catholic families to warrant a priest thought of Squire MacVicar. A saint! said the old gentlemen, on the doorstep. Father Tom decided not to visit his brother in Christ for some time. His stubborn Scots loyalty had been aroused in behalf of young Mr.

Gregor and his very young wife, who was expecting a child. And there was a vague thought hovering like a bee over his mind.

There were only forty Catholic children in the village, ranging from a month to twelve years in age. There were but sixteen in the catechism class. The Catholic families were, in the main, middle-aged or older. The younger did not breed more children than their Protestant neighbors.

Within a few days Father Tom had settled down in his parish and had met all his people. He could not understand himself, and often marveled. Whence had he acquired this new strength, this new spirit, this new sense of authority? He wrote his parents: "I have not coughed since I came here. The air is very salubrious, if cold. I have the heartiest appetite and am in good spirits. You would not know me." In fact, the young priest did not know himself.

On Friday afternoon he brought out the ladder, filled a basket with slates, and climbed on the steep roof of his rectory. It was odd, he thought, as he hammered and chipped away, that no one seemed about; his hammer echoed all up and down the street. He did not know, until later, that he had scandalized his own people and was embarrassing the Protestants, who thought it "fair dreadful" for a clergyman to be crawling and hammering all over the place, his coat off and his pullovers tucked in. No one, of course, offered to help him or do the job. The men were "sae busy" and were too tired at evening. Besides, there was a bad conscience among both Catholics and Protestants. They covered this by telling themselves that the clergy should be above wanting a tight roof. The old prophets and holy men had lived in caves or in the desert or the forests, and had thought nothing of it, their minds fixed only on God. When Mrs. Logan repeated this opinion to Father Tom, he said, "The old prophets and holy men lived in warm climates, not in sae Godforsaken a place as this. I'll not hae a leak over my head in the winter."

Auld Bob expressed it as his opinion that the new priest was an oppressor of the poor and would not pay wages, and sacrilegious into the bargain, and had no respect for his calling, if one could consider "Romans" as having a calling at all. He had fair stolen the slates from him, Auld Bob. This was an example of what the "Romans" would do if they ever seized control of Scotland again. His friends agreed, though doubting that Auld Bob had lost anything on the slates.

The good clear weather was holding; the stone cottages along the street reflected the sun like mica; the dark cobbles gleamed; the sky had the hard jewel look of polished aquamarine. But no one was about. Father Tom whistled some dolorous ballad about lost maidens and cruel fathers, and then changed to an even more dolorous ballad concerning a young gallant sailor lost at sea. The more tragic the ballad, the happier he became, as he felt all his muscles stretch elastically in his labor and the cold wind ruffled his hair. For, as everyone knows, the true Celt reveals his contentment in singing of the more disastrous events of life. It is when his throat throbs the hardest that his heart is the happiest, a matter a mere Sassenach could not possibly understand.

The roof was very steep, but young Father Tom skittered up and down it, feeling more exhilarated by the moment, his heels and toes digging into the gutters for purchase, his knees gripping on the slates for support. Aha, he thought, godliness is entwined with hard labor; to labor is to pray. He opened his mouth to sing a particularly direful phrase which had to do with the dying of a lass in a wave rushing from the sea, and the fact that at sunset she could be heard calling, calling, calling—— Joyously, the hammer becoming brisker, the priest's eyes filled with tears at the thought of that desolate and childlike wailing as the blue and scarlet dusk came down.

So engrossed, he had not heard the calm clatter of a horse's hoofs on the cobbles, and so did not hear the clatter stop, and was not aware of the horseman sitting below him and watching him with interest. He almost lost his footing when a loud and sardonic voice said, "Nae wonder the lass doesna come hame, with a song like yon to greet her, and such a singing."

Father Tom, halfway up the roof, leaned heavily on the slates and cautiously glanced over his shoulder. He knew who that tall, gray, tweed-clad man was instantly, for he remembered the phrase Mrs. Logan and others had used: "A lordly man with a lordly air." His face immediately suffused with various tints of magenta. His mouth fell open boyishly.

"A fine occupation for a priest," said the lordly man with the eyes like bits of pale and polished stones.

Father Tom's heart beat a little tattoo of embarrassment, and then he was angry. "You'll know of a better, perhaps?" he said, and did not stammer once. Mrs. Logan twitched the curtain and surveyed Squire MacVicar with horror, and thought, for a moment, that he had a truly "divilish" grin on his face. But she was also ashamed for the priest.

"Sich as praying for souls with the auld women—Parson," said the Squire.

"And sich as praying for the souls of auld men—if such are not lost, the noo," said Father Tom, and reminded himself that he must be contrite for that smarting answer—much later.

The man laughed sourly, but his eyes took on a harder stoniness. "We havena lost our spirit in the cloisters," he said.

"I hae a good faether," said the priest, wondering if it would be entirely sinful if his basket of slates slipped and fell like leaves onto the horseman, whose horse was as black as coal and whose coat resembled the better satins.

Squire MacVicar thought that over, his face darkening moment by moment. "And what will ye mean by that remark?" he asked at last.

Father Tom reflected. He would be doing the wee minister no good by inspiring new hostility in this very grim and very hostile man with the fine upright figure and the arrogant face.

"Sae very subtle," he said. "If a lad hae a good faether he'll not be afraid of the world when he is a man."

"Um," said the Squire, suspiciously. Father Tom resumed his dexterous work. The Squire moved his horse closer until his eye was on a level with the low eaves. "Not sae bad," he remarked. "And where will a priest-lad be learning to manage slates?"

"My Dada," said Father Tom, and made the street ring with his hammer.

"I see," said the Squire with a touch of contempt.

" 'Mary, call the cattle hame, the cattle hame, the cattle hame!

Mary, call the cattle hame, across the sands o' Dee!' " sang the priest, his voice throbbing calamitously.

"Good God," said the Squire, putting his gloved hands over his ears. "And will ye be assaulting the ears of the puir people with that voice when ye celebrate the Mass?"

Father Tom paused. The bee that hovered over his mind twanged a little nearer and sharper.

"And arouse the dead at Matins?" said the Squire.

"I hae no complaints," said Father Tom, looking down soberly at the horseman.

"Not even at a Solemn Mass, lad? Not even at the Gloria?" The Squire chuckled nastily.

"I see," said Father Tom. "My kirk hae had the pleasure of your worship's company, perhaps?"

"Not I!" said the Squire. "I do not like mummery."

Father Tom said, *"Quare fremuerunt gentes, et populi meditae sunt inania?"*

The Squire snorted. "I know me Latin, laddie."

"And as ye know your Latin," said Father Tom, innocently, "ye'll know, too, where that hymn occurs, and the occasion."

The Squire smiled that dour smile of his. "Ye think me a fool? It is Midnight Mass, Christmas, the entrance hymn."

Father Tom looked down at him with a beautiful affectation of admiring boyhood. "And ye'll have such words and hymns in the Presbyterian church, perhaps? Aweel, aweel! If so, then the day of ane Fold and ane Shepherd is near at hand!"

The Squire scowled up at him in deadly silence, and his sharp cheekbones reddened. Father Tom smiled at him in immaculate innocence, waiting. The Squire cleared his throat. "I am a traveled man," said the Squire. "I hae been in many's the cathedrals in the Popish countries." He waited a moment. "I do not like your tone. I am not 'raging,' nor do I 'plan vain things.' "

"Very, very good," said Father Tom. He looked into his basket. "Now, if I should ask your worship to refill my basket with the slates, would ye do it for me and save me a scrambling doon?"

"Give it doon," said the Squire in an irascible voice. So Father

Tom leaned down and gave the Squire the basket, and the Squire, astonishingly, swung from his horse and filled the basket with slates. "Ye'll have a pile here," he said. "How many blasted holes do ye have in your roof?"

The priest surveyed the work he had already done. "Fifteen," he said.

"But there's more here."

"Aye. I hae another job to do, another broken roof to make tight."

"Not one of my hooses!" said the Squire, handing up the basket. (Mrs. Logan, peeping from behind the curtains, could not believe her eyes.)

"No," said the priest. "Yours are all fair tight, I take it."

"I take care of my ain," said the Squire. "Have you a quarrel with me aboot it?" When Father Tom did not reply, he said, "And is there none of your ain to do the roof for ye?"

"The men," chanted Father Tom, "are sae busy, with the sheep and the shops and the lambing."

"Perhaps we didna like the parsons we got," said the Squire.

"Some sheep, the fractious ones, perhaps do not like the shepherds, sir. But the shepherds will guard them from the storm, for a' that. Our Lord did not promise us obedient sheep with good manners and kind hearts full of duty. Many a sheep hae a divil."

"A fine Christian sentiment, that!" said the Squire. "A Popish sentiment. We'd not allow the minister to say that of one of us."

"Calvin did. And there was Knox, a braw man with his tongue. Are the sheep teaching the shepherds in this village, sir?"

"Oh, be damned to ye," said the Squire.

"It isna for ye to say," said Father Tom. He became engrossed with his work. He scrambled about, examined critically, chipped here and there. He waited to hear the horse go away, but there was only silence except for his own brisk noise.

Then the Squire said, "That slate there ye are holding, it's nae good."

"Can a man expect goodness in all things, in this world?" asked the priest. He examined the slate. "Ye are right, sir. I was cheated. It was your Auld Bob, a rascal."

"How much did he charge ye?"

"Seven shillings for thirty."

"Ye say he cheated you? Laddie, ye cheated him!" The Squire gave his harsh chuckle again. "He doesna like Romans. Ye fair diddled him!"

Father Tom did not reply to him. He was frowning at the slate. Ah, well, he could halve it and put it near the eaves in a little place. He chopped.

"I like a man of parts," said the Squire.

"I can lay bricks, too," said the priest.

"Can you, now! And nae doot build a whole hoose?"

"Aye," said the priest with pride. "A good hoose."

"Stick to your last," said the Squire. "Ye are in the wrong pew."

"Our Lord was a carpenter," said Father Tom. "Will ye give me some nails, too?"

So the Squire, growling, dismounted again and handed up some nails. "Ye'll not dine well, after the offerings," he said.

"Nae doot," said the priest. "Ye will have a hand in that the noo. Ah, weel, the good Lord went hungry too, and hadna hoose to guard His head."

"Ye hae a rash tongue, laddie. What business is it of mine if ye starve? I'm not a Roman."

"I hear rumors," said Father Tom. "It's a hard hand ye have on this hamlet. Ye smile, and a man has a full stomach. Ye frown, and a man dines on oatmeal with nae milk or treacle." He looked down at the Squire. "There's some who hae a great empire, and some who hae an empire the size of a man's hand. Both are not content."

"I am a just man," said the Squire, strangely furious.

"So say all the tyrants. There's nae difference between ye."

"Ye'll mind that tongue of yours, lad, or the village will be seeing the last o' ye."

"Oh? Ye'll know my Bishop then, and ye sip your whiskey together?"

"Blast you! I am a man of righteousness and justice, but I'll nae endure a mock from such as ye."

Father Tom slowly and carefully turned himself about so that his back leaned against the steep pitch of the roof.

"And, so you are a man of righteousness and justice? You admit that, yourself? There's no humility in ye, but only pride, which is the sin above all that drove Lucifer into hell. 'Here the Almighty hath not built for His envy.' Nay, Squire MacVicar built his ain little hell."

The Squire colored deeply, and then turned ghastly white. He grasped his crop and started up the ladder and Father Tom watched him come in sober silence. The Squire's head rose to the level of the priest's knees and the priest could see his eyes even more clearly in that stark light, and they were evil with rage and vengeance.

"Ye are a man much older than my Dada," said the priest. "And I canna kick your face or strike ye back. It is a' your advantage."

The Squire looked at his crop, then at the priest, then he hurled the crop down to the ground, and the two men stared at each other in silence. Finally the Squire spoke, very softly, "And did ye think I'd raise my hand to a priest?"

"And why not? Ye hae lifted your hand many's the time to a man, have ye not?"

The Squire looked at him again, then looked away. He let his eyes rove over the new slates which had been fastened in place. "There's one not sae good, near the chimney," he said.

He climbed higher on the ladder. He was still deathly white, and the priest could see the tension about his mouth.

"I'd not have taken ye for a man of spirit," said the Squire. "Ye are but a lad, a puling bairn, fresh from his mother's breast. And where did we get this fine high spirit?"

"Here," said Father Tom, making a gesture that encompassed the village.

"It's good for something then, my hamlet."

"Ye may own the land and the hooses, but ye do not own the souls, nor do ye own any man unless he lets ye. I will pray for such a man."

The Squire grunted. "Then, ye'll pray for a' of them."

"And ye, too, while I am aboot it."

The Squire's face changed again. "Ye'll not be saying your nasty

prayers aboot me!" he said. "I want none of your Popish prayers! I
hae done with——" He paused. Then he climbed still higher, and
pointed to the chimney. "Ye'll hae that falling and bashing in your
saucy head. It's fair falling now."

"I know that. I will buy some mortar and mend it."

The priest turned slowly again, chipped off a damaged slate and
replaced it. The Squire watched him. "I'll give a man his due," he
said. "That's an unco good job ye are doing. There's many could
learn from ye."

"I need more nails," said the priest, and the Squire, as if musing,
went down and fetched more nails. Father Tom began to sing; the
Squire winced, then joined in, and one voice was boyishly tenor and
the other deep bass:

> "Oh, never, never, Scotia's realm desert,
>   But still the patriot, and the patriot bard,
>   In bright succession raise, her ornament and guard!"

They ended on a loud and lusty note. Not a soul appeared,
though the street had rung with melody. They smiled at each other.
"I dinna take it back," said the Squire. "Ye hae a fearsome voice. Ye'll
shrivel the eardrums o' the communicants."

The bee was humming very fast over the priest's mind. "I'll be mair
enchanted to shrivel yours," he said. The Squire's face became harsh
and cold. "Hae ye done?" he asked, as the hammer paused.

"Aye, I hae done," said the priest, and he followed the Squire down
the ladder. They stood face to face now, both tall even for Highlanders, but one massive and the other lean. "Ye'll be needing some
meat on those bones. A plucked fowl," said the Squire. "Will ye
come to tea tonight?"

"No," said the priest. "There is my sermon, and tomorrow is Confessions."

"Sunday, then?"

Mrs. Logan heard this exchange, and put her hand over her
rounded mouth of astonishment.

"No, and I thank ye," said the priest. "And I canna come Monday;
I hae the other hoose to make tight."

"I will send ye a man," said the Squire. "It isna right for a priest to be mending other folks' hooses. Shameful."

Father Tom had a tantalizing vision of the Squire's "man" appearing at the manse to repair the wee minister's roof, and he smiled longingly. Then he was surprised over this entire episode. Ah, but the man had a way with him, for all his tyrannies and his hard, proud and righteous heart, his lack of humility, his arrogance. And, the bee was very insistent in Father Tom's mind now, buzzing quite noisily.

"I'll come Tuesday for tea, sir," he said. "If it will please ye."

"Tuesday, then, it is," said the Squire. He swung lithely up upon his horse, who was nuzzling the priest curiously. The young man patted the silken nose. "Ye hae a bonnie face," said the Squire, with abruptness, and pulled on the reins and cantered off down the road.

The odd encounter was all over the village not too long after the lingering twilight, via the avid gossip of Mrs. Logan. The pub chattered with it. The Squire had "taken" to the young priest. By the time it was truly dark the Squire had also helped to "bang on the slates." There were excited rumors among Father Tom's flock that the Squire had promised to replace all the plain glass windows in the kirk with ones similar to that which he had already given. There were even rumors that he would be "converted."

"We'll hae a saint o' our ain at last, Ian MacVicar," said some of the Catholics optimistically. A little boy, born at midnight, was named Ian in honor of the first "saint," who was somberly drinking too much whiskey at that hour. At two in the morning he was dead drunk and slept on a sofa in his parlor. It was often that he did this, and his housekeeper was loyal and devoted and so no one ever knew. "He hae his sorrows," she would tell herself, shaking her head. She cooled a glass of barley-water and took it sympathetically to her master in the morning. It was sae sad to suffer from a delicate stomach.

The two Masses were attended encouragingly that Sunday. The communicants swarmed to the Communion rail. That afternoon Father Tom, feeling that things were getting on very well indeed, called on his brother in Christ, the Reverend Mr. Bruce Gregor, and his Betsy. The rectory was as tiny as Father Tom's own, but less cared for, and the slates were higgledy-piggledy all over the roof. However, there was a beautiful little garden like a rainbow with late summer flowers, and when he entered the house the priest was immediately impressed with the air of love and innocence which pervaded it.

The young pastor was shyly delighted, and brought his very young wife by the hand. She was most obviously pregnant, and timidly tried to conceal her state. The rumors had been quite right, thought the priest. She was a very lovely lass, with light brown curls, very large dark eyes, a complexion like a tearose and a mouth the color of a particularly bright carnation. She was as small as her husband. It was evident that they loved each other devotedly. Their very presence lighted up the mean little parlor like the sun itself.

"Gooseberry tarts, my Betsy's," said Bruce, with pride. The girl blushed. They all blushed together. The tea was hot if a little, and necessarily, weak. There was loaf sugar and a pitcher of cream, and not only the boasted tarts but fresh hot scones and current jam and a lump of butter. Father Tom had not forgotten his share of the feast; he had asked Mrs. Logan to boil a large section of the ham. She had then wrapped it in a white tea towel which she had brought from her own house. There was no doubt that she thought it imprudent of him to be visiting the wee minister, who lived outside almost everyone's pale. Squire MacVicar would not like it at all.

The minister tried to hide how desperately hungry he was, therefore he began by insisting that he was not hungry, that he had had a fine dinner, cooked by his Betsy, and that the priest must eat the major part of the ham, himself. Betsy would "taste" a little. But Father Tom stoutly insisted that he had a large joint for dinner that day, and would not be famished for a week in consequence. So, at first with reluctance, then with youthful avidity, the minister and his wife fell upon the ham and ate it with an expression of touching rapture on their faces. Father Tom, feeling rich and overstuffed and elderly, could have wept with sympathy. This did not keep him from enjoying the scones and tarts, however, and he ravaged them. There were only sixty-one years among the three of the young people about the tea table, if that many.

It began to rain, and the minister threw a small lump or two of coal on the fire. The room chilled and darkened. Betsy lighted a paraffin lamp. The little kettle sang over the coals. Betsy drew the curtains. The boyish clergymen sat before the fire and sipped their tea. Father Tom regretted that he had forgotten to bring the whiskey the Squire had left for him. It would cheer the minister, and the priest would enjoy the thought of him drinking his father-in-law's whiskey. Betsy went to the scullery to wash up.

The minister stammered, "I hope ye'll not be taking it as impertinent," he said, "but I hae heard that the—that the—Squire—himself, himself, hae invited you to tea in his hoose on Tuesday. It is but a rumor, perhaps?"

"No," said the priest. "He was very civil." He smiled an un-ecclesiastical smile. "And I hae insulted him."

The minister's mouth opened in consternation. "You were nae afraid of him, then?"

"Him?" said Father Tom, superbly. "A man of mean temper and pride, but a human soul for a' that," he hurriedly added.

The minister apparently considered that a vast overstatement, and stared gloomily at the fire, his fine red hair like a copper nimbus over his long head. Then he turned awed and fascinated eyes on this doughty priest.

"I envy ye your courage," said Bruce Gregor.

No one, at any time before this, had envied Father Tom's courage. On the contrary. He sat up very tall in his stiff chair and his white collar glimmered. He looked every inch the Older Man. He waved his hand deprecatingly. "A petty tyrant, and it is naebody's fault but the villagers that he is so."

The roof began to leak a little and the minister regarded it with dismay. "It didna leak in here before this," he said, and ran for a pan to catch the drops. "Only the bedroom and the scullery," he said, as he came back with the pan. Father Tom stared at the whitewashed ceiling and marked the spot accurately with his eye. He wondered if he should tell the little minister that a "man" would repair the roof tomorrow, the "man" being himself. No. They would be embarrassed enough when he wheeled his barrow here and demanded a ladder. He said, "Ye hae a ladder, Bruce?"

"A ladder?"

"So if one comes to repair the roof he'll not need to bring his own," said the priest, patiently.

"A ladder," repeated the minister, reflectively. He called, "Betsy, hae we a ladder?"

She assured him, from the scullery, that there was a ladder "aboot." The young minister sighed. "But none will come to the manse, Tom. There were but eight folk in the kirk this morning. Four shillings in a' in the plate."

Father Tom thought of the ham. At least these young people would have meat for a few days, and he regretted all the jam and butter and scones he had eaten.

"The auld faether—he was fair afraid of the Squire," said Bruce. "But his people came to the kirk——" He looked at the priest questioningly.

"It is a serious sin to miss Sunday Mass, unless for serious cause," said the priest.

"Eh! That must be a wondrous thing, to hae such authority," the minister said, wistfully.

"God is the Authority," said the priest, with some surprise, for he knew little of Scots Presbyterianism. "The duty to obey is man's. A man hae no merit of his own, save that Our Lord grants him through His own merits. A man must labor with God in the saving of his ain soul."

The wee minister seemed somewhat confused at this. "Aye, but God hae predestined man before his birth to heaven or hell, and it comes to me sometimes that it is possible that the Squire is predestined to heaven and Betsy and me to hell."

Father Tom thought this idea entirely unlikely. "A man hae free will," he said, cautiously, and suddenly remembered the Presbyterian doctrine of Predestination.

"Ah, that he doesna have," said the minister, sadly. "Not entirely, but only within the framework of Predestination. Man is the puppet of his predetermined destiny."

Father Tom had been taught not to engage in arguments with other clergy concerning points of faith, for that was not "prudent" and only incited enmity. But he was a young man and the very thought of such a stern belief depressed him and upset him. Life was hard enough, God knew, but how much harder it was if the shadow of hell lay on a man's spirit so that he believed that no merit he could acquire, and no faith he could be given, could save him if his Lord had determined to cast him into eternal fire.

"Ye mean," said the priest, appalled, "that one such as the Squire, who hae no heart and only virtue, is assured of heaven if it were determined before his birth?"

The minister nodded. "Aye, that, he hae virtue, full and over-flowing, though nae heart. I am a sinful man, I know, and oft do I wonder where my destiny lies. Hell, mayhap, for I am rebellious at times, and is not rebellion the sign of Satan?"

"What is it ye rebel against?" asked the priest, feeling as if he were in some heavy darkness full of pits and dragons.

The minister sighed and sighed. "I rebel that none here hae the courage to come to the kirk because the Squire hates me, and he hates those who will stand with me. The hamlet's life depends on his ain good will. I rebel that my Betsy mourns to be with her faether, whom she loves, and he willna have her the noo. I rebel when she, who is with our child, pretends to have no appetite so that I may hae something to eat. I rebel that man's heart is sae hard and there is no kindness in him, but only darkness. 'Man is desperately wicked and evil from his youth.' The Master showed the way, but man willna follow it, and laughs at his shepherd. I rebel that I, the minister, am sae futile! And have sae little spirit. I rebel that the Squire terrorizes the countryside so that nae man dare oppose him, and that the Squire will let nae man have a little joy and merriment in his life, in the name of virtue."

All these things did not seem "rebellion" to the priest, and he said warmly, "That is nae rebellion, Bruce! That is good and not evil. The Squire is a bad and wicked man, for a' that he does in the name of virtue. Evil is an excess of virtue, sae often times. You have too scrupulous a conscience, and scrupulosity is oft an error."

The minister was a little shocked and sat back and stared at the priest. "Tom! A man's conscience canna be too scrupulous!"

We are not speaking the same language, thought the priest in distress, and it came to him, in a startling fashion, that semantics could be a stony barrier between man and his brother, not bringing them together but holding them apart. He had never thought highly of Socrates, so bent on his exact definition of terms and his exact semantics that he had lost touch with the warm heart of man, but now he conceded that Socrates may have had a point. Father Tom thought of the Tower of Babel. It had not only been the cause of new languages among men but had confused the same language which all spoke in common.

It was a relief to the priest when the lovely little Betsy shyly rejoined the two young men. She appeared tired. She sat down and looked earnestly at the priest. "I hae heard my faether is not sae well," she murmured. "Did he appear so to you?" Her eyes were full of wretched love.

"He seemed," said Father Tom, with his new grimness, "unco well indeed." He wanted to add the Scots saying, "The divil takes care of his ain," but that would have been not only un-Christian but would have upset little Betsy.

He could not resist, however, saying to the minister, "God does not 'determine' a man's immortal fate when He creates that man's soul. God gives man free will. If He did not, then He would be the creator of evil and not of sublime and absolute good."

The minister was freshly shocked.

"He gives man the choice," went on the priest, firmly. "He knew, when He created the soul of the Blessed Mother, that she would accept Christ as her Son, but she had the free will to accept or not. God is omniscient, but man's will is his own."

The minister was embarrassed at this sudden spout of dogma, and ashamed that he had put the priest into this position. His innocent eyes filled with tears. "I am not even a good host," he said with miserable contrition. "I thought to make ye my friend."

"I am not a good guest," said Father Tom, contrite also. "We each hae his belief; we shouldna step on toes. Forgive me. Ye are not only my friend but ye are my brother."

Touching relief flooded the minister's very young face, and he held out his hand frankly. Never before had he extended his hand to anyone, because of his shyness, but had always waited to see if handshaking would be pleasing to others first. The two clergymen shook hands, Betsy curtseyed timidly, and Father Tom, now definitely feeling he was an Older Man—in fact, quite elderly—took his leave, thinking.

The next morning, cold and early and stark with strong northern light, found the priest trundling his noisy barrow to the manse, to the high excitement of the watchers behind the curtains. He knocked smartly on the door, and Betsy, sleepy-eyed and pale, answered. "A good morning to you, Mistress Gregor," said Father Tom. "And may I hae the ladder we talked of yesterday?"

Betsy looked at the barrow filled with slates and topped with hammer and nails, and swallowed. "Ye?" she murmured. The priest nodded with that wonderful new firmness of his, and, speechless now, Betsy gestured towards the back of the manse. The priest fetched the ladder and set it up against the eaves, carefully removed his coat and hat and laid them on the gate. He flexed his muscles, filled his basket, and climbed. Betsy came to the foot of the ladder and called up faintly, "Faether, if my Dada hears of this he will drive ye from the hamlet."

"He'll drive nae man from this day forward from the hamlet," said Father Tom, examining the roof with a keen eye. Betsy stared up at him with enormous and very dazed eyes. "It's nae proper for a clergyman," she murmured.

"Not proper to labor?" said the priest. "I must disagree, Mistress Gregor."

"Bruce will nae like it," she said.

"Bruce will like a sound roof," he answered in a tone of authority, which immediately made the girl respectful. She retreated within the tiny manse.

The Protestants were appalled at the thought of a "Roman" repairing the manse, and the Catholics were indignant and embarrassed. A priest, roofing the manse of a heretic! "I'll nae hold up my head again," declared Mrs. Logan to a neighbor, after she had run to her pub to spread the news. The pub was not officially open, but people were there as to a common gathering place for the dissemination of scandal. But Mr. Logan was thoughtful, and as he blew on a glass and polished it he said, "It will fair madden the Squire, and I dinna find it in my heart to shed tears for his worship." He had no love for the Squire, who, though he was "invested" in numerous pubs in surrounding hamlets, constantly inveighed against drinking. A fair hypocrite he is, thought Mr. Logan, resentfully. A mair one I niver knew. If it were not for the Squire there would be more merriment in the village, and more open conviviality. Now a man had to drink almost in secret to avoid annoying the Squire, and secrecy, thought Mr. Logan, was the mother of sin. And the Sundays! It was "mair" like death than death itself; even the bairns dared not laugh in their prams on the street. It was the Squire's doing. It was sinful, but the Catholics, themselves, dared not take happiness and relaxation on Sundays in the hamlet, not even playing horseshoes or singing softly on doorsteps. Did Our Lord want man to suffer on the Sabbath? Nay, nay!

Father Tom found the same isolation about him as he worked on the roof that he had found when repairing his own. Curtains tweaked, but no face appeared. The hammer rang. Father Tom began to sing. He fervently dedicated his heart to Old Scotia in passionate off-key. He throbbed over ballads concerning the sufferings and deaths of true Scotsmen at the hands of the Sassenach. " 'Scots wha hae wi' Wallace bled!' " he cried to the strong cold wind. " 'Welcome to your gory beds!' "

He aroused even the invalids from their beds so that they tottered to the curtains to see the scandalous sight of a clergyman hammering and chipping away and scrambling about a roof. "Lak a beetle, wi' no respect for his calling," was the general consensus. But eventually some very aged gentlemen, of both religions, gathered before the manse and added their quavering notes to the rousing choruses. Sometimes Father Tom would pause to lead them with his hammer from above, like a conductor of a symphony. It was very scandalous indeed.

Suddenly the old gentlemen in their caps fell silent, and Father Tom looked down to see the Squire on his horse.

"A guid morning to you, sir," said Father Tom, saluting with his hammer. "I hae not forgotten I am having tea with you tomorrow."

The Squire's face was an interesting lavender and his eyes sparked with something that was not mirth. The old gentlemen meekly pulled their caps off, then drifted slowly away, not entirely away but to a small distance.

"In the name of hell what are ye doing?" asked the Squire in a soft voice.

Father Tom looked surprised. "I am mending a roof," he said.

"Get ye doon from there," the Squire said, even softer.

Father Tom fitted a slate and hammered it cleanly into place. The clatter echoed in the deep and shining silence. Then he said, "No."

"Ye are doing Our Lord's work, are ye?"

"Aye, that I am."

"Get doon!" The Squire had not raised his voice, but the old men retreated another few feet. The hamlet held its collective breath.

"I take it," said Father Tom, critically examining another slate, "that ye dinna want me for tea tomorrow?"

"Get doon!" The Squire drove his horse almost up against the house.

"No," said Father Tom. He looked at the roof. "A fair shame it is, that the wee minister's manse is not fit for man or beast. That beastie of yours, he lies sweeter in his stall than your daughter lies in her bed in this hut."

"Damn you!" said the Squire. "Shall I pull ye from the roof?"

No one, not even the most irascible old priest, had ever spoken to Father Tom in such a tone and so he did not know that the sudden hard beat of his heart and the hot swelling of his face were the result of intense wrath. He crouched on the roof and held his hammer tightly.

"Ye shall not pull me from anywhere," he said. His teeth suddenly hurt; he did not know he had clenched them together and was speaking through them. "A wicked auld man with the evil in his heart! D'ye think I do this to shame ye? Ye are not that high in my regard. I bought these slates before I hae the misfortune to lay an een upon ye, and for this purpose. Along with ye, man, to your knees and contrition!"

The lavender changed to thick purple on the Squire's face. His whole big body vibrated. He said to the nearest old man, "Tammy, get the constable."

The old man scuttled away with a frightened face. Father Tom drew one deep breath after another to stop the wild roaring of his heart, then resumed his work. The blows on the slates were extremely hard, and one shattered and flew in chips. The hamlet watched. Father Tom tested the chimney and made a note in his mind to get enough mortar for the stones. His face was wet with cold sweat, the icy sweat of anger.

Then the constable arrived on his bicycle, a small man with a very large red mustache and ears that protruded from under his cap. He dismounted and looked up at the Squire, who pointed at the priest with his crop. "Order that—that priest from the roof which isna his property, George!"

Father Tom looked down over his shoulder at the bewildered constable and smiled a little. He was still somewhat breathless. "Inform yon auld laddie that it isna his property either, Constable," he said.

The constable swallowed nervously. It so happened that he was one of Father Tom's parishioners. He said, "Faether, will ye come doon, please?"

"Why?" asked the priest. "Is it a crime I am committing, then?"

"Faether, it is scandalous," the constable pleaded.

"It is that," the priest agreed. "Scandalous that a minister of the Gospel should live under a leaking roof, and not a man in this hamlet brave enough, or guid enough, to mend it. A braw lot of laddies ye are!"

The constable turned a bright pink. "Faether," he said, "it isna seemly. Hae ye permission to do this to this manse?"

Father Tom paused. He had not considered this aspect of the

question. Then he saw Mr. Gregor's bicycle approaching at a frantic speed, and he squatted on the roof until the minister had reached the house and had taken in the situation thoroughly. The small man appeared overwhelmed with shame, fear and misery. The priest smiled at him reassuringly.

"Bruce," he said with affection, "I hae taken this occasion to mend the roof of the manse. Hae I your permission?"

The Squire kept his back and the rear of his horse to the trembling young minister and gave no sign that he was there. But the minister looked at that formidable back, then up at Father Tom and moistened his pale lips.

"There's none to hurt you mair than ye hae been hurt," said the priest, gently. "There's none to fear but God."

"I——" began the minister. The door opened and Betsy's white face appeared. There were tears on her cheeks. Her father accorded her no more recognition than he had given her husband. "Betsy, my love," said the minister, in despair.

The girl advanced to the doorstep. The old gentlemen had been joined by several younger men, some women and a number of children. She looked at her father's hating and disgusted profile, then at her husband's tremulous face, then up at the priest.

She said in a clear young voice. "The good Faether is mending our roof, Bruce. Will ye thank him kindly for us?" She put her white hands over her swelling body, and her eyes, steadfast and brown as a burn in spring, fixed themselves on her husband's.

Bruce looked at her long and earnestly, and she smiled. Then an astonishing thing happened. The young minister appeared to grow at least three inches taller and four inches broader. The features which had always been gentle became stern, and in that moment the minister's youth left him and he was a man.

"How can a man thank one sae good as Faether Tom?" he said. "I can only pray for him, that God will bless him."

The priest closed his eyes for a moment. Then he said to the constable, "Ye see, I hae permission."

The constable removed his cap and scratched his head. Then he remembered that he was The Law. He said to the small crowd,

severely, "And hae ye no better to do this early in the day than to
hinder a man in his work?"

The crowd raised the smallest but surest of cheers, smiled, and
dispersed a few more feet. The constable straightened, and gave them
a frown from under his red eyebrows. They stepped back ten or
twelve more inches.

"And you, sir," said the constable to the Squire, "is there ought
I can do for ye?"

The Squire touched the crop to his horse and it jumped forward.
"At five, tomorrow!" Father Tom called after him. The Squire rode
off down the road, and the horse's hoofs struck fire on the cobbles.

"Ye'll come in for tea when ye are finished, Tom?" asked the
young minister, who now stood on the doorstep with his arm about
his wife. He was so tall and strong now, and she leaned against him.

"Gladly," said the priest. The hammer banged. "Sing us another
song," said one of the people.

So the priest sang:

> "Here's freedom to him that wad read!
> Here's freedom to him that wad write!
> There's none ever fear'd that the truth should be heard,
> But they wham the truth wad indite!"

The minister joined in the rousing chorus, and the walls of every
house echoed back the singing. Betsy looked at her husband with
pride and joy.

"Oh, there's none ever fear'd," sang the priest, "that the truth
   should be heard,
But they wham the truth wad indite! Indite! Indite!"

As the little crowd joined in the lusty singing every eye turned
down the street to the Squire's house.

The westlin wind came in with a roar that night and drove the
summer from the land with its lances of lightning and its drums of
thunder. But the roofs of the rectory and the manse did not leak
though the slates rattled with gusts of hail and water flowed over

them in miniature rivers. Father Tom lay contentedly on his hard bed and listened to the storm, secure in the knowledge that his house was safe, and the manse of the minister was safe, too. The sea rushed at the high headland on which the village perched, and roared away furiously, and all the air was filled with its salt and the scent of the pines. The hills crouched under the lightning, and echoed back the thunder. It's nae night for man or beast, thought the priest as he fell asleep.

The one Mass was well attended the next morning, for all the rain and the wind, and as Father Tom turned to bless his flock he saw the gleam of pride in many an eye in that leaden light. They were proud of him! Almost everyone came to the Communion rail, and the prideful eyes beamed upon him. Our ain priest! they seemed to say. And all he had done was to mend a roof.

Mrs. Logan informed him, when he entered the rectory shrugging water from his shoulders, that he had a visitor. "It's auld Jim," she said in a curious voice. "A bad lot, that Jim."

Father Tom doubted that there was any "bad lot" in the hamlet save for Squire MacVicar, that man of monolithic virtue. He could not recall any "auld Jim." Mrs. Logan, sniffing as she warmed the kippers, said that Jim was a heathen, not even a Presbyterian. He had probably not even been baptized. He had had nary a wife or a bairn, but had lived what Mrs. Logan discreetly described as an un-Christian life. He was a roisterer, a son of Satan, himself, and second to the Squire in money. He had been born somewhere "aboot," but where exactly no one ever had discovered. He had a small farm which he did not cultivate, and no animals but a herd of sheep. His money? He had been a smuggler "in the lang ago." Somewhere in England, it was said. But she, Mrs. Logan, should not complain. He spent much time in the pub and was one of its most valued customers.

"But it's the foul mouth he has, Faether, and there's many who crosses himself when auld Jim passes, or makes the sign against the evil eye."

"Why should he come to me, then?" asked the priest.

Mrs. Logan shrugged. "Not to be shrived, and ye can bank on that, Faether!"

She insisted that the priest have his breakfast before seeing his visitor, "who is smelling up the parlor with one of them cheroots from London, Faether." So the priest ate his kippers and a boiled egg, after downing a monster plate of oatmeal, milk and treacle, and drank his good hot tea. Mrs. Logan complained only once about the ham which had been given to the wee minister, but her eyes were proudful too. To think it was our ain priest who had driven the Squire off like a bad schoolboy, and never turned a hair!

Father Tom opened the door of his parlor cum study, where it was icy cold. He hesitated on seeing a large cloud of smoke rising from a chair, then glanced back at the kitchen. Mrs. Logan affected to be totally absorbed in washing up. The priest closed the door firmly, shivered, and advanced into the tidy room. "Ye wish to see me?" he asked.

The cloud moved and a short fat figure rose from under it, a rough figure in coarse but hearty tweeds. Then the priest saw an uncommonly fat round face, very old and very jolly, and the naughtiest and brightest blue eyes he had ever encountered. For some reason he wanted to laugh, for laughter was etched all over that ancient red face. Not evil laughter, but the virile mirth of a man who has greatly enjoyed life and who was continuing to enjoy it robustly.

The short stout figure extended a short fat arm. "Jim Ferguson, my lad," said the old man in a booming voice that echoed laughter. "Ye'll be the priest, Father Weir?"

The handgrip was as strong as a youth's and the priest winced a little. He assured Mr. Ferguson that he was indeed the priest and what could he do for his visitor? Mr. Ferguson settled back in his chair, blew another cloud of smoke, then offered Father Tom a cheroot. The priest had never smoked one. He accepted the cheroot and Mr. Ferguson lighted it for him, smoothly bending to strike a lucifer on the sole of his excellent boot. The priest puffed; the cheroot was excellent.

"I would join your kirk, sir," said Mr. Ferguson.

Father Tom sat up straight. "Why?" he exclaimed.

Mr. Ferguson wagged a pink finger at him. "I swore, as a lad, that never would I join any man's kirk unless that man had blood in his veins and not milk. I hae," said Mr. Ferguson, "a low opinion of the clergy, Roman or Protestant."

"Oh," said Father Tom. He puffed again. A fine cheroot, this.

"I'll not be offending you, sir?"

"No," said the priest, after a moment's thought. "Every man to his ain opinion. But why do ye want to join this kirk?"

Mr. Ferguson gave so infectious a chuckle that the priest found himself chuckling also.

"I heard of the row ye had with the Squire, and there's a man I hate," said Mr. Ferguson, cheerfully. "A man of virtue, to turn a good man's belly. I hae known him for many a year, and never hae I seen him but what I puked. So, ye drove him off, and gave him word for word! Him, who always had the clergy crawling at his feet and whimpering like a wean."

The priest reflected as he smoked. "Now," he said, "that's an unco strange reason for wanting to enter Mother Church. Are ye a Christian, Mr. Ferguson?"

"No, thank God," said Mr. Ferguson, with gusto.

"Ye have had no religious training?"

"None," said Mr. Ferguson, pridefully. He nodded at the closed kitchen door. "No doot Mrs. Logan has told ye of me. She dinna know the whole truth!" He chuckled mightily again.

The priest cleared his throat and waved away a rich cloud of smoke. "Ye are thinking of this time in your life, Mr. Ferguson, and your immortal soul?"

"Not a damned bit of it!" said Mr. Ferguson.

The priest sat up. The man must be all of eighty. "Ye believe in God, then?" said Father Tom.

"Not a bit," said Mr. Ferguson. "But I'm a man what listens. I'll listen the day to ye, my laddie, courteous as a Sassenach banker."

"Don't ye *want* to believe in God?" asked the priest, a little desperately.

"Now why?" asked Mr. Ferguson, all sweet reason. "What hae He done for me? I done it all by mesel', and I'll not tell you how."

Again he chuckled and shook his head happily, remembering his youthful years.

"But why do you want to enter this kirk?" Father Tom's voice rose a little.

The old man pointed his finger at the priest. "You," he said. He cocked his head like a fat old rooster. "Do ye, now, believe in God?"

"I do that!"

"Aweel, then," said Mr. Ferguson, all sweet reason once more, "it is enough for auld Jim. Ye believe and so auld Jim will believe."

"There's a wee bit more to faith than that," said Father Tom, baffled.

"Tell me then, and be quick about it, for there's another storm coming up." Mr. Ferguson sat back in his chair and waited brightly.

The priest's thoughts whirled. No one in the Seminary had ever spoken of any such situation as this and how to manage it. And here was an ancient soul definitely for the burning. Father Tom looked into the cheerful blue eyes, the naughty, not evil eyes, and at the sturdy and friendly face which openly admired him.

"Suppose, then," said the priest, "that we begin with the catechism." He got up and went to his little store of catechisms, and the old man watched him carefully. "Nae much meat under those skirts," he commented. Father Tom, assuming the utmost dignity, put the catechism into the wide red palm open to receive it.

"I canna read," said Mr. Ferguson. He winked. "But that didna keep me from getting rich."

"Is there someone who could read it for you?"

"My auld lassie. She reads well enough, and writes."

"I—I thought ye had nae wife, Mr. Ferguson."

"Nor do I have, sir. She's just my auld lassie. I hae had her for forty year or more. Bonnie, still."

The priest was shocked. Mr. Ferguson looked at him with friendly expectancy.

"You mean—mean," stammered the priest, "ye hae not married—your auld lassie?"

"No. I dinna believe in it." Mr. Ferguson was just slightly impatient now.

"Ye are living in sin!" the young priest blurted in horror.

Mr. Ferguson was interested. "Are we, the noo? What is sin, sir?"

Father Tom was aghast. The old man was actually primitive! A heathen, indeed. "Sin—sin—is disobedience to the Laws of God, Mr. Ferguson! And God doesna approve of men and women living together and they not being married."

"Aweel, aweel!" said Mr. Ferguson. "He is like the Squire, is He?"

"No!" Father Tom almost shouted, and Mrs. Logan, her ear against the door, recoiled in trepidation. "God is *not* like the Squire!"

"Then," said Mr. Ferguson, somewhat startled, "He's the Man for me." He eyed the priest a little anxiously. "I hae not offended you, sir? Ye see, anyone like the Squire would turn a man's belly. There were two little lassies here in the hamlet who were left orphans; no faether, no mither. No hame. So they obliged the lads, and Squire MacVicar drove them away and when the winter went the poor wee things were found dead in the forest yon. I wasna here; if I had been here I'd hae given the lassies some money to send them to Edinburgh to open a shop or some'at. Bonnie wee things." The blue eyes filled with anger and tears.

"The quality of mercy," thought the young priest, in confusion. The virtuous man had driven two children to their death; the bad man would have saved them.

"They had a handsome grave the noo," said Mr. Ferguson. "The auld minister that was let them be buried in the churchyard, and there's a fine stone on their graves. The Squire tried to stop it, but no man can stop auld Jim!" He sighed, gustily. "The Squire wouldna give them bread, the wee bairns, but auld Jim could give them a stone. With their names on it, as a reproach to the Squire and the divils in the hamlet."

Father Tom knew all about the problem of evil, or at least thought he knew something. But he had never heard of the problem of virtue before. Who was the evil man, the Squire or Mr. Ferguson? He decided, after a moment's study, that the Squire was the evil man, and Mr. Ferguson, who "lived in sin," was actually a good one. Dear me, the young man thought, there are great problems in this world and sometimes one does not know where he is.

He said, "But the Squire, I hae heard, does good things for the hamlet, the school, and the auld folks, and the food——"

Mr. Ferguson waved a dismissing hand. "It's a reputation for virtue he would have, but I know him for a bad man. It's a bad face on him, and a bad heart in him."

The priest was inclined to agree, then hastily shut off the thought. He had not the slightest idea of how to manage this matter, so he closed his eyes and prayed for help. When he opened them he discovered that Mr. Ferguson was regarding him with concern.

"Are ye sick, sir?" said Mr. Ferguson.

"Why do ye ask that?"

"Ye closed your eyes and leaned back." He fished in a very large pouch and brought out a bottle of whiskey. "A wee drap."

"I was praying!" said Father Tom, considerably nettled.

"What for?" Mr. Ferguson was deeply interested.

"For you!"

"Now, that's fair good of you, laddie." He considered this for a moment. "Why?" he asked.

Father Tom had never wanted to swear in his life before but now he felt the need of a good oath. He groaned inwardly and reminded himself to make a perfect Act of Contrition tonight. "Ye need it. Ye are a sinner, Mr. Ferguson."

"Am I now?" Mr. Ferguson was more interested than ever.

"Do you not know right from wrong?"

Mr. Ferguson turned that about in his mind with great concentration. Then he nodded eagerly, wishing to please this peculiar young man.

"I do that!" he said. "Ye never steal from a puir or a good man, and ye never kill unless the bas—the divil wants to kill ye first. And ye hate the Sassenach."

The priest looked mortally pained. Then he remembered the mission priests in darkest Africa. They had to start from absolute bottom, as he would have to start. Ah, it was no different! God had answered his prayer. He smiled palely.

"Ye and your—your—auld lassie will have to be joined in lawful wedlock," he said. "Before ought can be done. What is her name?"

"Florrie." Mr. Ferguson's face became fond. "She was in a hoose in London. The bonniest lassie in the whole hoose."

The priest winced. A heathen and a Magdalen. "Florrie what?"

Mr. Ferguson scratched his thatch of vigorous white hair. "I dinna know," he confessed. "I didna ask."

"And ye have lived with—with—her for forty years?"

"Forty-one. I mind me it was a Christmas Eve I met her."

The priest winced again.

"Ah, that was a lively night!" said Mr. Ferguson enthusiastically. The priest raised his hand. He had no desire to hear about that "lively night."

"Will ye bring her to me and be married before me?" (Was that correct? Father Tom asked himself with new wildness.)

"I will that!" cried Mr. Ferguson. "If it will please ye, sir."

"It's not I to be pleased. It is God."

"Good," said Mr. Ferguson. "He is your God, and He will be mine. Hae a wee drap?"

The priest felt he needed a wee drap very badly, and so he took the bottle, wiped the top with his sleeve, and drank slightly more than a wee amount. He wished his Bishop were not so far away. But then, the priests were far away from their Bishops when they were in Africa, too.

"Will—er—Florrie want to be married to you, Mr. Ferguson?" The whiskey was very warming and comforting in this dank little room.

"Oh, Florrie willna say me nay in anything, sir." Mr. Ferguson was very happy as he saw color coming back into the young man's face. "Never a cross word from her. A mair lovely woman was nae born. My bonnie Florrie. I talked aboot ye last night to her, and she fair fell in love with ye. She was in your kirk, sir, when a little lass."

"A Catholic!" Father Tom's spine became rigid again.

"Weel, yes. But she doesna know much aboot it. She hae the paper, but that's a'. Lost her mither and faether when a wee bairn, and left on the street."

The priest groaned aloud now, then took another draught of the whiskey. God forgive him, but he needed it.

He said resolutely, "Bring your—your—lady—tomorrow, Mr. Ferguson, with the paper, and I will witness your wedding." (Was this creating scandal? But the natives in Africa—— Surely the priest wedded them first. It was only right.)

Mr. Ferguson leapt to his feet like a lad. He seized the priest's hand. "That I will, sir! Gie me the time, and we'll come. And then ye'll let us in the kirk?"

The woman was Catholic, even if she knew little or nothing about it, and this ancient would wed her, and she would learn, with him, all that they should know. Father Tom desperately hoped, again, that this would not be a cause for scandal. But, what else could he do? He could not instruct an old man in the Faith who was living in sin. The wedding must come first, after the baptism. It would be like baptizing an infant.

"Will ye be baptized?" asked the priest.

The old man stared, confused. "Christened," said the priest. Mr. Ferguson nodded eagerly. "That I will. Florrie hae told me. Last night. She doesna want to go to heaven if I canna go, too."

More than a little dazed, Father Tom saw his guest to the door. A fine carriage waited outside. And a coachman! Mr. Ferguson was staring with disapproval at the church. "It doesna look braw," he commented. "I will build ye a new kirk, sir."

The priest, more dazed than ever, watched the ancient march rapidly to his carriage, and bounce up into it like a troll. Then Father Tom returned to the kitchen to find Mrs. Logan with a very red face and a sheepish smile. "I hope," he said severely, "that ye heard everything, Mistress Logan. If not, I will tell ye. And it is a serious sin to gossip or repeat what ye hae heard in this hoose." He walked away sternly, noting how the poor woman's face had fallen.

The westlin wind had dropped by tea-time, and the sky, though dark as lead, did not threaten more rain. The flags of the road were wet and puddly. Father Tom made his way to Squire MacVicar's house.

As he walked the priest pondered on what he had learned of the

Squire's truly magnificent charities, and his great solicitude for the old, the sick, the crippled and maimed of the village, the blind and the suddenly destitute. (The priest had an insight as to why the Squire had been so vindictive to the young orphaned girls who had "obliged the lads" when left without funds. He was against "sin." The girls had not appealed to him in their stunning plight. In the Squire's view, this was unpardonable, for was he not ready at all times to succor the helpless?) Among the many other things he had done was to establish a small and sound and free library, a thing unheard of in those parts. The school was truly fine. One of the small rooms contained replicas of works of art, all pure however. The children were served hot soup and bread and meat or fish for their midday meal, so that none should starve and none should be forced to race home in the furious winter weather. The Squire had attempted to buy up the old houses from their individual owners, so that he could renovate and repair them and "keep them up." As a Scotsman, thought the priest, he ought to have known his country-men's fierce pride in property, but he had failed in this instance.

The streets were kept in splendid order. He paid the wages of the constable, the teachers in his free school, the cleaners of the streets. He had introduced a method of farming among the farmers which prevented the erosion of their land, and lent them money at low interest to keep the bankers in the cities at bay. He had established a small bowling green outside the village. In short, there was nothing he had overlooked to make the villagers happier and healthier and literate.

However, he had been a tyrant. His word was law, even above that of the mayor's, whose salary he had increased without benefit of taxes on the inhabitants. He had not suffered sin tolerantly, and his intolerance had been far in excess of the usual Scots in-tolerance. He could not close the pub, for that would have aroused more opposition, and would have endangered his small czarship. He opposed drinking. He violently fought against smoking, would permit no man, however old or weary, to smoke in his presence and enjoy his pipe.

He was feared, though praised. When a harmless lad such as the

priest had challenged him his very beneficiaries had raised a small
cheer; they had beamed at the priest at Mass—the Catholics. They
had beamed at him, all of them, in the little shops, on the streets.
There was, thought Father Tom, no love for any despot, however
benevolent, especially among the Scots, and the priest rejoiced at this,
knowing his Edmund Burke. But despots, whether benevolent or
cruel, never learned that the love for liberty was steadfast in every
man's soul except for the naturally craven and servile, who had suppressed their gift from God in pure greed and the satisfaction of
immediate appetites.

There is no understanding man! thought the young priest suddenly,
and in that moment he lost his youth forever, and the souls of the
dead and wise old priests gathered to help him, as they always
must. His thoughts depressed him. He had believed that man was
intrinsically simple, that good and evil are definitely defined with
a wide area between them, that men have the capacity for gratitude
and that they prefer the true and pure above the false and the
impure, and God above the devil.

He paused a moment to look at the sky and earnestly pose a
question at its cold and darkened imperviousness. An enormous
answer began to stir in the depths of his mind but it was still
shadowy. He went on, still pondering, and very slowly. A dog barked
somewhere, and the stark hills behind the hamlet echoed the lonely
sound. The sun was dropping; it was a scarlet smudge in the wester-
ing sky, amorphous behind the clouds.

Why, thought the priest, had Squire MacVicar, a literate and
intelligent man, come to this isolated and desolate spot to live, this
hamlet poised on the lip of a cliff rearing up from the sea? What
was here to stimulate and fill his mind? What companionship could
he have among these small farmers, shopkeepers, sheep-herders, wool-
gatherers, whiskey-makers? What voice answered him in accents he
knew and in words that were not utterly plain and simple? He was
obviously a man not only of substance but of education and breeding.
Why had he come here of all the places in the world?

The priest had reached the Squire's house. It was no larger and
no more ornamented than its sound small neighbors. But the gardens

in front and in the rear were crowded with color and with the dark thickness of old trees. There was even a greenhouse! The knocker on the oaken door was not the simple one of the other houses—iron. It was a fine affair of polished copper in the shape of a sea nymph's head. The doorstep was of copper, too, covered with small drops of crystal water. The priest lifted the knocker and the sharp sound was repeated all up and down the winding street.

A little woman with a cold and costive face appeared almost at once, a white frilled cap on her gray hair, a white frilled apron over her black bombazine dress. She stared at the priest inimically. "And what would ye want—sir?" she asked, in a most forbidding voice, glaring with contempt at his habit.

"The Squire hae invited me to tea this day," said the priest.

She rejected him with her bitter eyes. "He hae told me nothing of it."

"Ask him," Father Tom suggested, and was surprised at the irritability of his voice.

She hesitated. Then her face changed. "I will gi'e ye a little advice," she said. "Come another day. The Squire—he is not himself."

The priest thought. Had the Squire ordered that he be turned away? He said, "Hae he told ye not to admit me?"

She shook her head. "Nay, not that. He is joost not himself."

"Sick?"

She was so relieved at this offer of delivery that she answered too quickly, "Aye, that! He is sick."

The priest gently reached over her shoulder and pushed the door open. "Then, I will see him. He hae invited me, and will wonder that I did not come."

He stepped into a small hall, bricked and shining with wax. A series of small rooms led from it. The priest was now familiar with the design of such houses and he went at once to the room he knew to be the parlor.

Here the gloom of the day was intensified to a heavy dusk. And the air was filled with the unmistakable acrid odor of whiskey. It smelled like a busy pub. The draperies had been drawn over the little windows. Shapes of furniture could hardly be seen. Only the smallest of coal fires glowed on the polished hearth, and it was like a red eye in the dimness.

The housekeeper thrust herself past the priest and stood in front of him and shrilled, "Master, it is nae my fault! He would force himself! I did try to keep him oot!"

What little light there was in the house flowed from the hall and outlined the tall thin figure of the youthful priest. He felt himself under some grim inspection from somewhere in the parlor. Then he heard the Squire's voice, thick with drink, and slowly harsh. "Let him be. Come in, man, come in, and rejoice your eyes. Be off, woman."

"Tea, Master?" she asked timidly.

"Nay, no tea. If he willna drink whiskey with me, he willna have anything. Light the lamp before ye go, woman."

The little woman scurried into the parlor and lighted one lamp. Its dull and murky light only increased the airless gloom. And there was the Squire, himself, slumped in a big chair, a bottle at his side, one on the floor, and a glass in his hand.

Father Tom was shocked. He could hardly believe that this great and rumpled man, monolithic in his chair near the fire, uncombed, unbrushed and very much unshaven, was the Squire MacVicar he had known, arrogant, and lordly and straight as an oak on his horse. The fierce eyes were sunken and reddened; the chin lay on the chest. The big nose had a squashed look. The mouth, only, retained its strength.

"Ye dinna like what ye see, perhaps," said the Squire. He pulled himself upright in his chair. He might be excessively drunk, but he was conscious, and now there was even a little malign amusement in his dragging voice. "And ye will be the first to know, other than Mistress Foy, that I am a drunkard."

The priest stared at him with a sudden and mysterious pity, profound and painful. And the Squire stared back at him, his eyes glinting with mockery and contempt. The Squire said, "Weel, now, come ye in and seat yourself, and join me in my celebration."

"Ye invited me," murmured the priest.

"Sae I did," said the Squire. "Weel, come ye in. Are ye waiting for something, ye loon?"

The priest went into the parlor and sat down near the Squire. With one part of his mind he acknowledged that the chair was large and soft and that the rest of the furniture could be described not only as luxurious but elegant. But his eyes were fixed on the Squire. He was about to say, "Perhaps I should come another day," when he was stopped. It was as if a strong hand had been placed firmly over his mouth.

"Hae a drink. It will do ye good," said the Squire, and fished about on the table at his side for another glass. He found it. With the careful and intent precision of a very drunken man he filled it almost full and extended it to the priest. Father Tom took it; the Squire watched him. The priest sipped the whiskey. It was the very best he had ever tasted. The cold in his bones, which had come not only from the weather, began to ease.

"Ye like my whiskey?" said the Squire.

"I do that," said the priest, and it was as though someone else were supplying his words and he was only repeating them obediently.

The Squire's filmy eyes wandered about the room very slowly, focusing now on a table, now on a picture on the paneled walls, now on the floor, now on the fire. They finally came back to the priest. "Ye will be telling of this to the town, nae doubt," he said.

"Ye know better than that," said Father Tom.

An extraordinary change came over the Squire's face. He sat up very straight. He appeared galvanized by some unknown wrath and hatred which overcame even his drunkenness. "Ah!" he exclaimed. "It is true, ye will not tell! But in your black heart ye will condemn, ye will turn away, ye will lift your pure skirts! Ye will pray for me, perhaps, but in your wicked superiority ye will think I am a lost soul! I know you priests! Damn you, do I not know ye!"

The new mysterious prompter in him made the priest take another careful sip of the whiskey, roll it on his tongue, then swallow it with a judicious expression.

"Very good whiskey," he said.

The Squire stared at him, watched him for the slightest quiver, the slightest look of repugnance, the slightest fear.

"Damn ye," he said, in a soft voice.

"'Tis not for ye to say," said the priest. "Nae man is condemned by any but himself."

"I know your jargon!" shouted the Squire, and he struck his big knee with his fist. "'Nae man is rejected by God! He, himself, rejects God and estranges himself from Him!'"

"That," said the priest, lifting his glass to study the whiskey in the light of the fire, "is nae Presbyterianism." He drank a little more, and took an instant to marvel at his new self. A month before this he would have shrunk in fear from the Squire; his shyness would have made him retreat, trembling. Yet here he sat, before a wild and drunken and blasphemous man, and could speak calmly and feel only the most aching of compassions!

The Squire refilled his own glass. The whiskey splashed on his hand. He said, speaking aloud to himself in a rough, pent voice: "Why do I bother with this silly, stripling priest, this lad with the down on his cheek, this piping creature just from his mither's skirts? Why do I not throw him from my hoose, this puling mouther of lies? Why hae I suffered him sae long, in my hamlet, this trouble-maker, this scorner of authority? What is he to me?"

The priest was silent. He turned the glass in his hand. He looked at it. He sat quietly in his chair, listening as if he were in the Confessional.

"Damn ye!" shouted the Squire. "Why do ye not answer me?"

"It is not I ye question," said the priest.

"Who, then?"

"God," said the priest.

As if that Name had been a terrible precipitant, the Squire jumped up from his chair, and so violent was his movement that it overturned with a crash. He fell upon the priest and seized him by the shoulders and shook him with even more violence.

"Oh, curse ye!" he stammered in fury. "Look at me! I am a priest! An ordained priest! A Monsignor! That I am! And who are ye!"

The glass fell from the priest's hand and shattered on the hearth.

A cold horror filled him. His mind whirled. He wanted to rise, to flee. But it was more than the Squire's powerful hands which kept him pinned to his chair. It was more than fear that dried his mouth, his tongue, his palate. He could not believe what he had heard, but he knew he must believe it.

The Squire released him after another savage shake. Then, like a man possessed, he sprang away. With almost demonic strength he dragged a long narrow table into the center of the room. He flew to a cabinet against a wall and tore from it long lengths of altar cloths, white and fine as silk and flowing with lace. He flung one upon the table. He rushed to the cabinet again and brought from its depths a candelabrum and put it upon the table; he brought forth a tall and exquisitely beautiful crucifix, with the Corpus gleaming on it with the gleam of gold. He put this on the table, too. He brought out a huge Bible bound in leather, glinting with gold letters. He brought out a chalice, pure gold, an exquisite Tabernacle, a ciborium, fine linen, a Monstrance such as the young priest had never seen. They glowed in the lamplight and the firelight.

Moment by moment, before the young priest's aghast eyes, there appeared the high altar, complete in every detail, every article of the most elaborate artistry, and brilliant with golden lights. He sat, unable to move; he told himself he was witnessing blasphemy, but he could not move. He was terrified, but far in his mind there was a comforting and reassuring murmur. I knew; in some way I knew, he answered the murmur meekly, and trembled.

Now the raging Squire went to the cabinet again. He pulled from it an alb and a vestment which shimmered with silver and exquisite embroidery. He put the alb on over his clothing, and it fell about him. He lifted his hands to the crucifix.

The Squire said, in a loud and agonized voice: "Make me white, O Lord, and purify my heart so that, being made white in the Blood of the Lamb, I may deserve an eternal reward!"

He staggered. He caught the edge of the table, steadied himself. He looked at the crucifix. He caught its base in his hands. He bowed his head against the holy Feet. He groaned, "Sanctus. Sanctus.

Sanctus." He groaned over and over, until every object in the room vibrated with that loud and awful groaning.

Slowly, still half staggering, he turned about and faced Father Tom. His eyes were wild and far, as if looking at a sunset, and anguished.

He began to speak, faintly, distantly. *"Dextera Domini fecit virtutem dextera Domini exaltavit me; non moriar, sed vivan, et narrabo opera Domini!"*

He reached for the shining vestments and put them on. He stood, robed as a priest. He stood, tall and brilliant, his face tormented.

Then he saw Father Tom. His mouth fell. His face became that of a stricken old man. He staggered to the priest and fell to his knees and covered his face with his hands.

"Bless me, Father," he moaned, "for I have sinned!"

Father Tom, in Grandmother's parlor, sighed this night. "If I had run, as I had first wanted to do, then this man's soul should have been lost. Great are the mysteries and the mercy of God!"

The Squire's story was the story of demonic pride.

From his earliest boyhood he knew he had a vocation for the priesthood. But his teachers in Edinburgh had been doubtful from the start. They admitted that he had great devotion and piety and absolute faith. But, there was his pride. He was of a proud, haughty and wealthy family, and of the Clan of MacGregor. The ancient blood of Scottish kings ran in his body. The ancient pride was even stronger. He had tried to be meek and simple. Eventually, he had convinced even the Bishop that he would make an excellent priest. The Bishop, of the Clan of MacGregor himself, knew what it was to be proud. He had transmuted his own innate pride to the joy of serving God and His Church. He had thought this would occur to young Ian MacVicar also. So, the aspiring priest had gone to his Seminary, and had tried to subdue his arrogance and his hauteur. He had, over and over, reminded himself that his Lord had washed the feet of His Apostles. But, in his heart, he had thought it a demeaning gesture. He had even thought, in the recesses of his heart, that Christ should not have walked with the humble, the obscure, the illiterate, the sinful. He, Lord of all, should not have condescended to such rabble, the howling, sweating rabble of the market place and the fishing waters. The mighty Lord of Heaven had incomprehensibly associated with the outcast, the mean, the inglorious, the laboring.

At one blasphemous moment years later he had questioned God. Were such of His Kingdom? If so, he wanted nothing to do with it. He committed the sin of Lucifer.

By this time he was not only a priest. He had been elevated to the Monsignori. Moreover, he was a conscientious administrator, excessively scrupulous, excessively inflexible.

Paradoxically, while he despised the obscure, the simple, the illiterate, the seemingly worthless, the unimportant, he was merciful towards them. He poured out much of his fortune in their behalf. It was only when they, with no excuse of blood, no noblesse oblige, no station, took on an ignorant arrogance and bragged and oppressed in their stupidity that he became ruthless. It was very uncomplex to him: the humble should realize that they are humble; the ignorant should understand their ignorance; the unimportant in the world's eye should be aware of their unimportance. Their Lord had been humble and meek and gentle of heart. They acquired stature if they followed Him in humility, meekness and gentleness. But when they became rich beggars on horseback they should be pulled down, the reins taken from their hands. It was notorious that when given a "little brief authority" they trampled their fellows.

Ian MacVicar said to his Bishop, "There is nothing so vile as a stupid gross man in a position of authority, or in an assumption of authority and importance."

The Bishop was inclined to agree. He did not think it proper that a man without training in the arts of civilization should aspire to public office, or authority. That led to chaos and eventual despotism and madness. It was notable, the Bishop admitted, that the most ferocious of tyrants almost inevitably rose from the base and the men of no family. It was also notable that they were merciless to their former companions and hated them, and that they hated, also, their new associates for their nobility and station, and envied them and tried to humiliate them. For the man of low breeding knew in his heart that he had no right to the position he occupied and so avenged himself on all men.

"It was the market rabble of Jerusalem who howled to Pilate, 'Give us Barabbas!'" said Ian MacVicar to his Bishop.

"But," said the Bishop, "it was the aristocratic Pharisees who incited the market rabble, the subtle, well-born and cynical Pharisees. A man should remember that."

It was a long time before he knew that the young priest was a Pharisee. It was a long time before he understood that he and Ian had not been speaking of the same thing at all.

The Bishop tried to be patient. He tried to explain, sympathize and enlighten. But Ian had gone too far in his pride and his anger, which now embraced almost all mankind. He was harsh to sinners and cowed them; he absolved, but with contempt. He said Mass with an expression that implied that those who knelt in the church were committing blasphemy by their very presence before the Most Holy of Holies. He was furious in his authority; some of the Sisters fearfully considered him mad, as time passed. He terrified his curates with his scorn for their lowliness, their simplicity, their gentleness with the stupid and bewildered and the sinners. He strode through his parish like a tyrant, condescending to speak only to those who bowed low before him and treating those who met him eye to eye with a violent look on his face. He would look at the quiet faces of those to whom he administered Holy Communion and they would be affrighted by his glance of outrage and disgust. The Bishop sent for him again, and this time the old man was censorious. Ian must go into retreat, there to learn the humility he lacked, there to learn that all souls were precious to God, and loved by Him, and it was not for Ian to judge, and judge so cruelly and with such vindictiveness.

At this sentence of discipline Ian almost lost his mind. He tore off his clerical collar and flung it at the Bishop's feet. He tore off his cassock, and hurled it at the Bishop. He did this with silent violence, not uttering a word. Then he looked at the Bishop with naked rage and hatred, and said, "I am done with it. I will serve no God who is alleged, by you, to love the wretches I have in my parish, and in the parishes before, and the trollops, and the drunkards and the filthy and the evil and the illiterate and the fools! No longer will I be commanded to pray with the old women and listen to their senile whimperings; no longer will I sit in the Confessional to hear vile little sins worthy only of dogs and not men. No longer will my eye be offended at the sight of these creatures who claim to be mankind, but are but the most degraded of animals! I shall give the Sacred Host no longer to the unworthy and the criminals, or the sly, whining beasts who smell of whiskey and peat and manure! This is not for me——"

He had flung himself from the Bishop's aghast presence and had walked in his bitter proud silence to his rectory and, not speaking to his curates, had packed his bags and had left without a word.

His stricken family turned their faces from him. Independently rich, broken in heart but not in spirit, he fled from them to the most obscure place he could find, his wrath undwindling, his outrage growing, his bitterness increasing. He wanted no more of the Church, or even of God. He would find a place where he could rule, reward the humble suitably, strike down the presumptuous, and where his word was law. He would be a full man again, among men of his choosing, and not a prudent priest who must always suppress his nature. He would marry. He would beget children in whom he would instill his own pride and haughtiness, and make them rulers in their own right. And so he had come to this remote and isolated hamlet and had set up his own laws and his own rule, his own measures of justice, his own penalties, and not a man would dare say him nay nor question his word.

He had, in short, as Father Tom had so innocently said, set up his own little hell, devoid of God. He had exiled himself. He had, in all ways, excommunicated himself.

His grandfather, the richest of all the family, must have understood. He left Ian his fortune, to the embitterment and fury of the other members.

Virtuous, secretly merciful, just, Ian had many of the attributes of a saint but one: he had no humility. He had stubbornly thought that saintly humility had meant, exclusively, wallowing in the gutters with the vile and the sub-human, not to raise them, but to be one with them. This he could not do, when he was a priest and when he was not a priest. He had not understood in the slightest.

When he was past his youth he married. After six months of marriage he was paradoxically horrified, and withdrew from his bewildered young bride. He led the ascetic life of a priest. His wife thought he did not want her, and she had died in her misery. He had a beloved daughter whom he had looked upon, in the dark and bitter places of his heart, as an eternal virgin, pure, undefiled. She had married and he had almost lost his mind. Not until it was almost too late, on the day Father Tom had come to his house, did he realize that he had never once spoken to his child of his own history and that he had never given her his old Faith. He had only blamed her for his own sins, and threw her from his house and tried to obliterate her from his memory. She became a symbol to him of his apostasy, of his excommunicated state. She was a violation of himself.

No one in the hamlet had known, of course, and no one had understood this complex and wretched man. Every man had feared him; his own agony fed on their terror. At each gesture of servility, at each craven and humble word, at each glance of a fearing eye, he had become more arrogant, more hating, more ruthless. His own son-in-law had trembled at the sight of him. Earlier ministers had crept from him. Earlier priests had considered him a cold and brutal man, and their personal enemy.

Then Father Tom had challenged him, in the innocence and purity of his soul. Father Tom had not been afraid of him. Father Tom, for all his shyness, had accepted him. Father Tom had even looked on him with a boyish affection. This had shattered Ian MacVicar. He had determined to try to subdue this childlike courage, to trouble this youthful soul, to throw the young priest into bewilderment, and finally into sniveling subjection. Within a few short days he had utterly failed. And Father Tom had brought to him, in stunning revelation, what it was indeed to be a priest.

Father Tom did not understand, himself, what he had done to Ian MacVicar, but the wise old priests around Grandmother's fire knew exactly. Father Tom, as an old man, could only say, "He had reached the breaking point, that poor man. He was ready for his saving." The other old priests smiled and glanced at each other.

Old Father Tom said, "I had never thought to encounter the problem of intrinsic virtue. But there it was, and I was confused and startled."

"And what did ye do?" asked Grandmother.

"He had confessed to me, that gloomy, windy and raining day in that lonely and isolated place. And then I wrote to my Bishop, and then, fearing that I hadna expressed myself rightly, I went to my Bishop and laid Squire MacVicar's case before him. I was afraid that I hadna behaved myself in the proper fashion. But the Bishop smiled. He wrote to Ian, himself, and Ian went to him."

Old Father Tom lighted his pipe. "Ian was a priest again in all ways. He spent the rest of his life in such humble and isolated places as that hamlet, as a parish priest. I saw him only once after that time. He was the happiest of men, and the most loved. When he died all mourned, even those who were not of the Church. The Bishop, himself, sang the Solemn Requiem Mass.

"He gave half his fortune to his daughter and the wee minister. The authorities in Edinburgh then thought the hamlet 'beneath' the minister and brought him home. They had a lovely son."

Father Tom worked at the dottle in his pipe. "The son was named Ian. He became a priest." Father Tom smiled at his friends. "Strange and wonderful are the ways of God!"

Chapter Ten

It was still early, though the darkness outside pressed itself solidly against Grandmother's house. Everyone considered the tale of Father Weir and his problem of virtue, and Squire MacVicar.

"There is nay black or white," said Grandmother, as if in relief.

"Oh, but there is!" said a priest, Father Joseph Shayne. "There is sin and there is innocence. Those who believe that they meet, somewhere, sometime, are what the philosophers are beginning to call relativists. In short, they are dispensing with values, with the Absolutes of God, with all moral laws. No matter how intricate the subject and the men, there will invariably emerge, after study, the fact that there is but sin—or innocence. It is true that the innocent in their innocence sometimes commit evil, but if the evil is not in their hearts or in their intentions, then they are not guilty.

"It is true that the wicked sometimes do good, but that is not their inner intention, but the mercy of God. For what is black cannot become white, and what is white cannot become black, except through intention.

"It always comes back to the inner soul of man. What did he intend? Good or evil? His outer acts do not always follow his intention.

"At one time I came into contact with a situation which appeared to be evil, but it was not truly evil. I must tell you, dear friends, if you have patience."

FATHER SHAYNE AND
THE PROBLEM OF EVIL

"To the very young, the absolutely innocent, the truly saintly, evil is no personal problem. Ah, they'll be thinking, this is good and this is bad, this is light and this is darkness, and where is the man who cannot see, for his soul's sake? But the Fathers of the Church have known always it is not the simple thing. They've discoursed on it through the centuries, and many there are of our divided brethren who have come to the conclusion that Satan is a useful fantasy, evil only in the ignorant eye of man, and if there be a problem of evil it can be solved by government fiat and humanitarianism. But, and this I am telling you, my children, this night, evil is not an abstract, but also it is not very clear. This could be one of the machinations of the Evil One, himself. It is one of his confusions which he throws among us, so that we pause in our trouble and ask: What is good, and what is evil?

"And not always, as I tell you now, can we be sure. Only God can be certain. And that is why He is the All-Merciful, and All-Loving."

Father Joseph Shayne was sent to his second parish when he was thirty years old and tolerably seasoned, being one of the new kind of priest just emerging in the Isles, sharp, quick, slightly worldly, tolerant and considerably polished. He had a high sense of humor, courage, strength, and he looked on man and the world with an eye that was becoming urbane. He was just the man, thought his Bishop, to manage the small but rather luxurious parish some twenty miles from London, and not too far from Windsor Castle. The village, containing some three thousand souls, housed retired colonels and other officers of rank, elderly and comfortable widows from London, gentlemen farmers, slightly rich spinsters who had inherited money too late in life to take advantage of it, retired schoolmasters who had pensions and private means, prosperous shopkeepers, teachers, three physicians and several lawyers. What working class there was served these pleasant and kindly folk who lived mostly in the past and were very clannish, looking down their noses at London but going to town several times a year for shopping and visiting with old friends or dropping in at their clubs.

Father Shayne, thought the Bishop, would be very suitable in that village, though there were only about five hundred or so Catholic souls and none of them were gentry, except for a few here and there. The priest was Irish, but "respectable" Irish, as the English called it. His family in Dublin had been very comfortable, themselves, and he had lived a happy and leisurely and pampered childhood—he being the only son—and he had gone to the best Seminary, where he had associated with easy young men like himself and somewhat worldly priests. He was a Latin and Greek scholar, and liked to spend what time he had in translating Homer and Virgil for his own pleasure; he was also proficient in German, French and Italian. He had an eye for art, and did a little dabbling in water-colors, and knew good painting from bad. His Irish accent would not offend his new parishioners, and he had the good nature, deep, kindly, and pleasant, of those Irish who had never known poverty and hunger. In fact, some of his fellow-priests said, if he had gone to America he would have been a politician of no mean prowess.

The priest before him, who had just died, had been of another kind of Irish, gloomy and astringent, and there had never been any margin in him for compromise. He had never known when to turn an insult into a joke, a snub into a smile. "It is not, of course, my thought that you will compromise with principle, dogma or doctrine, my son," said the Bishop. "But one does not use one's head as a battering-ram, does one?" To which Father Shayne had replied, a little wryly, "One does not."

The Bishop briefed him on his new parish. Most of the villagers were Anglo-Catholics, except for the farm hands, the domestics and the shopkeepers and such, who were Low Church, or "Chapel." "But all were very pleasant to your late brother, my son," said the Bishop. "The gentry were especially kind. However, he upset them, antagonized them. I had, myself, several complaints from the communicants of your new church, St. George's, because the poor old lad was so adamant on so many matters that were not important at all. The Sisters did not care for him, either. Of course, the good Sisters are usually intolerant of priests, anyway, but they were particularly intolerant of poor Tom." The Bishop sighed.

"Prudence is necessary then, I am thinking?" said Father Shayne.

"Ah, yes, prudence! One of the major virtues."

Father Shayne agreed, but he could not help thinking of the old priests of his boyhood who were not prudent at all, and never knew when to hold their tongues if their consciences were challenged or a difficult problem arose, and who were like the prophets of old: fiery, fiercely dedicated, passionate with love for God, and let the devil beware. But these were new days, and if the Church were to prosper in Protestant England the priests must move with caution and urbanity. And prudence. Suddenly, and it vexed him, Father Shayne took quite a dislike to prudence and did not consider it, at least for a moment or two, as one of the more shining virtues.

The house was small but nice, the Bishop said, with a pleasant garden of flowers and trees and a vegetable garden. He could potter there in the evening, though a gardener did the heavy work. His housekeeper was an elderly lady who did not need the small wages, but worked in the rectory for the love of God and lived with two widowed daughters down the road, middle-aged women in quite comfortable circumstances. "You'll find many a quaint thatched cottage there," said the Bishop, "and there are three Old English inns. In short, you will like it very much."

It sounded, thought Father Shayne, who was still but thirty, like a cosy refuge for some benign old priest who had been sent out to pasture. He looked a little sharply at the Bishop, and the Bishop smiled back serenely and said, "Ah, yes, there is a squire there, of a fine old Irish family, and his wife and children. Mr. Geoffrey Gould. Unfortunately, poor old Tom did not get on with him, and so Mr. Gould is, I fear, a lapsed Catholic. Mrs. Gould is Irish, also, but Presbyterian, and from Belfast. The children are Catholic, of course. The parents were married in the Church, and I understand that

Mrs. Gould is a very lovely lady, and only nominally a Protestant. Poor old Tom was very fearful of her."

"Why, my lord?"

The Bishop tapped his lips with his finger, thoughtfully. "You might as well have the whole story. Old Tom knew, and it frightened him half to death. You see, Mr. Gould was tried for the murder of his first wife, in Belfast. The present Mrs. Gould was a girlhood friend of the late lady, and she also came under suspicion. Mr. Gould was acquitted. He then moved to that village near London, and only Tom knew the story. You see how insular those people there are. Anything that occurs outside England is not of the slightest importance, and none ever seemed to connect Mr. Gould with the rather notorious case in Belfast. I doubt they even read of such Irish doings in their newspapers, though the English dearly love to read of murders and find the whole subject entrancing. I've often wondered why. Perhaps it is because they have become so respectable and restrained and polite in this century of Victoria, and their ancient merry blood seethes unappeased in them, the merry blood that sends them out to conquer the world and have a riotous time while doing so.

"At any rate, Mr. Gould, who had three children by his first wife, married the present Mrs. Gould, a Miss Florence Osborne, a little over a year after his first wife's—er—murder. They then came to England, almost immediately, and have two more children. Mr. Gould is very rich; he inherited a great deal of money and is a shrewd investor. He lives very quietly with his family in that village, and is as popular as a reserved man can be. Mrs. Gould, however, takes part in all the Women's Fairs and what not, and the children are very happy."

The Bishop cleared his throat. "You see, my son, I am the third cousin of Mr. Gould, or rather a half-third cousin. It is very complicated to explain, so I will not attempt it. Mr. Gould is some twenty years younger than I am, and we have never met. I don't know if he even knows of the relationship between us." The Bishop cleared his throat again. "I am worried about him and his family. Old Tom just

about issued a Bull of Excommunication all by himself against
Geoffrey Gould."

"Why?"

"Well, he was convinced, acquittal or no, that Mr. Gould had
murdered his wife, or that the present Mrs. Gould had done so,
and Mr. Gould would not admit either the murder, a most mortal
sin, or that he had had guilty knowledge of his wife's crime. You
see, she was never tried."

Father Shayne whistled. "So, she can't shelter herself behind
'double jeopardy,' then?"

"No. I really don't know exactly what poor old Tom did want.
Did he want Mr. Gould to expose his wife, and then see her hanged,
and all those five children stricken down? I really don't know! And,
as Mr. Gould would not admit either to the murder or to guilty
knowledge of the present Mrs. Gould's crime, then he could receive
only conditional absolution from Old Tom. It almost drove him
frantic. He wrote me that he could hardly bring himself to give
Geoffrey Holy Communion, after he had heard the story from
Geoffrey, himself—which he did not believe—and finally Geoffrey,
to avoid a most disagreeable situation, stopped attending Mass. But
his wife brought the children every Sunday and at least once a week
besides. It used to shake Tom severely. He intimated to Geoffrey that
he'd be very pleased if Mrs. Gould did not enter the Church, and
Geoffrey, quite rightly, said that this was un-Christian and unchari-
table, and he as much as told the poor old fellow to go to hell."

"What made Old Tom think that either Mr. or Mrs. Gould had
committed the murder?"

The Bishop pursed up his lips. "He wrote me that his instinct had
told him that one of them had, or perhaps the two of them together, in conspiracy. Now, one does not distrust instinct, especially
Irish instinct, which amounts to what is called second sight. Old
Tom was particularly fey; we knew each other from our earliest
boyhood, and I remember the many times—— Well, that's not perti-
nent. But he became more fixed in his opinion as time went on. He
thought Mrs. Gould an evil woman, Satanic, though I understand

that she is a beautiful woman, young still. The late Mrs. Gould—er —died some seven years ago.

"Now, it is untenable that a man be driven from his own church, as Geoffrey was. It makes a very bad situation for the children, especially the first three, who had known their father to be very pious and devoted to his religion. They are already asking questions, no doubt, as to why their father does not go to Mass any longer. Soon their questions will become more pointed. You can't put children off, forever, you know. The oldest is fifteen, the youngest four. Their father will eventually inherit a title—baronet. The family has not only money but position. Oh, the whole thing is very tragic!

"And the situation needs to be managed with much prudence. Old Tom was one of those wild old priests who, when he was convinced of a thing, could not be moved from his position. One or both were murderers, or one was a murderer and the other had guilty knowledge of it and was keeping silent. Old Tom had some points: the quite early remarriage of Mr. Gould after the death of his wife. The fact that Miss Florence Osborne was visiting their house at the time. It was evident, to Tom, that the two wished to dispose of the poor lady because they were in love with each other, and wanted her out of the way, and that doubtless they had indulged in adultery while the late Mrs. Gould was alive.

"There is one thing he overlooked, however. The late Mrs. Gould was discovered to have a serious heart complaint after the birth of her third child. In fact, she almost died. She was a semi-invalid for a year thereafter, and after that she spent more time in bed than she did up on her feet. She had a nurse in attendance, a sweet girl from Cork who testified at the trial. Rose had left for her evening off, leaving Mrs. Gould in the care of her husband and her visiting friend, Miss Osborne. She did not return until early morning, to discover Mrs. Gould dead in her bed. She had died, the autopsy showed, of a tremendous overdose of her necessary heart stimulant. The nurse swore that she had prepared the drops in a glass for Mrs. Gould to take at midnight, the carefully regulated dose. Mrs. Gould had taken the medicine, and had died of it.

"Mr. Gould, after long questioning, was taken into custody. There was an inquest. It was decided that he had administered the fatal dose, for he admitted going to see his wife at midnight and giving her the medicine. So, he was tried. But, there was no apparent motive. Friends and neighbors and servants testified that he was a most considerate and kindly husband. He is a very reserved man, so they could not testify that he was overly affectionate towards her. One neighbor did testify, somewhat maliciously, that Mrs. Gould was not a lady of agreeable temperament, but the jury discounted that. A man does not kill his wife if she is a little irritable, especially if she is an invalid, or a little petulant. Unless he wants to be rid of her and marry someone else. Miss Osborne was questioned. She admitted that she had visited Mrs. Gould at nine o'clock that night, had made her as comfortable as possible, and had stayed awhile to chat with her girlhood friend. The nurse had just departed and had given Mrs. Gould her half-past eight dose before leaving. Miss Osborne was quietly vehement in her statement that Mrs. Gould seemed more lively than usual. She was to be awakened at midnight for her last dose of the night, and that was Mr. Gould's task. Mrs. Gould was also given sedatives regularly, for her heart ailment was sometimes painful, and so she slept considerably."

"Did the nurse testify that something was between Mr. Gould and Miss Osborne?"

The Bishop hesitated. "Well, the girl was young and a little fanciful. She said she thought Mr. Gould and Miss Osborne 'liked' each other quite a bit. They had known each other well since the first Mrs. Gould had married Geoffrey, and Florence visited them often, sometimes for a day, sometimes for a week. When queried what she meant, exactly, by 'liking,' the nurse said that Mr. Gould and Florence often walked together in the afternoons and played with the children happily. There is no question that Florence is devoted to Mr. Gould's children, and they to her. She is an excellent stepmother and wife and mother. Tom could not deny that.

"But there was no motive for the murder, if there was a murder in fact. The late lady had come of an excellent but very poor Irish family, and Mr. Gould was rich. He did not have to anticipate a fortune on his wife's death. On the contrary, he had supported her parents until they died, and was kindness itself. And you can't accuse a man of wanting another woman so badly as to murder his wife, when the only signs of affection between him and that other woman are walking together and playing with children."

"Could Mrs. Gould have died of natural causes, or have committed suicide?"

"No. The autopsy proved that she had died of a massive dose of her medicine. And only the day before, their priest had heard her Confession and given her Holy Communion. Not Extreme Unction. She was in no danger of imminent death; in fact her physician believed that she would gain strength and perhaps recover in a year or so. The priest made a statement to that effect, that Mrs. Gould appeared to be in much better spirits that day than for some time before. I followed the case closely, though I had never met the first Mrs. Gould."

"Could the nurse, thinking of her evening and night off, have been too hasty and accidentally have prepared the medicine in too large a quantity?"

"She was asked that. Now, she was a nurse from one of the better hospitals in Dublin, one of the finest and most modern, and her superiors thought very highly of her. She made a good impression on the jury in spite of her youth. Competent. Sure. Careful. Her references were of the best; she had never been known to be careless."

"She was fond of Mrs. Gould, my lord?"

"Well, you know nurses are very professional and discreet. She said only that sometimes Mrs. Gould was a trifle difficult, which, considering her illness, was to be expected. The nurse showed the charity of her profession. Besides, the girl has her living to make. To blabber and chatter would do her no good in the minds of future patients, and the doctors. Incidentally, the doctor testified and said that the nurse was most competent and careful, and she had been warned to give Mrs. Gould only specified drops of the medicine in half a glass of water every three or so hours. She had been with the family a year."

"Where is she now?"

"Ah, I know what you are thinking! No, the girl was not attached to Mr. Gould. And she holds a high position now in her old hospital. Her character is impeccable. And she is a good Catholic woman."

"Has your lordship any thoughts on the subject, or opinions?"

The Bishop paused. Then he said seriously, "I do not believe that Mr. Gould murdered his wife. I do not believe that Miss Osborne did so. After all, the medicine was administered by Mr. Gould at midnight, three hours after Miss Osborne had last seen her. I do not believe that Mrs. Gould committed suicide, or took the medicine of herself. Mr. Gould testified that due to the sedation he had considerable trouble waking his wife up, and the nurse said that was always so."

"Then, what could have happened?"

"I do not know. But now that I have been so frank with you, my son, you will understand why I am sending you to that village. Geoffrey, though half cousin third removed, is still my relative. I am afraid for his immortal soul. I am worried about his children. I am hoping that you will smooth matters out and bring Geoffrey back to the Sacraments. It will have to be done delicately, and with prudence. You are only ten years younger than Geoffrey; the present Mrs. Gould is only a few years older than you are. I really don't know what you can do, but I've always been impressed by your tact and diplomacy! You see, I don't intend that you stay in that parish very long. It can be very stultifying to a young man of your intelligence."

But Father Shayne was still engrossed in the story. "Did no one go in to see Mrs. Gould after midnight, to see if she required anything?"

"What a detective you would make, my son! Scotland Yard is the poorer for your being a priest. Yes. Mr. Gould did look in, at two in the morning. Miss Osborne was with him. They had spent a long time around the fire in discussion, they testified. They saw Mrs. Gould in the dim illumination of the night light. They could hear her light breathing. She was fast asleep, and she never awakened during the night, as the nurse testified, for Rose slept in a cot in the room."

"Could they have awakened her, and in her dazed condition have given her the fatal dose?"

"Yes, they could. That is why Mr. Gould, Geoffrey, was tried. They both testified that they did not do so. At two o'clock the poor lady was alive. And the examining physicians said she was probably dead two hours later, at the most. You must remember that though Mrs. Gould's heart was not strong, she was not truly dangerously ill. In fact, she was recovering slowly. So it was not necessary for anyone to look in at her after that hour. Moreover, she had a loud bell by her bedside. The doctor had ordered undisturbed sleep after the midnight dose. And the nurse was there at seven, three hours after the death. Mrs. Gould, she said, was a 'frightful' blue, which the doctors said could have come from the massive overdose, which smothered the heart, or perhaps had overstimulated it."

"If it weren't for the quick remarriage—those two must have had some fondness for each other, my lord."

"Well, Miss Osborne stayed to help Mr. Gould with the children for several months, for he apparently had suffered a shock, and the children loved the young lady. Love can grow very quickly under those circumstances. Besides, my son, a guilty man does not remarry as fast as Geoffrey did. He waits, prudently, for at least two years, to avoid suspicion. It is really very tragic."

Father Shayne thought much about this case, being normally curious, while on his way to the village. No one had given Mrs. Gould a fatal dose of her medicine. Yet she had died of a massive overdose. She was not likely to have awakened between two and four in the morning and have given herself that dose that killed her. She knew she was not to have it; besides, she was partially drugged all the time anyway. She had not committed suicide. Had there been the slightest suspicion of that the priest would not have permitted her Christian burial. No one had killed her, yet she had been killed. The servants had all been questioned. They had slept through the night. They had testified that Mr. Gould was most attentive to his wife, and was greatly shocked at her death. They had been brief and discreet. They were also above suspicion. None of them had had a reason to kill the poor lady, and they had been with the family since Mr. Gould and his first wife had been married.

It was going to be very interesting, in that parish!

It was, in fact, extremely dull. Pleasant. But infernally dull. Everyone was kind, even the working-class "Chapel" folk, who rarely took to "Romans." Everything moved as smoothly as cream over a custard, and Father Shayne regrettably began to think of the village in those terms. He was a vigorous and intellectual young man, and he found little to do beyond his regular duties. The old gardener had shown him at once that he did not care for interference in the garden, and implied that a city man would not be able to tell a vegetable marrow from a carrot, or a rose from a lily. It was high summer, and the weather was unusually beautiful. It was holiday time, also, and the Sisters were relaxing as much as they cared to relax; after all, they had to keep a stringent eye on the new priest. One never knew about these young men, all with new ideas and enthusiasms which could be disturbing to staid middle-aged ladies like themselves. There was some criticism at recreation that he did, did he not? hurry just a trifle when he said Low Mass. And he had an impatient gleam in his eye as he strolled about the village.

The village had practically no sin, at least as far as Father Shayne could discover from his small flock. It was comfortable, hearty, rosy, and quite friendly for an English village. Many of the old colonels and widows were on holiday in the Lake Country or were visiting relatives in other parts of the country, or were basking at the seaside. So were two of the lawyers; only one doctor stayed on duty. It was a healthy village, too. The countryside was beautiful, the farming folk courteous. Father Shayne had looked forward to some leisure, but not quite so much as this. Now that he had more than he had bargained for, he discovered that his books did not interest him as much as they usually did. Besides, the weather enticed him out. He could walk in his small and excellently kept garden, but he was always aware of the suspicious eye of the gardener, and hardly dared to bend down to sniff at his own roses. He liked to use his hands, but there was nothing to repair in his handsome little cottage. He tried painting some of the lovely vistas he saw about. And yawned, sleepily.

He knew by now that his Bishop did not intend to keep him here long. He understood that he was to do something about the Geoffrey Gould family. He was to be "prudent." And prudent he was, and no one spoke to him of the Goulds, who lived in a fine gray stone house on a fine isolated knoll just at the edge of the village.

Were they off on holiday, like most of the other gentry of the village? Father Shayne could not come out bluntly and ask about them, for he was not supposed to know anything of their existence. Sometimes, at Mass, he would let his eye flash briefly over the communicants, to see if he could identify anyone who resembled the Goulds. The older children would be down from school now; there were many children at Sunday Mass, especially. He waited for any of the Goulds in the Confessional. None came that he knew of. He looked at the church records; the two younger children of the second marriage had been baptized here. Alice, six years old. Gordon, four. There were records concerning the Confirmation of young Geoffrey, now fifteen, and Elsa, fourteen, and the First Communion of Eric, ten. Squire Geoffrey Gould, though having been practically excommunicated by old Father Tom, was noted in the records as giving yearly large sums of money for the support of St. George's, a sum which would have been respectable in the richest parish in London. He had bought fine new bells for the church only three years ago, which showed that he did not bear too much rancor against the former priest. He had also paid for the really luxurious kneelers, and had given a beautiful Oriental carpet which flowed from the step of the high altar down to the Communion rail, there to be greeted by heavy rose carpeting along the rest of the length of the rail. And that beautiful rose window over the thick and polished door, Italian and precious: he had given that also. In the memory of his late beloved wife, Agnes Brady Gould. (Had that raised the gorge of Old Tom?) The organ, of the most exquisite make, was a gift of Squire Gould; it had a beautiful deep tone and filled the small church with resonant thunder at High Mass. In short, everything of value, and loving offering, had been given by Squire Gould.

Conscience money? An effort at atonement? Father Shayne found, in those first two or three drowsy, sunlit, bee-humming weeks, that he was giving tremendous thought to the whole matter, quite out of proportion. He excused himself by recalling that the Bishop was deeply concerned.

Should he go to that distant house on a friendly call? After all, the Goulds were his parishioners. He would have an excuse. But something made him hesitate.

They were surely off on holiday! Father Shayne ate his breakfasts of strawberries with thick cream, nicely prepared oatmeal and kippers and eggs and good tea, and ruminated. Sometimes he would wander casually, just strolling, in the direction of the house. He saw no one but gardeners, no one playing under the oak trees, no flutter of girls' bright summer dresses, no wandering of Mrs. Gould, no sign of the squire. The glistening green lawns were empty, the bright windows blank. Yes, they must be away. Or, remembering Old Tom, of whom Father Shayne was not thinking too kindly now, they were keeping away from the church. This, of course, was not only a great sin, but was dangerous for the Gould children.

Father Shayne went to see the Sister Superior, a majestic old lady whose very presence intimidated him. He said, "Sister, I have records of a Gould family here, and their deep love for St. George's. Yet, I don't recall—are they away?"

She gave him a long, slow look, penetrating and thoughtful. Then she said briskly, "I think not. I've seen young Geoffrey and Elsa and Eric every Sunday at the ten o'clock Mass."

"Oh?"

"And little Alice, with her nurse."

"Oh?"

"Mrs. Gould is not Catholic. A lovely lady."

"Oh?"

She smiled at him tightly. "Mr. Gould was deeply hurt by Father Thomas McGinnis. Of course, that should not keep him from his religious duties. But one can understand."

"One can't understand not attending Sunday Mass," said Father

Shayne, sternly. Sister gave him an even grimmer smile. "After all, it is his duty, and a sin to be absent."

"One," said Sister, in his own tone, which made him flush, "can be afraid of Scenes, Father. I declare that it is quite sinful of Father McGinnis, and I told him so."

"Scenes?"

"It is not my affair, Father. There was some trouble between Father and Mr. Gould. I am not a busybody."

Rebuked, and feeling ten years old and with a distinct sensation that the Sister Superior had whacked him with a ruler for his impertinence, Father Shayne went back to his study, fuming. The old lady was definitely on Squire Gould's side, even though she understood, clearly, that he was committing a grave sin by absenting himself from Mass. But then, it was possible that Old Tom had actually forbidden him to come, a grave sin in itself. The Church receives sinners with tender warmth, not ravings. She asks only repentance and penance. Old Tom, then, not hearing of repentance and penance for what he believed mortal sins, had been outraged. It was a very untidy business, indeed, and very wrong of the Sister Superior to take sides with Squire Gould when she did not know the circumstances. Father Shayne wanted to call her and chide her, but he shrank from the thought. He was still smarting.

Father Shayne went for a walk through the village, admiring, as always, its smart little shops, its good buildings, its charming houses—even the poorer ones—all aglow with summer flowers, its clean and winding streets, its air of contentment under the summer sun. A pastoral, he thought. He was bored to death. He would be glad when the absent ones returned, though it would mean rainy autumn and winter.

How had Old Tom gotten the story from Squire Gould? Had it been in the Confessional his lips would have been sealed. He must have heard it confidentially, without the seal of the Confessional. If Squire Gould was at home, he was afraid to come to the rectory for more Scenes, for doubtless he knew that Old Tom had confided in the Bishop, and the Bishop in the new priest.

Father Shayne went to Windsor Castle on a fine day. Trippers

were down from London. He stood, yawning, in the long line. He
thought Windsor Castle extremely dull, too. The Queen was in
residence, of course; she hated Buckingham Palace. Her standard
flew from a gray tower. The only exciting things there were the
Grenadier Guards, with their bearskin hats and red uniforms and
ostentatiously stamping feet. He looked at the vast gardens, the view
over the wall. Lovely. But the priest was restless. The Bishop would
be waiting for at least the first letter, and there was nothing to write.
But—prudence, prudence. And, of course, discretion. Silly things,
really, when a man's soul was at stake. When the Church had not
been so prudent, she had gone, like her Lord, to look for the lost
sheep in the most perilous places, and had brought them tenderly
home. And "prudence" and "discretion" be hanged! Possibly more
civilizations had fallen to the barbarians through a policy of prudence
and compromise and gentility than anything else. Diplomacy was
truly Satan's most effective gift to governments.

Father Shayne, with some hot thoughts, bicycled back to the village. When he went into the rectory his housekeeper told him, with
a meaning glance, that he had visitors in his study. At once, the
priest had a sudden high hope, but it was squelched when he found
three children awaiting him. But, as he loved children, he greeted
them affectionately, and sat down near them, smiling.

The children consisted of a boy about fifteen, a girl probably
nearly fourteen, and a boy child about ten. The older boy, in a controlled voice, introduced himself as Geoffrey Gould, the girl as his
sister, Elsa, and the younger boy as his brother, Eric. Father Shayne
sat up, alertly, and his thin and intelligent face flushed with new
hope and interest. He said, "I think I overlooked you at Mass—at
Confession——"

"We were at Mass," said Geoffrey, gravely. He was a tall dark
youth, very thin and obviously very intense, for his fine olive-tinted
features were mobile and expressive. His black and curly hair fell
over his forehead, a little girlishly, the priest thought, or a little
Byronically. But he was obviously aristocratic, and his manners were
perfect. The priest glanced at Elsa, a lovely child, with a mass of
smooth golden hair, a still and saintly face, and remarkably beautiful

blue eyes. Her mouth, however, was in a continual tremor which she pathetically tried to suppress.

The younger boy, Eric, immediately caught the priest's alarmed attention. He sat politely enough on his chair, but he was in constant motion, frail though it was and controlled. A perpetual trembling kept his muscles in almost imperceptible rippling; his fair eyebrows, over his very wide dark eyes, jerked up and down; his silky brown hair kept dropping over his white forehead; his mouth quivered; his nose twitched; his hands jerked noticeably; his feet had a little jumping movement. When he smiled at the priest, his timid mouth actually lurched sideways.

All the children were abnormally thin, though otherwise they appeared healthy enough and were dressed expensively.

"I'd like to speak to you alone, Father," said Geoffrey. Immediately his sister and brother got to their feet. Then the priest noticed another thing; the girl, Elsa, leaned to one side and he saw, as she stepped back, that she had a limp. Not a pronounced one, but one quite bad enough, for her left leg was shorter than her right.

"Certainly, Geoffrey," said Father Shayne. "Your sister and brother may wait in the parlor." He went to the door and opened it. Elsa came first, limping, her pretty mouth tremulous; Eric followed, all jerks and movement. Had the poor child suffered from St. Vitus Dance? Elsa curtseyed as she passed the priest; the little boy bowed. Dear children! For some reason the priest's throat knotted tightly, as he followed the boy and girl with sad eyes. He closed the door then and returned to Geoffrey. The boy was leaning forward in his chair, his hands clasped tightly between his knees, and he studied the priest with a passionate intensity.

"It's about my father, and my mother," he began at once. "I tried to talk with Father McGinnis about them, but he immediately stopped me. He spoke of the Commandment to honor our parents. So, he never heard what I wanted to tell him. Father, do you think one should suppress the truth because of that Commandment? If you think so, then we won't bother you any longer. We will leave immediately." He moved forward on his chair, and his dark eyes were watchful and resolute.

"Will your truth be revealing the sins of others?" Father Shayne asked.

"Yes. But something is more important: my father's soul and peace of mind, and his return to the Sacraments." The boy's voice was strong and uncompromising. "If you refuse to listen, then we must go. We," and he hesitated, "have been approached very kindly by Vicar Martin, who believes that Father McGinnis behaved abominably to my father, as he did."

Vicar Martin was the rector of the local Anglo-Catholic church. He was a splendid and erudite gentleman in his middle age, and Father Shayne had chatted with him often. If such a man had come mercifully to that family, while they had been rejected by their own, then Old Tom had indeed "behaved abominably."

"Does Vicar Martin know what you wish to tell me, Geoffrey?"

"Yes. I told him, myself. Father Shayne, we don't want to leave the Church; we'd never be happy again. But we've been driven out, or, rather, Papa has, and where Papa goes, we'll go, too."

Now here was a dismaying problem. It could not be defined in such sharp terms as good or evil. Father Shayne was agitated. After a little thought he said, "Tell me, Geoffrey. And I know you wish this to be confidential. I want to help you. Frankly, your family has worried me. If I think you are about to commit a sin——" He stopped, for Geoffrey's face had changed, become a little cold and distant. Then the boy smiled. "If I sin, I will confess, and will ask you for absolution, Father."

There was an atmosphere about the boy as of despair, and this was piteous at his age. Abruptly, he lifted the thick hair from his forehead. Across the dark fine skin a long deep scar ran. Geoffrey let the priest look at it for a moment, then he dropped his curls over it. "My mother did that to me," he said, without emotion. "When I was seven years old. You've noticed Elsa's limp. My mother did that; she threw her down the stairs and broke her leg in several places. You've seen Eric; she beat his head against the floor until he was unconscious; he was two, then, and he almost died. He has a brain injury. My mother did that to us."

He looked at the horrified priest, who had turned very pale. "Have

I committed a sin against that Commandment, Father?" he asked, and his voice was the voice of a man.

Father Shayne paused. His heart was beating with outrage at these evidences of cruelty. Finally he could say, "Let me judge a little later, Geoffrey. Continue." Who had done these things? The stepmother? Or the real mother? It could not possibly be the latter!

"Your father!" exclaimed the priest. "Surely he knows what your stepmother has done to his children! Why did he permit these horrible things? There are the police——" Old Tom had been right, after all. The stepmother was evil; if she could do things like this to helpless children, then she could commit murder without the slightest compunction.

The boy studied the priest. Then his mouth twisted slowly, bitterly.

"I said, Father, my mother. Not my stepmother; we call her Mama Florence, and we love her, for she is good and kind to us, and loves us. You see, I'm the oldest. Papa thinks we were too young to remember, and so to help him I've pretended not to have known. Elsa and Eric don't remember. At least, I don't think so. We never talk about it."

"Your mother," said the priest. He was stupefied. Then he thought: The poor woman must have been insane.

"My mother could deceive anyone, except Papa and me," said Geoffrey. "She even had our priest believing that she was saintly. She had the most cruel face, and it was mostly laughing. She hated Papa. She hated us."

"Why, Geoffrey?" Father Shayne could hardly believe what he was hearing.

"I don't really know, Father. But I'm not a child. I know there are wicked people in the world, who love to do cruel and malicious things, and lie and slander and libel for the very pleasure of it."

It was dreadful knowledge for a youth to have, thought the priest.

"They aren't mad," said the youth. "They are just evil. Some of my teachers in school in London, good schoolmasters who never knew a wicked person when they saw one—they're so wrapped up in their teaching and soccer and cricket, such simple people!—believe that bad people are either mad or the world has been so harsh to them that they are only retaliating. It isn't true, Father. I've met some lads in my own forms who were evil just for evil's sake. Doesn't St. Paul speak of these people? You believe in absolute evil, don't you, Father?"

The priest started. The old problem of evil. He fell back on his doctrinal training. "Certainly, Geoffrey, I know that a great many people in this world are purely evil, and love evil, and do evil, and prosper in their evil. The Holy Bible speaks of them often. They aren't mad, or hurt. They are simply of the tribe of Satan."

The boy sighed. "Thank you, Father. My mother wasn't mad, and she had no grudge against the world. She thought Papa was a fool because he was kind and charitable and would not listen to her vicious lies against their friends, and her lies about her children. She used to accuse me of the vilest things, and Elsa, too, and we were then only eight and seven, and Eric was only two. Once I found some money under my pillow, quite a lot of it. I was seven years old then. I had just lost a tooth, and I wanted to put it under my pillow," and he smiled shyly at that childish superstition. "And I found the money there and took it down to Papa, who had put it there anyway. And my mother screamed that I had stolen it, and that she had missed it only that afternoon! Papa brought me back to bed, and he said to me, 'Your mother was only joking, of course, Geoffrey. Think nothing of it.' But," said Geoffrey, "I thought of it. It was only one of many such in our house."

The priest was silent. The boy went on.

"My mother despised Papa. He was rich, but she wanted much more. When she was in the wrong he opposed her. And so she made us children suffer, for she knew how Papa loved us. I know a boy at school who has a mater just like her, and he won't go home for the holidays. He visits relatives near Bournemouth. When Papa would do something for our church she would flare up and throw things about, such as Papa's collection of Meissen china. She did so love to destroy his treasures! But he always gave to the Church in both their names and then the priests would come to thank them and Mama was so gracious and smiled so prettily. She was very pretty;

she looked like Elsa, and people—how very stupid people can be!—loved her because she was so pretty. She was very charming, too, to her friends and the clergy, and even to the servants. You see, she almost always managed to go on her rampages when the servants were off, or on holiday, and the family was alone. So no one knew, except us. Or, perhaps, old Bailiff, our butler in Belfast. He wasn't a bailiff, of course, but he was so strict and straight that we called him that. I don't think Mama ever deceived Bailiff. He hated her. But at the trial, for our sakes, he said nothing."

The priest, the product of intensive training, had been listening and watching closely, and he knew, beyond the shadow of a doubt, that Geoffrey had been telling him the truth. His horror increased.

"You knew about the trial, Geoffrey? You see, I do know something about this, myself."

The boy stood up and began to pace the room in extreme agitation. "Of course I knew! Everyone tried to keep it from us, but I knew. They hid the newspapers, and I found them. Papa wasn't on holiday, as he had tried to tell me before the police took him; he was in gaol. Mama Florence—she was staying with us then—pretended that everything was so nice and serene, and I let her believe what she wanted us to believe. It was the least I could do for her."

"And you were only eight years old."

The boy gestured impatiently. "I don't know why people think boys of eight are utter idiots! Or infants. We know a great deal more then than we'll ever know again, about people." He paused. "I don't think Papa murdered my mother. But, if he did, I'm glad!" He clenched his fists, and his young face was distorted for a moment. "I'm glad! I'm glad she's dead! She might have killed one of us, if she hadn't died. No," he added after another pause, "she'd always stop short of murder. She was very cunning; she did what she did to us all in private, and carefully, and she knew that Papa would never expose her. For our sake! That was foolish of Papa. He should have taken us away, before it all happened to us. That's the thing I can't forgive—that he didn't leave my mother. But he explained to me, when I was a child, that even the worst of mothers are better than none. I don't believe it, Father, I don't believe it! And then after Eric was born, Papa said to me, 'You see, Geoffrey, that your mother wasn't responsible. She is so ill, and must have been ill for a long time.' I didn't believe that, either. She would fly into such awful rages, and scream and shout, when we were all alone, and threaten, and I think all that wicked anger hurt her heart."

"No one knew, the neighbors, the friends, the servants?"

"I don't know. Perhaps some did. But, at the trial, they wanted to protect Papa. Everyone loved him. They didn't want to tell about my mother, because then Papa would have seemed to have had a motive for killing her. He was acquitted for the reason that there was no motive for her—murder."

The priest rose abruptly and went to the window of his study and stared out at the furious blossoming of his garden. Without turning, he said, "Do you think she was murdered, Geoffrey?"

"I don't know. I don't think Papa did it—I don't know. If he did, then God understands. If Mama Florence did it, she did it for all of us. It isn't murder, Father, if you kill to defend yourself, or the helpless. The Church knows that."

The priest turned and went back to his chair, and studied the back of his hands. The problem of evil. He thought of these children, so terribly injured in body and soul. They would bear the marks of evil all their lives; they would suffer all their lives, even if the younger did not remember fully what had injured them, and who. In dark nightmares, in loneliness, in grief, in difficulty or in despondency, the evil shadow of half-forgotten or wholly forgotten pain and terror would loom over them, heightening their misery, increasing their burden. He, Father Shayne, had often knelt at the bedsides of old men and women, old far beyond the average, who in dying had cried pitifully, like infants, for their mothers, or had screamed out some torment or suffering they had endured as very small children, too young then even to understand, too young to have retained the nightmare in conscious memory. The body, the brain, forgot; the soul never forgot. And, too, he remembered how he had stood beside those stricken with grief or mortal illness, and how they would suddenly exclaim, "Oh, I had forgotten that! I never thought of it until just now! How can I bear it?" The memory, for moments at least, was even more dreadful than their present state, and must have haunted their dreams all their lives, unknown, unexorcised.

He said to Geoffrey, "Can you not forgive your mother, my son?"

The boy smiled at him bitterly again. "How can I forgive my mother, when the Church will not believe my father, or, if he did kill my mother, will not forgive him?"

"The Church requires true contrition, repentance and penance, Geoffrey."

The boy thought deeply, his scarred brow wrinkled. Then he said wearily, "How can my father be sorry that he rescued us from our mother? Yes, I know you will say that murder is a most mortal sin. But, he did what he did—if he did it—to protect and save us. How can he be sorry?"

He waited, but the priest did not answer. Then the boy cried out, "The problem of evil! That is what you are thinking! I have been studying it, myself, and sometimes you can't tell, can you, Father? You can't tell!"

My poor child, thought the priest. There is something that perhaps you do not know, that perhaps your father killed your mother not only to rescue his children but to be able to marry another woman. Perhaps. Who knew?

"Geoffrey," he said, "do you think there is the slightest possibility that your stepmother killed your mother?"

The boy was silent. He said at last, "I've thought of it. If she did, I'm grateful to her, too. She loves us; our mother hated us. We never knew why. I think she thought, in the beginning, that Papa was richer then than he was. I remember hearing her scream at him when I was a child. She hated Belfast; she wanted to live in London. She wanted to travel. She wanted to be free, she would shout at Papa. And then she would curse him because we had been born. We had imprisoned her, she said. If we had not been born she should have been able to do all the things, and go to all the places, which she had dreamed about when she was a girl in a poor family. She would curse us, in front of Papa, and slap and punch us.

"Mama Florence visited us on holidays and for a month in the winter. We've always known her; she went to school with our mother.

We've always loved her, too. She was very rich, herself, and she would bring us beautiful presents. Mama envied her, I know, envied her because she wasn't married and had no children. She envied her for being rich. The only thing, Mama would say when she was in a good mood, was that she was much prettier than Mama Florence, and then she would frown and say, 'Much good it did me, after all! Imprisoned in this house with the children I never wanted, and the wife of a man who has no spirit and no imagination!' "

"And your mother was Catholic, Geoffrey, and had not wanted you?"

"She wanted no one but herself, Father. Do you think that just because she was Catholic she automatically loved children, even her own? Oh, she would make a splendid show when the priest visited us! She would have us dressed up handsomely, and she would hold Eric on her knee, and she would kiss us, and the priest would look sentimental. The moment he had left she would drive us off, undress and go back to bed and moan. She was always moaning. I don't think she was so sick as the doctors said she was. She was very clever. She could deceive even them."

Evil, thought the priest, does not always have a stupendousness about it, or even the dark grandeur described by Milton. It can be meanly venomous and meanly ugly, viciously small. It can have the face of an asp as well as the face of a great fallen angel.

"My father was wretched with my mother," said Geoffrey, into the silence. "I can never remember him laughing before she died. Sometimes, at night, I'd look through my window and see him walking up and down in the garden, under the moon, and sometimes he'd do this with his hands," and the boy wrung his own hands. "The only time he smiled was when he was playing with us, and when Mama Florence visited us. Then everything was happy for Papa and ourselves. It was as if someone opened windows in a musty house and let the sun and air in. You do understand?" said the boy, awkwardly.

"Yes, I think so." The priest hesitated. "Did your mother ever resent your—the lady you call Mama Florence?"

The boy stared at him. Then his face colored quickly and brightly, and his mouth twitched with disgust. "I know what you mean! But it isn't so! They tried to bring that out at the trial; I read it, myself. Papa and Mama Florence would take walks in the afternoon together, sometimes alone, sometimes with us, or they'd take us for a treat into the city in our carriage. That was after Eric was born, and my mother was almost always in bed. Before that, my parents and Mama Florence would go together."

The priest fell into thought again, while the boy watched him with deepening impatience and despair.

"Geoffrey," said the priest, "if your mother had been completely evil how could it have been possible for your stepmother to have cared for her and visited her?"

"Oh, my mother had always patronized Mama Florence; they had been roommates at school. And my mother—I've told you this—could be very charming when she wanted to be. I've told you that Mama Florence was very rich; she was also an orphan. My mother loved rich people; she always wanted them about her. And Mama Florence had no family of her own, and I suppose she clung to my mother when they were girls, and then when my parents were married and had children she adopted all of us—in a way. You don't know Mama Florence! She is really the saint my mother pretended to be. You see, Father, she wants to enter the Church, to be with all of us, and because she truly believes. But Father McGinnis drove her off, too."

"'Drove,' Geoffrey, is a very harsh word. I don't think it was so severe as that."

"Then, you're prejudiced," said the boy, flatly, and got up with resigned despair. "Please excuse us. We'll go home now. It is no use, is it?"

The priest stood up also. He put his hand on the boy's tall shoulder. "I think it may be of considerable use. I haven't chided you, have I? I did not stop you when you spoke of your mother, with such bitterness and, yes, hate. Truth is truth. Geoffrey, I know you want to help your father. I want you to go home to him and tell him that you have told me everything, and that I'd like to see him. And your stepmother."

Tears came into the boy's eyes, painfully. "Thank you, Father," he said.

The priest watched them leave, these wounded children. He had blessed them tenderly. He saw how Geoffrey brooded over his brother and sister, with protectiveness, as he led them away down the road. They were healthy now, and lived in a home of love and happiness. But always, all their lives, they would remain wounded. It was necessary to teach them how to live with their wounds so that they would not be forever blighted. They needed, not suppression of the truth by their father, but full knowledge. An evil thing exposed to the sunlight shrivels up and dies. Sometimes. At the very least it loses some of its terror in mutual sharing. Silence is frequently, thought the priest, the ally of Satan. And it could be hypocritical even though with the best of intentions.

He went into the church and prayed for enlightenment, for help in untangling this awful web of evil, which was also mixed with much good. Evil was like a vine that grew on the trunk of a tree and mingled its stained leaves with the good ones. Neither overcame the other; they lived in a sort of neutrality. It was truly a confusing matter, and one not to be solved by saying nay or yea. Not always. It was not always absolutely clear. Give me wisdom, the priest prayed, the wisdom to see good from evil, and evil from good.

He expected Squire Gould and his wife to call the next day. But they did not come. Nor did they come the next day or the next. Should I call on them? thought the priest, thinking of Christ's searching for the lost lambs. He had almost made up his mind to go when one Friday afternoon, as he was preparing his sermon, his housekeeper announced the squire and his lady.

They entered the study together, the tall, slightly bent man so much like his oldest son, but gentler and sadder with his years, Geoffrey's fire dimmed in the dark eyes, Geoffrey's black curls streaked with white. He was slender and graceful, and Father Shayne's first impression was of great kindness, sweet temper, and enormous patience. His wife, Florence, tall and slender like himself, seemed plain at first glance, but when she smiled as she did now, she was suddenly beautiful, with fine, large gray eyes and a perfect complexion. Her light summer bonnet only partly hid smooth brown hair, and the mauve ribbons were tied under a firm yet feminine chin. The tight bodice of her pale mauve summer frock showed her youthful figure; ruffled flounces fell to her feet. She moved as gracefully as her husband, and sat down near him with her gloved hands on her furled parasol.

Father Shayne suddenly became aware that the two were studying him as keenly as he was studying them. "I am glad you came, sir, and Mrs. Gould," he said. "I have learned how much you have done for this church. I'd have called on you earlier——"

The squire said gently, "I assume that you know what Father McGinnis knew, Father?"

The priest was a little vexed; had Geoffrey disobeyed when he had been directed to tell his father of the children's visit?

"Yes," he said. "We may as well be frank. It saves time. I wonder if you know that my Bishop is distantly related to you?"

The squire smiled. "Yes. I always wanted to know him, and intended to seek him out in London. And then"—his smile went away —"difficulties arose. I did not want to embarrass him. Father McGinnis would frequently, and angrily, tell me that he had written his Bishop concerning me and my family." He paused. "Did the Bishop believe Father McGinnis?" He smiled. "Or shall we stop being frank now?"

"No," said Father Shayne. "This is a time for utter candor. I am here only temporarily, I believe. I was sent here mainly to know you. And help you. My Bishop does not believe that you are guilty of— murder." He glanced at Florence Gould. "Nor does he believe Mrs. Gould is guilty.

"Mr. Gould," he continued, "do you know that your son, Geoffrey, came here to see me and that he told me his own version and— experiences?"

The squire looked apologetically at his wife as he said, "Yes, he did. Florence, Geoffrey remembers. He remembers how he came to be scarred, and he remembers what injuries the other two received. He remembers everything."

"Oh, no!" said Florence, with deep sorrow and misery. "I thought he was too young. And you did so try to protect him, Geoffrey, and I did, too." There were tears in her eyes.

"I thought he hadn't remembered, myself," said the squire. "I was shocked when he told me last week. I had prayed so hard that he would not remember."

"But why didn't he tell us, the poor child?" said Florence, her voice breaking.

"Because he knew that we wanted to believe that he did not remember. He wanted to protect our lovely little daydreams."

"And Elsa and Eric?"

"I don't know, Florence." The father's voice dropped. "I'm rather sure Eric doesn't know. He was hardly two when it happened to him. And Elsa—you know how quiet she is."

"And what nightmares she has!" said Florence. A tear ran down her cheek. "I thought that they were just the usual nightmares children have, and I would comfort her."

"It seems," said Father Shayne, "that there has been something a little less than candor going on in your house, also. Mr. Gould, I am a priest, and I have frequently been at the bedside of the dying, and I've heard their cries and all they said. The mind forgets, for it can endure only so much. But the soul never forgets. In life, the memories of the soul color all existence. In death, they are sometimes unendurable. Do you want your children to keep their silence, to protect your tender sensibilities about them, or do you want to be candid with them, speaking without rancor and bitterness but telling the factual truth, so that they will have less to bear in their future lives, which will be hard enough, God knows."

They looked at him in mournful silence.

"Your son, Geoffrey, is not a child. Within a few years he will be a mature man. Someone, somewhere, will remember that—murder—case, and connect him with it. You ran away to this hamlet, to bury yourselves quietly, for your children's sake. But you can't immunize them from the world. I am not speaking only of Geoffrey, Elsa and Eric, but of your mutual two children, too. Will it be pleasant for them, to hear from strangers, that their father had been tried for murder? They will wonder why you had never told them. And they will begin, in spite of their love for you, to ask themselves questions. Such as: 'Is my father guilty? Is my mother guilty? Of murder?' Do you want that to happen?"

"Oh, my God," said the squire, prayerfully, "no, no!"

"Then you must begin to give the matter the most severe thought. I suggest that you speak to Elsa, soon, and tell her how she acquired her injuries. It is more than possible that she remembers. Speak to her reasonably, without blaming or exonerating her mother. Children, above all, like facts, for they are realists. Tell her you have forgiven your wife for what she did to you and your children, and that Elsa must learn to forgive. Then when she is slightly older, tell her the facts surrounding her mother's death. She will have more confidence in you from the very beginning, then. She is entirely too quiet. The child did not say a single word to me when she was here. Such silence in a child is a signal of danger. She possibly, even now, mistrusts you, for she may not have the charity of your oldest son.

"So, after a year or so, when she knows about her mother, tell her that no matter what she hears later she must believe you, and that you were not guilty of your wife's death."

The squire's dark face became very pale. He looked at the cane he held on his knee. Then, softly, he said, "Florence, will you leave us alone for a moment?"

His wife sat up very straight, her face white, and she cried, "No! Father Shayne is right. Let us be frank. Geoffrey, Geoffrey! You have nothing to conceal."

Father Shayne had become rigid with shock. He stared at the squire. "Mr. Gould, you did not kill your wife, did you?"

The squire still gazed at his cane. "I don't know," he said in a low voice.

"Geoffrey!" His wife's exclamation was loud and terrible.

"You don't know!" said the priest. "How is it possible that you 'don't know'?"

Florence was staring at her husband, her eyes wide and glittering, her breast rising on a deep breath. But the squire was looking at the priest, open anguish on his face.

"I simply don't know," he repeated. "Do you know the details of my wife's death? Yes. I'm glad I don't have to repeat it all.

"The day before Agnes—died—she had been up for several hours. Florence was visiting us. Agnes had unpredictable rages; she would be smiling and gay one moment and then the next she would be in a fury. It was—unsettling, to use the English manner of understatement. The house was always in a tension, for one never knew." The soft Irish voice faltered, became hoarse, as the squire remembered. "Geoffrey told me that he had told you all this. Agnes could be superficially sentimental and affectionate. Dear God, I have tried so hard to forget!"

The priest was still in a state of bewildered shock, but he said, "It never does any real good to forget. It is best to remember, and then try to forgive."

"Yes. Yes. You are quite right, Father——"

"Geoffrey!" his wife cried. "You didn't kill Agnes. You did not! You did not!"

The squire touched her arm briefly and said, "I don't know. Please let me continue, and don't cry so hard, my darling.

"Father Shayne, my wife was in good spirits the day before her death. She had confessed her sins to our priest and had received Holy Communion. She was feeling much better, though she had to take a mild sedative to relieve her pain. She was suffering from angina pectoris, and it is painful, I have been told. She was not in danger of death, but she was languid, a semi-invalid, though she persisted in believing that she was a true invalid. I think that was to discourage me," and he smiled sadly, "from asking for conjugal relationships. She never wanted children, and she disliked those she had. Oh? Geoffrey told you? How much the poor boy knows, and I never knew he knew. How piteous for him.

"I always believed that children should say good night to their parents, and so I brought them into my wife's room. Eric was a restless little boy, just under two, and he raced about the room in his usual way, which always annoyed my wife. He accidentally turned over a tiny table she had, which was covered with exquisite miniatures, objets d'art. They were badly smashed, of course, falling on the bare, polished floor."

The squire squeezed his eyes shut, tightly, as if to try to shut out the memory. "Geoffrey remained; Elsa—she could not seem to be happy in her mother's presence, had left, and now I know she remembers something. My poor children. So, only Geoffrey and I saw what happened after that accident. Agnes jumped from her bed, screaming, and before I could stop her she had seized Eric in her hands, had thrown him to the floor and was savagely beating his little head on it. Over and over and over. It happened like lightning. When I could finally reach them the child was unconscious. Unconscious.

"I carried him out of the room, leaving my wife still screaming behind me. Her nurse, who was having tea in the servants' hall, came running, and closed the door after me. I took Eric to his room, and then called Florence. You see, we didn't ever want the servants to know about—Agnes. We were afraid they'd then gossip, and that Geoffrey and Elsa would overhear them. I'm afraid, though, that they must have known something——" He opened his suddenly sunken eyes and looked at the priest.

"They knew," said Father Shayne, grimly. "That is why they testified so generously in your behalf at your trial, Mr. Gould. They must have been devoted to you."

"Well," said the squire, in a voice that had become an old man's voice. "How good of them. . . . I put Eric on his bed and his nurse came and I said the child had had an accident, had fallen badly. He was still unconscious, and his face looked—dead. The nurse wanted to call a doctor immediately, and then Eric opened his eyes, his color returned, and he began to cry. I thanked God. I thought I should not have to send for the doctor. Doctors' eyes are very keen. Our doctor would have known at once that the child had not had a mere accident; there were too many—too many swollen and bleeding places on the back and sides of his head. I thought it would be well for him, for he did appear to be quite normal.

"I told Florence, only. She would have suspected, under the circumstances, knowing Agnes. She knew how the other children had come to be so—injured. I had to tell someone!" cried the desperate father. "It was too much to bear alone! And I needed help with Geoffrey, who had seen it all. He had run screaming out of the room when Agnes had begun to—— So Florence spent hours with him that night, soothing him."

"And lying to him," said the priest. "You knew he was an intelligent child, and yet you lied to him. What he must have thought of you both!"

The squire groaned. "I know. Now. But how can you let a child understand the enormity of such a thing?"

"Children have much more strength than we have," said the priest. "They can understand everything. Except those they love lying to them. Children are not only realists but they are natural cynics. They expect anything from the world and are never surprised. They fear, but they expect; it is their instinct. But no one they love should ever lie to them, for they never forget lies, and they color all the rest of their lives. But, go on, please."

"Thank you," murmured the squire, stricken. "I remember when my mother died; I was Geoffrey's age then, about eight. I knew she was sick; I listened at doors, as all frightened children do, and as I suppose Geoffrey and Elsa did. I knew when she died, though I was not near her room when she left us. But my father came to me and said that my mother was very sick, and that someone, one of the servants, would take me to my aunt's home some two miles away. My mother must have quiet, my father said. Didn't he know that I could see his pale face and his red eyes? Didn't he know that I knew all about death? I loved him, but I never really trusted him after that, though I understood that he had lied to spare me. And so, I suppose, Geoffrey is the same. I wonder how I had forgotten!

"At any rate, Florence stayed with Geoffrey until he fell asleep, long after his usual bedtime. And I remained with Eric and his nurse. The little boy appeared to be quite normal by midnight, though the nurse was worried about the wounds on his head. He slept quite peacefully, however. But in the morning he took a turn for the worse.

"I stayed with him for hours. He was restless and feverish, and sometimes he appeared not to know me. I am so guilty! Of course, the damage had already been done to his brain—but still I am so guilty. Agnes, of course, had recovered her good spirits. She laughed about the episode, and I was afraid to tell her that Eric did not seem well. You see, Father, I was always trying to protect her against herself, too."

"I see," said the priest, severely. "Entirely too much protecting was going on in that house, and so inevitably it led to tragedy. Mr. Gould, did you, on that day, stop loving your wife?"

The squire looked at him directly. "I had stopped loving Agnes within six months after we were married. Had she not been expecting Geoffrey I'd have left her then. But there was my child to consider—and with such a mother. Then I was so happy over Geoffrey, when he was born, that I decided it was my duty, as a good Catholic husband and father, to try to reform Agnes, to lead her away from her violent moods and unpredictable angers and rages. For a time she did seem more kind and more content. I promised her a visit to the Continent when she had fully recovered from Geoffrey's birth. Then, she became pregnant with Elsa. She could not forgive me, though what she thought I should have done I do not know." The squire sighed. He glanced at his silently weeping wife. "These are not things a gentleman discusses in the presence of a lady, but you would not go away, Florence."

"I wondered how you could—possibly look at her!" said Florence, in a sick tone. "I often wondered, all through those years. For I knew all about Agnes by that time; that is why I visited so often. I thought I'd help you protect the children."

"Well. Well," said the squire, speaking in dead sounds. He tried to bring life back to his voice. "Florence and I were worried about Eric. We talked all day about calling the doctor, and we also talked of the scandal. Our doctor would have been outraged. He might even have called the police. He was that kind of a martinet. We had the other two children to think of, and even Agnes, herself. And, as the day went on, Eric did appear to improve, didn't he, Florence?"

"Yes. A little," said his wife. "We decided to wait until the next day to see if Eric would continue to improve or get worse. We didn't realize——"

"I'm sure," said the priest, wryly, "that those words are heard oftener in hell than any other. 'We didn't realize.' But please continue."

"You can imagine how agitated and numb we were, Father. We tried to conceal everything from the servants, too. We wanted to protect Agnes' name and dignity, and now I see it was all useless. They knew all the time.

"Agnes' nurse, Rose Hennessey, was a good nurse, though she was quite young. It was her evening off; she had friends farther in town. She worked very hard, for Agnes could be trying, to say the least. Now, she testified that before leaving she said to me—Florence and I were discussing Eric's condition in the morning-room—that she had prepared Mrs. Gould's medicine and that I should give it to her at midnight. I, myself, remember only that she said, 'Please give Mrs. Gould her medicine at midnight.' Florence does not recall anything else, either. We were too disturbed to listen fully."

The priest sat and thought. Then he said, "Was it customary for Rose to prepare your wife's medicine before she left on her evening off?"

The squire's hands clenched on his cane. "Before God," he said, with deep quietness, "I don't remember. I didn't remember then, either. That is why I don't know—Rose said it was customary, to save me the bother, and to be sure that the exact dosage, three drops, had been measured out. But, I don't remember! You must believe me. I don't remember. The last twenty-four hours had wiped all thought for anyone but Eric out of my mind.

"And so, at midnight, I went into my wife's room. She was more than half asleep. The glass, partly filled with water, was on her bedside table. I measured drops of the colorless medicine into the water and woke her up. She was in a very bad temper. She said she didn't need my ministrations; she kept up a babble of talk, even in her half-dozing state. She repeated, over and over, that she wished she had never married me, and that she had no children. She called me —various names. She ordered me from the room. I had come for only one purpose, she said." The squire's pale face flushed. "I left. And that is all, before God. But I cannot understand how a double dose could have killed her. The medicine was potent, yes. The doctors of the autopsy said she had died of much more, that a double dose might have caused her severe trouble but it would not have killed her. Florence! What is it?"

For Florence was sitting upright in her chair, with a look of profound dread and horror on her face. "Geoffrey!" she cried. "Oh, dear God, Geoffrey! I killed her!"

"No!" said her husband. He tried to pull her head to his shoulder, but she resisted him and drew away from him.

"Let Mrs. Gould tell her story," said the priest, in a sharp, loud voice. But his heart was hammering. The husband—he was protected by double jeopardy. But his wife was not.

"I never read the newspapers! I couldn't bear to!" said Florence, in a harsh and suffering voice. "And I only remember what you told me, yourself, that you had given Agnes her medicine. I didn't think you had added anything to it; you never told me!"

"Florence, my dear. Of course you didn't read the newspapers, and afterwards we never talked of the matter again. What is wrong?"

Florence turned desperately to the priest. "You must believe me! I didn't read the newspapers! And, like Geoffrey, I thought Rose had merely said, 'Please give Mrs. Gould her medicine at midnight.' You must believe me! The girl was in a hurry. She testified that she had prepared the medicine and that she had told us. I don't think she told us she had. I don't think, now, that she had ever done so before! Geoffrey," and now she turned to her husband, "we didn't remember that she had ever done so, and that is why—— After all, the girl had to protect herself, and it is possible that she actually thought she had prepared previous doses on her evening off. I don't know! Geoffrey, Geoffrey, you *must* let me speak!"

"Florence, you don't know what this means——"

"There are no eavesdroppers here," said the priest. "And what you are telling me will never be revealed by me, unless with your permission. Please go on, Mrs. Gould. There is something you want to tell me."

"Yes!" Florence's eyes were distended and feverish. "I always brought Agnes her nine o'clock hot milk, when the nurse was off. It soothed her, and helped to make her sleep. As Geoffrey says, she was in a bad temper, after being so gay all through the day. She was drowsing, but she half sat up to drink the milk. I saw the partly filled glass of water on her bedside, and the medicine, and I—I measured out three drops and put them in the water. She didn't see me. She just complained and sipped, and sighed and moaned. I hardly listened. She abused Geoffrey frightfully, and I tried not to hear. Then I took away her milk glass and told her that Geoffrey would be in at midnight to see that she was awake and to see that she took her medicine." Florence stopped on a hard, dry sob.

"Did you tell her, Mrs. Gould, that the drops were already in her glass?"

"Yes! I never came with Geoffrey at midnight to see Agnes. That was their time alone together. I said, 'Agnes, the medicine is ready, and good night, my dear.' Then I left the room. She did not acknowledge that she had heard me, and didn't answer me. She was in such a tantrum. I *thought* she had heard! But now I know she had not. Or, she had forgotten in her half-drugged state. Oh, my God, Father! I killed her!"

"Florence!"

The priest held up his hand. "Please wait," he said. There was something stirring in his mind, something vague. "Mr. Gould, you've told me that when you went into your wife's room, at midnight, she told you she didn't need your ministrations. While she was upbraiding you, she didn't notice that you had prepared her drops. Is that correct?"

"Yes. She was more than half asleep when I went in. I had trouble in arousing her." The squire's eyes had begun to brighten, pleadingly, hopefully.

"Did you actually see her take her medicine?"

There was silence in the room, taut, alert. The squire and his wife stared at the priest. Then the squire said, slowly, "No, I did not. Strange, I didn't remember, until now, that I had not seen her take it. I only said I had put the drops into her glass. I was not asked if

I had actually seen her drink the water! My own lawyers did not ask; neither did the Crown Prosecutor. Nor did the judge. It was assumed, by me, my lawyers, the prosecutor, the judge, that she had drunk it while I was still there. If I had thought—but the things she had said to me, vile things, shut out any conjecture, in my own mind, as to whether or not I had seen her take the draught. I remember that when I was testifying my mind was preoccupied with despair, wondering about my children, and the disgrace, and asking myself how they would survive if I were—hanged. I can see why I was not asked; I had said I prepared the medicine and then had wakened my wife to take it."

"Assumptions," said the priest, "have caused a lot of trouble in this world, and probably many hangings."

But the squire went on, as if he had not heard: "If she hadn't been so abusive, if what she had said had not been so unjust and so cruel, I'd have stayed there until she drank that potion. But she ordered me out. She said she didn't need my ministrations, and that she was capable enough, even though I wished her dead, to take excellent care of herself."

"Aha!" said the priest, rising in his excitement. "Is that exactly what she said?"

"Yes, it is."

"Mrs. Gould, did you tell Mr. Gould that you had prepared the drops yourself?"

Florence's face went gray with concentration. "I told Geoffrey to give his wife her medicine at midnight, and that there was a glass waiting on her table."

"But you did not say you had put drops in yourself, those very words?"

She stared at him, blankly. "Words, words?" she murmured. "No. No. I only said the glass was waiting." She turned to her husband. "Is that what I said?"

"Yes, my darling," he said. Then he hesitated, and they both waited. "Frankly," said the squire, "I wasn't thinking of my wife at all. I hardly heard you, Florence. Only dimly do I remember that you mentioned the medicine Agnes would be needing at midnight and that there was a glass waiting. If you had not mentioned it now I should not have remembered at all."

The priest walked up and down the room. "Mr. Gould, did your wife say anything more, at all, after she had said she didn't need your ministrations, and could take care of herself, and after she had abused you?"

"Help me," prayed the squire, almost inaudibly. He shut his eyes again, and concentrated. "She only said she would take the medicine when she wished." His eyes flew open. He half rose from his chair. "I didn't remember that, either! Until now!"

The priest sat down and smiled at the two extremely agitated people before him.

"Was she quite awake after she began abusing you, Mr. Gould?"

"A little later, yes. I was alarmed. She seemed so—extreme. In fact, I wondered, as I left the room, if I should suggest to her that she take a dose of her mild sedative. She threw a book she had been reading earlier in the day at me; it caught me on the shoulder. She shouted at me. I closed the door, and I could hear her anger even when I went down the corridor."

The priest smiled even wider. "She did not see you prepare her medicine; she did not know you had done so. She thought she had driven you off before you had the opportunity. You awoke her. She had no way of knowing that while she was still asleep you had measured out the drops. Rose had not told her that she had prepared the mixture; the lady was half asleep when Rose left. Rose told you, or she did not tell you, that the mixture was ready. She probably doesn't know for sure, herself, but she has possibly put it out of her mind.

"Mrs. Gould, I have heard that you were questioned. Did you tell the authorities—you were not asked to testify in court?—that you had put those drops into Mrs. Gould's waiting glass of water?"

"No. I was terribly upset, as you can imagine, Father. I didn't even think of it! It left my mind completely until today, when you questioned us. They never asked me if I had prepared any medicine, myself." The young woman spoke with quiet vehemence and even passion.

"And you never testified in court?"

"No. The Inspector from Scotland Yard talked to me in the house. Then, I heard later I had been under some suspicion, but if so I was never informed directly by the Inspector. He knew my aunt very well; he had known my uncle. In fact, I had seen him often when I was a child, when I was living in my aunt and uncle's house after my parents died."

The priest could understand. The Inspector had known the girl from childhood; he had known her character well. He could not believe that she had deliberately destroyed another woman's life.

Father Shayne said, "Before I pass my opinion, which I believe explains everything, I should like to ask you, Mr. Gould, if you were in love with your present wife before your wife died?"

The dark and elegant face flushed. "Yes. I was. I admit it."

"Geoffrey!" exclaimed Florence, and now her face flared into beautiful light. "You never told me! I thought you had learned to love me after Agnes died!"

He put his hand over hers. She was trembling. "My dear, I was a Catholic husband and father, and I loved my God and tried to obey His law. You were a young woman in my house, loving my children, and having affection for my wife. I could not tell you. I fought it. I struggled with it, and prayed over it. I knew it was wrong, but I could not help myself. I knew that the only thing I could do was never to tell you. I wanted not to love you; I used all my will to prevent you from knowing. I willed not to love you, all through those years, and I never let you know."

"You never let me know," said Florence, delighted and marveling. "Well, my dear, I loved you, too. But I didn't tell you, either. I knew what you were, honorable and good. If I had told you, before Agnes had died, you would have asked me never to come again. Would you not have?"

"I should have asked you never to come again, for both our sakes."

The squire turned to the priest. "I told Father Tom that I had loved Florence for years, for at least from the time I had stopped caring about Agnes. I told him I had never told Florence. He did not believe me. He did not believe anything. He was certain that either Florence or I had killed my wife, for adulterous reasons and because we wished to be married. Before God, Father, that is not true."

The priest laughed a little. "You are wrong. You and your lady, Mr. Gould, did kill your wife. So did Rose Hennessey, probably. Technically, therefore, the three of you are guilty of murder."

Florence made a small dim sound and put her gloved hands over her mouth. Her lovely gray eyes stared wretchedly at the priest. The squire started.

"And, technically, my friends, the late Mrs. Gould committed suicide. After you had left, sir, she prepared her own drops, and drank all four doses.

"But, the murder and the suicide were done unknown to any of you. You did not will the murder; you did not know you were committing murder; your consciences are clean of any desire to murder. The late Mrs. Gould committed suicide, without her will and without her knowledge, just as you had killed her without your will and your knowledge.

"You, Mr. Gould, could not help loving your present wife. But you fought it, prayed against it, willed against it. Therefore, you are not guilty of adultery even in your heart. God takes note of intention.

"Now, I should like to know what you intend to do about all this."

Man and wife consulted eloquently with each other with their eyes. Then the squire said, "I think I should return to Belfast and lay the whole matter before the authorities."

"You have a name to clear?"

"No. No one believed that I had killed my wife. I was acquitted; the jury was out only twenty minutes. And tea was served them during that time. No one ever believed that Florence had killed Agnes, either. The judge expressed himself as approving of the verdict."

The priest again walked the floor, musing. They watched him, anxiously.

He paused before them. "Should you go to Belfast, after all these years, you would revive the whole case. You could not be tried again, Mr. Gould. Mrs. Gould might, or might not, be tried, on a technicality. Rose would be harassed again, and her name soiled, and under suspicion. And your children? They are old enough now, most of them, to undergo torture and shame. You could not live in this hamlet any longer. Therefore, I should like to ask you just what you would accomplish? And, by the way, after the verdict—I am interested in the comments of the court?"

"Death by misadventure."

"Will you, then, go to Belfast, considering all these matters?"

"What would you advise, Father?"

"I have given my advice, that you do not lie any longer to your children. In all good conscience you can tell them that you did not murder your wife, nor did your present wife. I should leave it at that. No other person is under suspicion, and therefore you do not have to fly to his help. Of course, if such an eventuality should occur, then you must speak up. I doubt it will occur, however."

Their faces were full of joy. Youth returned to them in an instant. The priest said, "Your conscience is not urging you to return to Belfast, Mr. Gould, and reopen the case?"

"No! For now all the doubts I had, Father, about my guilt have vanished. That is what haunted me, and that is why I told Father Tom everything."

The priest shook his head. "You did not tell him everything, because he did not question you as I have. Old Father Tom was right, I am thinking. His instinct was sure. He knew murder had been done, and that is why he was so outraged because you would not confess. You did not tell him because you did not know the truth. You must forgive him. You must think kindly of him. For, he cannot be blamed."

He smiled at them. "I shall expect you at Confession, tomorrow, Mr. Gould. And at Mass, on Sunday. After all, you have seriously sinned in neglecting your religious duties. You have let your children suffer needlessly, under the false thought that you must protect them. Despite the attitude of Father McGinnis, you should have persisted, and not have believed that you had been driven away. Had you persisted, he may have come to doubt his very reliable instinct at last. You caused him much misery, and he was an old man. I am afraid I shall inflict rather extensive penances, Mr. Gould."

The squire cried out, "Not penances! Blessed privileges! Father, you have lifted despair from us! What can I say, or do, to thank you?"

Mrs. Gould shyly gave her hand to the priest. She was smiling radiantly, though tears ran down her cheeks. "And Father," she said, "I should like to take instructions. If you will receive me."

Father Shayne did not write the Bishop after all. He decided to go to see him and tell him everything. The Bishop would be very happy.

"So," said Father Shayne tonight, "evil had been done, by an evil woman, who had hated her husband and her children. Her evil had turned the thoughts of her husband to her friend. Her evil had resulted in innocent murder, and her own innocent suicide. Her character had made her children suffer physically and spiritually. Evil, too, had been done by Mr. Gould and his second wife, out of a loving desire to shelter those children, who had wanted only the truth about their mother from them. Their lives had been blighted.

"Not permanently, however. Geoffrey became a priest; he is now a Bishop, in America. Elsa became a joyous wife and mother." He paused. "But little Eric died. He died in convulsions, a year after that day in my study. Who knows but what he might have been saved had his father called physicians in time? Another evil had been done, out of a fear of scandal, and to protect a woman who should not have been protected. Had her husband exposed her when Geoffrey had suffered his injury from her, Elsa should have been spared her suffering and terror and blight. Eric would not have died. Yet, it was all done with the purest of intentions and with innocence and love.

"So evil, in this case, was inextricably webbed with good and virtue. It is all very strange. Yet, there was no evil intended, so there was no evil."

Chapter Eleven

The unwelcome summons to return home came the next morning, and Rose watched her luggage being packed and cried a little to herself. Cook was firm and disapproving when she made Rose a last cup of tea and presented the small cake she had just baked.

"It is not as if," she said, "you loved your Grandmother." (Nor she you, added the good woman in her thoughts. Rose, with the prescience of lonely childhood, caught the compassionate glance of Cook and understood.) "It can't be just the tales you hear from the old men at night around the fire."

But it was indeed the tales, like a great book opening wide and colored pages in a small drab life. "What is it, then?" asked Cook. "Drink your tea."

As Cook obviously did not fancy tales, Rose could only shake her head miserably. But Cook was shrewd. "Then it is the tales," she said. "I could tell you plenty, meself, if I were a gossip like some who run from house to house. What's it about the tales, Rosie?"

"They make me think of God," said the child, and blushed.

"Aha," said Cook, meaningly. "They 'ave you a Roman in no time if you listen."

Rose sipped at her tea. If those kind old men, who took such an interest in her and fed her dainties from their own plates slyly—forbidden dainties for children—were Roman, then she would be a Roman, too. No one else but Cook had ever been so kind to her before, or had cared much about her. "I could do worse," she said to Cook, pertly.

"Mind your tongue," said Cook. She paused. "I'd not say that to your Ma and Pa if I was you, Rosie. They'd never let you come here again."

Rose remembered never to tell her parents. The spring came, and the summer, the endless hot and dusty summer in London, and then a visit to Bournemouth with her parents. She waited impatiently for autumn and winter, and listened eagerly to the mounting irritability of her parents' voices as the gray dull days came and went.

But it was January before the explosion came, and Rose was off to Grandmother's again. "Again?" said Grandmother. "I niver thought that one of my lads had so much spirit."

She looked at Rose critically. "If it wasna for the red hair, like mine, I'd say you were unco unpretty, Rose." Grandmother was indeed an "auld child." She spoke cruel words deliberately; she had malice to spare; her moods were not to be trusted, and there was no mature kindness to which to appeal, no understanding. Yet Rose looked at her with affection, and she was startled, herself. Rose was not a child to be beguiled by magnetism and charm and affectations. She did not consider Grandmother handsome. She only knew that Grandmother was lively, her house beautiful, her dresses full of splendor, her jewels incredible, and that, all in all, she was enchantment.

Grandmother was eying her exactly as the parrot eyed her, her head cocked, her green eyes fixed on Rose's face, her mouth grinning. "It's not sorry you are to come here," she said.

"I like to come," said Rose.

Grandmother, of course, was deeply flattered. She considered it a personal tribute to herself. She patted Rose's head, and then in the manner of children she pulled Rose's hair sharply and unexpectedly, and laughed at the little girl's cry of pain. Then again, in the manner of children, she was superficially contrite. "I've got a present for you," she said, and took Rose's hand and raced with her up the stairs to her magnificent bedroom. Proudly, she gave Rose a little cardboard box, and, opening it, Rose saw a string of bright coral. Grandmother preened at Rose's exclamation of delight, and so almost loved the child.

"And by the way," she said, "there are two old friends of yours here again tonight, Father Hughes and Monsignor Harrington-Smith. Did ye know what the Monsignor said of you? He said one day ye'd be writing doon the tales ye hear, and they'd be a book." She laughed merrily.

That night Monsignor Harrington-Smith spoke of a concert he had attended in London, and particularly mentioned the harpist. "Almost as fine as Stephen Doyle, who played as an angel plays. I heard him when I was a very young man. We called him the Minstrel Boy."

"I knew him well," said Father O'Connor, and all looked at him in amazement. "He was in my parish. He not only played like an angel but——"

FATHER DANIEL O'CONNOR AND
THE MINSTREL BOY

"Yes," said Father O'Connor to the amazed faces about Grandmother's dinner table, "I am the priest of that 'legend,' and I knew the Minstrel Boy." He looked at his old veined hands folded placidly on the table. "It is sixty years or more, I am thinking."

"But I heard that from my grandmother, and she has been dead twenty years," said Grandmother, "and it was very ould to her then, and she spoke of it as long in the past, before she had been born."

Father O'Connor said musingly, "Legends do have a grand way of receding into the past, and becoming tradition, and it is more authentic for a man to say, 'My old Dada heard it from his Dada,' than to say, 'I saw it myself, and I swear it by the saints.' No one believes a *man*, entirely, but the world has a curious way of believing legends, and the oulder the better, as if time gave them verity. It was harder for the Apostles to bear personal witness to the life of

Our Lord, they who had had the blessed grace to see Him alive among them—and they died for the witnessing—than it is today for a priest to bear the witness through the Church, the Holy Bible and tradition. For the priest teaches what he has been taught, but the Apostles taught what they had known and had seen for themselves and so the people, many of them, did not believe the Apostles, and killed them. Do men fear that all men are liars, then? I do not know. It is very puzzling that men will believe legends, which were first told by dead men, if those legends are old enough. Yet, it was but sixty years ago when I knew Stephen Doyle and when I witnessed what happened to him."

"It could be," said Father O'Flynn, "that men believe that a story which does not die must be true."

"But there are the many," said Father O'Connor, "who do not believe in a personal devil, who does exist, in spite of the truth which has survived the millennia. But then indeed, it could be that Satan, himself, has been very busy through the centuries persuading men he does not exist. Always will evil do that, the better to deceive and destroy. What man will take up arms against an enemy he does not, with all his heart, believe is on his step?"

"And it was you, then, Father, who knew Stephen Doyle," said Grandmother, marveling, "you who would be less in years than my Grandma who told me the story!"

"Yes," said Father O'Connor, "I was not only Stephen Doyle's friend, but I was his witness.

"We all know how sad and poor the little remote parishes of Ireland were and are, and I have heard the stories of my brothers in Christ in this very house who starved and labored and suffered in those parishes among their people. But Darcy was, I am thinking, the saddest and poorest of them all, tucked away in green hills, with the earth poorly yielding and famine surely at hand next Tuesday. Never did I meet a man there who had more than two pounds to his name, and it was thought he was a nabob if he had those two pounds all at one time. The young men left to work in Dublin or Waterford, or emigrated to America with their young wives, for there was nothing for them in Darcy, where it seemed only the hopeless or the very hopeful, and the young and the ould, lived in a state of hunger and anxiety.

"Darcy made nothing to sell in the markets, though there had been talk of a Belleek manufactory setting up shop. Some men had come to examine the soil, and had gone away shaking their heads. But the people of Darcy, the hopeful ones, talked of the day when the manufactory would be built and the grand wages coming in. They talked of it all the years I knew them, and I had known them since I was a lad, for I had been born there in a sod hut with a thatched roof. And Darcy was my first parish.

"Each family in Darcy owned its little land outside the village, and everyone who could walk or crawl or see worked the bitter earth. As there was no money, there was barter. A man exchanged a basket of oats for a basket of wheat, and the miller ground the grain for a part of the flour, and he gave part of the flour to the shoemaker for winter boots for his children. The women wove their own linen and wool, and their husbands exchanged them for barley and oats and the ground flour, and for milk and cheese and a little beef. It was primitive and wretched and no one had enough to eat or enough clothing or enough peat to burn in the fireplaces. It was an occasion for rejoicing and celebration when a ewe bore two lambkins instead of one, though the second lamb had to be kept alive in the kitchen before the fire, for its mother would not have it. And if a cow freshened and bore two little bulls there was more rejoicing, for when the bulls were old enough they could be slaughtered and eaten. No cow was ever slaughtered until she could bear no more or give milk, and so it was with the ewes and the sows. The ladies among the animals were cherished to the very day when even a fool could know they had nothing to give the village any longer."

The men in Darcy also cherished their donkeys and their few horses, for these carried the stuffs of barter and pulled the plows. The death of a horse was a major calamity. How would a man replace it? Darcy was days' journey away from the nearest city, and inland where there were only blue lakes and not the sea where the ships came in. Horses were too tired, and too precious, for a man to use to ride even to the nearest village for a gossip with his kinsmen, so

Darcy remained remote and isolated. But it was blessed in one thing: the climate was quite temperate and even, sheltered by hills from what the worst winter could do, and so the grass in the fields and on the hills remained green and edible for long months. Moreover, though it was stingy with its yield of oats and grains it grew fine potatoes, and there had been years when Darcy had been almost entirely kept alive by those vegetables. It was one of the few spots when, during the Famine, the potatoes did not rot. It also yielded peat for the fires. It also yielded some gray stone, and the miller had a small stone house, and the tiny church and rectory were of gray stone.

"That sounds very grand, to say that my house and the church were of stone," said Father O'Connor. "But the church held seats for about thirty people only, and they crowded, and the late-comers had to stand at the back and the sides and in the one little aisle. Many was the time the weary young mothers leaned against the cold stone, weak with hunger, and holding their squalling infants, and many was the time when I consecrated the Bread that my words were drowned out by the infant wailing. Yet, I am thinking now, the sound must have been sweeter to Our Lord than what I prayed, and the whimpering of the choir, which was composed of two ancient Sisters and one little boy with perpetual bronchitis. For, you will see, we all had bronchitis and we coughed the whole year through. The climate was not too harsh, but the hunger was. We had no doctor; we had a very ould midwife, and many was the young mother who died with the child to whom she had just given birth. Sometimes the child lived, and this meant that the father must try to persuade a pressed farmer for milk, if he had no cow of his own, and sometimes a mother with a nursing infant would help. Yet, I have never seen a village with so many sinewy ould people. The hundredth birthday would bring the children, the grandchildren, the great-grandchildren, and the great-great-grandchildren, with a cake for the sake of respect, but it was considered no tremendous age. I have buried many a man or woman who had lived long beyond the mark of the century, and to the last they had done their share of work in Darcy. It would have been a shame on them if they had shirked for one moment. Ah, they were grand people, my own, in Darcy! And never did the Sassenagh know of them to collect any taxes, which was a blessing from God.

"There was no pub in Darcy. Each man contributed his share of malt and grains to the brewer, who made the beer, and he sold the beer for a length of wool or linen or a pair of boots. The beer was drunk by hearthsides, among friends. I never saw a drunken man in Darcy, or a slatternly woman. We had very little, but we had pride in ourselves and we had Faith, and we had love for one another. In all the things a man can be truly rich in, those we had. There are many who would say we had no ambition, except for the young lads and colleens who emigrated—but we had our God, and what more can a man have? Even if he suffers?

"I was a young priest, but even the men and women beyond one hundred spoke of me with affection as the 'ould Father.' They loved me and I loved them. They gave me what they could in fresh beef and bread and vegetables and though it was very little it was all they could do. The women scrubbed my tiny rectory, which had but two rooms, each only as large as a stall, and never was a rectory cleaner. The men planted flowers about it, and potatoes in the little garden, and radishes and even some lettuce. Those were the happiest days of my life."

Children were cherished in Darcy, though few survived birth or the year that followed, for they meant more hands in the fields, more hands at the looms. Children were riches in Darcy. And so it was that everyone pitied Peter Doyle and his wife that they had no children. Though they lived just a little better than their neighbors, with no helpless mouths to feed the first years, they were pitied. Peter became forty, then fifty, and Mary, his wife, looked towards her middle age, too. Both were strong and handsome people, with strong backs—but they had no children. Then when Mary Doyle was forty-five she finally conceived.

Like Zachary and Elizabeth, they could not, at first, believe that such a miracle had been granted to them. The midwife was consulted, and was at first dubious. Mary was practically beyond child-bearing age; she had reached the "change." But month succeeded month and Mary's body increased. Each morning found the ecstatic couple at Mass, and each morning they received Holy Communion. If their neighbors were skeptical, they were not. Mary would have a child at last. They did not hope for a lad; a girl would be equally welcome. They looked about them with faces of gladness, and at last the whole village was praying for them both. Father O'Connor visited them often, just to look at Mary's rapturous eyes of faith and joy. He wished, for the first time, that his church possessed an organ. It did have the ruins of one, far beyond repair; of course, there could never be any replacement, for lack of money. The two very ancient Sisters, and the little boy, did their best with their Gregorian chanting. But still, an organ would have been welcome on triumphant Sundays, to remember the miracle of Mary's conception. However, there were times when the Sisters and the boy outdid themselves, and the tiny church rang like a holy gong.

The whole village declared an unofficial holiday when Mary came to bed in her labor. The brewer recklessly broached a keg of beer for those who stood about the Doyles' little house. The Sisters knelt at Mary's straw bed, and Peter Doyle was almost beside himself with joy and fear and had to be upheld by Father O'Connor. It was a warm spring day, full of the fragrance of grass and soft wind, and there was the brightest sun. All appeared auspicious, in spite of Mary's agonized and prolonged labor. Everyone knew she was in extreme pain, she who had never borne a child before. But no one heard her groan or scream. She bore her anguish with smiles of rapture and gratitude. She was about to deliver her child. Each time her middle-aged body was convulsed her eyes would light up like candle flames, and she would clasp her sweating hands towards heaven.

The hours went by. The midwife's face was lined with anxiety. She walked restlessly back and forth near Mary's bed, praying and muttering. Then she called Father O'Connor. "She is dying," she said, with the abruptness of all village folk. So Father O'Connor gave Mary the Last Rites, to the muted distress of those who waited. Mary rallied at once. "My baby will live, Father," she said. A little later she gave birth to a boy child, and at the very moment he squalled his first breath she gave her last, humbly and prayerfully. Peter Doyle sat dumbly with his son in his arms and was so far away, as he looked at his dead wife's calm and smiling face, that even the priest could not reach him.

" 'Tis strange, and then again perhaps it is not so strange," said old Father O'Connor, "that Peter began to hate his little son. He had had his dear wife for twenty-eight years, his dearest and closest companion in misfortune, hope, love, misery and joy. They had lived alone in the oneness of being for the greater part of their lives, and they had known each other as children. Mary was as much a part of Peter's life as his body. In the deepest sense of marriage they had been as one, almost from their own births. Peter had never loved another girl, nor had Mary loved another boy. Their faces were as familiar to them as their own. They had exchanged their first childhood kiss, and their last. Peter had always been 'Mary's boyo' and Mary had always been 'Peter's colleen.' They had sat next to each other at school and had looked at each other's slates. They, too, had been only children. They were at once brother and sister and husband and wife. No one ever saw Mary, from her babyhood, without seeing Peter beside her. So, when Mary died Peter died also, though he lived thirteen years longer."

Father O'Connor sighed. "I knew it almost at once. I deplored it, but I understood. Without Mary, Peter was not truly alive. He worked his little field, and came home to his cottage, where his dead father's elderly aunt now lived to take care of the child. Ould Eileen must have been close to ninety then, but a strong and vigorous woman. She lived to be nearly one hundred and three, and then she died, and Stephen was twelve years old. Never, in those years, did his father speak to him, not in love, not in anger. Sometimes I talked to Peter but he would stare at me with his pale blue eyes and I knew that he did not hear me. On Sundays, he spent his hours near his wife's grave, mumbling to her and smiling and nodding. It's very possible he did not even know that he had a son, though later Stephen told me that his father had always hated him. Who knows the recesses of the human heart? Stephen worked in the field with his father, and if they had need to communicate it was only through gestures. It was a terrible life for a young lad, and Stephen came to manhood with bitterness in his heart and anger, for he was all alone. He believed his father held him guilty for Mary's death, and that his life was a curse. As his father had rejected him and would not know him, he was sure that he was detestable and not worthy of human love and tenderness.

"Stephen was a tall strong lad, like his father, but with his mother's dark eyes. There was always a storm in them, from his babyhood. Those we reject, reject us; it is a truth we do not recognize. Stephen came to school for what the ould Sisters could teach him, but he was a restless lad, always looking beyond the hills. I was sure he would emigrate to America or at least to Liverpool. But he stayed on, laboring in the field, earning a penny here and there helping the shoemaker or the blacksmith or the brewer. He worked well, but he hardly spoke. His father became older and more tired, and Stephen did not speak of him. He was Confirmed, and Peter was not there. Stephen sang in the choir on Sunday, but Peter did not hear. The Sisters loved Stephen, but they were frightened for him. He was such a quiet and somber boy and he never smiled. He also did not sin in the full meaning of the word. When he was in the Confessional he would mutter that he sometimes wondered if God cared for him any longer, but that was all. The colleens of the village looked at him, for he was a handsome black-haired lad, tall in his boots, and with fierce and shadowy eyes. By that time he was all alone, for Peter had died when the boy was thirteen.

"I remember me that it was past midnight when Stephen knocked on my door and told me his father was dying and had asked for the priest. That request was almost the only thing Peter had ever asked of his son. Peter made his last confession; I administered Extreme Unction. Then Peter asked for his son, and there were tears on his face. But Stephen was not in the cottage. It was a wild night of rain and wind. I returned to Peter, and remained with him for the little time he lived. When I had closed his eyes I had felt the wetness of his tears, and I looked for Stephen again. Then I went to the neighbors and asked them to stay with the dead man, for it was almost time for Mass. Stephen did not return for three days, and no one knew where he ran, and his father went to his grave with none of his blood to stand beside him.

"It was not that Stephen was a sullen boy then, or resentful or rebellious, for had he been so he'd not have inspired the good ould Sisters with such anxious love for him. One of them told me that Stephen was lonely and desperate, but very conscientious. He worked the bit of land his father left, and he worked at anything else he could find to do. God knows I had little money of my own, but I found him odd jobs in my garden. He would talk seldom with anyone. He had a habit of walking in the woods all alone, and once I saw him so when the wind was high and it was sounding like a thousand harps in the trees. I stood at my distance and watched him and never have I seen a face so suddenly glorious and joyful and listening. He was listening to the great and crashing music of the wind, and its wailing among the boughs and its rustling and shouting in the leaves. He was then but fifteen, and he had the look about him of a wild black colt.

"And once, in the spring, I saw him lying face-down beside a brook, his ear turned to the brown and hurrying water, and he was listening again, and smiling to himself and humming a faint song as to a thin trembling of music. I saw him often like this, in the woods and forest, beside the water, in the fields. What music he heard I did not know. I, myself, was shy and I knew shyness when I saw it and I was not at ease with Stephen, nor was he at ease with me. I did not even know the condition of his soul, for when he was seventeen he no longer came to Confession and only on Sundays to Mass. He was not in the choir now since his voice had changed. He sat in his silence at the end of the worn pew, and he left in silence, and alone. There were those who said he had gone queer in his head, but I did not think so. I prayed for the lad, and I tried to speak to him. He would listen respectfully, and make no answer. Except once." The old priest smiled gently. "He said to me, 'Father, it is not the grand voice you have at Mass, but there is one note like an angel's trumpet.' And then he hurried away. I had the most foolish thoughts after that about Stephen. I questioned the Sisters, but they told me that Stephen no longer had a voice and that they had known that since it had changed. But, one very ould nun told me, he would listen with painful attention to the choir, and wince if a note was bad."

Stephen was only seventeen when he came to Father O'Connor and told him he was going off "to the wars." "Now," said old Father O'Connor, "the Sassenaghs did not come to Darcy for the lads for their eternal wars and skirmishes, for the same reason that they did not come for taxes. The village was so small, so hidden, so isolated, and it did not have any business with its neighbors or the towns. The Sassenaghs just did not know about Darcy's existence. Had there been a smell of a half-crown in all the village the Sassenagh tax-collector would have been there. But there was no half-crown; it was doubtful if any of the villagers would have recognized such a coin had they seen it. People lived apart in those days far more than they do now, and rare was the newspaper that came to Darcy and rare was the news even of the nearest village. I had the only books in the village; I knew that Stephen read what few I had, for so I was told, but I never caught him in my cottage. He came and went like a shadow.

"But in some way a newspaper from Dublin had gotten, in a sad state, to Darcy, and it was far over a month old. There was another war, and fine wages were offered to the lads to join the Royal Army, and grand opportunities for adventure. So Stephen came to me and gave me the few acres of his land. I said I would not take them but would hold them for him, and so it was arranged that the men of the village would work that land, take half for their labor and give the rest to my church and the Sisters. I then asked Stephen why he wished to go to one of the Sassenagh's wars—and I do not mind now what war it was—and he only shook his head and said he must go to see what the world was like beyond Darcy. I mentioned that he might be killed and he said, 'Father, that would not be bad. For the likes of me, without kinfolk or friends or aught to care whether I live or die.' It was the first time I had heard the lad speak so, and he spoke with no bitterness or pity for himself, and it was one of the most tragic things I had ever heard. I saw his eyes full for the first time, and they were far and lost for all the storm in them, and then he was gone. The villagers marveled at his going, and again spoke of the queerness, but they soon stopped their gossiping, for they had not known Stephen at all, no more than they noticed a silent tree in its accustomed place. He was long forgotten at the end of five years, and the little sod cottage stood alone and gathered dust and the men worked the small bit of land and began to speak of it as 'the Doyle acres.' Not Peter's as it had been, and not Stephen's when he had inherited it. It was only Doyle's, and none remembered Stephen's face or what or who he was. He was forgotten except for myself, and the two ould Sisters died and took the memory of him with them.

"Then, as suddenly and as invisibly as Stephen had left, so he returned. A little girl who had no memory of Stephen told me excitedly that gypsies were in 'the Doyle cottage,' and that smoke was coming from the single chimney. I went at once, crossing the golden fields of autumn. It was another day of high wind, and it sang a different song than the one it sang in the other seasons, a song of lonely places and desolation and shadows that stood forever unseen by any man. When I came to Stephen's tiny house he was there on the doorstep smoking, and he was a man grown and tall and very pale and thin, and the only thing that moved about him was the smoke from his pipe. His eyes stared at me but he made no sign of recognition. He did not even stand, as all men stood then when a priest approached. He just stared at me emptily and smoked, and I stopped and he bent his head a little to one side. And then as I passed over the thick turf a beam of sunlight struck his forehead and I saw that near his right temple there was the most dreadful of old scars. It was long and dark red and twisted, and it pulled up one of his eyelids so that he had the strangest expression.

"I was about to speak when he said in his slow and uncertain voice, 'Who is it?' I stopped again. Surely five years had not changed me that much, even in Darcy! And so I said, 'It is your friend, Stephen, Father O'Connor.'"

Stephen slowly and awkwardly got to his feet and mumbled, "And a good morning to you, Father."

"Good morning, and a fine morning it is, Stephen," said the priest, anxiously watching the young man, who was now twenty-two.

"I know it is a fine morning, Father," said Stephen, "for the wind tells me it is. It tells me all about the sea where it was before dawn, and how the sails sing in it, and how the mountains thundered when it passed over, and the web of gold the gulls made when they flew in the sun, flying together in the face of the sun."

It was the longest speech Stephen had ever uttered to anyone in the village, and he was suddenly still and silent again, with a red wash running over his face and darkening the scar so that it was a wound again.

"I am happy that you have returned, Stephen," said the priest. "You never wrote me. I did not know you were here until this morning. Welcome home, Stephen." He held out his hand to the young man, but Stephen did not look at the hand and he did not take it. Hurt, Father O'Connor dropped his hand. "And where would you be getting that terrible scar, Stephen?"

Stephen said, "In the wars. I have seen most of the world. The Sassenagh owns very much of it. It was a bayonet wound I had, and then a blow on my head. How is my land, Father?"

"In grand condition," said the priest. There was something about Stephen that alarmed him. "Have you not seen it yourself?"

"I'll never see it again," said Stephen. "I have been blind for two years."

The priest had heard many sorrowful things in those years, but it seemed to him that this was the most sorrowful and he felt that his heart had been torn rudely in his breast. The lonely young man was now doomed to a deeper loneliness and the priest wanted to weep. Even the death of Mary Doyle had not been so tragic as this.

The two men sat on the stony doorstep and they smoked together in the autumn sunlight and the priest waited. Stephen finally told him, and with indifference, as if this dreadful calamity had happened to one he did not know but who probably had deserved it. It was somewhere in Africa, he said vaguely. And then his face changed at the mention of Africa and he told the priest of the endless dripping of the rain forests and the pounding beat of the mighty rivers when

the water poured down from the green mountains, and he told of
the songs and cries of strange and exotic birds, and the majestic
call of lions and the laughter of hyenas, and the grumbling neighs
of hippopotami, and the crackling of winds in palm trees and the
long deep groaning of hot seas. "I was like one who was mad, I'm
thinking," he said, with some sheepishness. "I could not get enough
of the listening. I lay awake to hear it. I did not know that God
had so many voices, for what was I but a raw lad from Darcy,
drunk on the music?"

He folded his hands together in a gesture of awe, and he turned
his blind but unblemished eyes on the priest and they shone with
memory. "All God's voices," he said. "There was not an ugly sound
in them, though some were terrible, Father."

He had gone to the wars, he said, because he wanted a harp.
Once he had heard a harp, when he was fifteen and an orphan and
he had ridden his horse into the nearest village and had heard an
old man on the green playing a harp, a little feeble harp, and he
was singing a ballad. "I forgot what I had come for, Father, to that
village. I had four shillings with me. I sat down on the grass with
the old man, and I gave him three of the shillings to play for me,
and I stayed with him and listened." It was not until he had returned home, in his dream, that he remembered that he had gone
to the village for some tool not to be bought in Darcy.

And then he had gone to a music hall in London when he was
a soldier, where an Irishman played a larger harp and sang the old
Irish ballads, and the harp was not being played by a man at all
but an angel. "An angel, Father," Stephen repeated. "And it was
my heart that was burning now for a harp of my own, so that I
could hear all the voices of God again under my fingers on the
strings."

The Sassenagh did not pay grand wages, as the paper from Dublin
had said. But Stephen saved what little he received. Then he was
blinded in Africa by some desperate native during a skirmish, and
after long weeks he was returned to London to a military hospital
and rehabilitation. He had been taught to weave baskets, to work
looms, to polish boots deftly and to sole them. "It was a very new

thought in London then," said old Father O'Connor, "and a merciful one, and it was all due to the ladies. As a usual thing a crippled
or blinded soldier was turned out on the street with only God to
have pity on him and help him. The ladies were determined that
those who had suffered disaster in the name of God and country
should receive a pension. They had partially succeeded, for now
Stephen would have a pound a month. It was little enough for his
eyes, but it was still a little."

There would be no harp now. Stephen had spent his small savings in the harsh and filthy military hospital in London for soap
and tobacco and a new razor and other such necessities, trifles which
a presumably grateful government did not see fit to provide for him.
And his hireling's pay had ceased from the date of his injury. There
was no complaint in the patient and uncertain voice of Stephen as
he explained this. He had never expected much from life, and he
had wanted only one thing, a harp. It was denied him now, and
still he did not speak even with that old infrequent bitterness of his
which had appeared sometimes before he had gone off to the wars.
In fact, he felt presumptuous that he had ever had any hope at all,
for he was only a lad from Darcy with a bit of land, and of no
importance.

"You are important to God, Stephen," said the priest, after the
mournful tale had been completed.

Stephen shook his head. "No. My Dada was right. I am nobody
at all, Father. And now will you kindly tell the people that I am not
helpless but can weave them market baskets for the babies, and can
mend boots and tend a loom?" He hardly expected money, for there
was so little money in Darcy, and he had his pound a month for
tea and sugar and his meagre needs. He hoped only to live out his
life in Darcy, and listen to "the voices of God."

There was little Irish anger in Father O'Connor, but now he was
bitterly angry. He was angry against almost everything and everyone
in the world, because of Stephen. He looked at the blind eyes, and
his own swelled with tears. He patted Stephen on the shoulder
and went to neighbors and told them bluntly of Stephen's state and
demanded their help. They were astonished at the severity of their

priest and hurriedly remarked that none had really known Stephen when he had had his eyes, and that he had always been an unfriendly lad, and what had they to give him from their own pockets? The Father knew their condition. They would work the land for half of its produce and—— "You will give the rest, not to the Church, but to Stephen, for he has never lived and few have ever loved him," said the priest, feeling like a firebrand and full of nameless indignation. He went into his infinitesimal church and addressed God in somewhat stern language concerning Stephen. Then he was immediately contrite. Still his heart burned. There was not, he assured God, a harp in Darcy nor for many, many miles about. Stephen had no money; no one in Darcy had any money.

Suddenly the priest was weeping and praying that somehow a harp would find itself under Stephen's fingers. Stephen would not starve, though he was blind. But he needed a harp. "For Thy celebration, dear Father of us all," said the priest, with a slight feeling that he was being somewhat exigent and a little wheedling. A priest understood, Father O'Connor explained humbly, that God's ways were not man's ways, and God's will was above questioning. "But hast not Thou, Our dear Lord, told us that Thou knowest our needs and that one has but to ask in Faith? If it be Thy will," said the priest, earnestly gazing at the small cheap crucifix over the main altar and suspecting himself of being a little demanding, "send Stephen Doyle a harp." He hoped, very much, that a harp would materialize itself, and that it would be God's will. He could not believe that he was asking a triviality, considering that love had been withheld from Stephen all his life, except for the love of God and the two ancient Sisters long sleeping in the dust. True, it was, that when Stephen had become a young man he had shown little, if any, interest in the Church. "But didst Thou not halt to give a blind beggar his sight?" he urged.

Within a week Father O'Connor had everyone who could pray at all praying for a harp for Stephen Doyle. It is true that everyone was bewildered. What did Stephen Doyle need with a harp? He needed many things, such as repairs to his house—— "Repair it, then," said the priest, and the men hurried to do so, grumbling under their breath. If Peter Doyle's lad had "flown off" to fight for the Sassenagh and had lost his sight, then it was both God's will and Stephen's own folly. What would Peter, himself, have thought of such a treasonous action? A good Irishman did not fight for Sassenaghs; he fought the Sassenagh instead. Everyone was willing to do what he could for Stephen; it was only Christian charity, though he had hardly behaved as a Christian before he had been blinded. He had said some very regrettable things concerning religion, an old man suddenly recalled. Oh, the Father could speak of Stephen loving "the voices of God," and where was that written anywhere, Father, but he had shown little interest in his neighbors and had rarely spoken to them and was not even grateful that his land had been kept up. He walked with his cane along the one mud-packed street and when a kind word was said to him he only mumbled.

"His Dada didn't love him," said Father O'Connor. "No one did, but ould Sister Agnes and ould Sister Mary Francis. God forgive me, but I didn't love him either. We were blinder than Stephen is now, for we were blind in our spirits. Let us pray for a harp for him."

"The cheapest harp," said a young man in a tone of authority, "is fifty pounds, in Dublin. And where is there four pounds in one place in Darcy? There's not even a horse which would bring the likes of five pounds, in Darcy, and even a cow would be considered dear at that price."

"Pray for a harp for Stephen Doyle," said the priest, feeling like a Crusader in the midst of heathen Saracens. The people shook their heads. Was the ould Father becoming daft? A harp for Stephen Doyle, when children were barefoot half the year and a bar of soap was cherished and meat available only once or twice a week! There was ould Granny Guilfoyle who needed a new crutch, and everyone was saving pennies to buy her one.

"It's not asking you for pennies I am!" shouted Father O'Connor. "Not a penny! I'm asking you for prayers! Prayers for a harp! God knows you ask for sillier things! Cleanse your hearts and pray for a harp for Stephen; will it cost you a single copper?"

Thus reassured that Father O'Connor was not going to rifle a single teapot or precious sugar jar for—a harp!—the people prayed sheepishly. And a strange thing happened as they prayed for Stephen. They began to love him, or at the very least they began to regard him with compassion. He was the object, now, of their prayers, though they had been figuratively flogged to their knees, and it is well known that if you pray for a man you begin to regard him as dear to you and important, and you forget all his faults and he takes on something of a lustre. One of the prettiest colleens in the village, one Veronica Killeen, took a great deal of interest in Stephen, and brought a hot loaf now and then to his house, baked with her own sixteen-year-old hands. She had been too young to remember Stephen well when he left Darcy and certainly he had never known her. And now he could not see her pink cheeks and big blue eyes and dark red hair. But she had a sweet voice and Stephen loved to hear her speak, and she had a fragrance about her as of freshly cut grass, and she sang as often as she spoke. Stephen would listen to her innocent songs and he thought of young birds in the spring, and he could hear her light and dancing step and inhale her natural sweetness of flesh. After a few weeks he could even talk to her easily. Her parents, though praying dutifully for him, were hardly pleased, for Veronica was being wooed by the blacksmith's son, a fine broth of a lad whose father was the "richest" in the village and who possessed the nicest house on the mud road. Moreover, he had two horses and three cows, and it was rumored that the senior blacksmith had a bachelor cousin in Dublin who owned a "nice bit of property." The junior blacksmith in time would inherit such incredible wealth. Veronica was warned by her parents not to take too much interest in a man so much older than herself—over twenty-two now—and one who was blind and who had fought for the Sassenagh into the bargain. Was that worthy of a true son of Ireland? Veronica tossed her red hair pertly, and her case was brought before Father O'Connor, who was not in the least unsympathetic towards the girl and chided the parents for lacking charity.

"Would you have her have a heart of stone?" asked the priest, sternly. He often discovered Veronica kneeling in the church in fervent prayer, and he suspected who was the object of her prayers. A lovely colleen, he thought, uneasily. But what did she see in Stephen

Doyle, pale and very thin, and older, and blind, and dependent on the kindness of his neighbors? He asked her and received the astonishing reply, "Oh, it is the great man Stephen will be!" the girl cried, and gazed at the priest with such radiant eyes that he was taken aback.

"We are all great in God's sight," said the priest. "But let us exercise a little prudence, Veronica. A sweet girl you are, and the apple of your parents' eye. Er—what does Stephen say to you, on his doorstep in full sight of the village, or walking with him down the road?"

Veronica was ecstatic. "He talks to me of God's voices, Father. I never heard them before, but now I hear them everywhere. He opened my ears, Father."

"He talks of nothing else?" asked the priest, who now knew a thing or two about human nature, and especially the human nature of young men and girls.

Veronica hesitated and blushed. "He talks to me of meself, Father, and I'm the oldest child of twelve children, and the cottage full to the roof with all of us, and no one talked just of me before."

All at once the priest thought of the idyl of Peter and Mary Doyle, who had clung together as if no one else but themselves were alive in the world, and so he only mentioned decorum and prudence again to Veronica and prayed that all would be well. He did speak to Stephen, who was making baskets and soling shoes—all done excellently—and Stephen had said, "Veronica is like my eyes. She tells me of things I cannot see, Father, and she is an angel."

Father O'Connor hoped that Stephen would continue to regard Veronica as an angel for some time to come, and not as some rosy apple for a man's eating. Stephen laughed gently, he who had never laughed before. "When Veronica asks me to marry her, then I will, Father. I will give you my promise that I'll not be asking her to marry me."

Father O'Connor received fifteen dollars—three incredible pounds —from a parishioner who had gone to America ten years ago. That was Christmas. It was a personal gift from a grateful and struggling man who had not found streets of gold in America's cities. So praying he was doing the right thing, the priest sent to Dublin for many books, not all of them of a purely religious character, and he gave them to Stephen and suggested to Veronica that she read them to his protégé—on the doorstep in fine weather.

The harp was farther away from realization than it had been in the beginning, but the people zealously prayed even though they had private questions as to Stephen's need for a harp! Now, a harp was a nice thing, to be sure, and Irishmen loved harps. But why for Stephen Doyle, who needed new blankets and a new plow? Surely these were more important than a harp for a man who did not even know how to play one and who had never read a piece of music in his life?

But if the people had changed, Stephen had changed also. He felt the very palpable presence of concern all about him, with the prescience of the blind, and he wondered at it. He heard kind voices, he who had never known kindness except for the old Sisters. He became a different man, no longer shy and running from another human being. He even developed some esteem for himself, and stopped believing he was detestable and unworthy. He even dared to hope that he would have true friends in time. He found himself talking not too awkwardly to the villagers who accosted him. He bartered his baskets for necessities and at Christmas he was speechless at little gifts, he who had never received a gift before. A fine stuffed goose, baked and delicious, found itself on his table. And, as he discovered simple human sympathy and concern, he dared to turn to the God he had felt had never known him or cared for him. His love for God, his reverence for the voices of God, seemed less presumptuous now, less blasphemous. He approached God timidly, at first with shrinking, then with the sure knowledge that God welcomed him as a son. He knelt with Veronica every day now, at Mass, and received Communion.

One day the priest told Stephen that when his father was dying he had asked for his son. "He was wishing to make some amends; he knew he had not been a kind father to you and that he had not loved you. But death opens our eyes. He called over and over for you, to ask your forgiveness, my son. But you had gone away, for three days."

Stephen, the somber and reserved, burst into the first tears he had shed since his childhood. "Always, he would tell me I had killed 'his Mary.' He never said 'your mother' to me, so it was believing, I was, that not only my father hated me but my dead mother near Our Blessed Lord's throne. I had divided love from itself. I had brought disaster, by being born, to those who loved each other dearly. That is the burden I have always borne, Father."

Then he said, "I had not gone far. I had hidden in a barn in the country. For three days and three nights, without food. I had thought me that if I went away my Dada would die in peace, without the hatefulness of the sight of me before him."

"Do you forgive him now, Stephen?" asked the priest, much moved.

"I never held it against him," said the young man. "I held it against only myself."

So Stephen, assured that his father had wanted him at the last, took another step forward in grace and faith, and the people of the village, by the time spring had returned, told each other that Stephen was "another lad." Even Veronica's parents stopped scowling at Stephen, particularly since the priest had informed them that Stephen had promised him that he would never ask Veronica to be his wife. He refrained, discreetly, from telling them the other condition Stephen had mentioned, that he would marry Veronica only when she asked him to do so.

The high summer came, with its yellow cloak of grain and its green leaves and its blossoms in the small meadows and its murmurs of mystery in the woods. Once Father O'Connor thought that as Stephen no longer spoke of a harp he had resigned himself to the probability of never having one. But after a fierce thunderstorm he told the priest, "I heard the music of creation last night, Father, and the singing of high strings, and the chattering of water on the trees, and then, at dawn, the sweet hymns of the birds. I know, without knowing how I know, that I could make a harp sing so, for God's delight."

He also said, "I know how the angels charm the ear of God, and my hands—they are idle." He held the strong brownness before him, though he could not see them, and he sighed from his heart. "I hear the angelic music at night, Father, when all is still."

It was over a year now since he had returned to Darcy. He was strong and well, and his tall wide frame was fleshed, and he had learned how to bundle hay and make hayricks as well as a man with eyes, for his hands had become his eyes at last. He was never tired of working. His dark eyes were bright with health. He laughed often, if softly, and sometimes he even joked. There was nowhere that he was not welcome, even in the house of the Killeens, who were impatiently pressing Veronica to marry the blacksmith's brawny son. Stephen was now twenty-three, no longer a youth, no longer even young. He was not even a shadow of the boy who had gone off to the wars for the Sassenaghs' shilling, and he was certainly not the crushed and hopeless man who had returned. The slow deadness of his voice had gone forever.

If it had not been for Stephen's yearning for a harp Father O'Connor would have been content that Stephen had finally been accepted by his fellow-man for himself, that he was understood by them, and that he had some measure of love. The priest prayed, thanking God that Stephen had been accepted into the brotherhood of kindly men, and he told himself that surely it was enough. After all, all men had secret yearnings which were never destined to be fulfilled, because of the wisdom of God who knew best. Those most precious yearnings would be granted in heaven, where the noblest dreams are, and uncorrupted by the world.

Old Granny Guilfoyle, who had had a broken hip for several years, decided to die on a late summer morning, two hours after midnight. She had been dying regularly four times a year, but as she always chose a lovely night to do so, Father O'Connor was not vexed with her. Moreover, she was far over one hundred years in age and earned her own living by weaving mats for cold floors. When she felt that she was dying again she would rap her one window sharply with her crutch and a devoted neighbor would come running. The neighbor's wife came for Father O'Connor this morning, begged his pardon and said that ould Granny must surely be dying now. She was lying with her eyes wide open and rolled back.

"Ah, and it's sure I am now that the angels have come for me, Father," she said to the priest when he entered the one stony room of her hut. Her voice was very strong and young—as usual when she was dying—and very happy. Everyone called her Granny, she who had never had a man of her own and no child. She was the pride of the village because of the sturdiness, common sense and virtue of her character, though, as the villagers said, "she had the sharp tongue on her, like knives." No one could ever recall that she had ever uttered a malicious word, though she was a grand gossip and knew everyone "inside and out." So as she was dying again there was a knot of people concernedly waiting near her open door, even at this dark warm hour of the morning.

As Granny had received Extreme Unction several years ago, she could not receive it again. She had sent for Father O'Connor to hear her confession and prepare her, through prayer, for the seat in heaven which had waited for her during these endless years.

"What makes you think, Granny, that you are going to die now?" asked Father O'Connor, yawning. Someone had lit the candles beside the bedside and had lifted the ancient woman on her rough pillows.

"It was the angels I heard," said Granny. She was small and crippled and her white hair was very thin, and her cheeks had long ago fallen inwards. But her blue eyes were the eyes of a healthy girl— as always.

"And did you now?" said the priest, opening his book. He knew that Granny slept little, and he suspected that she found the nights lonely when all about her the village slept and the moon rode high.

Granny's eyes snapped at the priest, who was young enough to be her great-grandson, and they were fiery blue in the candlelight. "It's mocking me you are, Father," she said with some sharpness. She leaned sideways to look at the page in the book, and though she had never worn spectacles she could see like a hawk. "It's the wrong page you have, boyo," she remarked reprovingly. She was quite right, and the priest hastily found the proper page. Granny settled down on her pillows with contentment. "Aye, I heard the angels, and it was no wind I heard. I heard their wings and their words."

As Granny had never remarked on any angelic visitations before, but had been convinced that her time in Purgatory would be very long because of her really nonexistent sins, Father O'Connor was a little curious. He was also an Irishman, and to the Irish the supernatural is always very close. "What did the angels say, Granny?" he asked.

She regarded him thoughtfully. "You'll be mocking me again, Father, but I will tell you the truth. Oh, it was the lovely voice the passing angel had! He said, 'This is the first time, I am thinking, when one was ever given before.'"

"Well?" said Father O'Connor, impatiently. "And what does that mean, Granny? 'Before' what?"

"Now, Father, is it for the likes of me to know what that meant? You have not been brought up proper," she added, somewhat severely. "Questioning, you are, an ould woman on her deathbed. The young are impudent these days. But when one angel said that, the other said, 'Great is the mercy of Almighty God, and it's hoping, I am, that it will not be misunderstood or treated profanely.' Oh, it was the lovely voices they had as they flew over me house!"

She looked at the kneeling friends near her bed. "You'll be leaving for a bit," she said to them, "while I am confessing to this boyo."

The neighbors retired obediently. Father O'Connor sat and thought. Then he shook himself. It was a strange conversation for angels to be having as they flew over a very old lady's house, and it meant nothing at all. Father O'Connor also doubted that angels would speak in an Irish fashion so that Granny, overhearing, would understand them. He was of the opinion that pure spirits spoke a language not to be heard by human ears, if they spoke in tongues at all. So Father O'Connor dismissed the angelic story and settled down to listen to Granny's long list of sins, practically all of them imaginary. She made a perfect Act of Contrition. Then the priest came to the most solemn part of all—the dispatching of a human soul about to take wing from its body at any instant. He hesitated. Granny was most decidedly not about to take wing or anything else, and he glanced up at her. He started.

For Granny was surely dying now! There was no doubt of it. The

color had gone from her skin, from her eyes, from her lips. The unmistakable shadow of death was on her face, like the gray shadow of
some unseen and hovering wing. But she was smiling serenely at the
priest and her hands were crossed over her breast. The priest hastily
called three of Granny's closest friends and began the prayer for the
dying. The mournful litany murmured through the room.

> "Lord, have mercy on her.
> Christ, have mercy on her.
> Holy Mary,
> All you holy Angels and Archangels,
> Holy Abel,
> All you Choirs of the Just,
> Holy Abraham,
> St. John the Baptist——"

"Go forth from this world, O Christian soul, in the Name of God
the Father Almighty, who created you; in the Name of Jesus Christ,
the Son of the living God, who suffered for you; in the Name of the
Holy Spirit, who has been poured forth upon you——"

No one knew precisely the moment when Granny gave her last
breath, for there was no death sound, no death agony. She lay on her
pillows smiling, and there was no change on her antique face even
when it was evident that she had gone. The neighbors began to
weep and there were tears in the priest's eyes. He had known Granny
all his life, just as he had known the oaks on their knoll, the brownness of the brooks in spring, the look of great rocks in the sunlight,
the broken and colored marble of April skies. His parents had known
her before him, and so had his grandparents. Granny had taken
much of Darcy with her to heaven, and silently the priest sent one
message to her in her flight: "Don't forget us, Granny, Pray for us."
He was always sure, after that, that she had momentarily paused to
hear him, and that she had nodded reassuringly. So he was consoled,
and happy.

He left Granny to the loving care of her friends. The knot of men
and women outside were sobbing quietly. Granny had never been
the picture of a gentle saint; she had not been particularly benevo-

lent, for she had despised shirkers and ill-doers and the whining. She had not been tender with children, for she had darkly considered children as potential citizens of hell unless their parents were dutifully strict about religious and family and village duties. But children had loved her; her doorstep had always been teeming with them, in spite of her way of cracking her thimble on obstreperous heads. And the village had loved her, not for the gentleness she had not possessed or any helpfulness she had ever extended, but purely because she had been a woman of upright character, absolute honesty and sense and pride. Never once had she been charitable about deliberate sin, and never once had she expressed any excuse for it. For these virtues alone she had been loved and respected.

At one time, when Stephen Doyle had uncertainly tapped his way past her house, she had called him sternly to her, and had said, "My boyo, God has taken away your sight so that you can think of Him, and never see an evil thing again." That was during the first week of Stephen's return. He had said nothing, but as the priest now left Granny's house he was sure that Stephen had thought of Granny's words many times.

The first pearly light of dawn was in the east, and Father O'Connor wearily hoped for an hour or two of sleep before the Mass. The summer had been neither too wet nor too dry, and so the mud road was not dusty and it was not soft, but evenly packed and comfortable to the foot. The little cottages that lined it were still dark, and the vast sky above them stretched widely to the hills bulking against the brilliant starlight. The village was far from the sea, but a wind brought a vague scent of salt. Then, all at once, the priest stopped to sniff, for surely that had been the fragrance of lilies and roses on the light breeze. It was an intense fragrance, and he remembered it from a visit to a holy cathedral in Rome—St. Maria Major. There was not a garden in this little village which grew roses and lilies, for the area was too damp for roses and the season for lilies had gone. The priest stood in absolute silence, opening his nostrils to the beautiful and powerful scent. As quickly as it had come to him, as quickly it disappeared.

Bemused, he walked on a few paces. The gray light of the dawn

had become a vague blueness in the village street. It was later than
Father O'Connor had thought, then. If he could sleep an hour he
would be lucky. He glanced up; he was standing before Stephen
Doyle's tiny cottage. He looked, and then he looked again, and his
mouth went dry.

For, standing close to the high step, and slightly leaning against it,
was a huge covered shape, somewhat triangular, and Father O'Connor knew what it was at once, hidden as it was. No Irishman could
ever mistake that shape; it was engraved on his heart. Trembling, the
priest approached it on the balls of his feet, blinking his eyes to see
clearer in that dim blue light of the dawn's beginning, and half expecting that the object would disappear with the next blink. But it
did not. It stood there, waiting and majestic, covered with what appeared to be purple velvet with a fringe of gold on the bottom. There
was a slight glimmering as of silk in the protective cloth, or gilt
threads. And it was the largest object of its kind that Father O'Connor had ever seen. Not even in Rome had he seen one so tall and
so broad. Once, twice, three times, the priest put out his hand to
touch the cloth, to verify what his eyes were seeing, and each time he
withdrew the hand as if he had been about to commit a blasphemous
act.

The light was becoming stronger; the velvet cloth shone softly;
the golden fringe glittered. The priest drew in a very sharp breath,
and was conscious of the cool morning wind on his wet forehead.
Then he put out his hand again and touched the cloth. It was, it appeared, the most delicate of velvets, like a butterfly's wing. And, in
the fine folds, there was a thick film of dust, as if it had come a long
distance, a long distance indeed.

All the priest's restraint left him, and he found himself hammering wildly on Stephen's door, and calling. It seemed forever before
he heard Stephen's slow step and tapping within the cottage, and
forever before the door opened. Then the priest fell silent, and he
could only point at the great object waiting so patiently for Stephen
Doyle.

"What is it? Who is it?" asked Stephen, as he stood in his nightshirt on the step, his large eyes wandering and blindly seeking. He

put out his hand to search, and it touched the top of the object, and the hand paused rigidly. The first fire of the sun suddenly struck the top of the highest trees. Stephen's hand began to move over the covered shape. He murmured, "A harp. A harp!"

"A harp," said the priest. "A harp for you, Stephen."

He put his hand on Stephen's arm, but the young man stood very still, staring before him emptily, his face white and quiet. "Who?" asked Stephen.

"That I do not know," said Father O'Connor. "But let us get it in the house, or all the street will be about us in a moment, I am fearing."

Stephen was a powerful young man and the priest was no weakling, himself, but it took all their combined strength to lift the harp over the threshold inch by inch. Once or twice the cloth must have brushed against the hidden strings, for as the harp was moved into Stephen's one little room, where he lived and slept and worked, a faint high singing came to their ears, a far sound as of voices behind the clouds. Finally it was fully within the room, near the one small window, and the priest, panting, wiped his forehead. Stephen fell to his knees; he ran his shaking hands over the shape, and he murmured over and over just under his breath, as if praying, "Who, who, who?"

"Let us see it," said the priest, forgetting Stephen's blindness. He found the pearl buttons of the cloth, and reverently unfastened them and lifted the cloth from the harp. Then he was struck dumb again with astonishment and rapture, and more than a little fear.

This was no ordinary harp; it must have cost someone thousands of pounds. Stephen sat back on his heels. "Oh, God, who?" he cried. "Tell me, Father, what it is like, this blessed harp!"

"It is as tall as a man, almost as tall as you, Stephen," said the priest, in a strange voice. "The frame is of gold, and an angel's head, as large as yours, is mounted on its top. And its strings are bright and shining like silver, and its base is white and gold marble! Stephen!"

It was not possible, of course, but the impossible had come to Stephen in the night. The young man laughed softly, and tears ran down his face. He put his fingers delicately on the strings, he who had never touched a harp string in his life, and instantly the room was filled with a sound of musical waters rippling under the sun. Then, as Stephen's fingers, those loving, caressing and knowing fingers, moved again more quickly, the room resounded with angelic voices, pure, rejoicing, calling, praying. Never had the priest heard such exultant harmony, such transcendent joy, such echoes which appeared to be composed of light made sound.

Stephen clasped his hands in a gesture of prayer and ecstasy, and turned his blind face to the priest. "Who could have done this, Father, for the likes of me, a man who is nobody, hidden in Darcy beyond the world?"

Yes. Who? Who had given this gift? Who had found this place unknown even to the Sassenagh and the mapmakers and the builders of roads? Who, outside Darcy, had known that Stephen Doyle, the lost and the sightless and the most humble, had wanted a harp? Who, in an access of the most stupendous generosity, had delivered this treasure in the night and had left no name, this treasure which could have bought all of Darcy and a handful of neighboring villages? Even the Queen, herself, would have looked on it with reverence and awe, this mighty glory of a harp, and the Holy Father, himself, would have delighted in its music. A treasure beyond the knowing of most men. The priest looked at the angelic face surmounting the frame and it seemed to smile at him. Then it was that the priest blessed himself and did not quite know why he did so.

The sun shifted through the window and struck the harp and it glittered and shone and sparkled in all its incredible magnificence, its priceless beauty. Then the old sexton rang the one bell in the church and the priest started. Mass! There were footsteps outside, still heavy with sleep, moving towards the church, and sleepy voices. "Oh, God forgive me!" said the priest, in haste. "Stephen, come with me to the church. We will speak of this later."

They walked the little way to the church together, and Stephen moved in a dream, murmuring again, over and over, "Who? Who? Who? Is it dreaming I am, Father?"

"If so, then I am too," said the priest, and skipped fast into his house, the villagers staring at his back. They questioned Stephen. What was wrong with the ould Father, with his white face and the queer look in his eyes? But Stephen could not speak. He could only smile, as radiant as the morning.

Father O'Connor had always known joy when he said the Mass, and his heart had always shaken in him when he consecrated the Bread, for he was forever awed and was forever wondering why God had chosen him, a starveling young man born in Darcy, to elevate the sacred Host, and to offer It to the Most High in sacrifice. But on this morning his joy and his wonder and his awe almost blinded him with tears and his hands trembled and his heart was one fire of rapture. He kissed the altar and said, "*Sanctus. Sanctus. Sanctus,*" and all his soul was in his words and all his worship.

He must have communicated what he felt to his little flock, the few men and women in the pews, for their hearts rose humbly with his and not a thought wandered, and those who came to the Communion rail moved like youths and maidens through flowery fields. It was remarked, later, that the ould Father had had a light on his face like an angel's. A man guided Stephen Doyle to the rail, and Stephen received, then bent his head upon the rail and knelt there, not moving for a time, until all had received. Even when gently touched he did not stir. A stronger and more urgent touch finally aroused him, and he stood up, his expression far and dazed and shining.

Within a few minutes all Darcy knew of the harp, and all the men, before going to their work, and all the women, before making the breakfast, gathered at Stephen's house, and one by one, like those entering a small shrine, they went within to see the harp and stare at it with open-mouthed disbelief, and in silence. But when they were on the street again, they looked at each other dumbly, these poor men and women of Darcy who knew no beauty in their lives except their love for each other and their love for God, and who had never seen a cultivated rose or a fine stained window in a cathedral or a jewel or a length of silk or velvet or a golden chain, or any of the daily beauties which surround more fortunate people. They had now been in the presence of beauty and they were overwhelmed.

Then it was that some women who had heard old Granny Guilfoyle's talk of hearing angels in the night remembered her words,
and they were repeated eagerly and mysteriously and joyfully. Every
soul was asked if he had heard the sound of wheels or strangers'
voices in the night, and each shook his head, freshly overcome. No
one had been in Darcy that night, nor the night before, nor any
night that anyone could remember, except those who had been born
there and lived there. Who would come to Darcy? Who knew of
Darcy? Only the Bishop knew, in Dublin, and it was not likely that
he often thought of it except when it needed a pastor, or a new Sister. And the Bishop would not know of Stephen Doyle. Who, then,
had brought this harp? "The angels," said some old women very simply, remembering what old Granny had said. "She heard them fetch-
ing it." They blessed themselves. "And they took her back with them,
God rest her soul."

The younger men and women scoffed, but remembered that
Granny had been no storyteller and had roundly declared on more
than one occasion that she had no belief whatsoever in the "little
people" and thought those who believed in them to be "queer in the
head." Granny's life had been as outright as bread and butter; she
had not even been particularly pious and took all sorts of advantages
because of her great age. She was devoted to no saint, not even St.
Patrick, and would remind shocked others that the saint had not
even been an Irishman but had come from some heathen country or
other. She would cackle highly at tales of demonic possession, and
would jest in a most irreverent fashion even with the Father, and
would often ask the Sisters what in God's Name had made them
"give up the world." She often depressed the poor and humble ladies
with her questions and her jokes, but more often she had made them
laugh and blush like girls. So, if Granny said she had heard angels
in the night, then it stood to reason that she had heard angels in the
night, and anyone who doubted the tale of a fine old lady like
Granny, who had never lied in her life, was practically committing
a mortal sin.

Eventually even the most skeptical, such as the brewer, was convinced.

Father O'Connor, in his little cottage, was remembering Granny's words also. Once an old priest had said to him, "If, under certain circumstances, the reasonable does not appear, and nothing can be explained in a rational manner, then the incredible remains and must be accepted." He went back to Stephen's house, but even when he was some distance from it he heard the music, striking on the heart like angelic voices, powerful and exalted, and sweeter than any of the voices of earth.

"Who?" said Stephen to the priest again.

"I do not know," said Father O'Connor.

Stephen smiled. "God," he said.

Father O'Connor wrote to his Bishop in Dublin and the Bishop promptly inserted a notice in the newspapers there asking if anyone had "mislaid a harp." He thought it a silly notice, and he wondered if Dan O'Connor had lost his mind or was having hallucinations. Nevertheless, he had to make sure. So he caused a notice to be published "concerning a lost harp" in the Belfast papers also, and then in Limerick. He waited four weeks and there was no answer. Then he sent two priests who were notable for their common sense and lack of superstition and who teemed with erudition to Darcy. One was an Englishman, and one could always count on a Sassenagh to believe practically nothing. The English priest had spent several years in Rome and was about to be elevated to the Monsignori, and his family was a wealthy one and he had been educated at Eton. Moreover, he was a convert. There would always remain some slight skepticism in a convert, the Bishop thought, then remembered that his blessed dear old mother had been one, herself, and he withdrew the thought. But he was glad that Father Lambert was to visit Darcy.

"Where is Darcy?" the two priests asked. The Bishop got out his map and could not find it. "But I know it is there!" he said, baffled. "The nearest big village is some thirty miles from it, and you can ask the way. Darcy." The autumn winds and rains had come, and the Bishop remembered lost Irish hamlets and the roads that ran with mud and water and were hardly passable by the strongest beast, and he looked at the immaculate Father Lambert and felt a human and deplorable pleasure. "You will be able to get the hire of horses in the

big village," he said, "but you'll be doing most of the way on foot, I
am fearing." The English priest looked a little taken aback, but the
Irish priest, who knew all about the hidden villages of Ireland and
had come from one himself, chuckled under his breath. "Big high
boots," he said, "and a callused bottom. That's what you need in
those poor, Godforsaken places, and it's a donkey you will be riding,
Father, and thankful for it."

Father Lambert had plenty of pounds, for though he had taken
the vow of poverty his loving parents kept him well supplied with
money in the form of gifts. A new cheque had just arrived. He saw
himself comfortably riding, from the last railway station, in a carriage, and invited the Irish priest, who exchanged a slightly un-
charitable and amused glance with the Bishop. "I'm an ould man,"
said the Bishop, piously, "and it's been long since I've seen a lonely
Irish village, and it's happy I am that you'll be there, Father Lambert, and will be returning with your story of this—harp."

Father Lambert thought the whole journey foolish. A remote Irish
lad had found a harp on his doorstep, and all the village was agog
with stories of angels in the night. He knew these Irish. They looked
for miracles as eagerly as Englishmen looked for sovereigns. Ah, well,
poor creatures. What else did they have in their worn and battered
lives in that wild country? This fellow priest, Dan O'Connor, another of the dream-struck, another of those who sought miracles in
common events. No doubt some shopkeeper in a nearby village had
heard of this Doyle's desire for a harp, and in some secret penance
for his sins had sent such an instrument to him. Doyle was blind,
was he? Sad. The people of Ireland were famous for their sudden
generosities, which had a touch of childishness in them. They were
a people who loved mysteries and stories. In a way, thought Father
Lambert, it would be a shame to destroy this particular mystery and
story with the light of cold fact. Then he remembered that he was a
rational Englishman, and prudence and rationality were high virtues
in the opinion of the Church. So he set out with his Irish brother in
Christ, who appeared to have some secret amusement of his own, and
this made Father Lambert coldly irritable. He began to look on the
adventure as a sort of joke on himself.

"I know all these things," said Father O'Connor, at Grandmother's fireside. "For Father Lambert, who became a Bishop himself later, told me of them. He was shaken, he was, when he and Father Conway arrived in Darcy, and no wonder. They were both brown with mud, and not even the donkeys could carry them the last ten miles, and they had dragged the poor shivering beasts by the halter the rest of the way. Father Conway was enjoying himself, I am afraid, but Father Lambert was not."

They arrived on All Souls' Day. Father O'Connor, Father Lambert was surprised to find, was an intelligent man, and not an ignorant one, and he had no explanations, no enthusiasms, no annoying mysticisms. He told his visitors the facts. They were big men and had to crouch in the tiny cottage, and Father Lambert, in great dismalness, knew that he would have to spend his nights sleeping on blankets on the cold floor. Father Conway did not find the situation to be outrageous. He listened gravely to Father O'Connor's story, while Father Lambert frowned impatiently.

Stephen Doyle, who was steeped in the ballads of his people, was rarely absent from his precious harp. He enchanted the village. He had but to strike the strings to bring everyone running. "How much, Father," said Father Lambert, "would you say the harp originally cost?"

Father O'Connor considered. Then he said, "If it was bought at all, then I should judge at least five thousand pounds, or even much more."

Father Lambert was incredulous. "Surely you are jesting!" he expostulated, having had a long view of Darcy. "Who would have given such a treasure to a poor peasant?"

Father O'Connor bridled. "The Irish are not peasants, Father," he said, with severity, and Father Conway, who was enjoying all this, chuckled that disagreeable chuckle of his again. "Stephen Doyle is no peasant. He is a man of mind and heart and love, and read all my books before he was blind, and the colleen he is to marry after the New Year is a pert girl who reads well and who reads to him at night."

Father Lambert was vaguely disgusted. He decided to investigate immediately; anything to get out of this dank little hut with its smell of peat and mutton, even if it were raining worse than in London. He and Father Conway, accompanied by Father O'Connor, who was not liking the English priest at all, went to Stephen's house. And they heard the glorious singing of the harp even over the wind and the rain. Father Lambert stopped in amazement, in the torrents, and said, "Is that it?" "It is that," said Father O'Connor, a little grimly.

Stephen, who had been warned of this somewhat ominous investigation, let the priests silently into his house. The day was dark, the air brown with wind and rain and wild with dead leaves, and a little peat fire burned on the hearth. And dominating everything, filling the small room with grandeur and majesty, overpowering the big priests themselves, stood the mighty harp in its gold and silver and marble, and topped with its angel face. It glowed and shimmered and shone and sparkled as never a harp has done before, nor since, and seemed, not an instrument of metal, but a living entity in itself.

Now Father Lambert had had the pleasure, before he had been a priest, of visiting the noblest opera houses in England and on the Continent. He had seen harps in Windsor Castle and in Buckingham Palace. He had enjoyed the sight and music of them in the homes of grand friends. But never had he seen a harp like this, not even at the Royal Opera House during a ballet in St. Petersburg.

Stunned into silence and awe, the two visiting priests moved about the harp while Stephen stood restlessly on the hearth, restrained only by Father O'Connor's gentle hand. The priests appeared afraid to touch the instrument. Then Father Lambert finally brought himself to it and struck the strings. Instantly the air was permeated with the holiest and most glorious of sounds, rippling and singing, and there was a murmur of bells in the background. Father Lambert fell back, white and amazed. And Father Conway involuntarily crossed himself.

"Play for us, Stephen," said Father O'Connor, and Stephen, with surety in his step, went to the harp and sat down on the stool near it and began to play. The harp sang like a bevy of angels rejoicing in a simple Irish ballad of Tara's Halls. Father Conway's eyes filled with tears. Father Lambert stood like a statue, and there was no color in his cheeks at all. Stephen's hands wandered from the ballads to some grave song that lived only in his soul, and they all knew, instinctively, that it was a salutation to the Queen of Heaven, herself.

"And what is your explanation, Father?" asked Father O'Connor when the three priests were back in the little rectory.

"There is none," said Father Conway. "You have told us of all the villages about Darcy, and we have seen them ourselves. No one in Dublin, however generous, or even in London, could have sent this here, to Stephen Doyle, for it is a treasure beyond price. And who would give this to such a young man, whom no one has known except those in Darcy, and perhaps a poor comrade or two in the wars? It is a gift—from a Queen, or an Emperor."

"There is a rational explanation, surely," said Father Lambert, but there was no certainty in his voice. "We will investigate further."

The quiet investigation went on for a year, and in the meantime Stephen married his Veronica, and people traveled from the outer villages on foot or in carts or on donkeys to look at the famous harp and to hear Stephen bring life and splendor and joy from its strings. Then, in the summer of the next year, the Bishop himself came, covered with dust from the hot roads.

The Bishop, of course, was stunned. But he questioned Stephen sharply. Had he known any grand gentlemen in the Royal Army? Had he been servant to some great person, who had been touched by his desire for a harp? Stephen had known no great gentlemen; he had told no one but Father O'Connor of his desire. The priest, himself, came in for some sharp questioning. All the answers were simple and sincere, and entirely true. The Bishop departed, shaking his head. He spent more time than usual over his prayers that night.

Father Lambert, that cold and distant Englishman, had not forgotten Stephen and his harp and he told his gentry friends about the whole matter, cautiously refraining, however, from mentioning that there was something mysterious about the appearance of the harp. Stephen Doyle, he said, had been given that glorious harp, and he was a musical genius and the world should know of him. It was sinful to keep such music in the folds of the hills in a part of Ireland unknown to the outside world. The world had a right to it.

When approached on the subject, with definite arrangements in the hands of the now Monsignor Lambert, the Bishop hesitated, prayed on the matter, then heartily agreed. He wrote to Father O'Connor.

By this time Stephen and his Veronica had a fine pair of boy twins and were utterly happy. They were astounded at the Bishop's letter. Stephen should go out into the wide world with his harp and play for grand persons in grand places? Why? They wanted no money; they had all they needed in the world.

"But the world does not have all it is needing," said the priest. "It is a sin to hide what is here, for who knows how many multitudes will be touched in the heart by Stephen and his harp? There is another matter: Stephen, why do you think God sent this harp to you? To keep its voice, and your music, from His weary children, to keep their gladness from the souls of other men?

"In short," said old Father O'Connor, remembering those days so long ago, "Stephen obeyed what he knew he must obey, and he and his harp and Veronica went out into the world, from country to country, and everywhere they went, the generals and the princes and the nobility and the great ladies stood and wept when Stephen's concerts were over. He had developed an enormous memory; he had only to hear a sonata or a song once to repeat it on his harp. He had no eyes to see the notes of music; he had only his soul to remember. It is not important to mention that gold poured into the hands of Stephen, for he kept very little and sent the rest to the Church for the teaching of priests and the missions. And he built me a fine little church in Darcy, and tore down all the mean little cottages and built tight ones for those who had prayed for him, that he might have a harp. For he knew it was their prayers which had brought the harp to him and had given his soul a voice.

"Had the harp come to him sooner it would have been too soon. For he had had to purge his spirit of its old bitterness and despair, had had to know the heart of his brother first, and had had to love that brother. But then, the harp could not have been sent earlier, for it should not have been received as it was, and Stephen was not ready."

"It is a fine legend," said Grandmother.

Old Father O'Connor sighed and smiled. "It is no legend. It is the truth, and it happened over sixty years ago, and I was there."

He thought for a while, and all waited for him to speak again. "Stephen Doyle died thirty years ago, with his wife and five wonderful children about him, and their children. The old wound had never truly healed, in his head. He developed a tumor in his brain and he died in agony, but also in peace. For there was nothing but faith and joy in his soul."

"And the harp?" asked Grandmother. "Where is it now?"

Father O'Connor hesitated. "It is very strange, but it is true. When Stephen was buried in the largest graveyard in Dublin the mourners, many of them in the most splendid carriages, returned to the house he had there. And the harp was gone. It had disappeared, Father Hughes, as completely as your famous C'est Egal disappeared from the greenhouse of your friend, and from the house of your aunt. No one ever saw it again."

"But, there must be some explanation!" said Monsignor Harrington-Smith, who had had his dread encounter.

"Is there?" said Father O'Connor. "If there is, then none of us will ever know. For myself, I am thinking of the old prayer, 'The Lord gives, and the Lord takes away,' in His own mysterious time."

A priest who had been quiet looked at Monsignor Harrington-Smith and said, gently, "And God permits things to happen which are very strange, as you have told us, yourself, Monsignor. And things of humor, for who can deny the Almighty a sense of humor, also, which makes life sweet? I am thinking of Mustard. No, not an edible, a spice. A name, and one most dear to me. I must tell you of him."

BISHOP QUINN AND LUCIFER

"I knew of the ould Bishop, his dear lordship, by second-hand," said Father Morley, "that is, his youth, for he was well on to ninety when I was ordained. And never was there a lovelier man, less than five feet in his boots with the heel on them to make him taller, and towering like a giant in his soul. You'd have thought him a saint from the cradle except for the gleam in his bright black eye and the big roaring laugh he had. He was as round as a pot, at ninety. It was himself that told me that when he had been but a spalpeen, a fighting broth of a lad, he was called Mustard, and Mustard he was called by his ould sister who lived to be over a hundred and lively as a cricket to the day God took her to be one of His own. Ye had to be gnarly and full of muscles," said Father Morley, "to live to be ould in those days, what with the Famine, the Irish winters and the Sassenaghs. There's not much hanging of the men and women for the wearing of the green these days, but when his lordship was a lad it was common. But never will the man live who will make the Irish knuckle under him, and the Bishop was no exception. And in his youth he was not holy at all, but a rowdy sinner.

"It was said that in pitched fights—before he was a priest, of course—the Bishop gave a good accounting of himself with the Sassenaghs, and many was the skull he broke with pleasure and with a shout of patriotism. And they armed with rifles, too, and he only with his stout blackthorn. His sister told me, and herself had the black gleam in the eye, too, that Mustard was everywhere at once, heartening the lads to battle and whirling his stick at the same time, and shouting to heaven in a voice like the trumpet. He was willing to die for ould Erin at the drop of the hat, and while fighting for the occasion he did his very best, and many was the Sassenagh who rued crossing him. 'Ah, there was niver a man like Mustard,' said his sister, Eileen, to me, and it was sure she was that he'd have driven the Sassenagh out of Ireland single-handed if he had not suddenly decided to be a priest. And it was regretting it a little she was, as she told me.

"The Bishop did not tell me of his young days, but only of his later ones. His house in Dublin, when he was a Bishop, too, was little and cold and almost as bare as your hand, but he was a man of fire and iron and piety and laughter, with a wise way of looking into the heart of you. I did not know him when he was eighty-four, but had heard of him. With an eye to his youth, he had kindness for sinners, and if they were patriotic ones, too, and a lad of seven and a man in his great age felt comfort in his presence, and understanding. Penances he gave, and repentance he demanded, as God's only due, but never was there a harsh word from him or a turning away. He had been a mighty drinker in his day, before the priesthood, and any layman or desperate priest who could not manage the drink had but to come to him for help and he would receive it, and from that day on he was master of his weakness. A man did not want to disappoint the good Bishop, who knew the hard road and had walked it, and who had been a sinner like themselves and who sinned no more. If a man hardly higher than a tall boyo's shoulder could conquer, then a hulking big man could do it, too, they were thinking.

"He was a Bishop when he was eighty-four, and he had been a Bishop since he was fifty, and hardly in all that time had he more than a few pounds to rub together, and his larder was always spare. He always asked for prayers for his intentions, and the intentions of the Holy Father, and he asked for prayers for the whole miserable world of men, and even for the Sassenagh, though he admitted that no true Irishman should be asked to love the Sassenagh. That was asking too much of human nature.

"Those were the days when the Irish farmer was little more than a Russian serf in the eyes of the English landlords, and each year food was taken from the farms to be sent to England, though the Irish were starving and the Famine was not yet over, and the potatoes were still rotting in the fields. If those who took the food were sometimes not seen again, and if the soldiers or the lawyers or the agents came alooking, no one had ever seen the missing men, and the lads and the women swore to it. Will ye call that a mortal sin? But there were babies in the cradles whimpering for food, or a young mother with her milk drying for lack of bread, or a father dropping dead of hunger in the very fields he was tilling, or ould people chewing on their knuckles in the chimney corners.

"The Irish do not forgive freely, and it is hard to forgive when ye must strike a spade through the frozen ground of winter in the grave-yard to bury your wife or your child or your mother, who starved to death, and the food going to England. The Irish will forgive England in time, but never will they forget the Famine, and they will never forget the colleens and the lads who had fled to America so they'd not eat the little left and could make some money to send home.

"It was during one of the worst times, one of the blackest winters, when the starving people rioted in Dublin and killed and were killed, many of them, and may all their souls be remembered in our prayers. For it is the English poet, Kipling, who wrote: 'Lest we forget, lest we forget!' And over two hundred young lads and col-leens were arrested and driven into the prisons waiting for trial, and the Bishop knew that scores would be hung for the desperate killing, though it was in defense of their very lives.

"The judges were Sassenaghs, and the judge who was to try those wretched young men and women had lost his favorite nephew, who was an English officer, in the riots. He was a hot man by nature, that judge, but now he was in a frenzy, for he was a childless widower and he had loved his nephew. It was sad, and it was ter-rible, and that I am knowing. And the Bishop, in his little wintry house, in the coldest of winters, knew it, too. The Bishop was eighty-four, but strong as a lion, and if he had one bare meal a day he counted that day as lucky. His sister, Eileen, kept his house, and she was over ninety, and many was the time he said he had no appetite so that she could have the potato, or the herring, or the wing of the fowl which they had been eating for over a week, and the fowl was not a big one in the beginning.

"The Bishop offered his hunger, and he was always hungry, in behalf of the poor souls in Purgatory. He would take nothing if it meant that some mother or child or ould folk was deprived, and so it was that he did not have a full meal often. He could have borne that, but his heart broke when he learned of the two hundred lads and girls in the prison, and the judge who would sentence them to death in revenge. The desperate young folk, who had fought and even killed to save their lives, and it had come to nothing but the scaffold and the public hangings as a lesson to them that had too many lessons."

The Bishop was eighty-four, and he was gaunt then from lack of food, and moved like a little shadow about his house, and fainted quietly at the high altar for a few moments in the mornings, but so quietly that he knew when it was coming and rested his head on the altar until his wits returned again. He wanted no one to grieve over him, they filled with grief, themselves, and weeping for their children in the prisons until the church was filled with their mourning. He could only bless them, and pray that they would turn their thoughts to a just God, and he knew that they would find no justice on earth, an earth which was becoming harsher and more appalling every day. He told Father Morley, and some other young priests, that perhaps it was his giddiness at Mass one day, and his faintness, that gave him a vision of days to come, and the vision was so frightful that he cowered and went to his house, speechless. "Ah," he said to the young men, "it will not come in my day, and that I am knowing, nor in your day, nor in the day of the priests who will follow you, but it will come, and unless men repent in those days, and do penance for their sins, then they shall surely die and their world with them. Do not ask me about that vision, for I cannot tell of it, for I have no words, and I am one who never lacked words in all my life."

Young Father James Morley was the youngest of the young priests he had ordained when he was ninety, and he was an orphan, and matters were a little better in Ireland than they had been and so his lordship often invited Father Morley to dinner. It did his heart good to watch "the boyo" tuck away the mutton stew and the suet pudding, the young priest who was small in frame, himself, and whose mother had borne him in the height of the misery. In consequence, James Morley was delicate of bone, like a young fowl, and the Bishop thought that he could feed the lad up and make him stronger. And one night, after supper, the Bishop told him a strange story to lift his spirits. James was struggling in the rectory of an old priest who not only had rheumatism and cataracts but was almost doting and had to be helped through every Mass. The church was in the poorest section of poor Dublin, so there was little to eat in the rectory. The people in the parish were rough and led dubious lives and were not given to much piety, and all this weighed on James Morley's innocent young soul.

"Man needs little in this world except just enough food, and a tight shelter, and some warm clothing, and above all, love," said the Bishop to his youthful and almost nightly visitor. "He needs to work so that he may be proud of himself and hold up his head, but he should not be expected to work all the hours that the good Lord sends so that he is too weary to live. He should have time to be a man and remember his God and his religious duties, for man is not only a creature. He is a soul, and the saving of his soul is the most important work of his life. But in the days when I was much younger, in my eighties, men worked from sun to sun, like beasts, and still there was little for them to eat, and there was only grief in their lives. They will tell of these things to their children and their children's children, and it will be with bitterness, and that will be a great danger to the world. But still many of these men will tell their children and their children's children that above all a man must be free, for God has made him so, and without freedom even more than enough food and clothing and shelter will be worse than the starving. A fat serf without the freedom God gave him is not a true man at all."

Father Morley knew that the Bishop was thinking of the vision he had had one day at Mass, and he hoped that now the Bishop would tell him of it. But the Bishop began to speak of the Famine, and the riots, and the wandering men and women who staggered through the countryside with their children, looking for an unblighted potato or a piece of bread. And he told of the two hundred young men and

women waiting for death in the Dublin prisons and he told of the
hanging judge and the scaffolds prepared.

It was almost more than the Bishop could bear. He prayed constantly. He wept his painful old tears, he struggled with rebellion, he
was contrite, and he would be comforted. But at the very instant of
the coming of comfort he would see the stern and desperate young
faces in the prisons, and hear the weeping and the prayers. He had
tried to enter those prisons, but he had been turned away. He spoke
of last Confessions and Extreme Unction and the right of men to
the final consolations of their religion, and the gaolers laughed in
his face and drove him off. He thought of mortal sins weighing
down many of those young souls, and he hoped that literal martyrdom would wash away those sins in blood. For the young people had
been fighting for their lives and food, but more than all else they had
been fighting for their right to blessed freedom and the right to
worship their God in peace and without fear, and to have their
country, which God had given them for their own.

The winter was extremely severe, as winters have a habit of being
when men are in despair or at war. So there were just a few pieces
of peat on the Bishop's hearth, and they gave but little warmth to
his old and shivering bones. He had no money to buy quantities
of fuel, and he was intolerably hungry, for he had not eaten for
twenty-four hours. The hour was ten at night and the snow and
wind were blowing, and Eileen, his sister, had fallen into her bed
in exhaustion and tears and weakness.

The Bishop, this night, was in more agony than usual, and he
was sobbing uncontrollably and praying in catches of breath. The
light of his one lamp, in his small parlor, was very low, and so
was the oil. He put his hands over his face and rocked in his sorrow.
Then, all at once, he felt that he was not alone, and he dropped
his withered hands and looked up with a bounding of his heart.

A young and very handsome man was sitting near him across
the faint red light of the hearth. He was the most beautiful young
man the Bishop had ever seen. He was also beautifully clad, in
check pantaloons of rakish cut, and his waistcoat was of lovely
brocaded silk in a red and green embroidery, and his black broad-

cloth coat was of the finest, his cravat of black silk pinned with a stone that glowed like fire. His figure was patrician and elegant and tall, his shoulders excellent, his white hands gleaming with gems. But his face held the startled Bishop's full attention. It was dark, as dark as a Spaniard's or even darker, and it had a classic splendor, with a full brow, a chiseled nose, and a red-lipped mouth and sharp cheekbones and dimpled chin. His eyes were extraordinary, like jewels themselves, and of the deepest and most shining blue, like the sky just at sunset. His hair was curling and dark and luxuriant.

The young man was smiling charmingly, and there was an expression of sympathy on his grand face, and though he was young his eyes held the shadows of centuries of grief and rage and hate, for all their innocent color and shape, and he appeared very wise. He had the air of a mighty prince, mightier than any emperor or king, and the look of power and invulnerable pride and certitude. So the Bishop, staring, knew exactly who he was, and he knew that this was no lesser demon, but Lucifer, himself, full of grandeur and terrible strength.

The Bishop's heart was loud in his ears, and thudding and trembling, and all his pulses throbbed in his hunger-stricken body. He knew the greatest terror of his life.

"Don't be afraid, my lord," said Lucifer, and his voice was like rolling music. "I see you know me. You are a very astute man. Do I seem very formidable to you, in all truth?"

The Bishop's mouth and lips and throat were as dry as dust. It was some moments before he could reply. "But this is just an apparition of you," he whispered. "You do not truly look like this." His mind and his wits swirled; he tried to remember prayers and exorcisms, but they were like dropping water in his thoughts.

Lucifer cocked an indulgent eyebrow, and his face glowed. "And how do you know I do not look like this, my lord? After all, I am an archangel, and I was considered the most beautiful of all—by Him. I was also the most beloved. Or, have you forgotten?"

Now, like all devout churchmen, the Bishop had often thought of Lucifer and sometimes his thoughts had fascinated him. Ancient church-fathers had speculated on him and his dreadful empire of the pit, this tremendous angel who had fallen from heaven and who was still an archangel.

"But," said the Bishop, "you are a spirit; you are purely spirit. How can I see with my eyes of flesh?" He clenched his tiny hands together, and trembled even more.

"Come, come," said Lucifer. "Men have often seen me, through the ages. You have read of that. But perhaps you do see me with your eyes of flesh, and with the eyes of your soul also. Am I as fearful as you have heard, and as ghastly?"

The Bishop looked at him fully again. He admitted, "No. But then, you take many forms, I have heard. You seem like a young man in his pride of youth——"

"I am in the pride of my youth. Archangels do not age." Lucifer was amused. "It is true that I have appeared to men in the guises they found the most familiar, and so they were disarmed, but they clothed me with their imaginations. You see me as I am, for you are an old man and you have never lied in your life, and have no delusions."

"It is true," said the Bishop, "that you are very handsome. But——"

"Women have always found me so," said Lucifer. "I am irresistible to endless multitudes of them. Men have found me congenial, from the very beginning. I am much less unbending than—Him." As he said that word his face burned more darkly, as if with inner fire. "I understand mankind, though—He—took on your flesh and lived among you. He understood men, but how many men have understood—Him? He humiliated Himself to the cross and to death, forgotten by those He had loved and saved, abandoned by His friends. I tell you, my lord: once men have known me and accepted me, they have never forgotten me!"

He held up his palm to the quaking Bishop, who, however, was humanly curious and whose heart was calming. "I have helped millions in their direst hours, when their prayers were unheard by—Him. I have never failed to respond to a man's cry, when he called to me. But millions have not heard His voice—in answer—nor have they been helped."

"That is a lie!" cried the Bishop. "You know it is a lie! Our Lord called you the father of lies, a liar from the beginning!"

"But, His Father mourned me," said Lucifer, and for a single instant there was the most profound and supernatural anguish on his beautiful face. "He called me Star of the Morning. I stood at His hand, and knew His glory—and I loved Him. I knew Him for what He was, in all that He was. I saw Him face to face; I knew the Beatific Vision. Tell me, my lord, has there been a man on this world, of which I am Prince, who can say that with truth?"

"No," admitted the Bishop. He thought for a few moments. "You have told me you loved Him. How, then, could you have rebelled against God, and declared yourself His enemy?"

Lucifer smiled very faintly, and with a contempt beyond the contempt of men.

"Your theologians, my lord, have pondered that, and have tried to explain it. They never will, with their brains of mud, with their little hearts and their feeble imaginings, with their tiny fantasies. That is between me—and Him." Again the anguish charged his face and all at once the Bishop fully knew the horror of hell, and the torment of it, and the loneliness. This tremendous archangel was the Terror, the awful Adversary of all that lived, but his grief was beyond all imagination, and perhaps greater than his hatred.

"I must ask you," said Lucifer, "not to speak of Him again to me. There are matters beyond endurance. Look at me. I am as wise as He, and as immortal. I shall endure forever, as He will endure. Enough. We shall not talk of Him again." His face was so terrible now that the Bishop felt that he was about to be consumed and disintegrated by its glow.

But he said, "Had you been as wise—and what blasphemy that is!—you'd never——" But the presence seemed to expand, to swell, and for a terrifying instant to fill every corner of the room, the howling world outside, the very universe. The Bishop shrank in his chair.

"What do you want of me?" he whispered. "I, a poor Bishop in my sorrow?"

"I want—you know what I want," said Lucifer, who was again

the most handsome man in the world, the most genial, the most charming, the most sympathetic and elegant.

"My soul!" cried the Bishop, and fumbled for his pectoral cross. Lucifer's eye saw the movement, and saw the cross, and his dark face darkened even more. He put up his hand against it, as if it shone like the sun. The jewels on his fingers appeared living, each one quivering with sentient life and throwing showers of colored sparks into the little room.

"Your soul," said Lucifer, and dropped his hand. He was smiling again.

"How was it possible to come into my house?" said the Bishop, having another thought. "I was in the midst of my prayers——"

"I am able to go anywhere," said Lucifer. "And I usually interrupt men in their prayers. For how dare men speak to——" He paused. "If there is blasphemy, surely that is the most intolerable of them all. Intolerable." All at once there was a most savage and enraged glitter in the splendid blue eyes, and the Bishop shrank again and fumbled for his cross.

"But let us discuss our affairs," said Lucifer, and he was again the most engaging of apparitions. "Your soul."

"Don't be ridiculous," said the Bishop, and even in his dread and fear he was indignant. "My soul is not for you, and if you were as wise as my poor baker you would know that."

"You were a very sinful and violent young man, many years ago," said Lucifer. "I never forget such men. I was often close to you in those days. I am close to you again, tonight."

The Bishop blessed himself hurriedly. Lucifer watched with fresh indulgence.

"You were in despair tonight," he said. "And despair is a cry to me. Or, is your memory failing again, my lord?"

"I was not in despair for myself," said the Bishop. He could hear the ticking of his clock on the mantel, very loud, very hurried, as if it had gone a little mad. He could hear the gale against the windows; it seemed filled with multitudes of lost and wailing voices, screams and cries and implorations.

"You were in despair for the sake of those foolish young men and

women who will assuredly die in a week or so," said Lucifer. "If you
had had faith you should not have wept so, and been so unconsoled."

"I have faith," said the Bishop. He could not take his attention
from the rushing voices in the gale, and he was trembling still
again until his clothing shook and all his flesh.

"Then, with your faith, go to the prisons, demand that they be
opened at a single word, and deliver the imprisoned," said Lucifer.
"Did not—there was some mention, was there not, that faith even
as small as a mustard seed could move mountains?"

The Bishop was silent.

"You do not have that faith, and that is why I have come to you."

"There is such a thing as God's will," said the Bishop, and his
old face was resolute and gray. "If it be His will——"

"You were not satisfied with His probable will," said Lucifer, "and
that is why you were wrestling in your prayers. You did not pray,
'Thy will be done.' You prayed that it would not be done, but that
your friends would be saved."

Then the Bishop knew that he had reached the ancient paradox
of man's prayer: "Thy will be done—but do not will it!" He pondered
on that, too.

"I was not asking anything for myself," he said at last. "I was
asking mercy for others, if it be His will."

"Were you?" asked Lucifer. "I listened to you for a long time.
You said nothing about—will. You asked for mercy."

"We are permitted that. We are urged to pray for that."

"We are getting nowhere," said Lucifer, with impatience. "I am
very direct in my ways, and you are discourteous, for I asked you
not to speak again of—Him. Your young people will die, in spite
of your prayers, unless you are willing to sacrifice yourself for them.
And did not—was there not a Sacrifice—to save many more than
these? Would you balk at a much lesser Sacrifice?"

Then the Bishop knew that he was being most subtly tempted,
by the most terrible and subtle Tempter of them all, who could even
speak of mercy and sacrifices and to the very heart of vulnerable
and suffering man. How many men, thought the old Bishop, with
new and horrifying insight, had given their souls to save others,

in their generosity and pity? Who knew? Lucifer, it appeared, did not always tempt men through their evil nature, but by the deepest impulses and the noblest sentiments which can live in the heart of humanity. He exploited the best that was in a man, and the most sacrificial. He implied to man that he could do what God would not do, or could not do. And the man who listened——

Lucifer was a liar. He could no longer speak truth. The Bishop, reassured, drew a deep and shuddering breath. "You could not save those young folk."

"You have forgotten. I always keep my promises. There is not the smallest legend that, having given my word to do what is desired, I did not keep it."

The Bishop had to admit that to himself. He could not remember a pact with the devil which had not been kept. For a price. It was very confusing. He could see the faces of those in prison, and could hear their weeping again. He could hear their voices in the gale. They tore at his heart. His eyes filled with tears.

He was so distracted that when he felt something brushing against his little knee he started violently and looked down. It was only the ginger cat, fat and huge, whom Eileen, with fond youthful memories of her old brother, called Mustard. Mustard, like all her ancient and aristocratic tribe, had her own fancies and her own bullying manners and disdains. Eileen kept her not so much as a pet but for her redoubtable ways concerning mice and rats. (Mustard, at this time, was the only plump member of the family.) Consequently there was esteem and respect between those the Bishop called "my two colleens." A lover of animals, the Bishop had greeted the advent of Mustard as a kitten, some five years ago, with enthusiasm and with endearing cries, and Mustard knew at once that she need not woo him but could manage him nicely and bully him out of tidbits by a mere whine. She kept her leg-brushing for Eileen, and her lap-leaping for her mistress, and all her purrs. She rarely even bothered to turn her head in the direction of her clerical servant, and affected to ignore his presence at all times.

The chair in which Lucifer was now sitting was Mustard's by right of appropriation. She permitted only Eileen to sit in it, and then would curl herself on her mistress's knees before the fire. Once the Bishop had absently dropped into it and Mustard had snarled like a tiger and crouched for the charge, all her ginger hair bristling and her golden eyes filled with fire. Since then he had avoided the chair. And she had never sat in his nor approached him voluntarily except when she decided that some rare delicacy he was eating should be shared with her.

"Mustard," murmured the Bishop, weakly, as the cat pressed herself against his legs. Even in this disastrous hour he could feel surprise that she had approached him. The pressure against his leg became heavier and stronger, for Mustard was not only big but she was powerful, and all at once the Bishop remembered the dog he had had as a boy, who would press himself like this against his little master when he had felt his master was threatened. It was incredible, thought the Bishop, vaguely, that Mustard, who was a cat and who disdained him, should lean against him as if protecting——

Mustard's head and shoulders extended beyond the Bishop's knee. Her back was arched stiffly and powerfully; her neck was stretched in Lucifer's direction and her great mouth was opened in a tigerish snarl and from her throat there issued a guttural and savage sound. Her golden eyes shimmered in the faint firelight, and they were distended and filled with hate, rage and fear. Her long thick tail was twice its size, and twitching ominously.

If the Bishop had thought, a few times tonight, that he was suffering from hallucinations because of hunger and grief, he no longer thought it. For Mustard was definitely seeing Lucifer and all his danger and terror. She was definitely protecting her old clerical admirer, and preparing to give her life for his if necessary, a most uncatlike resolution. She was horribly frightened; her stiff body was full of tremors. Nevertheless, she was threatening Lucifer, she a mere, haughty cat busy with the affairs of her life. Her snarling voice, brave and without a whine, was challenging the mighty Adversary.

"My cat," murmured the Bishop, "seems to see you."

"So she does," said Lucifer, staring at the animal. "But then, all animals see the unseen; it is only man, with his muddy eyes, who

sees darkly. The muddy eyes of muddy men! Yet—He—dishonored
the glory He had created by giving not only life to the image of mud
but giving it a soul, also! And then dying for it! Yet rare has been
the man who has possessed the valor, the decency, the honor, the
majesty and dignity, and the innocence of even the least important
of animals. The vilest of the vile is man, and his history is written
in the blood of his fellows. I tempted him, it is said. It needed little
temptation! Not even the most starving and the most lowly of curs
would have succumbed to temptation so easily. Ah, you will speak
to me of free will, which you will say only man possesses. But I
tell you that animals possess that free will also. If they did not,
that lovely cat of yours would not now have resolved to attack me
to the death if I lay a hand upon you, and that is not in the nature
of the feline family, which is eminently sensible in all its ways.
I have respect for animals, who do not betray or murder their kind
and do not war against their kind. I respect their noble innocence.
But for man," said Lucifer, his voice dropping to a sound of muted
thunder, "I have nothing but detestation and regard him with
horror."

The Bishop gaped. "You—you have *horror* for us? You?"

"Certainly," said Lucifer, with a contemptuous smile. "Are you
not the horror of all that lives? What animal does not flee from you,
and know you? What wild thing comes to you with love and trust?
The very worms wriggle away from your disease, your contamination.
Man is the enemy of everything that lives. And I am his enemy,
always, that unlovely thing, that degraded thing, that most unspeakable thing. You know I have sworn to destroy him, out of my detestation. When I heard, in the Councils of Heaven, that—He—had decided, long before your solar system and your world was ever created,
to give His Only Begotten Son for your salvation, I revolted in disgust and horror. Do you blame me? What angel or archangel with
intelligence would not have recoiled at the thought, and revolted?"

The Bishop, forgetting his fear, forgetting the constant snarling of
Mustard, pondered on this, for he loved philosophy and was a man
who liked to hear opposing viewpoints on a theological basis. After
a little he said, "It is true that we are terrible and monstrous. Never-

theless, if Our Lord was willing to take upon Himself our human nature and die for us so that we might be saved from death, then we must possess something worthy."

"Your souls," said Lucifer. "Your immortal souls. He—and I—we struggle for them. It has always been my intention to show Him conclusively that you and your world are not worthy of Him, and that you must die."

"You wish to triumph over God," said the Bishop, absorbed in the discussion.

Lucifer shook his head. "No. I wish to show Him His folly."

"That is blasphemy," said the Bishop in a trembling voice.

Lucifer smiled again. "No. Man is the blasphemy."

The Bishop contemplated Lucifer, and he put his hand on Mustard's arched back. A strange thought came to him and he voiced it: "You do not hate God. No, you do not hate Him."

"No," said Lucifer. "I leave that supreme monstrousness to man, who is the only creature who hates his Creator." His beautiful face changed, became charged with wrath and grief and awful loneliness. "The time is almost at hand when almost every man will hate Him, and that will be my triumph. I will destroy those who love Him—and they are always so few!—and this world, of which I am Prince, will be mine alone, in all its evil, all its utter godlessness, all its living blasphemy."

"That is not true," said the Bishop, who had begun to quake again. "You cannot do anything that God does not permit." He remembered his vision in his church, and his throat became dry and stiff with terror.

"But man will permit it, for not even God will interfere with free will," said Lucifer.

The Bishop shook his head, some courage returning to him. "I know the prophecies of Our Lord, and what He has said of the Last Days. You will not triumph."

"But, I shall have so many multitudes of souls!" said Lucifer. "All those souls who have rejected God and chosen their natural climate —evil. Not even He can save those who have rejected Him and have given me their fealty. Have you forgotten that He said, Himself, that many shall be called but few shall be chosen? My kingdom shall contain countless souls, but few there will be who will ascend to Him. Have you forgotten?"

The Bishop suddenly thought of the speculations and writings of the ancient Fathers concerning Lucifer, and their conjectures regarding him. Man was the cause of Lucifer's fall, they said. He was the cause of Lucifer's exile and great torment and despair; man, in effect, had created hell. No wonder that Lucifer hated man! Was it possible, thought the Bishop, as some of the old Fathers had speculated, that man, in his turn, might redeem Lucifer, by turning from him so absolutely and becoming so perfect in his life? What had a great Cardinal said? "We must believe in hell, for the Church declares that hell exists, but so great is the mercy of God that I doubt, my children, that there is any soul there." If this were true, then hell was only waiting, empty except for the angels who had followed Lucifer out of heaven, for the Last Days when Christ would separate the sheep from the goats. A sweating and passionate urgency came to the Bishop. The goats must be few, if any! If there were none at all, then Lucifer would be vanquished, would acknowledge his defeat, and in his humility—and perhaps gratitude—turn from his hatred and his destruction. He would turn to God again, this majestic archangel, and his hell would be no more, and there would be rejoicing in heaven. Lucifer, at his worst, had never been base or petty. That had been left to man.

The Bishop remembered the dialogues between God and Lucifer, always conducted with courtesy and understanding. Did God remember His Morning Star, the mightiest and most brilliant of His angels? Surely, for the Holy Bible so stated. Man stood between God and Lucifer, like a burning and muddy wall of death. God forgave, but Lucifer could not.

The white storm outside the Bishop's house roared into vast fury, full of shrieking and howling voices, and the Bishop came to himself with a start. Mustard jumped upon his knees, never taking her golden eyes from Lucifer, and she flattened her ears and her mouth gaped open, showing all her savage white fangs. She was on guard.

"Our little business," said Lucifer, in an almost gentle voice. "Your soul, my lord, for the lives and souls of your young people. I have eternity, but you have only a little time."

"Why should you wish my soul?" said the Bishop. "I am only an insignificant man, of no importance. Sure, and you should be wanting the souls of the pompous men of the earth, the kings and the emperors, and not of a miserable, starving old Bishop like myself, in a poor little country."

"Your humility is fascinating," said Lucifer. "What youthful sins you committed have been forgiven you. Since you became a priest you have lived a most holy life, and are blameless. Is not such a soul precious to God and Lucifer? If I gain your soul, then He has a great defeat. Our triumphs are not the petty triumphs of man. Well?"

During powerful stress the Bishop had always resorted to a small but priceless object, which never failed to comfort and console him. His eyes turned to the little chest which contained it, and fastened on the very drawer. He felt tears on his lashes. He pondered again. It had been said that Lucifer could read the most inmost thoughts of men. The Bishop visualized the item in the drawer of the chest and said, "You can read my thoughts, I am thinking?"

"Certainly," said Lucifer.

"Of what am I thinking, then?"

"You are pondering if you should withhold your one soul even if it means the death, and perhaps the hell, of two hundred others."

The Bishop kept his withered lips from smiling. But he could not help wondering. Why had Lucifer not read his thoughts, had not seen the small item in his mind? The Bishop's heart leapt with courage and resolution. It was a mystery, but he had no time now to wonder over mysteries.

"I cannot give you my soul, nor is it pledging it I am, for any reason," he said with quiet firmness, and he looked into Lucifer's marvelous blue eyes with the shadows of endless centuries in them. "But, I will give you my life for the lives of my children in the cold prisons."

"That is a wretched bargain," said Lucifer, with a little laughter. "What is your life to me, and is not your life God's and not yours to dispose of, my lord? Your very offer is a mortal sin, is it not?" Lucifer paused, and he was very thoughtful. "Was it a mortal sin, Bishop? If so, and you do not repent of that offer, then I can take your life in payment and your soul will belong to me."

The Bishop cowered. Lucifer held out his gemmed hand to him, smiling again, and every finger flashed. Mustard darted her head forward with a frightful snarl and her jaws snapped upon the hand. Lucifer contemplated the cat almost affectionately, then tapped the writhing head with the finger of his other hand. At once Mustard howled dreadfully and there was a stench of burning hair and hide in the air, and a wisp of smoke rising from Mustard's flesh. Crying aloud, the Bishop put his palm over the tormented head and the heat stung his skin. He clasped Mustard to his breast, but she struggled from his arms and stood on his knees, valiantly facing Lucifer and preparing to spring in spite of her agony. Now she was one ginger-colored menace, and utterly silent.

"A melodramatic gesture," said Lucifer with regret, "and one I do not usually make. I leave that to lesser demons, such as the souls of men. My apologies. Your cat did not need convincing, but you did. Time grows short," and he lifted his noble head and listened to the ferocity of the white gale along the eaves and windows and doors, and heard its wild battering.

"A cruel thing!" cried the Bishop, with tears on his cheeks. He clutched Mustard's rear legs to prevent her from leaping. "You are wrong; I had no intention to commit a sin, mortal or venial, in offering my old life in exchange for the lives of my young flock. I offered it as saints have offered theirs, to save others from the suffering and the gallows. It is not accounted a sin."

"I am no theologian," said Lucifer, "in such minor matters. Well, then, your soul? I am growing impatient."

"Not my soul," said the Bishop, resolutely. "My soul belongs to God, and never to you. But, I have a treasure which always I have held dearer than my lowly life, and it is that treasure I am offering you for the taking."

He held his breath and watched Lucifer intensely, wondering again if he could read his thoughts. Lucifer studied him in genial silence, and the blue of his eyes appeared to wash over the Bishop's face.

"My life and my joys and my sorrows are entwined with my treasure," faltered the Bishop. "All the years of my life. It is dearer to me than aught else in the world, and so it has been. Will you take it?"

"It is dearer to you than your life?" said Lucifer. "Then it is as dear as your soul?"

The Bishop did not reply. His trembling hands stroked Mustard's back.

"If it is as dear as your soul to your lordship, then the fibres of your spirit are entwined with it."

The Bishop closed his eyes in pain.

"It is said that I never feel compassion for any man," said Lucifer, "but strangely I feel compassion for your lordship. I am much underrated. What is your treasure?"

The Bishop dared to open his eyes, and he was again incredulous. He said with great softness, "But surely you are knowing, for do you not read the thoughts and hearts of men?"

"Um," said Lucifer, thoughtfully. Again the fiery blueness of his eyes swept over the little Bishop's wizened features, and the Bishop could feel its impact like a stroke of lightning on his heart. But he did not quake now. He waited.

"A fine treasure," said Lucifer. "It is, indeed, dearer to you than your miserable life. It is of no value except to you, and so it is of value to me. Let me consider a moment." The eyes did not leave the Bishop's face, and he stared back at this stupendous archangel and hardly let himself breathe.

"Done," said Lucifer, suddenly. He examined the hand on which Mustard's fangs had snapped. There was no trace of a bruise on it, or any mar.

The Bishop felt the sagging of an awful weakness, whether of renewed fear or relief he did not know, but it was compounded of both.

"I will not be giving you my dearest treasure," he said, "until my children are safe." He paused, knowing the deviousness of Lucifer.

"Safe," he repeated, firmly. "Not safe in death, not safe through a vile trick, which would not be safety at all. Free, alive, safe—in the meaning I have, so that they live out the years God has allotted them in hope and peace."

"I cannot guarantee the hope and peace for every heart and soul," said Lucifer. "It is for their own choosing. But I will set them free of the prison, free of the hangman, free of bondage. For your treasure." He held out his hand again, and the Bishop restrained Mustard.

"I am a man of my word," said the Bishop, "and you know that, I am thinking. Many was the head I knocked and broke in my youth, but never did I lie knowingly and with deliberation and the full consent of my will. So I promise you my treasure when you have completed the bargain. You have only to return and I will place it in your hand."

When Lucifer did not speak, the Bishop went on with more urgency: "I have given you my word. Do you demand payment before you have fulfilled your own word? That is not in any legend of you."

"You are asking me to trust you," said Lucifer, "I who trust no man. I believe you will give me your dearest treasure, and so it is a bargain." He stood up, and so tall was he that he towered almost to the ceiling and the room quivered as if with flashes of white flame. Mustard howled, but her rigid body still strained at the archangel in her desire to attack.

"Hush, my darlin'," said the Bishop, stroking the poor burned head gently. Mustard started, and the Bishop looked up. He and Mustard were alone, and the peat fire was very low and the lamp was guttering and the white storm shook the little house as a dog shakes a rat.

The door was flung open and there was old Eileen on the threshold of the room, with a patched woolen garment over her long nightgown. She blinked at her brother wrathfully. "And what is it you are doing, Bernard, at this hour of the morning and Mass but two hours away, at your age and with no food in your stomach for two days?"

"I—I was thinking," said the Bishop.

"Hah!" exclaimed Eileen, putting her veined hands on her hips. She scowled about the room. "And who was it you was thinking with, for did I not hear voices?"

"You heard voices?" said the Bishop.

"Your ould squeaky one, and another! It was not talking to Mustard you were!"

"What did the voice sound like?" said the Bishop.

Eileen glared at him suspiciously. "The voice of a man, ye ould fool! Or was it," asked Eileen with sarcasm, "the voice of an angel, he visiting you?"

"Yes," said the Bishop.

Eileen snorted. She loved her brother with all her heart, but he was younger than she and she considered him only a lad who needed watching and bullying. "Glory be to the saints!" she cried. "And it's bragging ye are, in your dotage and your sins, and making mock of your poor sister! Off to bed with you, for a little sleep." She sniffed suddenly. "And what is that stench, your highness? Your pipe?"

The Bishop tried to rise, but all at once he felt quite sick and undone. Then Eileen was fascinated by Mustard. "Look at the ginger divil!" she said, marveling. "On your knee, she who would niver go near you."

"A—a piece of fire fell on her head," said the Bishop faintly. "I comforted her."

Eileen bore down on Mustard, and examined the burned spot incredulously. "Well, then," she said, after a moment, "it's no great harm." She seized Mustard roughly and prepared to toss her onto the chair which Lucifer had occupied, but Mustard howled terribly, writhed in Eileen's arms, and sprang to the floor.

"Her own chair!" said Eileen. "And why will she not take it?"

Mustard scuttled under the Bishop's chair, her body vibrating. "Has the divil been after her?" said Eileen with disbelief.

"That he was," said the Bishop with his last strength. And he fainted in his seat. His final memory before he became unconscious was of the mighty roaring of the storm and the whimpering of Mustard under his legs.

When he opened his eyes again it was to a glare of sunlight flashing from deep snow, and the doctor was at his bed, and he felt sick to death. He could only think of one of his priests and he whispered, "Jack. Fetch me Jack. I am dying."

"Not a bit of it," said the doctor. "A fever, and hunger, but there's a fine fowl boiling in the kitchen which I brought with my own two hands. You'll be better for the soup and a wing." He was a kind old man and had very little money.

"No," said the Bishop, and blinked the fog out of his eyes. When he could see again he felt a warm comfort in his stomach and warmth at his feet, and a candle burned beside his bed and the moon looked in the window. Eileen, wrapped in a thick shawl, was dozing in a chair near her brother. She came awake at once, almost as soon as he had awakened.

He had had, she said with satisfaction, a good supper of chicken soup and potatoes, and had devoured it like a wolf, and it was now midnight and he must sleep. She put her wizened hand on his forehead and nodded with more satisfaction. The Bishop was dazed. He moistened his lips and tried to speak and moved his head to clear his wits—and sunlight struck on his eyes. It was another day. But Eileen said it was two days and the doctor was pleased that the fever had gone. The Bishop tried to sit up; weakness overpowered him like a wave and he fell back on his pillows and slept again.

When he awoke on another day, free of the fever and cool and with his wits about him, Ginger was sitting on the bed, on the Bishop's feet over the worn blankets. Her golden eyes gazed at him wisely. The top of her head had been lavishly anointed with Eileen's pet and odoriferous salve and the smell filled the little cold bedroom, which was full of quiet winter light.

"Mustard," said the Bishop, and remembered everything. His heart quickened with dread as his whirling mind assured him he had been only the victim of a feverish dream and sick hallucinations. A Lucifer did not come to a very old and starveling Bishop in his little house in Dublin. A Lucifer, the mightiest of all angels, did not waste time in seeking tiny souls; such souls are wooed by tiny demons. A Lucifer could read the minds of all men, and yet, in that dream, he had not been able to read the Bishop's mind, not even in the simplest matter. Lucifers are not deceived. "It is my wretched pride," said the old Bishop, "in my thinking that Lucifer would find me worth the tempting! Oh, it's the proud and wicked heart I have, the black, black heart, and me a Bishop!" He looked at his ring; it was so loose now that Eileen had wrapped the back of it with white yarn so it would not fall from his finger.

Then he began to weep, remembering the young folk in the prisons awaiting death for the crime of defending themselves and wanting the food of their labors for their children and parents, and for the greater crime of a dream of freedom and liberty to worship as they must. The Bishop turned his face into his fat pillow and the coarse linen was soon wet with his tears. Mustard moved uneasily on his feet, then she slipped down and nuzzled his neck gently. He turned his head and stroked the thick gingery fur and saw again the big healing burn on her valiant head. "Was it a dream, Mustard?" he asked her, urgently. Mustard whined a little, consolingly.

The door was flung open and there was Jack Morgan, the middle-aged priest, tall and big and with a ruddy, lighted face, and the fiercest blue eyes in Ireland. "Jack, Jack," said the Bishop, feebly, "I have been wanting you——"

The priest, exhaling ice-cold air and briskness and elation, knelt to kiss the Bishop's ring, and his eyes were dancing with exultation. "It is I who have been here every blessed day," he shouted in his ringing voice, "praying beside your bed and listening—your lordship will forgive me—to your feverish babblings about Lucifer!" The priest laughed richly. Before the Bishop could utter even a murmur, Jack Morgan roared on:

"Oh, it's the grand news I have for you, my lord, this morning! The grand news!"

The Bishop began to tremble, and he started up on his pillows.

The priest chuckled heartily, and shook his head with delight. "Ye'll not be believing it, my lord, but the lads and girls are free and safe! That Sassenagh judge—he was thrown into the deep snow from his carriage three days ago, and broke his da—— I mean his two legs! And it was Judge Rafferty who presided for the hearing, a Protestant but an Irishman, and may God love him!"

"Tell me!" cried the Bishop, when his priest stopped to rub his big knees and shake his head.

Jack Morgan's eyes glittered with joy and happiness. "It was Judge Rafferty who said the young folk had but defended themselves, and it was sympathy he had for them in spite of the stout blackthorns and their rioting against the peace and order of the Realm and Her Majesty's Government! It was regretting, he was, that the other judge had lost his nephew, but who could swear which lad had cracked his skull? It was the fortunes of war, said Judge Rafferty, and the accidents of war, and his was the straight face, and he said skull-cracking was an old sport in the world and there'd be no end to it. He'd cracked many a skull himself at rugby, and was it a crime in a war but not in a game? Ah, it was the smooth voice he had, smooth as cream and cold as new cheese on a winter's day, and the Crown Prosecutor protested and down came the gavel and the judge's wig fell over his eyes, and all laughed in the room. The judge," said Jack Morgan, with rising joy, "fined each lad one pound and each colleen eight shillings, and gave them a warning."

"Oh," whispered the Bishop, and clasped his hands, and was afraid to thank God.

"And there was a fine gentleman," continued the priest, "who paid the fine for them all, for where should the lads be getting pounds, and the girls the shillings, they who have not even copper pennies amongst them?"

"A fine gentleman?" quaked the Bishop, his heart jumping again.

"That he was, and no name he gave. He spoke of a patron. A gentleman like a Duke."

"Oh!" exclaimed the Bishop. "Was it a man with the face of an angel?"

Jack Morgan stared at him, puzzled. "No, your Excellency. A man with a big yellow mustache." He laughed again. "Are the angels growing mustaches now?"

"It is happy I am," said the Bishop, "that my children are free. But my heart is heavy that I made a pact with the devil for them, and had no trust in God."

Jack Morgan gaped. He was a man of good and earthy common

sense, and he thought his Bishop feverish again. So the Bishop put his hand on Mustard and pointed to her burned head. With painful word following painful word he told his favorite priest of that howling winter night. Finally he ended with a hoarse whisper, "Is there forgiveness for me, I am wondering, Jack?"

The priest rubbed his thick gray head, and stared at the Bishop, and coughed. He appeared bewitched by the tale, though he doubted its verity. He wanted to know of Lucifer's appearance, and the Bishop described him. The priest was enchanted, and the Bishop thought, with dismay: Is Jack a little envious, as well as curious?

"Well, well," said Jack Morgan, in a loud and burly voice, "it was not the devil, I am thinking, for does he not have horns and hoofs and does he not wear red, as red as scarlet?"

"I am no authority on his apparitions," said the Bishop. "And it's doubting, I am, that if he appeared so to man there'd be many lost souls, for very fear. I think I saw him, and it is all true, and he was the most beautiful creature I have seen in my life. For, is he not an archangel, and was he not the greatest of them all, with a face like the morning? And was he not full of grief and sorrow? I found it in my heart to pity him."

"That is a snare," said Jack Morgan, suddenly remembering that he was a priest.

"Sure, and that is true, perhaps," said the Bishop.

"It was not himself," said the priest. "If it was not a dream, it was an angel of God." And he blessed himself.

The Bishop smiled wryly. "Would an angel of God burn poor Mustard's head? Would poor Mustard, from thence on, refuse to sit in her favorite chair? No, it was Lucifer, and I made a pact with him for my children."

"Your soul?" exclaimed Jack Morgan.

"No. My dearest treasure. And he'll be calling for it soon."

The priest glanced nervously over his shoulder. Then he coughed again. "The devil takes only souls, my lord," he said. "He is not tempted by—treasures. For, does not all that is valuable in the world belong to him? It is not possible that he would make a pact with you for anything but your soul."

"He does not know what my treasure is, Jack."

The priest was greatly relieved, and his high color returned. "Was it the devil, my lord, he'd have known, and there is no doubt, for does he not read the minds of men like a book?"

"He could not read mine," said the Bishop. "I tested him, and he could not read it."

The priest was even more relieved. "Then it was not Satan, or even one of his demons—if there was anyone at all, and you with the fever and the hunger. For no human mind is closed to him."

The Bishop wanted to believe it was all a dream. Perhaps a coal had fallen on Mustard's head, when she went too close to the fire. And it was God's mercy, alone, which had saved the young folk and set them free, and the mercy of an unknown benefactor who had paid their fines. Nothing could happen, thought the Bishop vaguely, without God's permitting of it. On this comforting thought he fell into deep sleep, for he was still weak.

When he awoke again it was midnight, and he felt his ancient strength returning. He begged Eileen to go to her bed, she who looked not ninety now, but one hundred and ninety. It needed little urging; she put a clapper on the table at his head, and went, bowed and very old and lean, to her own room and bed. It was cold in the Bishop's bedroom, though the door was open to his small parlor so the heat of the fire could enter. Someone had been kind enough to send coals to heat the Bishop's house, or "palace," as the poor people liked to call it in their hopeful fantasies. The bed-warmer was cosy against the Bishop's feet, against the long wool stockings he wore to bed in the winter, and the candlelight flickered and there was a lamp burning on a table in the parlor, within sight of the Bishop's eyes.

He pulled himself to a sitting position with only one gasp, and he turned his head and looked at the crucifix on his wall, and then at his prie-dieu, and then he pushed his thin old legs out of the bed and tottered to the prie-dieu and fell on his knees and bent his head over his clasped hands. Could he ask forgiveness for a dream, for are men responsible for the nightmares of their nights and the phantoms of their fevers? If it was not a dream, could he still be forgiven? He had made no pact, in the meaning of the word. He had offered his dear treasure, and Lucifer had accepted it, and this was puzzling, for he must have known what it was and how could he then have agreed?

Mustard suddenly yelled and dived between the floor and the Bishop's ankles and cowered there, and the Bishop knew, even before he lifted his bowed head, whom he would see. And there, surely, was Lucifer, himself, more beautiful than memory, his clothing covered with a cloak of rich velvet edged with ermine, the velvet as black as night and the fur whiter than snow.

"I have come for your lordship's treasure," he said, in a very kind voice. "For, I have kept my bargain, as you know."

"Are you a dream?" asked the Bishop with fresh terror.

"I am every man's dream," said Lucifer. "Infant or ancient, saint or sinner, I am all men's dream."

"And you cannot be deceived?" said the Bishop.

"No, I cannot be deceived," said Lucifer. "May I assist your lordship to your feet?"

"No, no!" cried the Bishop, horrified, and shrinking. He pushed himself to his feet. He stared at the great, dark angel. "You will not want my treasure," he said, pressing his hands to his chest, in which his heart was shaking.

"Surely I will want it," said Lucifer, "for is it not dearer to you than your life?"

"And you are knowing what it is?" said the Bishop.

"Certainly. I know all things."

He looked smilingly at the Bishop, then courteously drew aside so that the Bishop could precede him into the parlor. The Bishop tottered to the threshold, then glanced back fearfully. Lucifer was regarding the crucifix in enigmatic silence, and there was a deep cleft between his eyes. The Bishop went into the parlor, his long nightshirt blowing about him in the drafts which no mortar could stop, and he supported himself with bits of furniture. He heard no sound, but all at once Lucifer was at his side.

"The treasure," he said, patiently.

The Bishop bent his head and went to his little chest of drawers and opened the one at the top. A silver-gilt box lay there, very old and dim. He took the box in his hands and his eyes filled with tears. He lifted the lid.

A delicate rosary lay on pink cotton-wool. It was made of silver-gilt, with pearly beads, and the cross was large and the Corpus was exquisitely cast in pure yellow gold. The rosary had been the christening gift to his grandmother by her own mother, ages ago, and in turn it had been given to his own mother on her christening day, and it was rarely out of her blessed hands until the day she died. She had told her son, long before he was a priest, that she must not be buried with it. It was her heart's desire that he have it as his own, and be buried with it, for he was very dear to her. He had received it from her, finally, when she was dying.

He had cherished the rosary because of his darling mother. He had received his First Communion with it in his hand. It never left his person, even during the skull-cracking days. It was with him when he was ordained as a lowly priest. He felt that it was a talisman, the guardian given him by his mother. Once he had lost it, it dropping through a hole in his pocket, and his distress had been overwhelming. He had prayed feverishly to St. Anthony for its return, and one day the sacristan had brought it to him, saying he had found it in a crack near the high altar. Yet every corner had been searched over and over long before. The Bishop considered it a miracle. After that he kept it in its box, waiting for the day when he would lie in his coffin, with the rosary in his hands.

Now his tears fell on the precious rosary, and he put his fingers gently over the lustrous pearly beads and the cross, and turned to Lucifer. He closed his eyes and mutely offered the box to him.

The box did not leave his hands, and after a little he opened his eyes. Lucifer was gazing at the crucifix, and he was frowning.

"You know I cannot take this," he said in a very ominous voice.

"It is my dearest treasure. It belonged to my grandmother and her mother before her; it was blessed, so long ago, by the Holy Father, himself, so I was told. It belonged to my sweet mother, who gave it to me with her dying hands. My heart is in it; it is the dearest thing I ever owned." The Bishop's voice trembled. "Not even for

bread would I have sold it. Not even for my life would I have sold
it. It is my treasure, for thousands of prayers were said with it, and
every bead is holy."

Lucifer looked into his eyes, which were filled with tears.

"Yes," said Lucifer, "it is your treasure. And it is this treasure that
you pledged to me. Tell me, my lord, did you know, when you
promised it, that I could not accept it, for very excellent reasons?"

The Bishop thought with all the honesty that was in him. Then
he confessed, "I do not know. I was in much misery; my mind was
not fully in order. But, I must speak truly: I hoped you could not
accept it."

"You hoped to deceive me?"

The Bishop again considered. "I prayed that I could. Yes, that I
prayed, though I had heard you could not be deceived and could
read the minds of all men."

Lucifer was silent. The Bishop said, "Did you read mine?"

The great dark archangel began to smile. "Shall I tell you that?
That will be my secret. As a penance, you will wonder all your life.
It will enliven your idle moments. There is nothing like endless
speculation to give interest to one's existence."

The Bishop gently closed the precious box. He looked down at it.
"I am speculating now, Lucifer."

Suddenly Lucifer laughed. It was not an evil, boisterous laugh, but
a hearty one, mirthful, delighted, masculine. It was incredible, but
the Bishop found himself laughing with him, and he had not laughed
for many months.

"Tell me," said the Bishop, aching with his laughter, "Did you
truly save my children?"

"That," said Lucifer, his beautiful face merry, "is something else
I will not tell you. Am I not called the Great Deceiver?"

His mighty blue eyes sparkled and flamed with his mirth, and
his teeth glistened in the lamplight.

"Farewell, Bishop Quinn. You will not see me again, not in this
life nor in the next. I have enjoyed your conversation as I have enjoyed the conversation of few others. You are not entirely honest,

but I doubt if that will be held against you, for I now hear the laughter in heaven."

He threw back his head and laughed again, that hearty and rollicking laughter. But suddenly he was sober. He looked at the Bishop.

"You will remember a vision you had, which you saw in your church when you were fainting of hunger. Tell no one of it!"

"Why shall I not?" said the Bishop.

"Because it is my truth, though it was prophesied by Another. You shall not see it, nor the young priests following you. But those not yet born will see it, and it will be my triumph, my final triumph. Many there will be who will try to escape it, but they shall not! For man is a curse upon the earth, which would be free of him, but would He listen to me, He Who knows all? No, He would not. Yet He and I know that it will come to pass on this earth, and we shall see," said Lucifer, vengefully, "who will triumph then! For in the womb of time there is breeding a race of men who shall be my total servants. Hail and farewell, Bishop Quinn, and rejoice that you shall not see that day!"

"And that," said Father Morley, "is the tale the Bishop told me, when I was young and despondent. I, too, wondered, for who could help it?

"I also have another thought: Did my blessed Bishop, by his deceit, which was caused half by fever and starvation and grief, lift Lucifer one step towards the heaven he had lost? He liked to think so, to the end of his life. But then, it may all have been a dream. Who is there to tell?

"However, when I strain my eyes upon the future, I wonder again. What horror is man preparing for himself, what suffering for his world? Be sure he is preparing!"

Chapter Twelve

"THERE WERE DOZENS OF OTHER STORIES I heard in Grandmother's house," said Rose to her husband, "and I remember some of them, and others are only fragments. But these are the ones I best remember, for they made such a difference in my life. Grandmother never returned 'to the Sacraments,' except on her deathbed. But the stories I heard from her friends helped bring me to them, and that's ironic when you think of it. I rarely saw Grandmother after I was eight. She left Leeds; she went everywhere. She wanted to see the whole world, and love it."

Her face saddened. "I can't help thinking of her lying there alone in the churchyard, she who had never been alone before. And I can't help thinking of the last years of her life, all her money gone, all her brothers and sisters dead, and no one to care at all whether she lived or died. She spent those last years with one of her sons, and they were quiet years. Knowing Grandmother, I feel they must have been a penance for all her sins. Do you remember how she looked when she was dead? Not peaceful or resigned. Just half amused, and—yes, relieved."

"Still," said William, "she had things in her life which we'll never have. She lived in a heroic and exciting and adventurous world, for all its faults. She lived when men were really men, and not tailored careful conformists. The priests you told me of: they were heroes. And heroes are always full of legends, themselves, and legends are invented about them. I think that modern man will be forgotten, for he has no heroism about him, in his thoughts or in his life. He's just a little nonentity, a mediocrity that wants only one thing: safety. That's why the brood of Satan is having its own merry way these days. There's no one to oppose it."

"We don't know that," said Rose, looking at the emerald on her finger.

"At least, they're not getting any publicity," said William. "No one hears about them, or knows about them, and that is just like not existing at all. All we hear of is the devils, and they're getting stronger every day, though our so-called intellectuals spend half their time assuring us that man is really good and noble and needs only to reform his social institutions to be absolutely perfect. As if man, himself, isn't responsible for the world he is making! But he loves to whine that he isn't responsible. He's not evil; it's just his neighbor."

"I think," said Rose, "that the worst thing in our modern world is that we have no dream. Our grandparents had one. It's really the one and only dream—God and His love. They built their lives on it, and that's why nations prospered then. Now I hear that the Americans are talking about 'new goals.' That's because they, and all of us in the world, have forgotten that we really have one goal, and that is God. We had a vision, but we drove it off. So we must invent petty little others, such as plumbing for the Hottentots, and fresh cows' milk for the bushmen, and television for the natives in the Congo, and social engineers for Angola. What silly little visions! We've become a world of children, with all the vices of children, such as immediate small pleasures, shrill insistence, tantrums and invectives against all authority. Worse still, our worldly authorities are no more than children, themselves, except when they are devils. A world of children and evil! I wonder what it was Bishop Quinn saw in his vision so long ago?"

"I think we all know," said William. "That's why we are so afraid. We did it all. We are just frightened because of our inevitable punishment, whether we are a Russian or an American, an Englishman or a Frenchman.

"You remember what the hanging judges always say: 'May God

have mercy on your soul.' Rose, somewhere in the world, among those who have dedicated their lives to God, there are men and women who pray that for us every hour. They are the heroes, though we don't hear about them. It may be at the very last that their prayers will, indeed, save our souls. They can't save our world, and that we know."